MW00965302

Rachael Treasure's first novel,
Australian publishing industry f
is now considered an iconic work of contemporary Australian
fiction.

Rachael is a rural business graduate of Sydney University's
Orange Agricultural College and has a Bachelor of Arts in
creative writing and journalism from Charles Sturt University
in Bathurst. She has worked as a journalist for Rural Press and
ABC Rural Radio.

Rachael Treasure lives in Southern Tasmania with her two
teenage children and her husband, Daniel. Together they are
restoring farming landscapes using regenerative agricultural
methods and Natural Sequence Farming techniques.

White Horses is her seventh novel.

Rachael Treasure

White Horses

[signed: Rachael]
xox

HarperCollins*Publishers*

HarperCollins*Publishers*

First published in Australia in 2019
by HarperCollins*Publishers* Australia Pty Limited
ABN 36 009 913 517
harpercollins.com.au

Copyright © Rachael Treasure Pty Ltd 2019

The right of Rachael Treasure to be identified as the author of this work has been asserted
by her in accordance with the *Copyright Amendment (Moral Rights) Act 2000*.

HarperCollins*Publishers*
Level 13, 201 Elizabeth Street, Sydney NSW 2000, Australia
Unit D1, 63 Apollo Drive, Rosedale, Auckland 0632, New Zealand
A 53, Sector 57, Noida, UP, India
1 London Bridge Street, London, SE1 9GF, United Kingdom
Bay Adelaide Centre, East Tower, 22 Adelaide Street West, 41st floor, Toronto,
   Ontario M5H 4E3, Canada
195 Broadway, New York NY 10007, USA

A catalogue entry for this book is available
from the National Library of Australia.

ISBN 978 1 4607 5757 4 (paperback)
ISBN 978 1 4607 1126 2 (ebook)
ISBN 978 1 4607 9379 4 (audiobook)

Cover design by Laura Thomas
Cover image by Merr Watson / Women Who Drone / Getty Images
Typeset in Sabon LT Std by Kirby Jones
Printed and bound in Australia by McPherson's Printing Group
The papers used by HarperCollins in the manufacture of this book are a natural,
recyclable product made from wood grown in sustainable plantation forests.
The fibre source and manufacturing processes meet recognised international
environmental standards, and carry certification.

For Daniel and Maggie

'*I have realised that the future depends upon the feminine principle in all things because all things are born of woman*'

Wisdom Keeper, from Jamie Sams,
The 13 Original Clan Mothers

#metoo

#metoomothernature

Chapter 1

The bell of the Widgenup Store door was still jangling as Drift walked in and Shaynene instantly started blabbing about the latest drama on her Facebook feed.

'Well, I'm *totally dev-voed*. Just *dev-vo-stated*,' Shaynene moaned from behind the counter cluttered with chewing gum and chocolate bars.

Drift swiped her wide-brimmed stockman's hat from her head, enjoying the cool of the air-conditioning on her brow, and thought, *Here she goes ...*

Shaynene threw her phone down theatrically, her melon breasts wobbling in her low-cut red tank top, causing the tiger tattooed on her left boob to jiggle too. She interrupted her monologue and swung around to the pigeonhole mailboxes and gathered up a large bundle for Drift.

'Your dad has *two* copies of his brainbox magazine in there — it means youse two must've been gone a while. What? Over four months? I've had two roots since. And not from the same bloke neither.'

Drift took up the *New Philosopher* magazines bound up in a rubber band with the other mail, relieved her dad would have something to distract him. She smiled at Shaynene. Hearing about Shay's life was like trying to follow the plot of a long-running, badly written TV soapie. Drift lifted the hot weight of her long hair from the back of her neck and wound it into a blonde knot,

1

waiting for Shay's verbal diarrhoea of daily drama. Today, her friend's short flop of lank hair was a chalky purple. The last time she'd seen Shay was when she and her dad had carted the first lot of cattle out from Pinrush Point. Back then, Shaynene's hair had been flame red on top, shaven on the back and sides.

'Such a shame. He was *such a spunk*,' Shaynene said, picking up her phone and staring at it again. 'Far too young to cark it. What a bugger. And *here* if you can believe it. Nothin ever happens here!'

'Who's died? One of the blokes you had sexual relations with?' Drift asked, framing the words 'sexual relations' in inverted commas with her index fingers.

'No! You dick.' Shaynene flashed a picture on her phone of a shirtless Islander man, boardies slung low on lean hips, dark hair long and surfer-cool. 'Kai Kaahea. You know. He's famous — with a capital F for *fucking* famous.'

'Oh, yeah, him,' said Drift, without a clue as to who she was talking about. Steering away from Shaynene's celeb news, she instead turned her attention to the chocolates on the counter. 'I didn't know they did M&Ms in chocolate blocks nowadays. How weird.'

'You friggin redneck on-the-road hobo! What rock have you been hiding under?' Shaynene said, looking at her with her dark gaze. 'They've been around for-*eva*! Honestly, you and your dad might act like professors of Pinrush Point, but you don't know *nothin*.'

There was a *chirrup* from the tinned foods aisle, and a bird the colour of custard slice and cement fluttered towards them. It landed on Shaynene's shoulder and nibbled one of her ear piercings with its curved grey beak.

Shaynene lifted a finger to stroke the vibrant orange blob on its cheek. 'Hello, Head Bob,' she whispered to the bird. 'I know she's backward ... but we still love her.'

The bird, true to his name, bobbed his head up and down. 'Blow me, blow me. *Faaaark*,' he screeched.

Drift cocked her eyebrow at him. 'That's new, Head Bob.'

'My little brother taught him,' Shaynene explained. 'Little shit. Disgusting language. Anyways,' she continued, tugging down her summer tank over her tummy rolls and fully taking in the sight of Drift, 'welcome back to town, cowgirl.' She clicked her tongue and winked at her. 'I'm lovin them Daisy Dukes, sister,' she said, pointing to Drift's ragged denim cut-offs and flicking an index finger under her own frayed shorts. 'We could be twins,' she joked.

Drift glanced at Shaynene's all-woman apple-round body and short-as-short shorts, which bit into thighs as juicy as delicious Christmas hams. Shay's toenails were painted a sparkling green, and peeking from pink rubber thongs was a new tattoo of a bluebird. Drift looked down at her own skinny legs; they seemed especially gangly today, teamed with her big clobbering workboots and thick socks. Next to Shaynene, Drift felt like a scrawny foal.

'What can I do youse for today, madame?' Shaynene asked, giving an expansive wave around the shop as if it were a New York boutique and not a remote general store cum post office that sold crappy gift cards, cheap 'made in China' billy cans for caravanning tourists, out-of-date chips and dried dim sims.

Drift nodded towards the bright glare outside on the main drag, where her father sat hulking in the rumbling LandCruiser flat-tray ute, still sweating despite the aircon. 'It's my birthday and Dad wants to get me a present.'

'Well what the fuck's he doin sittin in the cab? Why isn't he in here gettin somethin for you?'

Drift shrugged. 'You know what he's like. He's got his nose in a ye olde English book of sonnets, so he's gone all iambic pentameter on me.'

'Huh?' Shaynene looked puzzled for a moment. 'Poetry, huh? Well, whatever floats your boat.'

'At least he's out of his bush ballad phase,' Drift said. '*Oh, the weary, weary journey on the trek, day after day, With sun above and silent veldt below,*' she said tiredly.

3

'Jeez.'

'He's worse when he's on his horse. Hits me over the head with Banjo twenty-four/seven.'

'Better than being hit over the head with *a* banjo,' Shaynene said. 'One of my step-dads hit me on the head with a recorder once. They may be plastic, but those things bloody hurt.' She sighed. 'Poetry on your ponies. You two. You both oughta be working at one of them universities in the city, not stock contracting. Silly buggers.' Shay tilted her head. 'What's he wanna get you for your birthday?'

'Don't know. He gave me fifty bucks and said, *"But search in shop you wander for present and for cake!"*'

'Fifty bucks for food *and* a present, along with really bad poetry? Bloody tight arse. That's tragic!'

'The cocky hasn't paid us for the last lot of cattle yet,' Drift said.

'Meatworks being slow again?'

Drift nodded.

'Bloody aioli holies.' Shaynene reached for a KitKat, ripping it open and offering Drift a stick.

Drift shook her head. 'No thanks.'

'Skinny bitch,' Shaynene said, biting into the chocolate. 'What else did you get for your birthday?'

'I didn't get anything,' Drift said.

'Oh well. Happy birthday anyway, sweet thang. How old ya turning?'

'Twenty-one.'

'Jeez, woman! You can't be. You sure you're not turning eighty? You speak like friggin Yoda somedays. You never want to come out with me and you act like an old fart. Why don't you 'n your dad get your nose out of your bloody books and come out tonight with me to the pub?'

'I would … but … you know …' Drift's words faded. 'He likes to keep to himself.'

They both looked at Split Wood, out in the driver's seat,

staring ahead at nothing. He'd taken off his hat, so they could see the close-clipped grey-flecked brown hair forming a dark line on his pinkish bull neck. The tight expression on his face and his overweight form made it difficult to see the good-looking man he had been. It made Drift sad to look at him these days.

Shaynene put her hand on Drift's arm. 'Has he been OK, since … you know …?' she asked quietly, as if Split Wood might be able to hear.

Drift nodded. 'Mostly.'

'You're twenty-one now. Surely you can choof off and get on with your own life? He'd be right, wouldn't he?'

'Maybe.'

Then, as sudden as a whip crack, a siren shredded the hot air of Widgenup's main drag. A police car roared past, travelling well over the town speed limit, lights flashing. Followed by a second cop car. Then yet another. A fire truck came soon after, along with an ambulance and a State Emergency Services vehicle.

'Jeez!' Shaynene said, rushing to the window. 'Someone's called in the entire Cooperville cavalry!'

Above the girls' heads, beyond the store's spinning ceiling fans, helicopter blades whumped. At the unfamiliar sound, Head Bob squawked, taking off to the safety of his cage in the lunch room.

Shaynene reefed open the shop door, sending the bell stuttering again. She and Drift hurried out to the baking hot footpath, watching the brake lights of the emergency vehicles pulse at the end of the main street before turning down the mostly unused road towards Pinrush Point. Above them in a squintingly bright blue sky two choppers angled their noses purposefully in the same direction.

'Far out!' said Shaynene. 'They're headed towards your stock camp.'

'What's going on?' Drift asked. She could see her dad watching from the vehicle and reaching to turn on the ute's radio for clues on the ABC news.

'It's really happening!' Shaynene said, grabbing Drift's arm and bouncing up and down, sending the tiger tattoo into another jiggle in its jungle. 'They've started searching for him!'

'Who?'

'Bloody Kai Kaahea, you idiot. I thought you said you knew.'

'Kai who?'

'*I told you*. The pro surfer. They reckon he's gone missing off Pinrush Point. Swept out to sea.'

'Swept out to sea,' Drift murmured.

Shaynene saw the colour drain from her friend's face. 'Oh, sorry. I forgot.'

'It's OK, Shaynene. Ancient history. But I don't know this Kai Car Keys or whatever his name is. Wouldn't know him if I fell on him.'

'I would've liked to have fallen on him,' Shaynene said wistfully. 'I wish! If I'd known he was in this neck of the woods, I would've conned you into tracking his camp down! He was hotter than a Marble Bar pavement.'

Shaynene's eyes returned to the choppers, now just black dots.

'This'll be the biggest thing that's happened to Widgenup since that billionaire woman bought up all the land on the Point,' she said excitedly. 'Remember the fuss then? We ran out of frozen chips for the fryer. Those bloody journos were hungry bastards, and fucken fussy when it came to their coffee. But some weren't too fussy with their women.' She gave a giggle at the memory.

Drift smiled for her friend's benefit, watching the choppers disappear in the distance, while her stomach turned.

'You know what this also means?' Shaynene said.

Drift shook her head.

'It won't just be the news crews who will be here soon. There'll be a ton of groupie surf nuts showing up. Kai Kaahea is a god to them. They'll come to help look for him, or just hang out to worship him on the beach. All those fit young bods.' Shaynene poked her tongue out and waggled it.

Drift rolled her eyes. 'Friggin surfers. I hate 'em.'

But Shaynene still wasn't listening. 'Can I come camp with you on my days off?'

'S'pose,' Drift said.

Shaynene bounced again. 'C'mon, girl ... let's get your birthday present ... something to spruce you up, ya bloody cowpoke dag. And after work, I'd better go shave me legs and tizz up me southerly bits. And maybe recolour me hair? Do you think this purple suits me?' She hoicked up her breasts and dragged down her top, not waiting for an answer, to Drift's relief.

'G'day, Mr Wood,' Shaynene shouted, waving to him before linking arms with Drift and leading her back inside the store.

'C'mon, woman,' Shaynene said as the bell jingled dramatically, 'I get the feeling love is coming to this little arse-end town!'

Chapter 2

The Woods' stock camp, nestled between the road and the dunes down on Pinrush Point, was just as they'd left it that morning, with no sign of any urgent missing surfer chaos. Relieved, Drift got out of the LandCruiser with her shopping bags and reached to the Esky hitched by an occy strap on the back.

'G'day, clowns,' she called to the dogs as Molly, Hamlet and Dunno emerged from their sand-dug bunkers beneath the stock truck and danced on the ends of their chains. The horses on the tether line whickered, their empty hay nets pegged on the ground beside them like wilted black balloons.

Split picked up the box of beer and hoisted it onto his shoulder happily, as if he were carrying a premiership-winning footballer, then grabbed the mail.

'Go kick Gerald in the arse, will you? Get him going,' he said to Drift as he trudged in the sandy soil towards the caravan. 'That way I can get an early tea on.'

'No worries,' she said, relieved he'd given up on the Shakespearean speak for now. 'Then shall I go wrap up my *own* present that I bought for me?'

Split glanced at her, read her expression as cheeky, and gave her a wry smile. '*If presents be thy love of life, then wrap on,*' he said to her.

She pulled a sarcastic jokey face at him, but inside Drift felt a twinge of sadness. 'Getting her tea on' meant he would crack his first can. After the third he'd be reading bits out of his philosophy magazine to her in a desperate fashion, and by the sixth he'd be morosely ruminating on life, the universe and the stupidity of humans. Then he'd start on the topic of her mother.

She hated beer box nights.

As the sea breeze gathered strength Drift made her way over to the generator. They'd set it a distance away, behind the stock truck, to mask the riot of noise it made. She unscrewed the cap and checked the diesel level, wishing again her dad would buy them a new, beaut modern one.

'You gunna behave, Gerald?' she asked as she grabbed the ripcord. Gerald was a complex beast and sometimes took fifty shoulder-aching tugs to get going. This evening though, to Drift's surprise, he started first go, shuddering and spluttering to a wheezy kind of life instantly. 'Good boy. Is this my birthday present, you starting first pop?'

Drift made her way to the horses, tethered on a line strung between two wind-pruned paperbarks, and gathered up the hay nets. Minty nuzzled her shoulder as she did. The wind bit. A change was coming through. The nearby copse of sheoaks moaned eerily. Black clouds gathered far out to sea like an army waiting to attack, but Drift turned her back on the weather.

'Hungry, girl?' she asked, placing her hand on Minty's muzzle and running it over the horse's snow-flecked face. 'Me too.'

She thought of her 'birthday tea': a cardboard box of frozen herb and garlic crumbed 'fish' triangles that her dad would drop into the deep fryer along with the 'treat' of frozen crinkle-cut chips. She knew after eating she'd say, 'Thanks, Dad,' but she'd feel disappointment.

She wished her dad would stand long enough beside her in the froth of the ocean on her birthday to catch a real fish. But the old rods were now slowly rusting in the stock truck cab, time rendering their reels immobile. She imagined sizzling fresh-caught fish on an open campfire, her dad and her, side by side, like they had done in the old days. She let the fresh blast of onshore wind catch her thoughts and carry them away. It was her birthday. New cattle would be here tomorrow. Shaynene was likely to arrive in a few days as entertainment. Wilma the Wondrous was due for a visit too. Life was all as it should be, Drift tried to reassure herself. But, like the surge of the ocean just over the dunes she felt resentment for her father roll in her, images of him and his betrayal invading her mind.

'The thing about your dad is, you just gotta look beyond his grief and pain and love the Hell out of him, because he's doing his best and he loves ya to bits. But the trick is not to get sucked into his moods,' her elderly friend Charlie Weatherbourne had coached her afterwards, like a bush preacher and counsellor combined. Today though, Drift couldn't find that return to love Charlie spoke of. These days her dad seemed particularly irritating. She could see people mistook Split's moods as long-held grief for her mother. But Drift now knew better. The grief was actually anger; for her betrayal. Her neglect. Her unfaithfulness. The past being dragged into the present each time he looked at his daughter. Drift shuddered at the memory of what Split'd chosen to do to himself — and to her — just three short months earlier. As she worked to feed the animals, she blocked the horror from her mind.

With the hay nets filled, and Bear, Roger, Dunston and Minty happily snorting into their feed, Drift scooped out pellets for the dogs from a tin tub set beneath the stock truck. The sound caused Molly, the collie-kelpie cross with the feathery ears, to sit bolt upright, and sweep her tail on the ground, eyes bright with expectation. Young Hamlet splayed his long red teenager limbs and raised his waggling bottom. Dunno, the stray, sat rigidly in his odd-dog body, gazing at her, drool falling from sagging black lips that always reminded Drift of the edges of freshly knifed abalone.

'You are one uggerly dawg,' Drift drawled, 'but I love you, buddy.' Her palm caressed Dunno's excessively domed head, stroking ears that were too small for his face. He was black and tan and as big as a kelpie, but had gnomishly short legs, an overly long catlike tail and a barrel ribcage and brisket that should belong on a cow. Drift gazed into his dark too-close-together eyes and sifted through the joy the funny-looking dog had brought her.

When she'd found the pup that first year on the road, she had fleetingly thought her father had deliberately placed the puppy in the concrete culvert especially for her eleventh birthday. The pup was huddled in the shade, a shadow himself. After she'd scooped him up and wrapped the shaking puppy in her flannie, she realised his litter mates lay in a pile nearby, maggots already at work on the little bodies. With a jolt, she knew he wasn't a gift from her father. The puppy, she realised, was like her. Alone on the road and without a mother. Drift had jogged over to her father, who was equally surprised to see the bizarre-looking creature. He had stopped girthing his horse to lean his hands on his knees and peer at the tiny bag of dehydrated bones.

'Where do you think he came from?' Split had asked.

'Dunno,' Drift answered.

'What breed do you reckon he is?'

'Dunno,' Drift said, inspecting the pup.

'What's his name?'

'Dunno,' she had said again, lifting and dropping her little-girl shoulders.

'Well then,' her father had said, ruffling her curly blonde mop, 'we'd better go find Dunno something to eat and drink, and make him a bed.'

Drift's face had lit up when she realised what her dad was saying. He had gone back to his saddling, calling over his shoulder to her, 'Dunno if he'll live or not, but if he does, do you reckon he'll work stock?'

'Dunno,' Drift had replied, then giggled, already knowing the puppy would be hers for life.

Now she hugged Dunno good night and on her way back to the van looked to the aluminium-framed water tank: it sat lopsided on a hillock of sand. She ought to get Split to help her slide it onto the Cruiser now, along with the water pump, before the beer carton emptied. Big day tomorrow, she thought. The cattle arriving would be long-haul thirsty, but Drift knew her birthday reminded her dad of her mother, and when he was reminded of her mother life took a slide. She decided to just get the job done herself. As she strained to lift the tank up, she remembered the box of leg-wax strips and the bottle of nail polish she and Shaynene had chosen as a present, still nestled in the shopping bag. A shiver of amusement ran through her.

'Good on you, Shaynene,' she said quietly. A smile curved her wind-chapped lips. The water run could wait until morning, she decided as she went into the van to prepare for her best birthday gift yet.

Chapter 3

'*Behold you, a feast to be had!*' her dad pronounced as Drift entered the van. He proudly held aloft two dinted enamel plates laden with yellow chips, an orange number-21 birthday candle jammed into one of the fish fillets. The tiny fold-out table in the van was set with a tomato sauce bottle, plastic salt and pepper shakers, mismatching cutlery plonked in a pile, and a couple of sachets of tartare sauce Shaynene had thrown in for free. Looking at her father's birthday spread, Drift remembered the pain of blowing out her eleventh birthday candle — the first birthday with Dunno, but also the first without her mother.

'Happy birthday, bovine beachside maid,' Split said, giving her a loving shove.

'Thanks, old pilgrim,' she said, grinning back at him, pushing down the sadness and restlessness. She noticed three beers had been downed already.

He reached over and patted the back of her hand. 'I know I'm not so good with presents, but what did I get you?'

'You'll find out. It's a surprise for both of us, later,' she said, pulling a face at him. She wondered if he could tell her mood was forced. Drift wished he had for once given her a surprise. Her hand roamed to her wide hobble belt and knife pouch. Her most precious gift. She'd got it for her thirteenth birthday from her old friend Charlie. Charlie Weatherbourne was a legendary saddler and had long grey hair plaited down to her waist, so long it could almost be flicked and cracked like the stock whips the old woman made. Her mobile saddlery truck was cluttered with ancient but solid sewing machines set up in a cavern of leather smell, old tools and gypsy creativity.

Drift wished Charlie's dusty truck would arrive now like a mirage and deliver her the amazing birthday gift of her wise warmth and humour. For Drift's eighteenth, Charlie had given her a quart-pot holder, and a new saddle blanket with the coveted CW brand for old Bear, who was feeling the droving work a little more these days. But Drift and her dad hadn't seen Charlie for months now. She looked over to the unpacked shopping bag from the store. The gift in there would just have to do.

An hour later in the caravan's oily fish-fry air, Drift looked over to her father where he sat in a midden of empty cans and cast-aside books, their open pages flapping in the draught like stranded butterflies. Before he'd dozed off he'd jabbed his finger at the magazine.

'See! See!' he said. 'David Rabbitburrow has it right.'

Drift had glanced over to the article in the *New Philosopher* magazine quoting naturalist David Attenborough.

Her father excitedly began reading. 'Old Rabbitburrow said *Ten thousand years ago man regarded the natural world as divine, but as he domesticated animals and plants, so nature lost some of its mystery and appeared to be little more than a larder that could be raided with impunity.*' Her father looked at her in distress. 'That's exactly what we see when we go to all those desolate farms with all those shutdown, blinkered farmers and managers chasing the almighty dollar. Why can't anyone see this? That we're ransacking our very own planet?' He spoke as if in extreme pain.

Often she wondered why he worked in agriculture, when he said he hated modern-day industrial agricultural practices. He was always banging on about attracting a better class of farming client who understood the link between economy and ecology, but he never made any attempt to find those kinds of clients.

On nights like this Drift could see clearly just how addicted her father was to his pain.

Drift nodded to pacify him, knowing how much the world of humans cut him, but after this many drinks, there was no point conversing with him about it. Instead she simply agreed and told him to get some shuteye.

Soon, her father was in the deepest sleep, and the weather was really coming in, shaking the van violently. Above the roar, Split was making sounds from the back of his throat like a gigantic dying fly as he slept in his greasy roadside-found armchair, which stank of dust and motor oil. His feet were encased in polyester orange work socks that carried grass seed and the dirt of several days.

Drift caught the whiff of his socks as she moved nearer to where her dad's ankles were crossed on a machinery lubrication drum converted to a stool with a rough-sawn top. An almost exhausted bottle of Bundy Red was nestled between his legs, leaning into his rounded tummy like a sleepy child. Her father reminded Drift of a tranquillised bear; she was relieved the roar of his pain was silenced for a while. She poked him with her index finger on the shoulder. 'Oi. Dad? *Dad? Yo, shepherd who first taught thy chosen seed?*'

He didn't respond.

'Good,' she said, grabbing up the leg-waxing strips. She took one from the box and warmed it between the palms of her hands, listening beyond the thin shell of the caravan. Outside, the relentless boom-crash of surf beyond the dunes and the bucking wind brought rattling shudders as if the nearby turmoil of the missing surfer was being echoed by the sea.

She tried to push away the image of a man, a body, out there on the water, floating. Bloating. It made her shiver. It wasn't her business, even though Shaynene sorely wanted to make it theirs. Drift found comfort in the fact that tomorrow, adding to the sound of the ocean would also be the deep moaning bellows of the drought-starved Northern cattle arriving weak and shit-covered on the trucks, ready for their long paddock drove to recovery on rich coastal feed. Above all else, droving in this people-less landscape was Drift's favourite work, especially nurturing cattle back to health. But the shadow of her father's depression sat with her. She resolved to jolly him out of it, before he was swallowed again. And she knew just how to do it. Practical jokes were their tradition and there was more stirring between them than a Mixmaster, so Drift set about on yet another prank.

Slowly, she drew the cloudy paper apart, the pink smear of wax sticky like gum sap. She squatted in front of her father and gently pasted the strips above his orange socks, up his chunky black-haired legs, over his thick banged-up knees before stopping at his thighs just below the line where the tan ran out. Split stirred and snorted. Drift paused, watching his eyebrows furrow, but she knew his booze-soaked brain would soon lull him back into blackness. The box emptied as she papier-mâchéd her father and, when the last wax strip was pasted, Drift leaned back on her haunches to survey her masterpiece … There: her birthday present all wrapped. But she wasn't done yet.

Reaching into her pocket, her fingertips met with shards of hay and rolled bits of bale twine before locating the bottle of nail polish she and Shaynene had chosen. She held the bottle up to the grey light that shone weakly through the flyspecked gauze curtains, steadying herself as the caravan rocked in the wild wind.

'Perfect,' she said, holding the little brush up against the vibrancy of his socks and then his shirt. She supposed some women would choose the colour because it reminded them of orange trees fruiting in summer sunshine, or tequila sunrises by the pool. But not her. It was the same full-force orange of her father's hi-vis shirt: it spoke of their long days of stock contracting, working under biting sun, and the iron-hard nights they spent living in either a cold, rattling or sullenly roasting van, depending on the weather. First she chose her father's right index finger. Then she moved to paint the next, tilting her head as she ran the brush carefully, last, over his lined thumbnail.

This close to him, she saw the deep etchings of his square, rough hands, which were gnarled from filing horse coconut shavings from hard hooves and trimming the hard shells of sheep's feet. His were hands that didn't just speak of hard work, but shouted the fact. They were buckled and worn from thousands of cattle castrated and lamb's tails docked, ewes crutched, needles jabbed into hides, drench guns squeezed into mouths and ear tags crunched into cartilage. Mile upon mile of animals walked. Along roads, through races, up ramps. A never-ending stream of animal-husbandry work needing to be done in whatever weather, in whatever district that the road and the rhythm of the seasons took them. As she painted, she noticed how knotted his knuckles were, his fingers beginning to bend at odd angles with early-onset arthritis.

When she was little she had loved his hands. They had been so certain. Hands that gathered up their washing, dried fresh and crispy at whatever laundrette they could find in whatever town. His were hands that would never punch dogs when they barked on the back of the ute, like she had seen other men do. Nor would they ever whack a hard-worked horse on its soft muzzle when it keenly edged too close at the end of a thirsty day. Her dad's hands would lift a lead rope lightly, or stroke the warm back of a working dog steadily. They would slide over the back of her head, with protection and love.

His square giant's hands were such a contrast to the fading, fraying memory of her mother's. Her mother had thin mermaid fingers that strummed guitar strings and beaded shells onto fishing line and twined daisies into Drift's baby-soft long blonde hair. Harmony Wood's fingers were often wrinkled by the sea, or imprinted with a garden's deep brown soil, sometimes coated in gentle pastel shades from shelling vibrant peas or peeling the skins from steamed beetroot. Slim hands carefully placing eggs gathered into the frothy skirts that Harmony had dressed her in. Fingertips melding butter and flour bought from the wholefoods store in the nearest hippy-infused rural town for birthday cakes and biscuits.

Drift looked at the half-eaten yellow supermarket sponge cake sitting on a plastic tray next to the deep fryer. It had sickly sweet filling labelled 'jam' and icing sugar as fine as lice powder dusting its bald top. The number-21 candle, half melted, lay beside it, and the wish that her life would change was already released on the wild winds.

Drift knew she ought to clean it all away, not just because it would set her father off on a rant about how food corporations forced them to buy unsustainable packaging and chemical-permeated food, but also because of the mice that forever kept finding their way inside the van. No matter how many times she set traps and plugged holes with steel wool, they still invaded the space. Then there was the sand … always the sand that scattered over the worn lino floor each time they peeled work socks from their overheated feet. She knew she could never go back to that time when life held her mother at its heart. And a garden. Drift longed for a garden one day. But for now, with her father, there was only one choice: to keep moving forward on this long, endless road of work. But today, for whatever reason, forward felt like standing still.

She scrunched her eyes shut tight and twirled the birthday candle around in her fingers. 'Please change. *Life*. Please change.'

Chapter 4

After she'd finished painting Split's fingernails, Drift sat back on her heels and sighed. Through the tiny salt-crusted window, clouds scudded across a dull sky. It was January and supposed to be summer, but not in this part of the Western Australian countryside, where the weather blew in over vast, wild oceans and betrayed the seasons with a suddenness that jolted. The sinister shift in conditions had brought with it a grey angry surge that boiled incessantly against the jagged rocks, which Drift knew would be making life treacherous and near impossible for the search-and-rescue team assembled down at the end of the beach, where the more hardcore surfers camped. In a dusk sky a pale orange full moon was just peeking over the wind-trimmed scrub to the east. She hoped her birthday wish would work, doubly so with the power of the moon behind it.

'Happy birthday to me, Melody Wood,' she said, picking up her father's phone and taking a quick picture of him. She wanted to send the photo to Shaynene, but there on the wildly isolated Pinrush Point they were out of range. The shared joke would have to wait.

A sudden banging on the door shook Drift from her daydream with a start. She flew to the other side of the caravan and drew back the curtain. A police four-wheel drive was parked there. The gusting wind was so loud the animals hadn't heard the vehicle. The tether-line horse team stood with their ears

19

folded back, tails to the wind, dozing in a determined meditation against the weather. Even the dogs lay curled in balls beneath the stock trailer, noses covered by tails, unwilling to unfold themselves against the cold blast. Drift glanced towards her father, still sound asleep, before opening the door a little.

She looked down at the cops. An older policeman with grey hair and a walrus moustache braced himself against the thrust of the wind. Behind him a tall, lean, dark-haired young man with a classic chiselled face like an elite Aussie Rules footballer stood holding onto his police cap to stop it blowing from his head. Her eyes lingered on him.

The dogs at last sensed strangers and stood suddenly, barking. Piercingly, she whistled to them to be quiet without unlocking her eyes from the young policeman's. A small involuntary smile arrived on her face. She noticed slightly pitted skin that spoke of the torture of adolescent acne, but even with it he was still a babe-magnet, as Shaynene would say. He was the sort of good-looking man in uniform Shaynene would convulse over, shouting, 'Frisk me! Frisk me!'

'Could we come in?' the older man shouted just as a gust tried to rip the words from his mouth and steal the door from her hands. Even without the wind, she could barely hear him over the boom of giant waves beyond the dune. She looked back again at her father, sprawled senseless on his chair, and a flush ran over her face. Puddle-sized raindrops began to dollop onto the earth.

'Um ...' she hesitated, '... sure.' Her dad would kill her. Her birthday joke was suddenly not just backfiring but exploding in her face.

'Just a sec. Gotta, um, make some room,' she shouted, before shutting the door quickly; the rain began to teem down, bedraggling the officers.

'Shit, shit, *shit*,' she said at the sight of her father, his nails glowing like a brand-new Stihl chainsaw case, the pinkish wax strips plastered to his legs, fluttering slightly in the breezy van

20

like roadwork bunting. Drift couldn't help a laugh escaping. There was going to be hell to pay.

'*'Tis not so sweet now as it was before!*' Drift muttered to herself as she hastily grabbed his blanket from behind the curtain around his bed and threw it over his lap. Next, she gathered up the clattering cans and shoved them into the tiny sink, flinging a tea towel over them. She shoved the Bundy bottle under the chair and began to shake her father awake.

'*Dad!* Dad? It's the cops.'

As he waded through fog to wake up, she went back to the door. The police officers were in the same stance as she'd found them moments before, faces tilted against the onslaught of fat drops of sideways rain.

'Sorry,' she yelled. 'It's my birthday and it's a bit of a mess in here. Dad and I had a little party.' She gestured for them to come in, the young policeman taking the door from her to hold it steady as they stepped up and entered, pooling rain drops on the vinyl.

'Happy birthday,' the younger cop said loudly over the rain.

'Thanks,' she said glancing at him shyly. Once in the van the men seemed huge. The younger one was stooping his head, his cap with the chequered banding now in his hands, his hair as black as night, clipped short on the sides, but slicked back like an old-time gent. The older one, as thick and short set as a Murray Grey bull, looked imposing in his crisp blue shirt and jacket emblazoned with the badge of black swan and regal crown, darkened by rain.

'I'm Sergeant Dodge and this is Constable Swain, Cooperville Police,' he said, indicating his young offsider and flashing his ID. As he spoke, he looked around the van. Drift flushed at what he must be thinking about the mess. Her and her father's clutter of books, their sketches and paintings pinned all over the walls and cupboards, the tumble of clothing and livestock equipment, along with saddlery she was halfway through mending under the direction of Charlie Weatherbourne.

On the table lay the dirty plates, sauce smears like a bloodied crime scene. Cocaine-style spilled icing sugar on the table. Vaccination needles for animals looking dodgy. Her dad's philosophy magazines laid open and already marked with etched sticky notes. She wondered if she ought to pretend this was some kind of normal and offer them some cake. But then the officers' eyes fell to her father, who was awake now and had a deep furrow on his brow and a look of utter confusion. He was clenching his fists to hide his nails and shifting his legs uncomfortably under the blanket, blinking at the sight of the two cops standing in his van above him.

'This is my dad, Split ... er ... Dennis Wood, and I'm Melody. But you can just call me Drift. Everyone does. Um ... Dad's having a bit of trouble with leg cramps. The gout or something,' Drift stammered, as her father's dark eyes glared at her.

'Don't get up,' Sergeant Dodge said. 'We won't keep you long.' He cleared his throat as if about to make a public speech. 'You have probably heard a man's gone missing.'

Sergeant Dodge retrieved a photo of the surfer from his pocket and flashed it at them, Drift not taking in the image. All she could feel was the flame in her cheeks, not just from the fury her father was emitting towards her, but also because the young Constable Swain had not taken his eyes off her.

'We'll have a phone-reception booster set up for the duration of the search as of tonight, so if you have any information please call us. We're asking you to keep an eye out. A body washed up on the beach. Clothing. A board, maybe? That sort of thing,' he said.

Drift felt the chill of the past soak through her system as she watched her father's face turn ashen.

'Of course,' Drift said. 'How terrible for his family.'

Constable Swain added gently, 'There is hope he could've clung to his board and washed in somewhere on the current. But this change ...'

'Not to mention the sharks,' came the harder voice of Sergeant Dodge. There was an empty silence. Dodge's eyes roamed from father to daughter, as if he were looking for a piece of a puzzle he couldn't quite locate. 'Well,' he said, as he offered Split his card, 'thanks for your time. Better head back to base camp.'

Reluctantly, Split unfurled his fist to take the card. The sergeant's head tilted ever so slightly as he saw Split's hand, the orange polish standing out like flashing tow-truck lights. One dark, perfectly curved eyebrow lifted on Constable Swain's face.

'Thanks for stopping by,' Drift said a little too loudly, flinging the door open to the wild wind.

'It was nice to meet you,' Constable Swain said. He leaned closer to her and muttered, 'Your father? He's not Priscilla, Queen of the Desert is he? Interesting. Different.' He pulled a face at her and winked. His senior officer gave him a scowl but it did nothing to dim the glimmer in his eye as he looked at Drift.

She blushed as she watched his broad back walking away in the wildness of the storm, trying not to think of the missing man, her mother, or the fury she was about to receive from her father. She pulled the door shut and braced herself for what was to come.

Chapter 5

Normally her father would've dug deep into his repertoire of Shakespearean insults or used words like 'treacherous wench!' after discovering he'd been pranked. But this evening, Drift was shocked to hear him yell furiously, 'You little bitch!'

The words hit Drift like a slap. He had *never* spoken to her that way before.

'How was I to know the cops would turn up?' she said, tears springing into her eyes. Normally, Drift would've spluttered with laughter at the sight of him standing in the van with his perfectly colour co-ordinated hi-vis orange nails, workwear and the dangling wax papers. And normally he would've caved, joining in on the joke, but since the events a few months back, there was an undercurrent of blackness in Split.

'Why'd you let 'em in?' he yelled.

'How could I *not*? It's blowing a gale. We couldn't hear each other! And it was pissing down.' A blast of wind hit the van full force as if to drive her point home. 'Plus, how do I say no to cops?' Between them the memory flared of the past, her mother, and the police who had asked so many questions. The dark days when they'd had Child Services authorities relentlessly grilling Split on just how he could care for and educate his little girl on his own with such an itinerant life. If it hadn't been for Wilma the Wondrous, Drift would have been shoved into foster care in a flash. Both she and Split had been wary ever since of the powers of paper-pushers and police who seemed intent on challenging the choice of a widower and stockman to take his little girl on the road.

Split looked down at himself, ashamed. 'Look at me. They'll think I'm some kinda psycho. You're lucky you're as old as you are now or they'd have taken you away from me.' He glanced up at her, and she inwardly winced at the pain she saw in his deep brown eyes, but then a sudden anger flared in her.

'You *are* psycho,' she blurted, instantly wishing she hadn't when she saw the fear in his eyes that her words could be true.

They stood facing each other in silence, upset flowing between them and the shared knowledge of what had so recently happened. It was such a large elephant in the very tiny room. Eventually Split spoke, his face softening. 'What the fuck is all this *really* about anyway, Drift?' he urged.

Drift paused, biting her lip. She felt so furious with him. So let down by him. It surged in her like a monster wave. Maybe it was turning twenty-one and knowing she was glued to him, not for her benefit, but simply to keep him safe and alive.

'It's payback for the possum,' she lied, trying to sound light and steer the conversation away from the awful day a few months ago when she'd found him slumped over the steering wheel in the old ute in a cloud of carbon monoxide. She now shuddered each time she got into the bloody thing.

'Possum?'

She saw her father's alcohol-affected brain slowly retrieve the memory of the prank, the previous month on Gingun Station, after a three-day hot-as-Hell stint of cattle work. One night after work, Split'd hoisted the roadkill up into the branches shading their caravan, and sat as still as a rock, waiting for Drift to come out of the van. When she'd emerged with a nice cold drink, he'd dropped the dead possum onto her head.

Recalling Drift's scream of surprise, the cordial spilling over her clean clothes and the stench of the carcass that remained in her hair all night, Split nodded. He pulled a 'fair enough' face.

'The possum, eh?' he said, knowing it wasn't the possum at all.

Normally by now they would both be laughing about her 'birthday present'. They'd be in stitches 'unwrapping' him with every painful tug of the strips. Their father–daughter payback jokes had helped pass the days of hard-edged monotonous work for years. Their shared sense of humour usually drew them closer together, but this time, with the police again in their midst, asking about a person lost at sea, they were both lost in memories that sliced like razor blades on thinly healed wounds in both of them.

Neither of them had ever really recovered from that day when they received the news that Drift's mother, Harmony, had disappeared into the ocean. Split's pain was still as raw as if it were yesterday, and both remembered the agony of the tense wait for a body washed up on shimmering sand, hours dragging into days and then weeks.

The cosy coastal cottage of Drift's childhood hundreds of kilometres south east of here became her nightmare, the little girl calling out fitfully in her sleep for her mother. Her father would come to her, but it wasn't the same. Nothing was ever the same. Sunny mornings in the cottage were shadowed now by Split's dark silence as they sat before the grey, cold ash of the woodstove. He sometimes suggested returning to Tasmania, but they had stayed out west. Near the water. The hurt never leaving. When the memorial came and they'd gathered for Harmony's 'send-off' there was no need for a coffin. Drift watched her father endure the slow painful reveal of how Mrs Harmony Wood came to be in a sea so rough and so dark, bombed out on surfer drugs, partying with a crowd her father had no time for, while he waited at home for her, their little girl sleeping between flannelette sheets with stars printed brightly upon them. Dawn revealed a husband's heart, torn, and a young daughter, motherless.

Drift looked at her father's reddened face. The pain behind his eyes was so familiar to her. He'd kept her by the sea all her life, just in case her mother came back to them, pointing to the white horses and saying that Harmony might be riding them home. He'd sometimes whispered in the dead of night as he sat on Drift's bed that maybe she'd just cleared out. Maybe she'd faked it.

Now Drift was older, she was beginning to wonder why her father clung to his wife's memory so much. Harmony Wood had been like a carnival of colour but she was also a swirl of restless energy: alluring, yet unstable. She was like a fault line running beneath paradise. Both father and daughter had learned she could erupt any time. Sometimes savagely.

Now Drift realised she had spent over ten years of her life looking out to sea, hoping for a sign of a mother who didn't exist. She knew in her heart her father had created a fantasy of who Harmony had been in their lives. It was utterly futile for her dad to *still* be obsessing about her. To still be grieving and angry at her. Like she was an excuse *not* to live.

Frustration flared again in Drift. He'd fed her sweet hope like some parents fed their children sugar and so her addiction to the possibility of a happy ending had begun. For a long time Drift believed one day her mother might just walk back into their lives, balanced and healed. But lately she hoped for a sign that answered that enduring question, 'Is she still alive?' Maybe knowing the answer would bring her father back to earth. For the months since his botched suicide, Drift had borne the weight of having to be the adult and Split the child.

'I'm done,' she said suddenly. 'After this droving trip, you're on your own. I'm outta here.'

Her words contorted Split's face into an expression of shock. Then hurt. She and he were a team. A partnership. Inseparable.

She pulled on her dogger boots in silence, glaring at him once more as she banged her way out into the bluster of the evening. Drift let the wind unravel her hair so it fell in wild waves over her shoulders. It was too cold for shorts, but she soldiered on, wrapping her blue checked flannelette shirt around her.

Beyond the dunes, above the chop of a grey-sea horizon, where the storm was passing, the half-sunk sun was prising open the clouds and showering the low coastal scrub and white sand with a burst of orange. It lit the coats of the horses so Bear, the heavy-set bay, looked like a bronze statue. Drift stood staring in wonder as the two flea-bitten greys, Roger and Minty, turned golden white as if held in some magic spell and the paint patches on Dunston, her father's chunky brown skewbald horse, glowed like sunset clouds. She was awestruck by how a burning orange glow set the world alight like a candle in the gap between day and night, and wondered if the world really was this beautiful all the time. Maybe *this* was her birthday present, Drift thought. One sent to her by her mother. She could feel it. Like a hello … and a goodbye. She hugged her arms about herself and her lips turned up in a sad smile.

The door of the caravan opened behind her.

'Where the fuck are ya goin?' Split roared over the wind. 'When are you gunna get this shit off me?'

Drift had never heard her father speak to her in such a way … not even in the company of rough workers who peppered their sentences with swearing. 'You've lost it,' she yelled at him, turning her back and walking away. 'Like I said, you're on your own. I'm going to the sea. To sing happy birthday with Mum.' Her words were stolen away by the wind.

Chapter 6

The three droving dogs danced on their chains, looking at Drift beseechingly. Even in her state of upset they won a loving smile from her. Brushing her tanned hand over her forehead in a futile attempt to control the wildness of her hair, she stooped to unclip them. Dunno was the first off, leaping away with his splayed paws. Molly was banging the rim of the stock truck tyre with her tail, her gentle feathery collie-kelpie face framed by tufted ears. Unchained, she danced away on the sandy soil to the coastal grass to sniff. Drift waited for Hamlet to calm before she released him.

'*Steady*, sit,' Drift commanded. Even if she was mid-fight with her father, she wasn't going to muck up the young dog's training. Hamlet did his best to settle his adolescent self, but the chink of the dog clip sent him off in high excitement, his long red limbs jerking about like a frenzied kid doing 'the dab'.

'Hamlet, ya ning nong,' Drift chided, before going to the horse line. Laying a hand on Minty's grey soapstone shoulder, Drift untied her, flung the rope over her neck and fastened a knot under the headstall so she had some reins. She grabbed a handful of charcoal mane and as agile as a circus rider swung up onto the narrow high-withered back, spinning Minty around to make for the dunes.

On the other side of the van, her father clattered drunkenly outside, his eyes squinting into the sting of sand, the paper wax strips flapping forlornly. Drift didn't look back as her old man stooped over and retched up his dinner and booze onto a clump of marram grasses. As she rode away, the dogs came to her without so much as a whistle and locked onto her horse's hocks as if held there by an invisible thread. Together, they cantered along the narrow track that led between two hummocked dunes, the coarse grasses thrashing madly in the wind. She felt compelled to get away from him. Him and his dark, angry grief.

On the beach, the grey ocean bathed in half-light spread before them. White wave horses scudded over the surface of tumblesome water that stretched to a cold and distant horizon. Huge barrel waves heaved and boomed not far off the beach, sending spray and foam into the air. Sand blew in windborne rivers, stinging Drift's face. Squinting her summer-sky blue eyes, Drift settled her gaze on the monotone horizon, scanning the water's surface. Searching. Searching. Always searching, as if her mother was out there still. She told herself to stop it.

But what if she found that surfer's body? How much horror would it bring? With her imaginings of a bloated body beached like a dead seal came the shock memory of finding her father. Split's suicide attempt had happened east of Bunbury on a desolate drought-ravaged sheep property. They'd been bunkered in the caravan, cabin fever messing with their minds as long-awaited rain drummed relentlessly for two days on the bare soil, washing away any possibility of continuing the sheep work. Outside in the holding yards the flock was slumping into mud: bags of bones, dying.

Inside, Split had been reading too much environmental science for Drift's liking. And seeing the barren land turned to a quagmire tipped him over the edge. That afternoon, booze sodden, he'd already raved at the shocked sheep farmer.

'The planet's sixth extinction is on its way and your overgrazing is part of the cause!'

In the darkness of the low-roofed shearing shed, Split had stabbed his thick index finger at the skinny farmer, ranting. That was until Drift had placed her hand on his forearm. Lowering it slowly like a loaded gun. The farmer had narrowed his eyes at Split, looking at him as if he was a total arsehole, bonkers at best.

'Less than two hunnerd years, they reckon!' Split had slurred. 'Unless you blokes wake up and help turn it around.'

The farmer, his stance wide, a drip hanging from his nose as the rain roared on the corro roof, shook his head. Drift's nerves had jangled when she saw the agony in her father's eyes, and the fury in the cocky's.

'Extinctshon!' her dad ranted, booze sliding his words sideways. 'Not because of 'n Ice Age. Not b'cause of a meteor! But b'cause of human greed! Human schtupidity! How can no one see it? Why won't anyone wake up to it? Why won't you? *What's wrong with you people? Look at your land! Look at your livestock!*'

Drift had ushered the cocky out of earshot, soothing him, telling him the anniversary was coming up for them ... of her mother's drowning. The cocky had mumbled something about not bothering to stick around to finish the sheep then stepped out into the bleakness of the rain. Many knew of Split's mood swings on the grog, but he was such a calm, brilliant stockman, flowing animals seemingly effortlessly through the yards, that Drift had gone to bed believing the farmer would forgive him by morning and that when the clouds cleared, so would the moods.

Instead, Drift had woken in the middle of the night sensing something was wrong. Pushing back the bedclothes, stepping outside the van, she'd followed the low rumble of the idling ute, rain zinging in the headlights. As Drift neared, the glow from the dashboard light revealed an appalling sight: her father's face green and grey, head flopping forward, eyes closed, lips tinged blue.

'Dad! Dad!' She had reefed open the door. Screaming, grunting, crying, she'd used all her country-girl strength to haul him from the vehicle. He toppled, landing like a shot bullock in the rain and the mud. The fumes made her cough and retch. Grabbing his phone in his pocket, she called emergency services, adding up in her mind the insane distance they were from Bunbury. Then she found herself leaning on the horn repeatedly, hoping the farmer would come, bringing with him his silent, no-nonsense wife with her nursing skills.

As she pummelled her father's chest in the downpour and searched for his breath, Drift tried to imagine life without him. It was an impossibility. How could he have even thought to leave her like that?

On the beach tonight, on her birthday, she still ran her mind over the question. What had he been thinking? Before her, the sun had boiled into the sea during a lull between the hot–cold currents creating the storms. Behind her, over the dunes, silently and slowly sliding up into the indigo sky, came the giant orange disc of the full moon. It wavered in a halo and shimmered where its fan of light touched the darkening landscape. Drift felt the moon's pull but resisted the temptation to stay and gaze at it, wanting to put some distance between her and her father.

Instead, she turned Minty with her bare legs pressing on the mare's snow white sides, edging her towards the setting sun, into the frothing water's edge. The mare dropped her head, her nostrils rippling in a snort. The horse was well used to swimming with Drift after work on calmer, warmer days, but this blast of unseasonal chill and the thunderclap booms of the breaking surf in the half dark were making the mare edgy.

'C'mon, Minty. It's my birthday … treat me a little.'

The mare lifted her coal-black legs and danced forward, one eye cautiously watching the bubble and froth of each dying wave as it sighed back out to sea. As they edged deeper, and the surf surged around them, Drift saw dark tendrils of kelp wavering just beneath the surface like mermaid's hair.

'I'm twenty-one, Mum,' she said to the water and the drifting seaweed. 'Same age as when you had me. Can I leave him now? Do you think?' A shiver went through her just as the crash of a wave sent Minty in a spinning shy towards the beach. Drift squealed, exhilarated by the wildness. She urged the mare into a canter so that soon they were flying over the grey-sheened sand parallel to the madness of the choppy frothy waves, the three dogs, grinning wildly, galloping with her. Silver reflections turned to orange as the moon wove golden light into the melding of day and night.

After a time, hoof marks filled with moonlight, spilling out behind Drift and Minty, leaving a trail along the huge crescent stretch of beach. Birds, yet to roost on the faraway rocks, were thrown about in the air like unanchored yachts in a storm. Far out from the shore, white wave horses tossed their foaming manes and galloped on with the wind in the same direction as Drift. Eventually, she and Minty slowed to a walk, ambling along, the mare snorting down, Drift feeling the wind chill on her skin.

Darkness crashed down on the day. The land beyond the dunes could barely be seen, except for where the moon drooled a pool of ginger light over it. At the end of the beach, near the rocky headland, Drift saw the leap of amber flames: a bonfire. Floodlights in the dunes and the chug of a generator told her it was the base camp the cops had mentioned.

It was odd to see lights and so much activity out here, like a mini alien city had landed. They were miles from anywhere, on a coastal route few people visited. It was one of the reasons she and her dad brought cattle out here. Not many stockmen could be bothered chasing feed that was this remote, the profit margins too tight and the camping rough. Even few surfers bothered to travel this far for waves, when perfect barrels could be found closer to coffee shops and bars in more civilised centres.

Beyond this particular beach there was still another two hundred kilometres of unused, long-forgotten stock route that would offer up the rare opportunity for drought-starved cattle to survive and fatten enough to sell. The Department of Agriculture administrators had quickly rubber-stamped Split's droving licence, knowing no other stockmen had taken cattle there in years and that the graze would do the land good. Now the Woods had sole access to the peninsula's tall stands of marine couch grasses and protein-rich seed heads of poas. Coastal herbs of trailing jointweed and brookweed, along with washed-up ropes of iodine-rich kelp, gave the cattle a banquet of choices in healing their emaciated bodies.

With one lot gone away to market after six weeks on the route closest to Widgenup four months back, tomorrow a full B-double and dog trailer of cows and calves would be arriving in the morning to be taken further on, deeper into the dead-end headland. They weren't the Woods' cattle, but the money she and Split were paid for droving and fattening them was good — better money and better work than the grinding repetition of stock contract jobs like foot paring and calf marking. Drift tried to shake the words she'd delivered to her father from her mind. She loved this life. She wondered what on earth else she could do or where she could go. She ached for guidance.

Closing her eyes and feeling the horse beneath her breathe with warmth and life she asked, 'Where should I go? What should I do?' But no matter how hard she tried to hear her mother, she never could. It was as if her voice was muted by all that sea.

'Mum?' How strange the word sounded, spoken aloud. 'Anyone?'

Suddenly the mare baulked and propped, skidding and wheeling as if she'd seen a snake. Gripping her thighs to stay on, Drift cried out in surprise. The mare half-reared and shook her head, snorting. Normally Drift's calm droving mare withstood anything life threw at her — the sudden storm of a passing road train or the tumbleweed shock of a plastic bag on the wind — but tonight, as if charged with electricity, Minty fidgeted and danced.

'Minty! What the —?' She peered into the darkness ahead of her, the sand cast in shadows by the bright moon. Trying to regain her balance, Drift's fingers entwined in the rope and mane as the mare continued to prance. What was Minty shying at? Further on down the beach, over the sound of the wind, she could just hear music coming from the direction of the dancing flames. Guitars and voices. Drift knew that wasn't spooking Minty. Ears pricked, head lifted like an Arabian show horse, the mare was staring at the dunes. Drift followed her gaze and felt the hair on the back of her neck stand up. In that moment the world stopped still. The dogs froze, pricking their ears. For Drift it was just a glimpse, but the glimpse seemed to last forever — the image etched in her mind — like she was in a tunnel of time.

Squinting into the darkness, Drift could swear she saw a small figure about ten metres away on the white sand, framed by the darkened sky. The moon above the little girl was hanging, salmon-coloured, like scenery painted on an indigo-black curtain. The little girl was aged about six. She was wearing a white summer beach dress. Her small fingers were stroking the quivering ends of the dark dune grasses that danced about her, and her big eyes were locked on Drift. Big dark earnest eyes. Soulful eyes. Her little heart-shaped face, framed with long twisted dark hair, was smiling at her.

Then she was gone. Disappearing in a blink, gone with the crash of a wave. A blast of wind. A little girl in the dunes, appearing as quick as a lightning flash. There, bright and brilliant, and then suddenly no longer. Gone.

Chapter 7

The words were out of Drift's mouth before she'd fully pulled Minty up from the gallop.

'You haven't lost a little girl, have you?' she asked breathlessly.

Sparks shot up into blackness from the campfire as the men turned in surprise at her arrival.

Drift took in the group staring at her, a ripple of buzzing energy running through her as it did her horse.

An older man wearing a colourful Mexican poncho gazed at her, his back to a line of surfboards dug into the sand sheltering them from the wind. Three super-fit real-deal surfer dudes sat holding on to their beers, while a scrawny man stumbled over to her like an inebriated Pinocchio, all skinny limbs, wobbling head and glazed black-button eyes. 'Whoa, man! Are you a ghost girl? Is that a ghost horse? Whoa! You're freakin me out,' he said.

Pissed and stoned, Drift suspected, unimpressed. Behind him, wetsuits hung like shadowy ghouls from the roof racks of black shiny four-wheel drives. He staggered back theatrically and ran his puppet hands through his dark ginger curled hair. Drift ignored him, turning her matter-of-fact gaze on the older man. 'I've just seen a little girl. She was back there in the dunes. On her own. I thought ...'

'Bullshit. You thought you'd come hassle us,' the poncho-wearing man said. 'You know there's no girl.'

'What?' Drift replied, suddenly taking in how different this group was from the usual scruffy stoner surfies she and Split ran into on the road. These guys had flashy vehicles. Their camp and surf gear was plastered all over with sponsorship logos. Their clothing too. Their cool gazes held an air of disdain and she sensed their egos were as huge as the darkened Western Australian sky.

'You're just the first of so many about to arrive, pretending to get ripped up by losing him,' poncho man said.

Drift looked at him, puzzled, then realised he must be talking about the missing surfer. 'Do I look like I'm some ditzy surfer-crazed chick?' she flared at him, anger with her father and her mother's past fuelling her words. 'I saw a girl in the dunes. Too young to be by herself. Especially out here.' Irritated she jiggled Minty's lead-rope reins, wishing the mare would stand.

She glanced over to the bright lights of the emergency-services camp set up in a small sandy lay-by behind some low boobialla trees. She could see people in their uniforms moving about. Maybe she ought to go tell the searchers about the girl instead of talking to this lot. Maybe the girl had wandered out of that camp, or she'd come off The Planet, the cattle station that ran most of the length of the Point road beside the stock route. Surely the girl had to have come from that property, if not from here?

'You saw a what?' came a voice from the shadows. A young man walked into the rim of the campfire light, lugging an Esky. He had a shock of blond hair and classic broad shoulders — a typical Aussie lifesaver look. Another perve-worthy boy in Shaynene's book, thought Drift. He dumped the cooler.

Poncho man grabbed the neck of a beaten old Maton and sat it on his lap, beginning to tune it by ear. 'She wants to know if we've lost a girl. I know you've deliberately lost a lot of girls, Digger, especially young ones,' he said sarcastically, not taking his gaze from her.

The lifesaver boy, Digger, narrowed his eyes. 'Is she taking the piss?'

Drift studied the men's tense faces. 'Look,' she said in a more gentle tone, 'I've heard that you've maybe lost a mate, but I just saw —'

'A mate?' the poncho man suddenly scoffed in his American accent. 'He wasn't *just a mate*. He was the greatest surfer ever put on this planet. And here you are hassling us about some lost girl … fuck off.'

The other men averted their eyes as they heard his voice choke with anger and pain.

'Settle down, Mo,' said lifesaver man. He looked up at Drift. 'You're from the drover's camp, right?'

Drift nodded.

'Why hello, cowgirl,' said the pissed puppet man lasciviously, moving closer, offering a wavering handshake. She lifted Minty's neck rope, bending her so puppet man had to wobble out of the way of the horse's rump, his yellow caffeine-toothed smile turning to an offended sneer. She returned a tough-girl gaze. This one was creepy. Minty's ears flicked back and forwards. She threw her head, eager to get out of the wind and the weirdness. Drift sat back on her, trying to reassure the mare by slowing her own breath.

'Helloooo?' puppet man said questioningly in his Aussie drawl. 'Why aren't you goin off your tits by now?' He looked at her as if she were stupid, sweeping his arm around to indicate his mates.

'Beg yours?' Drift said.

'Anyone home in there?' He tapped his temple with his index finger.

Drift looked at his expectant face, puzzled.

'What rock have you been under?' he asked.

'Sorry?' she said, still perplexed, thinking back to earlier today and Shaynene's similar comment.

'Leave off her, Gup, you tosser,' snarled Mo as he set down his guitar.

Gup ignored him. 'You have just been introduced to *the* most famous group of surfers on the planet. Der.' He began to reel

off their names and their world-superstar-pro titles, until Digger
pelted him with an empty can.

'Shut the fuck up,' Digger said. 'Why'd you think we came
this far out to the Woop Woop? To get away from all that shit.
And now Kai's gone … This is fucked.'

'And the rest,' said another surfer in a drawling Southern
American accent.

Drift shrugged. 'Famous doesn't have legs round here,'
she said entwining her fingers in Minty's mane. 'Not with me
anyway.'

She softened her gaze with compassion at the older man, Mo.
'Look, if we can do anything to help, Dad and I are around. Just
sing out.'

She caught the briefest glimmer of gratitude in Mo's eyes
before he shut down again. He waved her away as if dismissing
a servant.

'Just keep an eye out, will ya?' Drift said. 'This is a little
kid out here on her own, I'm talking about. It's a big stretch of
nothin country.'

Slowly, she swung Minty towards the bright lights of the
search-and-rescue camp that thrummed with the generator and
collective voices further along the beach. As she rode over the soft
sand towards the fringes of the makeshift camp, Drift wondered if
the girl had been real. Had she dreamed her up? Could she really
belong to the cattle station, The Planet? She recalled the blokes
earlier today in Widgenup, gathering around her father outside
the pub and bottle shop, kick-starting the same conversations
they had every time they spotted Split Wood and his daughter.

'Takin another lot of cattle south down the Point again?'
asked one.

Split had nodded, reaching for his tobacco and papers.

'Seen that mad bitch billionaire who done the dodgy deal
with the government to shelve the mining?' asked another.

Drift had turned her face to the pavement and rolled her eyes.
Did these people realise their lives really were just on loop — day

in, day out — doing the same thing, thinking the same thing, talking about the same thing?

'Town could've boomed with jobs and progress if that rich greenie cow hadn't interfered and stopped it all,' said a hairy old man, his grey eyes reflecting a life wasted on too much grog and negativity.

'You ever seen her? She never shows her face around town,' one fella spat, showing his disgust.

Her dad finished rolling his smoke. He stuck it behind his ear and squinted, then shook his head. He put his worn leather CW tobacco wallet back into his top pocket. 'Last time Drift and I was there, we seen nothing for weeks but the arse end of cows, a few stinkin dead roos and one square shittin wombat,' he'd replied, ditching his normal talk and settling for stockman speak.

'When I done a bit of road work that way I seen these fancy black four-wheel drives comin and goin from Perth,' a gap-toothed man said, 'and these big white trucks too. Even seen big planes landin in there.'

'Probably dealing drugs.'

'Law unto herself.'

'Bitch,' one added as a finality.

The men then shrugged and changed the subject to the weather. The Yankee woman didn't hire locals, so they mostly left her to her sprawling swathe of not-much-good-for-anything sandy coastal country and dubbed her mad. Now as Drift sat on her horse on the blustery isolated beach, she wondered how mad. Mad enough to have some little kid running about in the dark in a white dress?

She ought to find out, she thought as she rode right up into the makeshift camp to find Constable Simon Swain ducking out from the awning of the police van to greet her. Local SES volunteers in overalls stood beside police officers and glanced up briefly at the pretty girl on the horse before returning their attention to the maps spread out before them. Some were looking at laptops, charting tides and currents, and monitoring weather and winds. On the sheened sand where the waves frothed, lit by portable floodlights, surf crews were hauling a white inflatable rescue craft back onto a thin-framed yellow trailer.

Constable Swain stood on the gravel in his sturdy black boots, his long lean body casting a narrow shadow. 'So you just met that lot,' he said, indicating towards the surfers' camp.

Drift looked back over her shoulder. 'Yep.'

'Arrogant bunch.'

'Sure are,' she agreed. They exchanged shy smiles.

'What brings you out?'

Drift looked down at him. 'Constable Swain, right?'

'Simon. Call me Simon.'

Drift felt a buzz run through her. She paused and turned her mind towards the reason she was here. 'I saw, at least I *think* I just saw, a little girl. Back there in the dunes. I wondered if she was missing. Or part of this crew?' She glanced about at the rescue workers, some making ready to tow the rescue boats further up the beach. She realised no one would bring a child to anything like this, and suddenly felt foolish. Had she imagined the whole thing after all? She soldiered on in retelling Simon what she'd seen.

'It's something I'll need authority to investigate right now,' Simon said, looking back towards the hub of the camp. 'We're really busy here. Unless someone is reported missing, it's unlikely we take action. Just let me go check with my senior officer.'

As Drift waited she looked up to the moon and the pool of orange that spilled on the surface of the sea. She wondered if that Kai fella was out there, somewhere. Out there with her mother? She felt tears rise, but shoved the emotion back down inside.

Simon arrived back and stood a way off from her, his boots looking even blacker against the white glowing dunes. 'I'm clear to go with you,' he said.

'Good. I won't keep you long. We'll find the spot faster via the beach. Want to dink? She's super quiet. At least, normally she is.' She stroked Minty's neck. 'This night feels anything but normal though.'

Simon shook his head. 'There's one thing they don't coach you out of in police training … and that's horse phobias. I don't like horses. Terrified of them.'

Drift at first thought he was joking, then she saw the tension in his expression. He swallowed. He truly was scared. She smiled reassuringly at him. 'How about I ride back to camp and meet you there?'

Relief spread on Simon's face. 'Sure. I'll pick you up at your caravan. See you soon,' he said, just as a wave boomed.

As Drift cantered Minty back on a loose rein along the smooth sand, she felt the cool breeze lift goosebumps on her thighs. The January moon was breathtaking. It made her think of her birthday wish for change. It was a wish made on the very same day a man had been suddenly swallowed by the sea and a young handsome policeman had knocked on her door. Drift felt another tingle, like silver stars sprinkled through her body, as she and her horse cantered home over the darkened sand. Here it was. *Change.*

Chapter 8

Drift tied a relieved Minty to the horse line and pulled a nosebag over the mare's ears just as the lights of the police car glanced off the sides of the caravan. She whistled the dogs, tying them back up, keeping one ear on Gerald to gauge if he was running right, his diesel stink blowing past her on the brisk breeze.

'All the four-wheel drives were taken,' Simon said as he got out of the car. 'They're doing a night-time beach patrol further down the Point while the tide's lowering. I'm sorry, but we'll have to go in your ute.'

'Sure. I'll just let Dad know,' she said, looking over her shoulder as he followed her to the caravan.

She had hoped her father had gone to bed and was slumbering behind his drawn curtain. She wanted things to be back to normal with him, but as she opened the door, the light spilled out, so too spilled out her same feeling of frustration when she saw him: head back, snoring in his chair, his slack mouth revealing the black tunnel down his gullet. Some of the wax papers, ratty from the wind, were holding fast to his legs, among red pinpricked oblongs of chicken skin where Split had pulled some off. His fingernails glowed orange in the van's dim light. Drift clenched her jaw. Nothing had changed. She tried to duck inside without Simon following her, but he caught the door in his hand and peered in.

'That sure is something you don't see every day,' he said, glancing from Drift to the vision of Split Wood. Drift groaned internally. The cluttered caravan was not only filled with her weird-looking drunk father and infused with the smell of deep-fried fish and diesel, but also seemed to shout 'crazy people'.

Both father's and daughter's artwork and poetry plastered many of the cupboard doors. Painted and sketched scenes of cattle, horses, trees and coastlines were pinned to every available flat surface, along with looped writing recording glimpses of life on the road. She and Split often scribed a captured thought about a sunset or a grey-blue morning. Art would be the last thing the constable would expect to find inside a stockman's van, Drift thought. Along with a failed cross-dressing cowboy.

'What happened to him?' Simon whispered, transfixed.

'My birthday. That's what happened to him … along with a little father–daughter payback. Put it this way,' Drift said, trying to grin at him, 'practical jokes are a family tradition.'

'Interesting tradition.' Simon grimaced. 'I might wait outside when you wake him.'

'What for?' asked Drift. 'He looks savage but he's a big bloody softie underneath that beer belly of his. Are you terrified of trans stockmen *and* horses?' she teased.

He looked blankly back at her.

'Trust me,' Drift said, suddenly serious. 'It's not his fault. This is all my doing. I was angry at him.'

'Is that meant to make me scared of you now?'

'Maybe?' she said with a 'try me' edge to her voice. She realised she was flirting with him. She *never* flirted. She didn't even know she *could* flirt. Maybe Shaynene was rubbing off on her.

'I think now I'm afraid of both of you,' said Simon, taking in the hulking form of her father in the tiny caravan.

Drift began poking her father's belly with her index finger. She felt a fondness for him, and yet at the same time a rage. 'Dad,' she said loudly, 'Oi, Dad!' There was no response, so Drift suddenly ripped one of the remaining wax papers off.

Her father woke with a jolt and a cry. His red-rimmed eyes took in his daughter standing over him, her face brazen. 'Fuck!' he bellowed. 'You've got a nerve.'

'Where's your eloquence now? I show no mercy,' she said, ripping another strip from him.

'Drift! Stop!'

'It's the best way! Plus you'll be able to take up cycling after this. You'd look good in Lycra. Wouldn't he, Simon?'

Split's bleary booze-drooping eyes travelled to Simon. He hauled himself up straighter in the chair when he saw the fit, handsome young cop again standing on the mottled rug in the doorway.

'Dad, you remember Simon?'

Split read the amused expression on the policeman's face. 'You just can't help yourself, can you?' he said, glowering at her.

'Just showing him the local entertainment — the Pinrush Point Pantomime,' she said.

'Don't tell me he has one of them smartarse phones and you've taken pictures of me and put me on the web tube or whatever it is.'

Drift rolled her eyes. He was playing dumb again. She hated it when he put on his ocker stockman's mask. 'Now there's a fine idea,' she said. She scooped up her hair and wound it in a knot as she spoke. 'Simon's helping me look for a little girl. I saw her on the beach. It was really weird. I thought she was lost, but she didn't seem lost.'

Her father looked at her through narrowed eyes. *Simon?* He cleared his throat. 'A lost girl? What do you want me to do about it?'

'He needs our four-wheel drive. Maybe you could get out the spotty. Take a look with us?'

Split stared at his daughter. Was she off imagining things again? As a child she often told him how the trees were speaking to her, or that the rocks were libraries and were telling her stories, or that the wind was singing to her and instructing her to go south, not north, or to stay put, or move on.

Split Wood knew what it was like to be raised in a practical no-nonsense family, when you lived with your head in the clouds. He knew the pain it caused. He wanted his daughter to be different from him. He wanted her connected more to the hard-edged reality of the world than he had been. So he tried not to entertain her fanciful imagination. He'd been caught out in life being like that. He didn't want that for her.

If he'd been realistic he would've seen through Drift's mother when she'd first turned up in his tiny Tasmanian timber town, like his family had. But because he was a soft-souled dreamer, Harmony had blinded him, manipulated him, belittled him and captured him. With his gentleness in his big son-of-a-saw-miller body and his creativity carved out of him due to his hard heritage of chainsaws and log trucks, Split knew the dangers of being a dreamer in the real world. He saw both Drift's and his own creative streaks as a kind of gentle eccentricity … a harmless eccentricity … but one that made them open and vulnerable to needy, unhinged people like her mother. And at risk of being accused of being mad by the more conservative people in the world. Safer to stick to themselves. Safer to live a hard practical life that kept you grounded, otherwise others might dub you crazy, like his own family had. Was this mystery girl yet another figment of Drift's vast wild-girl imagination?

Drift read his sceptical expression. 'I *saw* her, Dad. *Really*. We need to go look for her.'

'I'm not goin nowhere. Not like this.' He gestured at his legs.

She was tempted to correct his grammar, just to let him know she was mad with him for continuing to put on his blokey ocker persona for the policeman.

'Well, let's sort you out,' she said. 'Hold still, Dad, this won't hurt a bit.'

'Arrrgh!' cried Split, convulsing in his armchair as a forest of dark hairs came away from his thigh.

'Last one,' Drift said eventually. She sat back, surveyed his red bumpy skin and gave a wolf whistle. 'Would you like some lotion?'

'Bugger off.'

Split hauled himself up from the chair and, like a big half-skinned grizzly bear, ambled over to the water container and turned the tap, downing a glass in three gulps and going again.

'She's not as wayward as she comes across,' Split said to Simon, indicating the books contained on the upper shelves of the van.

'And you're not as thick,' Drift retorted.

'If it wasn't for Wilma, though, she'd be as wild as a brumby.' Drift delivered him a look.

'Wilma? You mean the mobile-library lady?' Simon asked.

'The one and the same,' Split said.

'I know her.' Simon smiled. 'We see her often on the road around Cooperville. Great lady.'

'Sure is. She'll never get a speeding ticket from you ... not in that old bus, anyway.'

They all chuckled thinking of the giant silver bus that backfired and clunked on its slow journey from remote school to remote school and isolated station to isolated station.

Wilma had helped Split and Drift shape her home-school lessons into a more formal model of education. But Wilma had also pointed out to Drift that there were bigger, more important lessons to be learned, taught by Mother Nature herself every day and every night. Birth and life and death everywhere, every minute. There were lessons of great beauty, Wilma said, to be seen along their journey from the swathe of stars that changed with the passing moons, to the fresh grass that sprouted in different types of soil. Then, as the seasons turned, the grasses grew long and butter coloured, passing away with the wind and the wet into a fresh cycle of green. Rhythm and music could be learned from the birdlife that chorused every morning. Then again, at dusk, the revelry and rivalry of birds going to roost closed down the day. Drift learned all this and more. She also learned the beauty and efficiency of rotting roadkill and the carcasses she studied while sitting on the back of her horse. Maggots making the lifeless skin of roos move again in a thrilling, repulsive wave of frenzied flesh eating and bone cleaning. She saw decay of the grass stems as they were trampled into the ground along with her animal's manure, which fed the soil for their return, should they find a new droving contract in the future.

Wilma and her dad had selected books to bolster Drift's knowledge of life on the road. She'd told Drift that road lessons were a reminder that, 'Everything dies in physical form, but energies live on.'

'Including us,' Wilma had said once. 'It's no big deal. It's the natural law.' Wilma's, Charlie's and even Split's lessons always seemed more important to Drift than the ones listed in her home-school syllabus books. She knew tonight was a chance for learning. This time, the big lessons.

'C'mon then,' Split said relenting, 'let's go look for Drift's ghost girl.'

*

An hour later, after scouring the dunes without finding tracks or footprints, they arrived back at the caravan. Drift cut the ute's engine. She could feel the burning warmth of Simon's thigh next to her as he sat wedged between her and her gigantic father. She stayed a moment longer than she needed as her dad clambered out of the old cruiser.

'That was a waste of time and diesel,' Split said as he slammed the door.

Drift felt embarrassment burn her cheeks: the girl *must have* been in her imagination.

'We'll see if we can get someone on The Planet radio tomorrow and ask them if they have a child on the loose,' Simon said kindly, but she could tell he was following her father's lead — both doubted there ever had been a girl out there at all. She gathered up the hand-held spotlight, getting out of the Cruiser. Split silenced the barking dogs with an irritated whistle.

'Well,' Simon said, glancing shyly at Drift as he ran his thumbs under his police belt and hoisted it higher on his thin hips, 'I might see you about.'

'You might do,' Split said. 'Cattle coming in tomorrow. Tell your crew — there'll be stock on the road in a few days.' Her dad's tone was jagged like barbed wire. Drift could sense he knew the policeman was hovering for a reason other than searching for missing people. Split was well used to men hanging about longer than they needed around his daughter. Even in the oversized men's workwear, torn jeans and flannie shirts she wore, there was no hiding the fact she was as naturally beautiful as the wild lands that had shaped her. What Split wasn't used to was Drift hovering back. She'd been completely uninterested in men, unlike that crazy Shaynene from the Widgenup Store. Up until tonight. As Split thought about what she'd said earlier about clearing out, he sighed a little too heavily before nodding a 'see you later' at Simon and walking to the van. He was getting a hangover. He could feel life as he'd known it slipping away from him tonight.

'Turn Gerald off, will ya, before you come to bed,' he said to Drift.

'Sure,' Drift said.

Split shut the van door.

'He's a complex beast,' Drift said, glancing up at Simon. 'Sorry about him. Moody.'

'Sergeant Dodge remembered him. I know he tried to ...' Simon's words filtered away like sand.

Drift looked to the toes of her boots, ashamed. What a weird pair she and her dad made. How must they look to the world?

'Yes. That. Well,' she said, 'big day tomorrow. Better go.'

In a moment, Simon took her hand. His fingers were smooth and thin. His palms cold. 'If I can ever do anything. You know. To help?' he said, nodding towards the van and her father.

She snatched her hand away. 'Do I look like I need anything?' she said defensively.

Redness flared on Simon's cheeks. 'Sorry ... I ...'

She shook her head. 'No, I'm sorry. It's just ... well ... nothing.'

Simon gave her a sad smile. 'Maybe I'll see you around,' he said. His words hung like a question in the air.

'Maybe,' Drift answered, just as Gerald coughed the last litre of diesel through his system and the van light shut down, bringing the relief of silence, before the roll of waves filled up the sound space. The light from the big orange moon was the only thing that guided Simon Swain to his police car parked near the dunes. Drift watched the tail lights as he drove away and she wondered why the entire world felt tilted tonight.

Chapter 9

A buttery sun edged up over the scrubby horizon and gleamed on the portable steel cattle yards. Drift turned her face to it and breathed in the new day. The world seemed more peaceful and settled than yesterday. The morning birdsong told her it was a normal summer day in January. Despite that, her mind still spun with the vision of the little girl in the wildness of the dunes, and the memory of meeting handsome Simon in the crazed wind and rain. She also felt deep emotions stir with the fact the sea had yet again swallowed someone whole, just like it had her own mother years ago. Drift sought peace by looking up at the pale cloud-like remnant of the moon disappearing beneath the horizon. She tried to breathe in the calm way Wilma had shown her when she was little.

Suddenly a low-flying sea plane buzzing like a blowie swept over the water. Next a helicopter arrived above her. The horses jerked on the tether line as it swooped near, their heads lifted, eyes uncertain, Roger pulling back on the line.

'Steady, Rog,' Drift said as she looked up and saw a TV network logo on the side of the chopper. A man in dark clothing leaned out with a camera, like a sniper. She ducked for cover on the other side of the truck, swearing under her breath at the invasion and the upset it was causing her animals. Next a line of cars streamed past on the road, like it was peak hour in Perth.

Shaynene was right — a storm of people was about to arrive, all because of the missing famous surfer. Drift wondered about this Kai whatshisname. Where was he from? What were his family thinking right now? Would they come out here and camp by the shore for days, the way her father and she had after her mum went missing?

Far off in the distance Drift heard the low engine of a stock truck. She climbed to the top rail of the cattle yard to look along the hillocking dunes. Suddenly, a blaze of lights appeared over the dull dawn ridgeline rise, the faulty orange clearance bulbs of the truck looking like an oncoming disco.

'Bugger,' she said when she recognised the rig. Kelvin Waller was her least favourite trucking contractor. She'd begged her father to get the other Cooperville stock carter, but he must've had another job. She braced herself for Kelvin's ugly unwanted flirtations and for the rough way he handled the drought-eroded cattle.

Within her though ran a pulse of excitement at the prospect of nurturing the new herd back to health by hooking them on to the diet of saltbush, shrubs and seaweed, and to steady them down to trust and calm. She loved watching them curiously reaching out to tug at unfamiliar sedges and rushes, tasting each plant to see if the bare twig rush or sea heath offered them any kind of medicine.

Drift went to the underbelly of their stock truck and tugged open the large rusted metal compartment, dragging out her stock saddle and blankets. The dogs stood around her, their tails in a low wag, ears pricked to the sounds, noses attached to the cattle scent thread. They knew it was game on. Bear, the jaded old gelding, tossed his head and laid his ears back as Drift approached him.

'I know, mate,' she soothed, slinging the woven saddle blanket onto his broad back, 'I'm sorry, but it's your turn today. Ya grumpy ole bugger.' As she lobbed the saddle over Bear's high round back, she reached under for his girth, scratching with her fingertips, feeling for any signs of girth galls, where the white patches of hair from past sores had healed. She cinched up the saddle, the horse's ears flattening further. She pushed yesterday from her mind. She had to focus. The work was about to begin.

The loud explosive shush of engine brakes was followed by a wave from Kelvin in the cab. Drift raised an unenthusiastic hand back at him, and cocked an unimpressed eyebrow as he blew her kisses and grinned a gap-toothed smile before he began logging his hours. The cattle bellowed from within their metal confines and the stench of cow dung gave the fresh morning air a tang that Drift inhaled like rose scent. An electronic reverse beep sounded as Kelvin angled the dog trailer towards the open panels of the steel yards. Their small portable set-up would be barely big enough to hold the arriving herd, but Drift knew they would have cattle scattered throughout the dunes if she didn't contain them somewhere to start with.

From the far end of the panels they had run a secondary yard fashioned from rusty steel droppers, tread-in upright posts and old electric tape hooked to a solar battery. As ramshackle as it looked, it had a good dose of volts through it. Normally they didn't let cattle out into the electrified yards and onto the road for a couple of days until they'd settled, feeding them instead on hay. She'd seen how poorly handled cattle could rip through the tape and tangle it over the landscape like a giant cobweb. After she and her dad had calmed the cattle they would then flow them between the two enclosures, teaching them the system of pressure and release from the horses and dogs.

Each beast had to learn its place in the herd when it came to walking onto water and fresh feed and to respect the portable fences and dogs. Order in the system translated into better weight gain at the end of the drove. And better weight gain meant more money for her dad. But for both Drift and Split the money was the least important thing. Succeeding in healing and calming the animals meant everything to them, and watching the landscape respond to the periodic mob grazing was their own private study in the generosity of Mother Nature. Drift knew these poor beasts needed to get on to tucker straight away and there could be some rodeo riding ahead if they were stirred up. She suspected instead though that they'd be weak and compliant, hunger driving them to put their heads down right away. Time would very soon tell.

Dropping Bear's split reins over a rail Drift looked at the empty plastic troughs that remained tipped over outside the yard. They should've carted the water yesterday. It would be a job she could tackle when Kelvin headed back for the second load. It would mean driving to the fresh waterhole on the roadside that she realised was right near the surfers' search-party camp. Maybe she would see Simon? The idea brought a flush to her cheeks.

As she stood in view of Kelvin in the side mirror, she raised her hand just before the truck almost touched the mouth of the unloading ramp, the wheels sinking a little from the overnight rain. Kelvin jabbed the brakes a little hard. Hooves scuttled on the metal floor as the truck rocked. Drift muttered under her breath, then hauled in a panel so it sat flush with the truck's side, before angling up two thinner panels to act as a makeshift unloading race. Drift whistled her dogs and positioned them well away. They sat quivering with excitement, their bellies pressed to the sandy soil, keen eyes locked on the cattle within the trailers.

Kelvin hauled his heavy body down from the blue shiny cab. 'G'day, honey pot.' He went to the dog-trailer's end, pulling the pins and sliding open the back door.

Drift grunted a reply and turned her attention to her young dog. 'Stay, Hamlet, *you stay*. Good boy.'

Even with the noise of the first cattle coming off the truck, Hamlet held firm on his spot, quickly glancing at his mistress and wagging the end of his tail. She'd worked hard on his 'stay' and today she was glowing within to see the little fella had it nailed.

There was only a makeshift ramp, so the cows had to do their best to jump down onto the raised area she and her dad had created a few years back using shovels of sandy dirt, rocks and a few scavenged lengths of timber. It was still a fair drop despite their efforts. Drift shook her head as Kelvin tried to speed up the process, forcing the cattle along with his harsh voice and waving his Humpty Dumpty arms, holding an electric prod in one hand like a power-hungry prison guard, sending the cloven-hooved beasts scrambling and slipping on the wet flooring.

'You got to be somewhere in hurry?' she asked pointedly.

He stopped, his short legs set wide and his big belly casting a comically large shadow over the ground as the sun rose above the scrub behind him and painted the world in a salmon-coloured glow. Beyond them, over the dunes, the sea was waking itself up to a deep blue.

'Girlie, I bin driving all night. Only place I'm hurrying now is home. Might even get one from me missus if the lazy bitch is still in bed when I git there and she agrees to roll over. Then I gotta turn around and do it all again for you with the second load.'

'Yeah well, if you let the cattle take their own time, you'll get home faster,' she retorted.

He knitted his thick black eyebrows down over his piggy eyes and glowered at her. 'Where's your father?'

Drift flicked her head in the direction of the van. 'He's in baking me a birthday cake,' she said, knowing her old man was still on the camp toilet behind the blue tarp, his bowels giving him grief over yesterday's food and grog binge.

'It's your birthday? Well, bugger me!' exclaimed Kelv as he moved towards a cow that hovered on the precipice of the drop. The sullen bag of bones looked to the ground then anxiously out to her herd mates, who were now trotting around the yard enclosure, seeking a way out between the rails, snorting at the dogs a good distance off.

They were a mottled mix of all kinds of breeds, including brindle Brahman cross and toffee-coloured Santas, and Drift could see she would have her work cut out for her with some who would take an extra day or so to soothe down to quiet. She knew the hard-edged farmer who had sent them and it didn't surprise her they were this stirry. The last herd they'd been contracted to put on the long paddock had been the same way. At least there were no dead ones in this load so far. She looked back to Kelvin. 'My birthday was actually yesterday.'

'Then why's he cooking you a friggin cake today?'

'Round here it all gets done in its own good time,' she said with a jibe in her voice.

'Yeah well, missy, I'm not on your time.' For good measure Kelvin stabbed the baulking cow through the w-strap rails of the truck, jiggering her with his electric prodder. The brindle Brahman bellowed, leaping forward, ripping her hip on the truck door on the way out. She slammed to the ground and her legs flailed hopelessly as she lay cast on her side. She let out a moan of distress.

'Stop complaining, you old bag. It was a soft landin,' he said, his eyes narrowed at Drift. She had recently earned a reputation with the stock agents and sale-yard boys for being a frosty young upstart. But who could blame her, the truckie thought, being raised on the road by a weirdo like Split Wood.

Drift swore again under her breath, wishing her dad would hurry up and get here.

'How old are you, darlin?' Kelvin asked as he zapped another cow caught up in the corner.

'Twenty-one. And will you stop doing that?'

'Ahhh!' he said lasciviously, as the cow bucked and roared to the ground. 'A proper grown-up woman.'

A flash of memory of her attraction to Simon last night, and Drift felt her cheeks burn red again.

'You're younger than me,' Kelvin said. 'Hop up in there darlin and open the divider door for me? Go on. There's a good girl. Swing a leg over.'

She looked at him with distaste as she climbed the side of the railing and lobbed up into the truck. He turned the jigger towards her and waved it through the truck sides at her.

'I could give ya a little birthday spark, eh? Light your candle for ya?'

He pointed the metal tips of the prodder close to her jean-clad thigh.

She glared at him and hit it away. 'Bugger off.' Hastily she dragged open the bottom gate and stood back waiting for the first cow to find her way through the opening, the rest flowing behind her. Above her on the top decks more cattle stirred, the other cattle in the front trailer becoming increasingly restless.

'Oh well. Seeing as you're a bit mentally menstrual today, darlin, I'll give ya a hand to drop the top ramp,' Kelvin said. 'It's a heavy bastard.'

Next he was in the confines of the trailer, leering at her as he passed.

'I left 'em pretty loose up the top. Should be easy enough,' he said, reaching for a shit-splattered pin that would drop an internal ramp. As they stood out of the way of the fresh flow of cattle, Kelvin looked at Drift.

'They're a bit on the skinny side, but knowing your father and you, we'll need four truck 'n dog trailers to get 'em out. You're good at putting the weight on 'em.'

Drift couldn't help but feel pride in her swell even if the compliment was coming from a prick like Kelvin. She knew she and her dad were good at what they did. She knew when the cattle left their care they'd be in the best of nick, both mentally and physically. It made her feel sad she'd told her dad she was giving the game away and leaving. What on earth would she rather do than this? Apart from putting up with wankers like Kelvin bloody Waller, life was good.

'I like a bit of weight on a rump, myself.' He spun towards her. 'Let's do a little rump test on you,' and he reached to grab at her arse.

She felt the hard hold of his big ugly hand. Before she could hit his arm away, he'd dragged her to him, gripping her CW belt and hauling her close so she could see the blackness of the pores on his hooked nose, and the gleam of the ugly gold caps on his teeth.

Laughing, Kelv licked his slug-like lips. 'Oh you are ripe for the picking, girl. You sure is ripe. I'll give you a birthday kiss.'

Despite her strength and her fight to push him away, he was like an immovable boulder. As she struggled he sneered at her, 'Word is, you don't put out for no one. Shaynene thinks you might be a lezzo. Maybe you need a little warming up. You're too old to be a virgin.'

He covered her lips with his stinking mouth. She felt the warm rancid poke of his insistent moist tongue slide over her gritted teeth. When he pulled away he leered, 'You taste fresh. I'd like to pop your cherry.'

Drift had never known men were strong enough to overpower her. She'd never known they could feel this terrifying and repulsive. Her mind raced as she struggled to get away from him. In the sweat of panic, Charlie's voice at last sounded in her head.

'People say, "grow some balls",' Charlie had once told her, and scoffed. 'Remember, Drift, men's balls are bloody soft and squishy and that makes 'em vulnerable, despite what the tough ones think of 'emselves. Whereas women: oh the strength of women! You're better off to grow a pussy — those things take a pounding in more ways than one! We are powerful. We bleed every month and don't bloody die. We bring new life with our babies. We're the tough ones. Never forget that. Grow some balls,' she muttered. 'That's a joke to folks who have ovaries.'

Remembering Charlie's words, a guttural cry of rage erupted from Drift as if it had been stuck in her throat like barbed wire for aeons. Determination rose in her as she rammed her knee into Kelvin's nuts with a conviction she'd never felt before. As he curled over, howling, she ran through the truck and screamed, 'Dad! *Dad*?'

'You bitch,' Kelvin said through a gurgle of pain. 'We're just havin a bit of fun. You were putting it out there, little ho.'

At the door of the truck she saw Kelvin's prodder where he'd left it, wedged in the railing. She grabbed it up and ran back to where he was clutching his crotch; like a swashbuckling swordfighter she seared it onto his thigh. Kelvin cried out, his body convulsing like a high-pressure hose on the loose, his round pug-dog face red with fury and pain. Drift threw down the prod and, like the terrified hunted cows, jumped clumsily down from the truck, her chest burning, her breath ragged. Involuntary tears spilled as she swiped her mouth with the back of her hand, trying to erase the disgusting taste and touch that lingered on her skin.

She watched from outside the trailer as Kelvin, walking crab-like, released the rest of the xylophone-ribbed cattle from the truck, fallen cattle hauling themselves up from the slops, staggering off in their shit-covered hides. Bags of bones with sunken eyes from dehydration. Hip bones jutting out. Walking skeletons, still trying to mother up and give milk to their calves. Drift was crying now at the shock of being violated, made worse by the sight of the cattle. It had happened right under her father's nose. *Where was he?* How could he leave her exposed to this? All she felt now was broken trust. She stood with her arms around herself, her dogs sensing her distress and hovering near her legs.

Kelvin emerged, cramping along. 'You'll fucking pay for this,' he growled. 'Tell your father I'll see him for the next load tomorrow. I've got unfinished business with you, missy.' Then he was up in the cab, firing up the engine, swinging the big rig in the direction of Widgenup and back on to Cooperville.

She found her grey-faced father squatted down near the van steps.

'Kelv gone already?'

Drift didn't answer.

'Sorry, I'm a bit battle weary today,' he said.

Drift looked at his pathetic form and felt hot tears rise. 'Where the fuck have you been?' she blurted.

He looked up suddenly at the sound of her cracking voice, shock on his face as he registered her expression. 'Are you OK?'

'No,' she said, turning abruptly, calling her dogs to her.

He followed her over to the LandCruiser, where she was already pulling open the door. Red-hot shame burned in her.

'What's the matter?'

'Him.'

'Him who?'

'That Kelvin. He …' she stammered '… f-felt me up. In the truck.'

'No,' Split said incredulously. 'Old Kelvin, flirting with you? He wouldn't do that to my daughter.'

'Flirting? Dad! He *grabbed* me. He stuck his tongue in my mouth! It was disgusting.'

Split reached for his top pocket and took out his tobacco, studying her face, brow furrowed. She couldn't believe it when he calmly laid a cigarette paper in the palm of his hand, rolling the tobacco in it. His greying hair shot up at all angles, puffy bags under his reddened eyes, lines etched deeply on either side of his mouth, like someone had sketched him into the world with thick charcoal. He dropped his gaze from hers and, smoke rolled, went to the railing to survey the herd like he was Sir Sidney fucking Kidman. He lit the rollie and dragged on it.

'Dad?' she said, her voice breaking, 'What are you going to do about it?'

'I'm not much of a father,' he said in a tone that scared her. 'This planet is too crazy for me. Everyone is nuts. It's like the last days of Rome. We're all on the slide.'

Suddenly he was sobbing. His big shoulders shuddering. 'I'm just plain old no good in this world. They all warned me this was no life for a little girl. I shouldn't have tried to keep you from the world. I'm sorry. You're right to want to leave me.'

Drift, shocked, felt her chest tightening. Wasn't he going to do something? Avenge her? Fight for her? But he kept on crying and crying, like a baby. Ragged animal-like sobs as he dropped his head onto his arms. Wasn't she the one he ought to be comforting? She was about to relent and put a consoling hand on his shoulder then stopped herself. Anger flared again at his impotence, overtaking her deep pity for him.

'Stuff this,' Drift said, turning away. She began jogging towards the beach.

'Where you going?' her father called weakly after her.

'Where the fuck do you think?' she replied, as if her life was on loop. To the water, she thought. Always to the water. To search the white horses.

Drift stood at the high lip of the dune, her dogs at her heels, the beach stretching out before her in early-morning silence, looking subdued as if it had a hangover after a massive night of partying. Gumtree branches tumbled about in the surf, trying to reach the shore like shipwrecked sailors. Long strips of bark blown from faraway trees had caught in the giant tendrils of great bull kelp tossed on the beach like storm-drowned seals. Great chunks of sand had collapsed and washed away so that dark shadows lay along the uneven beach. A few kilometres away the wide ribbon of a rushing creek frothed with strong tannin-brown floodwater and severed the beach in half, flattening the waves where fresh water poured out to sea. On a better day, she would've grabbed up her watercolour pad and captured the beauty on paper. But today was not one she wanted to remember.

If her father wouldn't help her, then surely Simon would. The beach, cut now by the outflow of the estuary, meant there would be no reaching him at the search-party camp that way. She thought of the card his boss had left with them last night and the new phone tower. Maybe she could call them. But the thought of going back to the van to use Split's phone broke her. She couldn't see her dad like this. Drift felt the same storm surge of emotion that had raged overnight as desolation settled in her soul.

'Mum? Where are you? Help me.'

Only the call of a seabird on the wind answered.

Chapter 10

As Drift drove towards the stock-route waterhole, she tried to focus on the beauty of the thin stormwater rivulets still ribboning their way across the landscape. Despite her mental efforts, residual grubby feelings of Kelvin's unwanted touch brought fresh tears and jagged breaths. Confusion swirled over her father too. He'd once been her hero. Her rock, until grief and life's disappointment over time had eroded his strength and equilibrium, like waves wearing down a sandstone cliff. To Drift, after his suicide attempt, Split was now just shifting sand: unstable, unreliable, detached, selfish. Surely his reaction to Kelvin proved that? It made her more restless to get away, somewhere, somehow. She knew he was in the midst of some kind of breakdown again, but how was she meant to deal with it on her own? Or even make a life on her own? Especially when she doubted herself so much. She scoffed at herself: seeing little girls in sand dunes on moonlit nights. Believing she could talk to her mother through all that water and read the land like the ancients had. 'Drift Wood, you're a freak,' she muttered.

As she turned the corner on the narrow single-lane dirt road, the surprise of a makeshift mini city captured her attention. Tents, vans and caravans had mushroomed overnight around the beachside car park near where the pro surfers had camped on the beach.

Amid the huddle, a tall flimsy-looking communication tower had been erected, piercing the blue sky, bringing a phone signal to isolated Pinrush Point. Behind Drift's ute, surfer-fan traffic began impatiently tailgating her. Ahead, the beachside had become cluttered with surfer cars capped with boards. People were milling about or sitting in groups as if they were at a trendy outdoor music festival. Drift half expected to see a coffee van or gourmet ice-cream truck show up.

'What an odd bunch,' she said through the open window to Dunno's reflection in the side mirror.

The police, busy with crowd control, had set up bunting of no-go zones near their camp area. She could see the cops roadblocking any newcomers. Despite their efforts, the surfer fans were simply setting up camp on the other side of the barrier amid the boobialla trees and sea grasses. To Drift, it looked like madness. She swore under her breath and dropped back a gear when she approached the line of stationary cars. She hesitated a moment but then swung out wide of the traffic jam, driving on the wrong side of the road, one tyre on the sand, headed towards the orange bollards. A sign before her shouted in big blocky text, STOP. A policewoman with a stern expression stepped forward. Drift braked, leaning her elbow on the window and looking up at her.

'What do you think you're doing?' the cop asked.

'Just getting water for the cattle,' Drift said. 'I'm from the drover's camp a few K thataway.' She jabbed a thumb back towards the north.

The cop looked at Drift from under the brim of her cap, slowly summing up the dinted, dusty ute with the lopsided sticker on the grimy window that read, *Dogs make me happy — you not so much.* She saw the pretty girl's genuine face under her large ragged black hat, the working dogs sniffing the air, wagging tails and grinning at her.

'OK,' the cop said. She moved the bollard and waved her through. Drift watched her getting smaller in the rear-vision mirror, disappointed it hadn't been Simon policing the traffic. Maybe he was down the beaches on one of the spits or out in one of the boats? The emotional fire within her over Kelvin had cooled now that she'd seen the crowd. She was far too shy to walk into a search-and-rescue camp with all those people during the bright light of day to go see a hot-looking cop she had only just met and tell him about a gropey truckie. First a ghost girl, now a sexual assault claim. He'd think she was a nutter.

She thought back to last night in the van and how Simon's gaze had lingered on her. Maybe she'd imagined it. Drift didn't know how to tell if a guy liked her or not and she knew Shaynene was the wrong one to ask. There'd been a few keen young ones on occasion working in the yards with her, in the shed, trying to have a flirt, but with her dad there, and their young-man goofiness, she'd never let them in much. Besides, blokes with any nous knew not to try it on with Split Wood's daughter. In the past, before his slump, her dad had cut down any man making inappropriate comments about her. His glare was enough to freeze ducks mid-flight, and he could razor-cut flesh with one single sharp comment. Kelvin must have sensed he wasn't up to protecting her any more. What a sleazebag.

And why now, having met one nice bloke, was it she was feeling this kind of tidal surge of longing that felt so much like desire? Until now her dogs and her horses and the road had been enough. Lately, it seemed, men of all types were finding her attractive, even in her rough-as-guts workwear. Even Simon had seemed to. But after seeing Split last night, Simon'd already implied she was some kind of welfare case. A normal guy like him would never go for a misfit like her. Would he?

As for Kelvin, Drift told herself in no uncertain terms to 'get over it'. Just like Shaynene had. On her last trip to Pinrush, Shay had told Drift that Kelvin had cornered her near the magazine section in the Widgenup Store where he bought his nasty trucker porn.

'He bloody well called me over to help him select what mag to buy,' Shaynene said incredulously. 'Big tits or bleached arses? I mean, *seriously*? Who makes this shit up? Who would want to *buy* it? I told him it was for losers. Then he'd pretended to reach for a mag and he rubbed his hard ugly wood in his trousers up against me leg! Ark! It was fucken gross.' Shaynene made a face like she'd just drunk off milk.

'So I whipped out me phone and caught me 'n him in a selfie with him going for me tit.' She'd bellyached with laughter when she'd shown Drift the photo. 'Classic, huh? I threatened to send it to his wife and that shut the dirty fucker up. At least until the next time. Seriously, I've had to train Head Bob as a guard bird. He goes ape whenever Kelvin comes in, flies over him, and goes for his bald patch with his claws and beak. It's fucken funny.'

Drift smiled at the memory. 'Fucken funny,' she told herself in the rear-vision mirror, but her blue eyes looked haunted. Shaynene hadn't seemed that freaked out about Kelvin's unwanted attention the way she was now. Was she overreacting?

Relieved to be alone and away from the surfer hub, Drift pulled up at the stock-route watering hole and got out, feeling a sudden surge of gratitude for her reliable, faithful dogs.

As she let the dogs off their short ute chains, she pulled each one to her, nuzzling her face to theirs. Happy for the attention, the dogs leaned into her and wagged their tails low.

'OK,' she said at last, 'go for a run!' They flew from the ute with extra zing. Except Dunno, who rolled off more like a log, trying to look dignified as he landed.

'You bloody nong,' she said, patting her leg to call him over. For a time she stooped, just holding him, listening to his breath and the sounds of the watery world around her at the burgeoning waterhole. Chuckling at him, she set to work, lowering the inlet hose down into brackish water that was still swelling from storm rains. She climbed up on the ute to put the outlet into the tank. Above her, a single cloud hung in the blue sky over to the east. As she looked at it, she wondered why she felt the world of humans so heavily. Why couldn't she be more like Shaynene, finding everything 'fucken funny' and flirting with everyone and anything, including old women and babies?

As her dogs lapped at the water's edge and scooted about, she told herself to lighten up. She took a deep breath, feeling the soft morning air expand her lungs, allowing the wind to whisper in her ears of how beautiful it was to be out here, just her and her dogs. It was something Wilma had encouraged her to practise when she was out of sorts — to take time to appreciate the natural beauty of the world around her. 'Gratitude heals all woes,' Wilma often said when her father began one of his self-pity parties. Lately, with her dad constantly in her ear about urban sprawl and industrial agriculture's war on Mother Nature, she'd found it hard to be grateful when most places were now brutalised by humans. But not here. This spot was exceptional in its beauty. She cast her gaze about.

The billionaire woman's station, The Planet, lay on the other side of the waterhole behind high sturdy fences that would've cost a fortune — extra high star pickets, electric outriggers, square-panelled stock tight wire and glimpses of buried rabbit wire at the base. Whoever she is she doesn't mind spending a dollar on fencing, Drift thought. The owner clearly wanted to keep unwanted grazers like rabbits and roos out. Judging by the locked electronic double gates over the cattle grid she'd passed at the property's entrance, human strangers weren't welcome either. What went on in there? Whatever they were doing, Drift thought, looking at the lush landscape on the other side of the fence, they were doing it right. They knew how to run country.

Since the rain, the landscape was singing with vitality. Birds, insects and frogs were vibrating a symphony through the still air. Drift could swear she could actually hear the plant life growing. The scent blowing across the land was sweet and fragrant.

The dogs too were picking up on the vibe of the place. A puppyish Hamlet play-bounded through the waterhole's shallows. Drift matched his moves, kicking up droplets of water, grabbing the scruff of his neck in play, laughing as he made wolfish noises. Old Dunno lay on his wonky back, writhing happily on the grass like a break-dancing wombat. Molly sat with her eyes half shut to the sun as if she were in meditation, contemplating the breath of life.

A distance away, a flock of ducks trawled about the leaves and small sticks that had curved themselves around the base of old-timer wooden fenceposts where the racing water from the previous night's storm had receded. Frogs chattered in the filled-to-overflowing wetland waterholes on The Planet side of the fence. Drift caught the wave of euphoria and began to splash through the shallows like Gene Kelly singing in the rain, kicking up water-stars, laughing and dancing with her dogs. Mud spattered the backs of her bare legs as she ran and spun until she was out of breath. She sat on the ute's tray, her three dogs settling down, panting in the shade of the vehicle to cool off.

Beyond the fence, wavering golden seed heads, healthy clumping shrubs and the blanket covering of grass and wildflowers formed a meadow, pretty in its diversity. It was such a stark contrast to the barren, dry country Drift was used to passing on their way down to the route. Reluctantly, she fired up the pump, the hose jiggling to life, the motor drowning out the blissful sounds of nature. She shut her eyes, the sun on her eyelids, her mind at last stilled by her slow practised breath. She lay back on the dropped tailgate, tracing her fingertips over her bare belly, staring at the blue above, dangling her legs, longing to be a child again so the complex emotions she now felt would disappear. She dropped her hand down and there was Dunno's head, ready and waiting for a pat. Absent-mindedly she stroked his ears and floated off to a familiar future dreamplace with a garden and gumtrees and a house with a red corrugated-iron roof.

A while later trickling water interrupted her trance: it was spilling over the top of the water tank. She shut the pump off, pulling up the inlet hoses, the dogs already clambering on the back, bustling each other out of the way for the best spot on the crammed and cluttered tray. From up high, Hamlet barked suddenly once, his eyes trained to the distance. It was a 'someone's there' bark. Drift followed the dog's gaze. Through some trees, far off in the distance, a lone rider on a white horse moved at a slow amble through the landscape. Maybe she could let them know about the lost girl.

'Helloooo?' Drift shouted and waved her arm in the air, but the rider was too far off to see her and clearly didn't hear her. She watched the figure disappear, drifting into a thicket.

'Friendly,' she said, a little disappointed she didn't get to talk to one of the workers from The Planet. She was more curious about the place than ever now.

As she pulled out slowly onto the road, the weight and slosh of the water slowing the ute down, she turned her attention to the fact she would soon be passing the search-and-rescue camp again. Travelling at a snail's pace with the heavy water, back tyres swelling, engine complaining from the weight, Drift took her time passing. She waved at the roadblock cop. More media buses were there now, with satellite dishes on top like white upturned umbrellas. Beyond the camp, a gap in the dunes revealed the black dots of fifty or more surfers bobbing in the water. Above the blue, another chopper buzzed by. More cars were pulling in. As she passed, a group of pretty young girls setting up a tent beside a sloping dune waved cheerfully at her and began pointing and gushing at the dogs. Drift re-gripped the steering wheel. There was no way she was walking into that, Simon or no Simon. Those surfers last night had been enough for her. She dropped back a gear and rumbled on towards the cattle camp. As the ute vibrated up and over a rise Drift saw something that prompted a beaming smile on her face.

'At last!' she said with surprise and joy. 'Wilma!'

Chapter 11

The bookmobile door flew open, but to Drift's surprise it wasn't Wilma standing there. Instead Shaynene leaped out.

'Surrrrrprisse!' she shrilled. She wrapped Drift up in a gigantic bear hug, the sweet waft of her latest discount-chemist fragrance by Taylor Swift forming a strong olfactory cloud around them.

'I hitched a lift with The Wondrous! Come on! We've got Tim Tams!'

She hauled Drift by the arm into the bookmobile. Before they climbed the fold-out stairs, Drift glanced over at her father who, without a word, had started filling the troughs. The hungry cattle were ripping into hay set within the giant metal feed ring, and now the smell of water had them moving over to the rail and mooing thirstily. She could almost forgive him, the way he remained motionless, holding the hose as it drained into the trough, deep in thought, concern on his face as he studied the state of the animals. He seemed to sense her watching and looked up. A sad smile came to his face, his eyes dark and vacant.

He called to her over the bellow of the cattle, 'I'm OK. You go on ...' He waved her away. Drift signalled a thumbs-up, love and pity for him swelling in her, along with the worry that he was disappearing from her into his dark internal mire, and he might try again to leave her. She then felt a stab of deep resentment. He needed to man up. To tackle the hard issues with her. To get a grip! Why couldn't he talk to her about what he was going through? About what happened last winter? Or even just comfort her about Kelvin?

'Has he got those roos back in his top paddock again?' Shaynene asked, tapping her temple with her index finger when she saw where Drift was looking.

'I reckon he might,' Drift said.

'So he didn't like our birthday-present idea?'

'Nope,' said Drift.

'C'mon, he'll be right. Wilma's waiting.'

Entering the mobile library, Drift instantly felt her tensions ease.

'Drift, my darling!' came Wilma's warm tone. Drift was gathered up in a gentle, centred hug that wrapped her in the scent of rosewater. As she was folded into a large, loving bosom, the grateful memory of her first meeting with Wilma Schnitzerling came to Drift's mind. It had been their first year on the road. They'd found Wilma not far from the Kingenrup crossroads, holding a wheel jack in her hand and standing beside a bus sagging down on one injured tyre.

'What's your puppy's name?' Wilma had asked, her eyes alight with delight.

'Dunno,' Drift had said, snuggling the pup into her arms.

'You haven't got a name for him yet?' Wilma had said, the remains of her accent still hinting at her Eastern European heritage.

'Noooo. His name is *Dunno*!' Drift had said with a little giggle.

Wilma's round homespun face had bloomed with laughter. As Split knelt to loosen the wheel nuts, Wilma laid a gentle palm on Drift's back. 'Would you and Dunno like to see inside my library on wheels, if it's OK with your dad?'

Drift looked to her father and then to the round lady who had a halo of brown fuzzy hair. Drift nodded and beamed a gappy-toothed smile. Split hadn't seen his child smile like that in months, not since her mother had disappeared. He had nodded at Wilma, then turned away, his face crumpling with pain. Drift had seen it. The kind librarian saw it too, and she had quietly ushered the little girl with the puppy up into the mobile library.

Inside Drift had sucked in a breath when she felt the world of magic the bus held. Books wall to ceiling made it a cosy, mystical space, insulated from noise and the heat outside. Colour hung from the roof in the form of mobiles and puppets. The floor too was awash with vibrant rugs and rainbow-coloured cushions.

Since that day Wilma had become like a book fairy godmother to Drift. She would turn up suddenly out of the blue, her arrival as surprising and beautiful as a shooting star sprinkling dust into Drift's world ... only noisier. The bus's engine sounded like fifty Harley-Davidsons rolling by and blew smoke like a steam train, but when it was shut off, and Drift entered, it became a quiet haven and the world expanded through the books she found there.

Over the years Wilma's Aladdin's book cave had found Drift in all weathers in stockyards, shearing sheds or on stock camps or roadsides. Wilma matched her bus and like its metal sides she shone with light, even on grey days. If Drift and Split were on remote droving contract jobs, Wilma would still track them down, tramping through tatty roadside grasses on her thick marching legs, hopping over cow dung in her summer dress and lace-up Caterpillar workboots, books clutched in her hand, calling out Drift's name. Drift's spirits would rise to see Wilma's vibrant floral frocks blooming like an English garden in the outback dry.

For Drift's twelfth birthday Wilma had given her a massive old library-issue dictionary that had clouded, cracked Contact covering it. Well-thumbed though it was, it became the favourite of all Drift's books. Her dad called it 'her pillow' as she always seemed to fall asleep with her face on it, waking the next day using words like 'exquisite' and 'manifestation'. Today Wilma was already piling her selection of titles for her and Split, along with birthday gifts, into Drift's outstretched arms.

'Happy birthday!' she said, passing Drift a package. 'Sit. Sit!'

'I'm goin the purple one,' Shaynene said dragging a jellybean beanbag forward. 'Matches me hair.' She launched herself into it, and for a moment Drift thought the seams of the bag would burst, spreading polystyrene balls throughout the bus. Wilma went to the kitchenette that lay behind a vibrant green curtain and soon returned with a mug of hot chocolate each and the promised packet of Tim Tams.

'Ta, darls,' Shaynene said as she took a mug from Wilma and bit the corner from a biscuit before dunking it. 'I wish my old bitch of a mum was as nice as you.'

She wiggled her bum further into the beanbag. Her bright brown eyes were hooded heavily with thick black eye makeup and purple eyeshadow that matched her hair. Her eyes shone excitedly as she spoke rapidly to Wilma and Drift.

'Turns out this Kai disappearance is the biggest news since, since …' she thought a moment '… since Lindy Chamberlain's "a dingo ate my baby" and Schapelle's "I didn't have drugs in me boogie board bag". It's going ape back in town. Me boss barely gave me the time off because it's crazy at the store. He said if I'm not back by tomorrow I've lost my job and he'll put Head Bob in the deep fryer. They've closed the road now at Widgenup to stop more people coming. It's like a concert you need tickets for! So glad I could hitch a lift with Wilma, otherwise the cops would never have let me through! I can't *wait* to get to the camp area. Will you take me in your ute, Drifter chick?'

Drift smiled at her. 'Sure, as long as you don't expect me to hang around.'

'Booor-ring,' Shaynene said rolling her eyes. Glancing at Wilma she said, 'Tell her to lighten up.'

Today Shaynene wore a ridiculously short denim mini-skirt and Drift could see the pink camouflage-patterned boy-leg shorts beneath them that cut into dimpled fake-tanned inner thighs. Her undies matched the straining camo-print bra that was clearly visible beneath a black Daffy Duck singlet. Chunky pink and silver Kmart jewellery rattled on her wrist. She was done up to the nines, Shaynene-style, clearly on the hunt. Wilma passed Drift the other mug, kicking a red beanbag nearer Shaynene's.

'Sounds terribly exciting, Shaynene,' Wilma said, 'if you're into that kind of thing ... but some of us like a quieter life. Don't we, Drift?'

Drift took the mug gratefully from Wilma and sat. 'We sure do. I've just driven past the camp. It's nuts down there,' she said. 'The traffic will be such a pain when we let the cattle onto the route. I wish they'd all just bugger off.'

Wilma gathered up her own hot chocolate and sat in a yellow beanbag between the girls, her floral-clad bottom making the beans rustle.

'Aren't you going to open them?' she asked, nodding to the presents Drift had sat on the floor beside her.

'Oh yes!'

The card was of an orange sunset, painted in watercolours by Wilma herself. Inside she'd written, *Happy 21st Birthday my darling all-grown-up Drifty girl. As you walk the earth now as an adult woman, always honour your truth. Love Wilma.* Drift felt goosebumps lift over her skin as a surprise memory of the girl in the dunes came to her mind.

'Honour your truth? What do you mean, *truth*?'

'Ah,' Wilma said, 'there's a tricky question. Let me see ...' She paused as she thought, then continued. 'Love is always truth. But you can only find love with a still, *quiet* mind that is beyond your noisy *thinking* mind.'

'Oh, I'm seeking love,' Shaynene said, as if she were auditioning for *The Bachelorette*.

Wilma looked at her kindly. 'I'm not talking about romantic love. I'm talking about love that gives you peace, and kinship with all life and knowing you're whole regardless of having a partner or not. The truth of life is about the rhythm of nature ... and our oneness with it and all others, not what mainstream society or the media tells you love is. Love and feeling whole, above all, is the only light to follow. If you do that, only then can romantic love thrive long term.'

'Yeah, yeah, whatevs,' Shaynene said discontentedly.

Wilma looked at Drift, reaching out to touch her arm. 'I think you know how to feel truth innately, Drift, by being on the road and out under the stars so much. Not many people have lives that give them the opportunity for stillness that you have out here. If you can keep your thoughts in check and your mind still despite the white noise from the outside world, you can keep your heart open. As you get older and the world pushes in, you need to remember how to keep your centre and honour your truth no matter what circumstances you find yourself in.' Drift knew she was referring to her father and his choice *not* to still his mind and push away the pain of his past.

'How come she knows and I don't?' Shaynene butted in.

'Everyone knows it deep inside themselves,' Wilma answered, 'but the more you allow the external world to influence you, the less you hear your inner voice. So most people forget.'

'You're sounding like friggin Oprah now.'

Wilma smiled. 'Both you girls, as you move through life, you have to consciously choose to keep your hearts open. Truth comes from the open heart, the inner light, not the head and the "blah blah" of the mind's ego.'

'Faaaar out, Brussels sprout,' Shaynene said. 'It's a bit different to the world according to my mum. She just tells me, "Life sucks, so take what you can get. You eat, you sleep, you root, you shit, you die."'

Wilma laughed. 'We all have our own lessons to learn, Shaynene, and that includes learning *not* to listen to our parents sometimes.'

Drift tried to hang on to the words Wilma had told her about keeping her heart open. Everything that had happened recently — her father's suicide attempt, her disappointment with him, the disgusting morning with Kelvin, the memory of her mother lifted from the seabed by the missing surfer, and her restlessness — all made her heart constrict. The world had become threatening. Dark memories shuddered through her. Now it seemed her life hurt, and that was the truth.

Suddenly Drift wanted to tell Wilma about her truth — the vacant look she'd just seen in her dad's eyes. That he was slipping again. She wanted to tell Wilma everything. About the ghost girl, her feelings stirring after meeting the policeman, the awful time unloading cattle with Kelvin, the need to pull away from her dad for some space, but how could she abandon him? But with Shaynene here, she didn't feel like she was able to talk freely. Shay and Wilma had already moved the conversation on by the time Drift caught her spin of thoughts.

'Well I don't read no books,' Shay was telling Wilma. 'So I guess I'm buggered. I'll never learn nothing.'

'We can only get some of our knowledge from books,' Wilma said. 'Most of our wisdom comes from movement through life and, like I said, getting out of our heads, where our ego lives, and living from our hearts instead.'

Wilma's vibrant gaze was settled on Shaynene's face, but Shaynene was already reaching for another Tim Tam, and squirming a little in the beanbag, clearly itching to get to where the action was.

'Yeah, yeah, you're right, Wilms. Bring it on then. I'm gunna live life. Flat-out full-throttle live it. Just get out there and do it,' Shaynene said. 'Speaking of doing it, hurry up and open them,' she said to Drift, flicking a hand at the presents, 'so we can get our backsides beachside.'

Drift ran her fingers under the sticky tape of the golden tissue paper that covered her birthday present. For years, like Charlie, Wilma had been supplying her with surprise presents. What started out as strawberry Freddo Frogs to accompany the books grew into substantial gifts: pretty summer dresses and colourful cotton socks along with art supplies, sketch pads and brushes.

As Drift unwrapped her presents she smiled to see a collection of new bras and undies, a pair of cool surf shorts and a bikini.

There was even a supply of prettily packaged organic pads and groovy period-proof undies.

'For your superpower women's business,' Wilma said, pointing to them. Drift grinned back, grateful. It had been Wilma, years before, who had taught Drift that as a woman she was inextricably linked with the moon, and she was to be proud of who she was and the cycles of energy her body gave her every month.

'Fancy pants,' Shaynene said, giving them a twirl on her index finger.

Drift then held up the pretty patterned blue and white swimwear and Wilma could see the young girl's eyes shine.

'Do you like them?'

'Oh, yes,' Drift breathed.

'Seeeeexy,' confirmed Shaynene. 'You'll pull a few surfers in those. You got the body for it, ya wormy bitch.'

Drift laughed as Shaynene tried hopelessly to cover one of her giant breasts with the tiny triangle of fabric.

'They'd see my tat in this. And a bit more than they bargained for,' she said.

The third present were books. One about plants as medicine for livestock and another on horse-colour genetics that explained why white horses were called grey.

'Fantastic,' Drift said excitedly as she thumbed through it. 'I love it, thank you! I love all the presents!' She leaned over and hugged Wilma.

Shaynene glanced at the books and pulled a face. 'Genetics. Great. Whatever floats your boat.' She reached for her back pocket. 'Here's my present to you. No balloon, no party!' She held a small packet in her outstretched hand.

Drift took it, glad her friend had thought to bring her a gift. Thinking it was a chocolate from the store, she was about to unwrap it, then she looked at what really lay in the palm of her hand: a shiny foil packet. The writing read *Pecker-up Condoms — Cola Flavoured*.

'Gee, thanks,' Drift said flatly.

'Extra thin for his pleasure. Ribbed for hers,' Shaynene said, winking.

Drift felt her cheeks burn. 'As if I'll need this.'

'As if you won't,' Shaynene said, sniggering. Wilma cocked an eyebrow. They fell silent until Drift spoke.

'Wilma?' Drift asked, trying to sound casual.

'Mmm?'

'Do you have any books on ghosts?'

Wilma paused as she raised her mug to her lips. 'Ghosts?' she echoed, the steam of the hot chocolate rising. 'Why?'

Drift lifted one shoulder in a shrug. 'Oh, no reason. Just, you know …'

'No,' Wilma said, 'I don't know.'

As Shaynene groaned and rolled up and out of her beanbag, she said, 'Jeez, Drift … you and your bloody ghosts and spirits. As my mum would say, you sure as Hell aren't the full tickety-boo. But I loves you anyhoo. Now come on, give us a lift down to party town, will you?'

'But … I can't … Dad … the cattle … Wilma, can't you?'

Wilma shook her head. 'I'm not going anywhere. I've already driven too much today. There are regulations with the government, you know, about how many driving hours their employees can do.' She winked at Shaynene. 'Plus, Drift, your dad won't be going anywhere with the cattle until the second load arrives — they could arrive this evening or tomorrow. I'll stay and give him a hand now to make ready. So off you two go. Live a little.'

Drift looked at Wilma's insistent gaze and realised if she did stay, she might encounter Kelvin again. 'C'mon then,' she relented, and gathered up her things.

'Don't forget your best prezzie,' Shaynene said, chucking the condom at her.

Chapter 12

As Drift pulled out from the stock watering hole for the second time that day with a re-filled tank, an unimpressed Shaynene folded her arms across her ample chest and frowned, the tiger seeming to scowl too.

'Dunno why you always have to be working,' she grumbled. The sun was now high in the sky, summer fully reinstated. Light glimmered across the blue water beyond the dunes.

'Are you talking to me or the dog?' Drift nodded towards Dunno, who was framed in the side mirror, his odd oval-shaped pink tongue lolling to the side of his wide black rubbery mouth.

'Very funny. Ya dick. Dunno dunno how to speak human,' Shaynene said.

Drift gave Shaynene a gentle shove. 'Stop your grumbling. By me working, you stay undercover longer as part of the drover's team. The cops are more likely to let you hang about if they know you're part of my crew.'

'True,' Shaynene said, sitting upright, hoicking up her boobs and tugging down her denim mini-skirt as they neared the camp headquarters.

'I sure do look like a stockman!' she joked.

She flipped the ute's sun visor down and slammed it back up again when she realised it didn't have a mirror. 'So you're staying here with me then?' she said, dexterously applying her bright pink lipstick blind. 'It's just for one night. After that, Head Bob gets crumbed and fried by me boss.'

Drift shook her head as they rolled past a large gathering of people sitting on the beach staring at an even bigger group of surfers who bobbed out on the water, seal-like, around a wreath that floated like a giant lily pad in the middle of them. A small plume of smoke rose from it and wavered like a ghost. Choppers above filmed the floating prayer circle. On the beachside, media men and women loitered nearby, their dark townie clothes marking them out as aliens in this vast, wild landscape.

They hovered near their media bags looking bored until the next live report; some stooped and smoking; others had their heads bent over mobile phones; and another few sat in their cars, the engines running, aircon on, as the heat of the day lifted sweat from them.

'Are you mad? I'm not hanging about here. The cattle are gunna need more water, and quickly.' Drift looked up at the glaring sun. 'I can't stay. And we've got the rest of the herd coming soon.' An image of ugly Kelvin flashed through her mind. Drift shuddered. She wondered if the signal would work on their phone so she could insist her dad change truckers. 'I can come get you when I do another water run tomorrow. Then you can hitch home with Wilma, get back to work and Head Bob's life will be spared. I'm not here to chase missing surfers.'

'You're not meant to chase the missing one, dufus. You're meant to chase the ones who are alive and on land,' Shaynene quipped. Drift thought of the missing man and felt a shiver as if the shadow of a sinister bird had swooped overhead.

As they neared the cordoned-off police camp, Drift recognised the figure walking towards her.

'Hi, Simon.' She smiled as he stooped to look through the window, leaning a tanned forearm on the roof of the ute.

'Hello,' he said, looking directly at her. In the intense light of full sun, she noticed his face, despite the peppering of acne scars, was rather like a shop mannequin's, with its perfectly classic, even, almost expressionless features. Perhaps his mask was the police training? Or was it perhaps just him? The faint pitted scars on his cheeks made him seem young and vulnerable. And he was seriously shy, judging by the way he was blushing at a very forward Shaynene.

'Why hellooooo, *Mister* Police*man*,' Shaynene said, leaning over Drift to get a better gander, dragging her top even further down as she did, so her tiger looked set to bite him. She eyed him up and down as if he were meat.

'This is my ah … ah … assistant, Shaynene,' Drift stammered.

'Assistant?' Simon said.

Shaynene poked Drift hard in the thigh with her index finger. 'Dick,' she muttered quietly.

A banging sound began on the back of the ute as Dunno's tail thumped a wag with his sloping weird-dog arse. He was dragging his top lip up in a doggy smile.

Simon frowned at him. 'Is that a working dog?'

'Yes, D-Dunno,' Drift stammered. 'Sort of. He does work. A bit, but mostly he likes being on the ute.'

Simon looked momentarily puzzled.

'His name's Dunno,' Shaynene explained. 'Dunno where he came from. Dunno who he belonged to. Dunno what breed he is.' She shrugged. 'Dunno?'

'Ahhh! I see,' he said, still seeming confused.

'They're normally my lines,' Drift said, smiling up at Simon. As she did, she surprised even herself by the involuntary sparkle she knew was in her eyes. It raised a smile on Simon's face. Even Shaynene gave her a surprised glance. In the silent gap as chemistry between them fizzed, the blond pro-surfer from the night before came jogging up the beach, concern written all over his face.

'Mate,' he said to Simon, a little out of breath. 'Those fucken bitches are back hassling us again. You're going to have a homicide on your hands if you don't kick them back out of our camp. Mo's gunna kill the lot of them.'

'Sir, those women have as much right to be here as you do. Mind your manners, please, around the ladies.'

Drift felt Shay's elbow.

'Why hellooo,' Shaynene said slowly, as she looked at the tight-T-shirt-clad sportsman. Then she recognised him and began to wiggle in her seat like a dog with worms, and let out a small high-pitched squeal. Drift thought Shaynene was set to wet her pants. Clearly she knew the celeb. Shay began squeezing Drift's forearm as tight as a carpet snake squeezes a rat.

'Oh, hi again,' the surfer said as he recognised Drift. 'Drover girl.'

'Hi, Digger.'

'You know him?' Shaynene gushed in an all too obvious whisper. 'You know *Digger Corbet*? Oh my God! *You know him! And he knows you! Oh. My. God!*' Drift tried to unclamp Shaynene's clutching hand. This time it was her turn to poke her with a finger.

'I'll be right with you,' Simon said to Digger, then he turned back to Drift. 'I've been wanting to talk with you. About the time Kai Kaahea went missing.'

'Me?' Drift said, suddenly perplexed. 'But Dad and I were up in town early. We weren't even —'

'Sure she'll talk to you!' Shaynene butted in, unbuckling her seatbelt and leaping out of the ute. 'She'll come and give you a statement.'

Simon glanced at Shaynene. 'I don't need a statement ... I just want her to recall the weather conditions before you went to town. If you noticed the currents, saw anyone, that sort of thing,' he said, his eyes locked on Drift again. Drift wondered why he hadn't asked her before. It would be good to get him alone. Then she could tell him about Kelvin. She looked into his eyes.

'Sure,' she said. Then she felt the sizzle. Attraction radiated from him. He *did* like her.

'It's OK, we'll *both* come with you,' Shaynene said to Simon. She grabbed Digger's hand and pumped it up and down, standing way too close to him.

'Shaynene,' she said with a big grin on her face. 'From the shop. Back that way. *So, so, so* good to meet you!'

'Right,' said Digger. 'Shaynene from the shop. Great.' He pulled his hand away. Drift now felt compelled to get out of the ute too — Shaynene on her own was a crowd-control issue, and she felt Simon needed back-up.

As Drift stood before Simon, she noticed again his height and his narrow frame. A small zing ran through her. Then an awkward silence descended. Simon seemed torn by what to do next. He didn't look at Digger as he spoke to him, but kept his focus on Drift's face.

'Is it OK if these young ladies come along while I sort things out with your unwanted visitors?' Simon asked. His gaze remained upon her. Drift was going to have to nickname him 'staring Simon' if he didn't let up with that. She felt a pulse of confidence. In her limited experience, when she was around Shaynene, most men fixated on Shaynene's knockers. Drift had never noticed the gaze of a man before in the way she was feeling it now from Simon. She then saw that Digger was smiling at her too. What was going on? What had shifted from one day to the next in her? Did she have a sign above her head that said *Life change needed; ready to date men*? She didn't realise that the men standing before her were intrigued by the unusual wild-haired cowgirl, drawn to the way she stood so strong on the earth in her boots, in ragged cut-off jeans and a faded soft pink singlet with a peeling number 11 that curved over her shapely breasts. Over her singlet she wore an unbuttoned old blue checked flannie to protect her arms from the sun. There was nothing vain or needy about her, with her muscled, wide shoulders and working-woman no-nonsense hands. But it was her face, where their eyes lingered. Ultra-blue eyes framed by long lashes, and innocence and honesty written in the dusting of freckles on her face.

Embarrassed by their scrutiny, Drift reached into the ute and jammed on her hat.

Shaynene tugged her top lower. 'We promise to behave,' she said, giving Digger a wink.

'I've got cattle to water. Can't be hanging about here for long,' Drift said in a voice as dry as dust.

'Sure, the girls can come,' Digger said. 'No iPhones,' he quickly added, his sea-blue eyes narrowing at Shaynene.

Drift opened up her palms. 'I don't own one.'

Shaynene felt the press of the phone that she carried tucked down the side of one of her cowgirl boots. 'I don't either,' she lied. 'You can frisk me if you like.' She rubbed her palms over her tight-fitting clothing, turned her round bottom to them, patting her back pockets provocatively.

'See? No phonesie,' she said.

'OK, follow me,' Simon said.

'With pleasure,' Shaynene muttered as the constable and the surfer set out in front of them. She elbowed Drift and nodded towards the men's backsides. Drift rolled her eyes.

'Hot, hot, hot!' Shaynene said, fanning herself. 'The afternoon is getting very, very *hot*!'

They walked between two orange cones and past a policeman who was guarding the pro-surfer area. The cop nodded at them, giving Simon a smile.

On the beach Mo stood in front of a group of girls. He was embroiled in a yelling match with the tallest, skinniest one, her long mane of brown hair lifting in the breeze. The other pro surfers sat beneath an annex attached to one of the fancy four-wheel drives — they had towels over their heads, sheltering themselves from both the sun and the prying lenses of the media who were cordoned off a good way back. It was not far away enough though to hide the heated exchange from the long lenses the reporters had trained on it.

'He can't just fuck me and dump me,' the girl yelled as she gestured towards the pro-surfer crew. 'I'll sell my story. About what a prick you are, Arnie Gordonson.' The girl flung her arm in the media's direction. 'World's biggest arsehole!' she yelled. 'I wish it was you out there missing —'

Mo stepped forward to shove her, but Simon dived in, grabbing him by the shirt. In an instant Drift saw how Simon seemed to get taller. Broader. Braver. More purposeful. Beside her Drift noticed Shaynene's cheeks turning crimson, her chest rising and falling as if hyperventilating. She clutched Drift's forearm as she noted the surf gods sitting in the shade. She was again making small high-pitched noises of excitement and gritting her teeth.

'Keep your pants on,' Drift muttered to her quietly.

'That's enough now, Mo,' Simon said. He turned to the girl. 'Miss, this area is out of bounds to the public.'

The girl's eyes flared at him. '"The public"? I wasn't "the public" last night! Was I, Arnie? *User*!' The sun glanced on her nose piercing as she swiped away silvery snot with the back of her hand. As one of her girlfriends put her arm around her, tears arrived. Drift saw her body soften and her anger melt away as her shoulders folded forward. The girl leaned on her friend, crying as they steered her away.

Drift looked over at Arnie. His face showed no remorse; instead he was high-fiving the lanky dark-haired American. Drift could feel how jagged the energy of the men felt collectively, like a group of meanly bred young colts with too much testosterone and not enough alpha mares in the herd to keep them on the straight and narrow. Drift knew these men had forgotten their manners. She'd seen it time and again in her world, when she and her father lobbed into stockyards and shearing sheds. Drift looked at the groupie girls wandering off sulkily. She was again reminded of how grateful she was to have been raised the way she had, by Wilma, Charlie and Split, to be aware some men could behave badly in groups.

With Mo calmed down, the media finished with their rapid-fire photo frenzy and began to tail the girls, certain they had another scoop of surfer scandal. Simon gestured for Drift and Shaynene to join him in the shade of the annex.

'I'd advise you, Mo, to get your surf team out of here as soon as possible. Chopper them out. Charter a plane from The Planet? Anything. But if you go by road there'll be media mayhem and a million more headaches.'

'We're not going until you've found him,' Mo said.

'There's nothing to be gained hanging about here,' Simon said gently. 'We're doing all we can. The crowd issues are escalating. It'd help us to have you away from the scene. They're reducing the search to a skeleton crew in a day or so, anyway.'

Mo's face fired with anger. 'You can't just give up looking for him!' His cheeks were a mottled grey and red, and the stubble on his jaw now almost a pepper-and-salt beard. He had bags under his eyes like inflatable dinghies. Drift looked at him and thought how unhealthy he seemed — not just physically, but also in his spirit. If Charlie Weatherbourne spied him she'd say something like, 'If he were a steer, I'd be giving him lots of roughage. Clean his system out.' She'd not like him as a leader in her herd, she decided.

'But he can't just be *gone*?' Mo said. 'You have to stay and find him.' He squared up to Simon like a bull, but Simon stood his ground and kept his cool. 'He could still be out there,' Mo continued. 'He's a strong athlete. A master at swimming and of the sea. I'll sue you cops if you don't do everything, *every damn thing*, to find that boy!'

'We're doing all we can, sir.'

'Bullshit!'

For a moment Drift thought Mo would cry. He turned to the sweep of blue before them and clutched his hair. 'He can't be gone!' His voice almost broke.

'You mean, you can't *afford* for him to be gone,' the American surfer sneered from beneath the cover of his brand-name surf towel. 'You're bust and broke without his contract. In fact, we all are.' Mo swung around to the dark-haired guy who continued,

'We all know Kai's been carrying us with his prize money and his sponsorships and pretty-boy image. You're sunk — we're all sunk without him.'

'Well, if you lot focused. Won a few,' Mo shouted, swiping his arm in the air.

'Won a few? And that's all you care about? If you hadn't pushed him so far,' said Arnie, standing abruptly.

'Me?' Mo spat. 'You lot were part of it too. How else do I pay for your expensive habits? You shitheads cost me a bomb!' He glanced cautiously at Simon.

Drift cleared her throat, and looked coldly at the surfers and then Simon. 'If you don't mind,' she said to him, 'I've got thirsty cattle to get to.' This was no time to raise her issues with him about Kelvin. She wanted out of here.

'I know,' Simon said, his face set like stone. Suddenly the radio hitched to his belt crackled. An unintelligible string of words barked from it, but Simon understood them. He spoke into the receiver that was clipped at his chest. 'Copy that. On my way.'

Simon looked darkly at the surfers. 'Kai's parents have been found and notified,' he said. The news seemed to ripple through the men and all of them dropped their anger down a notch. 'They'd been uncontactable on a flight out of New York to Hawaii. I suspect they'll need to talk to you,' Simon said to Mo, 'in person. So you'd best make plans to leave.'

'Ahhh!' came a voice, as Gup weaved unsteadily out from behind the vehicles with a beer in hand. 'Hello, Cunt Stubble,' he said antagonistically. 'And if it isn't horse girl. And who has she here with her?' He sidled up to Shaynene, eyeing her voluptuous form. 'Gup Jones,' he said, offering her a handshake.

'Shaynene. From the shop,' she said. 'Back thataway. Widgenup.'

'Ahhh, I remember you!' Gup said, looking at her breasts. 'Tiger girl. I called in there on our way down. Grrrr!'

'*I* don't remember *you*,' she said, eyeing him suggestively. 'Which is unlike me. I would normally remember someone like you. Bit early, isn't it?' she added, looking at the beer.

'It's after midday. Sip?'

'Thanks, Mr Surf Pro,' she said, taking a swig.

'Pleasure's all mine,' Gup said. 'Although I'm not a pro. These guys are, but we're good mates. Right?'

The other men didn't respond. Drift could tell from the way Shaynene was turning to him, and he was locking onto her, there'd be more *Home and Away*-style romance dramas unfolding.

Simon cleared his throat. 'Come on, I've got to get back.'

'Me too,' said Drift.

Shaynene stood her ground, gazing up at the sunburnt lanky Gup, who was grinning like a village idiot at her.

'She's OK,' he said to Simon. 'This one can stay.'

'This is not a fucken picnic,' Digger snapped from where he was leaning on the side of a vehicle.

'I know that, numbnuts,' Gup said with nastiness in his voice. 'Don't blame me for the shit we're in. It was Kai's choice to go out on his own. I tried to stop the arsehole. He knew the weather was comin in and the rip was a bad one.'

'Well maybe you shoulda tried harder,' Mo muttered like a rumble of thunder.

'Don't you tell me what I shoulda done,' Gup exploded, pointing his finger at him, still holding his beer. 'You were the one keeping him hooked on that shit. He wanted to go. To get away from you.' All the men's eyes slid to the police officer.

'Is this a conversation I'm supposed to be hearing?' Simon said in his bland tones. 'Are you suggesting Mr Kaahea was under the influence of narcotics at the time of his disappearance?'

Mo leaped forward, scruffing Gup by his shirt front and pinning him to the side of the four-wheel drive — the annex wavering, the media pack springing to life with cameras again. 'You little shit! You're a fine one to talk.'

'Do you think this is a fucken picnic for me too? Cut me some slack, arseholes. I'm not taking the blame for this. No way.'

Gup freed himself and turned to Shaynene as if he had joined her soapie TV set. 'Let's blow this joint, baby.'

'Where we goin?' she asked, her face beaming at the situation she found herself in.

'I don't know, darlin,' Gup said as if he were Elvis in a B-grade movie. 'Anywhere but here.' He handed her his beer.

Just before she disappeared with Gup around the side of the vehicle, Shay gave Drift a delighted smile and a not-so-subtle thumbs-up. Drift pulled a face to say, are you sure? Shaynene grinned more. There'd be no talking her out of it, Drift knew. She looked to Simon for help. He gave nothing away. Instead his steady gaze fell upon the rest of the surfers.

'I'll be bringing the detectives down in ten minutes unless you begin to pack up and leave. If you aren't all gone by tomorrow, I'll start investigations you obviously don't want started. If there're illicit substances in your camp or drug use in your team, we'll be doing more than a search and rescue.'

Mo swiped a hand over the stubble of his jaw. 'Sure thing, officer,' he mumbled. Simon extended his hand in the direction of the ute as an invitation for Drift to go with him. Her head bowed as she turned from the surfers, she wondered why on earth she'd been swept into the eye of someone else's storm. Trudging through sand scuffed with the chaotic events of the past few days, Drift rolled the scenario around in her head. A man missing. And for her, maybe a man found? Relieved she was leaving the madness of the surf camp, Drift felt glad to reach the ute and her panting overjoyed dogs.

'It's got nothing to do with me,' Drift said to her dogs firmly. But as she started up the ute to return to camp, she got the oddest feeling that, for some reason, this had *everything* to do with her.

Chapter 13

The following morning Split Wood swung open the gate. From his paint horse, Dunston, he watched as the cattle spilled out from the yard, led by the only black cow in the herd, who clearly had a dash of dairy to her along with some wilfulness.

A distance away, Drift noticed the cow and made a mental note to watch that one. As the cattle took to the road, the sun was just breaching the scrub line, and Drift breathed out. After the past couple of days, it was reassuring to be back in the saddle, back into life as she knew it; she wondered why she had ever wished it away.

Life felt safer in the saddle. With a new herd and a fresh stretch of road she wondered at the restlessness she'd felt. Minty bowed her head and pawed the ground as if to say, 'Hurry up.' Just a jiggle of the reins and a smooch sound between Drift's lips and the mare stopped her fidgeting. The yards were badly pugged from the recent rain and, with the next load of cattle coming, Split had made the decision to let the first lot out onto fresh tucker sooner. It was risky in Drift's mind, as the cattle hadn't had time to settle, but she wanted to get on with it. There was nothing like droving work to get her dad out of the dark cloud he sometimes slipped into.

'You sure you want to let them out?' Drift had asked him the night before as he pushed Wilma's camp-oven chicken stew around his plate. 'The police are about to pull the pin on the search. The traffic's gunna get heavier tomorrow.'

Split had shrugged his shoulders. 'They'll be up to their guts in mud if we leave 'em.'

He returned to his silence. It terrified her. She wished he was still in his spoken-poetry phase. After lights out she'd heard him rattling around to find his not-so-secret stash of whiskey. He took it to bed with him like a baby needing a dummy. His snoring, waking her in the middle of the night, told her he'd be rough tomorrow. She reached over to the bottom drawer and turned on the night light and moved aside her most precious artwork, fingertips finding the one photo of her mother that remained. She looked at it. Harmony, with her long spiralling seaweed hair, her pixie face and clothing that suggested she belonged in a love-all-as-one hippy commune, yet she held a vanity and defiance within her stance. The photo had given Drift no comfort. In his bed, her father stopped breathing for an uncomfortably long time, before he shuddered in a noisy snore. Drift sighed, putting the photo back, switching off the light.

Now, as the lead black cow began to jog, taking other cows and calves with her, Drift let rip with a determined, high-pitched whistle. She knew in handling stock, she had to put her personal turmoils aside and find calm. Her dogs at Minty's hocks cast out to the lead as she cantered Minty on from a standstill.

Hamlet and Molly soon had the leaders blocked up, and were manoeuvring the beasts in the direction they needed to graze, south along the road towards the searchers' camp. On the northern side of the road Wilma had angled her bus as a visual block and was now standing squarely on the side of the road, one hand on her blue-flowered hip, the other arm raised as a shade to the arriving sun. Drift knew Wilma needed to get back up the track to the next town for a scheduled school visit, but she could tell she was hovering, dragging her stay out because of the state of Split.

That morning as she set down a dish of stodgy spoon-holding porridge in front of Split, she'd blamed the wayward Shaynene — who hadn't come back last night — for her hanging about. But all of them knew she was delaying her departure because of Split's slump.

'I said to that girl we needed to head out early, and I told her you two are too busy to be taxiing her around,' Wilma had tut-tutted. 'Get the cattle sorted and then we can go find her.'

Drift could sense Wilma's tension. 'Hurry up, you grumpy arse,' Drift called to Split now from the back of her horse, trying to force good-natured stirring into her tone. Dunston was swishing his tail as Split swung him to shut the yard gate and gather up a sluggish droopy-eared cow and her little toffee-coloured calf who had both made a beeline for the grasses away from the herd.

With Drift working the lead and her dad at the rear, the stop-start pace of the cattle eased quickly once the hungry beasts discovered the fresh pick along the wide, flat coastal dirt road. Still though, the black cow got too pacey, so Drift sailed her stock whip around her head, shattering the stillness with a loud crack, sending waterbirds scattering upwards on a nearby lagoon on The Planet. The cow, who had a high whorl on her brow and poppy eyes, propped on her front hooves looking at Drift and the dogs in surprise. Her calf at foot had the same slightly off-centre energy as her mother.

'You'd better settle yourself, lady,' Drift said to the cow, turning Minty to block her, Minty's energy lifting to meet that of the wayward mother. The cow's freedom-feeling of not being yarded fought with her instinct to eat. The desperate hunger of the whole herd was causing a disquiet and a restlessness in all of them. Drift hoped they would soon settle down into some kind of order so that all of them, including the stirry black cow, would lower their heads calmly, instead of nervous sniffing and snatching at roadside vegetation.

Drift looked to her left, where the sturdy high fences of The Planet ran beside the eastern side of the road. She smiled at the fancy new fencing. She was grateful for it flanking the herd, making her job of keeping the cattle steady so much easier. Soon, she was able to relax more, with Minty splashing slowly through puddles in the table drains, while Hamlet sniffed at the water, leaping over it in an ungainly way with his too-long teenager-dog limbs.

Drift pulled Minty up to watch the lead cattle graze, and as she did she was once again astounded by the beauty of the property beside her. Standing brisket-high in healthy grassland stood about fifty glossy bronze Santa Gertrudis cows. Curiosity had drawn them out of the shadows from a clump of gums. They edged forward, ears cast keenly towards the passing herd, gathering speed as they approached the fenceline.

'Hello, girls,' Drift said, smiling as she took in the impressive bloom of the cattle. Such a contrast to the concentration-camp emaciation of her road herd. Hamlet pricked his ears in surprise when he saw the frolicking cattle on the other side of the fence. Health and good vigour rippled through them — the cattle practically shone gold in the emerging sunlight.

Drift was so used to seeing animals hungrily haunting bare country that had been raped by whitefellas for generations, on soil that had been grazed down to its bones. It was nice to see such a vibrant herd. She noticed the watering systems of portable troughs fixed to poly pipe that followed the fencelines for miles, and the infrastructure of movable electric fencing, powered by solar. It was simple yet innovative. There it was, all laid out before her. The sort of farm Wilma and her dad discussed, and one Drift had dreamed of. It was a management system of time-controlled grazing like she had read about after Wilma had printed out her Google searches on holistic farming. She now knew it had to be seen to be believed. Dry though it had been until the storm, there was no 'drought' here. The country and the cattle shone with life, particularly now a good couple of inches had been dumped on the well-covered soil filling a chain of ponds that were surrounded by lush water plants.

The curious cattle at the fence eventually wandered away and Drift sat listening to the still day, silent save for the tearing of grasses by the mouths of the near-starved cattle. All of a sudden, though, the peace was shattered. A black speck, once far off in the sky, was soon overhead. A chopper, hovering low. Then another. Roaring, thumping, whumping above the same line of the road. News crews on the hunt for more live feeds. They tore the air and set the cows on edge. Before Drift knew it, Minty's head was high, her eyes wide in her skull. The cattle were running, their eyes rolling white from the shock of the loud weird otherworldly noise and the giant metal insects that skittered above. A few head broke past Drift in a panic. The black cow's eyes popped even more. Hamlet got a rush of young kelpie blood and began barking and singling out the black beast. At full gallop the cow aimed at a low spot in a deep drain that ran under the fence into The Planet. She hit the base hard, pushing a panel of ring-lock up, flipping herself through the plain wire. The fencing shrieked. The calf zig-zagged away from the teeth of the dog, then back to her flailing mother, smashing into the fence beside her. Both threw their legs about like beetles on their backs, reefing the screaming fence staples from the posts.

Split was now shouting above the noise of the chopper, shaking his fist at it, leaning too heavily on his reins. Panicked, Dunston reared. Split threw himself forward in the saddle, slinging his arms about his horse's neck. The chopper swung back over to capture the action of the big man on the flighty horse.

The choppers swooped close again, and Drift watched in horror as chaos unravelled their day. Their horses were used to road trains, to flapping tarps of grain trucks hurtling by; used to shotguns and whip cracks and roadside rubbish that came alive and took flight in sudden breezes. Dunston and Minty had been mustering on properties where choppers were used, but with the energy of the storm still firing the air and the freshness of the cattle, as well as Split's dark mood, Dunston lost his calm. He was scuttling sideways away from the cattle with her dad barely on board. The dogs began to take charge, and as a pack they pushed too hard. Drift's whistles for them to sit fell on adrenaline-filled ears that refused to hear her, particularly over the mini-storm of wind the chopper blades stirred. Molly and Hamlet surged the cattle into a wall of energy as they fled collectively from the aircraft and the dogs. Even Dunno grabbed some of the action, snapping at hocks voraciously like a wolf.

The black cow, her nose bleeding, made a second lunge for the underbelly of the fence strung over the waterway, pushing her head under, angling her neck and shoulders upwards till the fencing wire shrieked, then snapped. Drift watched helplessly as the cattle behind her spilled over each other, tumbling like floodwaters through the broken fence into The Planet.

Seeing the leaders headed for freedom, the tail enders went with them, leaping over the section of the fence that now offered an escape to the other side. It was as if it were a portal to paradise. The drover's herd merged with the purebred Planet cattle, bunting and bellowing as they collided in social uproar.

Split had managed to right himself and rein Dunston in. With a crack of his whip, and a roar, he got the dogs under control. Horses breathing hard, Drift and her dad watched the perfect Santas mixing with the rib-thin mottled drought cattle. Drift was still spinning Minty in circles so she wouldn't bolt from the chopper that continued to sweep along the shoreline. It dived close once more, before hurtling away south towards the camp.

'Idiots!' Drift screamed after them. Then she turned to see the last of their cattle make their way into the billionaire's land over the tangled mangle of fence. Bear, who had been watching the whole thing with a long stem of grass hanging from his drooping mouth and a surprised expression on his docile face, saw the rich pickings the cattle were tucking into and casually ambled over to the fence, snorted at it, then with big disced hooves trumped over the wire, catching his hoof in the ring-lock, casually tugging it free, allowing the taut top wires to drag over his back, then snorting down to eat the diverse pasture on the other side.

'Not you too, Bear,' Drift said, wishing she had been riding him and not Minty. Drift glanced to her father. His hairy chest was heaving, but his expression of frustration and fury was morphing into amusement. Wilma too was grinning as she trudged her way along the road towards them.

'A pox damn you, you muddy rascal!' he yelled to the sky in the direction of the choppers, shaking his fist. 'Away, thou tedious rogues!' Then his belly started to shake with laughter. Wilma and Drift exchanged a glance. The excitement had momentarily shaken a cloud away from him and into another mood. Wilma stood at Dunston's shoulder, looking at the fence and the cattle, who were galumphing in and out of the gumtree copses.

Drift slid down from her horse and handed the reins to her dad.

'What are you doing, valiant maiden?' he asked as Drift stepped over the flattened fence, picking up a fallen branch beneath a nearby tree. The cattle were scattering in several directions, helping themselves to the fine native pasture, the home herd sniffing after them, tails still aloft.

'I seeketh my cows, Dad, what do ya reckon?'

The banter was back.

'Shouldn't we try to contact them first?' her dad asked.

Drift rolled her eyes. 'Are you becoming a notable coward?' she said, squinting up at him.

'Yes,' chimed in Wilma, 'are you?'

Split cast them both a dark look.

'Well, we can't just leave them,' Drift persisted, lugging the branch over and laying it on top of the crushed section of fence. 'We gotta take the lot of them into the billionaire's yards and draft them.' She set more fallen branches down to press the remaining wire flat and took her reins from her dad. Carefully she led Minty over the fallen fence. 'Coming?'

'I'm not going in there. I've heard she's a nutter.'

'You've told me yourself, Dad: don't ever listen to gossip. And look at the place. It's regenerative ag management for sure! A solution to everything you've ranted to me about all my life!'

'I just don't think we ought to go barging in there moving their cattle about. It feels bad.'

'There is nothing either good or bad but thinking makes it so,' Wilma said, tugging on his trouser leg.

Split looked down to her, annoyed. 'They say in town that she runs some kinda weird religious cult.'

'And who might "they" be?' Wilma quizzed.

Split pointed to Drift. 'You might come out all brainwashed, wearing a long skirt and married to an eighty-year-old man with fifty wives.'

Wilma scoffed.

'You two hold the cattle here and I'll go get some panels,' Split said, running his hand over his stubbled jaw. 'We can make some kinda yard and separate them that way.'

'Who's the nutter now, Dad? That'll take forever and we need the panels for the next lot coming in. We gotta let her know her fence is down and that her cattle have been in with our pox-ridden lot.'

'A few steelies, a few gripples, a strain up, and she'll be as good as new,' he said, surveying the tangle.

'Even still, we gotta tell her she's had road cattle in with hers,' Drift said. 'I'll just have to go marry the eighty-year-old cult leader without you giving me away. You're just chicken or is thou a cream-faced loon?'

'Pull your head in. And don't you pinch my Shakespearean insults. You know I've got to hang about for Kelv. He'll be here with the second lot.'

Drift's face clouded at the mention of his name. Her dad hadn't taken steps to change the truck contractor like she'd hoped. Like she'd expected he would.

'Well if it's still him bringing the cattle, I'm gone for sure.' This time there was not a jot of stirring in her tone. It was flat with fury.

Wilma looked downcast. Last night Drift had told her about Kelvin and the ghost girl. In the quiet of the night, she'd offered up some words of advice and solace. 'Often when these awful and strange things happen, it's the Universe giving us a nudge. It's an invitation to grow and to change. What can feel like the worst thing in the world, or the strangest, can later be our greatest gift in moving us forward.'

But Wilma's words were lost on her now. Nothing felt good at the thought of Kelvin. Drift swung up into the saddle, disappointment in her father surging again.

'Wilma?' Split said. 'Tell her my plan's best. You can stay and help.'

'Not on your nelly,' Wilma said, her voice clipped too. 'Shaynene and I were meant to be out of here an hour ago. And you owe me — it's lucky I had nail-polish remover.'

Wilma climbed through the fence and patted Drift's leg, sensing the pain had been raised in her again. 'See you soon, beautiful girl. Stay away from crazies.'

Drift smiled. 'Oh, I'm well used to them,' she said pointedly to her dad.

'You want me to grab Bear?' Wilma asked.

'Nah, he's good for conversation, aren't you, Bearsie?' Bear, part thoroughbred with a bit of cob thrown in somewhere, was the most laidback of all the horses. He was more like a dog. When she said his name, he swished his tail and shook his head and snorted in response, but didn't stop grazing. He had the thickest, longest mane. During winter his hocks feathered and he lived up to his name by growing a shaggy brown grizzly coat. When she was younger, her legs sticking out from his broad flat coffee-table back, Drift wound Bear's mane into braids, copying the same pattern in her own hair. She reached for the lead rope that was knotted under Bear's neck and undid it.

'You don't know if the homestead and yards are five K away or fifty,' her dad warned. Drift didn't answer, just turned her horse and began riding, her dogs at heel, Bear falling in step beside her. She wanted more than anything to see this magical property and to find its heart and to meet the people who made it happen — and to distance herself from her dad and his inadequacy. Looking out at the vista before her, she legged Minty into a trot and went to gather up the boxed herd of cows and calves.

Chapter 14

Her dogs were tonguing hard and Minty was in a lather as Drift battled to get the two herds to flow as one along the wide-open road. She wished her father had come with her. The Santas seemed to know the direction of the yards, but the road cattle kept breaking, tails up, gallivanting away like African warthogs. Bear, let loose, trotted on slowly in their wake, sometimes slowing to a dawdle and nibbling at the banquet of grass, shrubs, flowers and forbs, then casting his ears forward and calling out when Drift got too far ahead.

She wanted to give Minty a rest and swap horses, but the restlessness of the cattle meant there was no time to switch. An hour in, as they followed the road, dogs panting, Drift began to wonder if she'd made the right decision. What if there wasn't a homestead at the end of this road, substantial though it was? What if the station's heart was hundreds of kilometres away? She reached for the water bottle hanging from her saddle and took a swig. Had her anger with her father and fear of seeing Kelvin made her too rash?

She checked her pocket for her usual emergency stash. A busted muesli bar rustled. A fly buzzed by. They passed a trough and the dogs dived in.

After finishing her snack, Drift whistled them out so the cattle could drink. The cows and calves milled around; few were thirsty, but they seemed to calm and to group. Drift leaned on the front of her saddle and stretched her legs out of the stirrups. She scanned her surroundings. On the other side of a slow-turning windmill the open grassland was closing in with clumps of gumtrees. Amidst them she caught a flash of white. She blinked and looked again. A few cows cast their ears forwards, alert to what lurked in the dappled shade of the trees. As the shape moved she saw it was the white horse again, and the rider.

'Hello?' she called, a little tentatively, wondering if she was seeing ghosts again. Through the low-slung branches, that gleamed the same white as the horse, she saw the rider emerge. The horse was solid, had charcoal legs and a dark mane, much like Minty's. The rider wore the same blue shirt she'd seen the day before at the waterhole.

He continued to weave in and out of the low scrub.

'Hello!' she called more insistently. 'We've had a bit of a box-up. Any yards around here?'

The rider hesitated. Then he turned, rode a little way towards her and pulled his horse up in the deep shade of a larger gum. He wore a huge stockman's hat, old style, that sat at odds with his trendy blue reflector sunglasses. His black bushy beard made him even more shadowy beneath the large tree. His long lean limbs and relaxed seat in the saddle told her he was a Territory-style stockman, possibly Indigenous.

'Err … Thataway,' he said, swivelling in the saddle and pointing. ''Bout three K.'

With the ease of a pro-rider, the stockman wheeled his horse in a single-hoof hind-quarter spin and then cantered away into the thicket. Bewildered, Drift watched him go. 'Super friendly,' she said to her animals. 'Chatty. Showy rider too.' She shrugged, relieved she was only a short ride away from help.

*

An hour later at The Planet's cattleyards Drift stood alongside property owner Sophia Gaier, knowing it had been absolutely the right decision to come. Drift had been surprised by Sophia's warm welcome, and relieved by the casual way Sophia had accepted the news that stray cattle were now amidst her pristine studs. The elegant woman folded her long, toned arms over the wooden railing and surveyed the boxed herd.

'You've done me a favour, darlin, truly you have,' Sophia said in a thick American accent, evoking the cowboy movies Drift and her dad liked whenever they found a telly. Drift noticed Sophia's turquoise-painted nails, and her strong hands, which looked like they did their fair share. Her long black hair, streaked lightly with grey, fell in a thick, wavy ponytail between her shoulders. Around her neck she wore a pretty patterned western paisley scarf trimmed with little green pom poms. She had a beauty and a grace Drift had never seen in any woman. Sophia's brown eyes were large and soulful, framed by long black eyelashes, like a doe, but piercing when she looked at her, like a she-wolf.

Drift tried to gauge Sophia's age. Her tanned skin was smooth and, like her cattle, she shone with good health and vigour. She must be over forty, Drift thought, but she could be mistaken for thirty. She could be the same age as her dad, and yet she looked much younger. She was so beautiful, Drift could barely take her eyes off her.

Under silver sunlight-sheened gumleaves, Minty, Bear and the dogs seemed to be settling in, easy in Sophia's company. Hamlet now lay in the shade nearby, occasionally clacking his teeth at passing flies. Even the cattle were camping, lying down and chewing their cud in the shaded yards.

Drift felt as if she'd stumbled into another world. Literally another planet. The place was incredible. The work area was an oasis of serene beauty, despite being cattleyards. Around them sculptures in rusting metal were interspersed with native garden beds that continued along the curved gravel road leading to more working spaces. Everything seemed relatively recently built, but was so beautifully crafted in old timber it looked settled in the land. Drift couldn't help commenting on the beautiful yards: to be encased in steel that rattled and was either freezing cold or firebrand hot had never felt right to her.

'We love the yards too,' Sophia had responded. 'Here, we like to put the ecology and the animals first. Fresh grazing every day or so, and, when the animals are handled, it's done gently. They're mostly good creatures, but this lot busted out last night over the tape. Cheeky girls,' she said, pointing to the coffee-coloured cattle. 'I was gonna have to get Serge to go get 'em in anyway, but you've done it for us. We've got a nice surprise social visit happening too with you turnin up, darlin. We don't have many visitors from the sleeping world often.'

'Sleeping world?' Drift asked.

Sophia laughed, her teeth white and perfect in the sunshine. 'I'm sorry, darlin — it's Planet speak. It takes some explainin, which we can do over an iced tea. Do you like iced tea?'

Drift's mouth opened and closed like a gaping fish out of water. Iced tea? She'd never had iced tea.

'Best to let the cattle cool down before we draft 'em anyhow. C'mon, honey, come meet The Planet people, and you can introduce us all to your dogs and give your horses a spell.'

Drift's mind flashed to her father, back on the roadside. She hesitated but Sophia was looping her arm through Drift's, continuing to talk.

'Here on The Planet, our animal companions are as much a part of our family as we are. Your dogs would like a rest, I bet. Bring your pretty mare and your big hairy boy too. They can rest in the stables too, next to Alphie.'

'Alphie?'

'He's my dreamboat pony. I'm sure your mare will love him. What's her name?'

'Minty. And the gelding is Bear.'

'Your Minty's in for a treat. Alphie's a real gentleman.'

'But ... I really should ...' Drift said, again thinking of her dad sweating, straining and bashing droppers back into soil to fix the fence out on the coastal road.

'Ahh, we don't have the word *should* here on The Planet. You either will or you won't. Or either *you are* or *you're not*. No shoulds. That word just makes us feel sad and obligated. Whatever or whoever it is you "should" go back to can wait just a little while. I promise, we won't be long,' and with her little lecture out of the way, Sophia led Drift on.

As they walked towards the heart of the property, where the homestead and outbuildings were nestled among gardens and gums, Drift felt as if she'd truly stepped into paradise. Sophia's calm, purposeful personality was carrying her along effortlessly, and it was a relief not to be going straight back to the moodiness of her father. Nor did she want to risk seeing Kelvin Waller again.

Drift gazed about. She'd never seen a farm like this place. She'd never met a person like Sophia. All around, trees had been planted in meandering, curved patches, rather than the linear shelter belts most farmers routinely placed alongside fencelines. The 'straight-line thinking' of humans, which Charlie Weatherbourne often spoke about, was nowhere to be found here. Here, nature was allowed to speak.

The curved tree clusters wrapped around the hub of the farm, enveloping the buildings and home paddocks in deep shade. The soothing energy of the life of plants was everywhere. Swamp gum, black box, yellow box and melaleuca, mixed in with ironbarks and red gums wearing skirts of sedge and daisy bushes and feathering native grasses. In the paddocks, the 'tree gardens' were dotted about too, and in shorter pasture, which clearly had been grazed recently, there were rows of squat mobile sheds around which chickens scratched, fluffed feathers or sun bathed.

The same electric fencing and trough systems Drift had noticed on the boundary could be seen in the home paddocks, where she glimpsed a flock of turkeys and, in another paddock, roaming pigs. Sophia pointed out two black and white patched cows that were clearly milkers, their calves bunting their udders. Sophia explained that Constantina and Gwendolyn had already been milked that morning by The Planet people.

'We are proudly completely off the grid, and almost one hundred per cent self-sufficient, but not in the old-style escape-from-everything hippy sense. Some of the most brilliant minds and most open hearts in the world are bunkering down here to experiment with food, fuel and power systems. It's exciting times. And over time, we hope to wake the people up in the sleeping world.'

Again there was that term. Drift frowned. 'Wake people up?'

'Yes, to the truth.'

Sophia saw Drift's questioning look. 'That we are all one, darlin. We can't keep living with corporations and corruption. You see, my dear, we are like individual waves in the ocean, but we are each part of the same ocean. Simple quantum science. We are all interconnected. Once people wake up to this, they will stop doing harm to each other and the planet. The old systems are crumbling. We're exploring the new.'

They rounded a large vertical-board barn and Sophia announced, 'We're here.'

The horse barn was built from recycled timber, like the yards, and had lovely round windows and rusty-red painted finishes. There was not a bland steel-kit shed in sight. All the buildings had a classy beauty to them, with their hotchpotch honey-coloured timber walls from re-purposed materials and trellises of fruit trees that grew up the expansive sides of the sheds.

On other wooden buildings climbed plums, nectarines, figs, mulberries, peaches and persimmons. The plants hugged the buildings, trained by thin silver wire, their trunks sunk into straw-laden garden beds. Small corrugated-iron tanks sprouted off the side of every roof, and pipes dripped life-giving water to the plants.

As they walked, Minty's and Bear's hooves clopped over flagstones, and the mare tried to snatch at some plants growing in giant halved wine barrels. The large yard was clearly the hub of the farm activities. Here, more pots were scattered about, burgeoning with strawberries, blueberries and citrus. Others had spinach and lettuce plants in them, along with dollops of colourful flowers and laden miniature fruit trees.

Sophia saw where she was looking and plucked a strawberry and handed it to her. 'The people who come to work here like to snack. Easier to bring the food to them.' Drift took the plump, shiny fruit in her palm. 'There's more, of course, in the commercial experimental garden and the greenhouses, but this food here is for Planet people. The other produce for sale is in another section of the farm.'

Sale? Drift had never heard of The Planet selling food. She wondered where. And how. She'd heard the locals gossiping suspiciously about how they never once saw a beast come through the selling system from The Planet or a single grain through the wheat silos. There were plenty of jokes that the cattle were simply 'beamed up' to feed aliens. Drift actually did feel like it truly was an alien world. The place felt so different from anything she'd ever experienced.

A golden retriever ambled over from a shady spot near a wound-up hose, fanning his pretty feathery tail as Drift's three dogs greeted him with a flurry of tail wags and legs lifted on the pots.

'Oi,' said Drift to the cocked-leg dogs.

Sophia waved her hand. 'Never mind them. All the dogs do it. That's why we put the plants up high.' She smiled. 'That's Joel. His little mate, Zen, a Jack Russell, was killed by a snake a few months back, so he's been a lonely boy. All the other working dogs snub him. He's glad to see your three.'

Sophia hauled a stable door open. 'This OK for your horses? It's big enough for two.'

Drift nodded, amazed at the quality and finish of the stalls. She led Minty and Bear forward and they snorted their way in, their eyes adjusting to the dimmer light, sniffing at the fresh bed of sawdust.

Minty began to paw at the ground.

'First time in a stall?' Sophia asked, and Drift nodded and gave a shy smile.

'They'll like it once we give them each a hay net. The sawdust is from the farmed trees we've begun to mill ourselves. Fresh as fresh for 'em.'

Drift was about to ask how big the property was and what kind of timber they grew, but then a horse in the next stable caught her attention. She couldn't help but gasp when she saw the chestnut stallion, ears pricked, greeting the newcomers with a nicker. He was a thickset quarter horse with a wide white paintbrush swipe down his nose. His eyes were curious and kind.

'Wow,' Drift said, then began unlooping the girth cinch and hauling off Minty's saddle.

'I know. He's something, isn't he? Alphie's a bit of a star round here,' Sophia said, as she and Drift stood for a moment taking in the horse's perfectly square, muscular, yet curved form.

'He's daddy to some pretty little foals. All of 'em turning out level headed but with plenty of cow-keen in 'em. Now what did you say yer name was, sweetheart? I didn't catch it the first time.'

'Drift … as in driftwood. It's my nickname.'

Sophia tilted her head and raised her eyebrow ever so slightly. 'And what was the name your mama gave ya?'

'Melody.'

'Melody,' echoed Sophia in her low, soothing voice. 'It's got such a pretty ring to it. A song.'

Drift couldn't help flinching a little.

'Don't you like being called Melody?'

'I'm not so sure. I rarely hear it.'

Normally she didn't like to hear the name. It belonged to a little girl from long ago who had a mother. But coming from the beautiful full mouth of Sophia, it was as if she heard her name anew. It was pretty.

'I'll call you Drift, if that suits you best,' Sophia said, waving her hand in the air elegantly so a silver ring stamped with a horse shoe flashed in a beam of sunlight. 'Come and meet my

Planet people. We don't have staff or employees here on The Planet, although everyone gets paid mightily well here, indeed, both in food and the folding stuff. Instead, we have interns, and future farm participants. We are all here to learn what Mother Nature needs to teach us. Tell me, Drift, do you know much about holistic farming? I notice, without sounding rude, mind, them cattle you have with you sure don't know much about it. You could play a tune on their ribs, poor darlins.'

'I know,' Drift said, feeling at once guilty even though the guilt about the state of the cattle was not hers to own. 'I do know about holistic farming. Dad would be a total devotee, but we don't own land. Just work for others. Others like the owners of those poor girls back there, and they don't seem interested in changing.'

'*Yet*,' Sophia said. She patted a wooden keg mounted on its side on steel legs.

'You can pop your saddle and gear on here.'

As she hung the bridle, halter and lead rope on a hook and set down her saddle, Drift's mind ran with questions again. What about the stallion she'd just met? Surely a horse of that calibre would be known around the local camp drafts and cutting events? She'd never heard of his foals. What was this place? 'Curiouser and curiouser,' she heard herself say.

'Come, Drift, dear,' Sophia said. 'The Planet people will be at lunch. It's a good time for you to drop in. You'll get more than iced tea. You can sweet-talk Serge into drafting the cattle after you've had something to eat.'

'I think I've already met Serge,' Drift said.

Sophia frowned. 'You did?'

'Yes. When I was bringing the cattle in. He was on a grey horse with black mane and legs; a dead ringer for Minty.'

'Dead ringer?' Sophia echoed, puzzled.

Drift smiled. Clearly the American, despite having been here a long time, was not up with some Australian lingo. 'Yeah. The horse your stockman was riding looked just like Minty.'

'You saw our stockman?' Sophia asked, tilting her head.

'Yes. He pointed me in the right direction. Barely said a word.'

Sophia paused. 'Ah ... that would be Eli,' she said eventually.

'The horse or the man?'

Sophia laughed. 'The man. I'm surprised you saw him. He likes to keep to himself,' she said. 'Did he say anything else to you? Did you talk long?'

'No,' said Drift, 'he seemed in a hurry to get somewhere. I kinda got the sense he wasn't the talkative type.'

'Ah, that'd be Eli,' Sophia said. 'Now come on. Let's go eat.'

Chapter 15

Following Sophia a few steps behind, Drift watched the swing of her wavy ponytail catch the sunlight as their boots crunched on a wide red gravel pathway. Overhead fronds of peppercorn trees formed an arbour of peaceful green. There was no hurry in Sophia's step. They arrived at a large double-storey stone and timber homestead with a wide bullnose-roofed verandah with covered pathways linking it to other cottages. Great flourishes of purple and white flowering bougainvillea sprayed colour over the buildings, screening huge water tanks to the side of the houses.

On the main verandah, Drift followed Sophia's move, kicking her doggers off amidst a scattering of boots that lay on the flagstones. As Drift bent over, she glanced up to see a curved green lawn flanked by lively native flowerbeds containing more rusted farmyard junk that had been masterfully turned into beautiful artful sculptures.

Kids tumbled and cartwheeled, chattering like young magpies on the lawn. Sophie smiled and waved at them, then rolled open a large timber sliding door and ushered Drift and her dogs in.

Drift found herself standing in a vast room with honey-coloured wooden beams and slow fans turning high above them. A long table was lined with people all eating, talking and laughing in the cool of the room. There were more kids, some of whom ran to Sophia for quick hugs, faces lit with delight, before scampering away again.

Large artworks of Western Australian native flowers beamed from the walls in vibrant, splashing oils. On a cool slate floor, a cheerful, cruisy pack of working dogs ambled over with low wagging tails to greet them. Molly, Hamlet and Dunno sniffed cautiously. With such a friendly canine welcoming committee, even the tucker-obsessed Molly failed to immediately lock on to the delicious collage of food smells that wafted throughout the room. Instead she was utterly distracted by an effervescent little collie who was flirting with her and dancing on his white ballet feet.

'Munro, stop being such a ladies' man. She's not interested,' Sophia said to the dog as he enthusiastically sniffed at Molly's rear end.

Glancing around, Drift noticed how many young people her age were in the group. On most farming properties she and her dad worked at, it was rare to find more than one or two young people, but here there was a bunch. Also, unlike Widgenup, where everyone was pretty much the same brand of whitefella, this station was a real global mix.

One girl had beautiful large dark brown eyes and long plaited hair like rope that fell over a shimmering pink sari. Beside her Drift noticed a group of Australian Indigenous people passing platters to brightly dressed Maori people — or they might have been from Samoa or even further afield. A little Asian girl toddled past into the arms of her mother, who had just placed even more food on the already groaning table where people were feasting on salads, fruits and meats.

In the middle of the table chunky loaves of bread had been sliced thickly and laid on big wooden platters next to golden homemade butter cut in thick wedges. Drift stood in wonder. What was this place? *Was* it some kind of cult? No: Drift could feel there was no fear in these folk. These people seemed free: like the birds that swirled the skies at dusk, they had an uncomplicated, connectivity and lightness to them.

'Planet people!' Sophia announced above the chatter, tinging a knife on a glass as if about to make a wedding speech.

Gradually the room fell silent and all eyes turned to Drift and Sophia. Drift felt she was in a spotlight beam, even though everyone was smiling. She blushed red. Holding her hat in her hands she looked to the toes of her work-worn socks, noticing one toe poking through.

'Meet Melody Wood ... Or also known as Drift, and ...' Sophia swung her arm to the dogs as a cue for Drift to introduce them.

'Dunno, Hamlet and Molly,' Drift said shyly, pointing to each one.

'Dunno, Hamlet and Molly,' Sophia echoed more loudly.

A collective call of 'hello', 'welcome' and 'hi' rose up from the group.

'Greetings!' was added belatedly by an old man raising a twisted hand at her, his eyes cloudy, but his smile clear. A younger man with tousled sandy hair was chuckling as he dipped bread into his vegetable soup.

'Dunno and Hamlet,' he said. 'Classic.'

Drift noticed the cute upward turn of his nose and his striking green eyes. What was with her lately? Was she turning into Shaynene — a serial perve?

Her thoughts were interrupted when a little kid collided with her legs and stretched her arms up in the air to be picked up. Drift automatically stooped and scooped her up, surprising herself. She'd never had much to do with kids before, and, with her mother's track record in parental devotion, Drift planned on steering clear of having them in case. Still, this little kid was super-cute. The child began gently lifting Drift's lip and trying to jab a strawberry past her teeth.

'I think Maisie wants you to eat that. Come,' Sophia said, plucking the child from Drift's arms and hugging her. 'Drift, you sit next to Serge and tell him about your interesting morning.'

Sophia swivelled the child onto her hip and reached between a couple of young women, grabbing a plate that had a grey-blue bird with an exceptionally long swirling tail on it. Drift noticed all the plates were different and patterned and colourful, as were the glasses and cutlery, as if gathered from all corners of the world.

The entire place jangled with colour, like glossy, glassy bangles. As people shunted along a bench seat adorned with vibrant cushions to make room for her, Drift glanced at the dark-haired, dark-skinned man she now knew as Serge.

Like Sophia, it was hard to pin an age to him. His black hair was glossy and streaked with grey, his face set with a beautiful bone structure. He waved his fork at her as a greeting and smiled as he chewed.

'Drift's cattle got a fright and flattened the boundary fence, Serge,' Sophia said. 'Her dad's patching the fence, but we've got some drafting to do after lunch. She kindly brought our escapees in with her stock-route cattle.'

Serge nodded as he finished his mouthful. 'You like the road?'

Drift was surprised. She thought Serge would ask her about how the cattle got a fright. Or how many head there were to draft. Or how bad was the busted fence. But his dark, dancing eyes searched hers for an answer when she echoed, 'The road?' She shrugged. 'Yes. It's my life, I guess. I love parts of it.'

He smiled. 'Roads lead places. Where are you headed?'

Drift frowned and felt a little helpless. She'd never thought about it. It was only in the last few days that she had begun to dream of another life and travelling a new road. 'I dunno. Just fattening cattle for a bit. South, I guess, until they're ready.' Internally she kicked herself. Her intelligence and verbal ability had dried up like a shallow summertime dam.

Serge nodded but looked right at her. It was as if he had read something in her that she herself didn't yet know.

'Well, welcome to The Planet. The West's best-kept secret. Surprised?'

Drift nodded. 'Yes. Very. What actually goes on here?'

Serge smiled. 'Now that would take some explaining.' He reached for a jug in the middle of the table and picked up a glass from a collection on the tray. 'Have some iced tea? Do you like iced tea?'

'I'm not sure whether I do or I don't.'

'Well life's all about trying new things ...' He winked at her as he poured her a glass.

As Drift was offered platter after platter of food to choose from, she listened in on the lively conversation around her about food, family, farming. As she bit down on some fresh salad she realised it was the most delicious food she'd ever tasted.

Relaxing into a conversation with Serge, she sketched in how she and her dad had come to be on the stock-contracting circuit, even telling him about her mum going missing, possibly drowned, skirting around the edges of the truth about how it had affected her father. She mentioned seeing the little girl on the dunes, asking Serge about her.

Serge shrugged his shoulders, saying it may have been possible it was a Planet child, but unlikely. 'Life's mysteries reveal themselves when they are ready,' he said. 'Or not.'

Next Serge told her about his boyhood in Argentina, Drift leaning into his story, so engrossed that she was surprised to see Sophia back by her side. Time must've flown. She suddenly remembered her dad and wondered if he was OK.

Sophia cast her a warm smile. 'C'mon. Let's give you a quick tour before you head back to your father.'

Drift wondered why a mega-rich woman would trouble herself with a stranger like her, but she was on her feet in a flash anyway, even her dad forgotten. 'I'd *love* a tour!'

Serge gathered up her empty plate. 'Meet you in the yards in about half an hour.' He reached out and squeezed Drift's hand warmly. 'Nice to meet you, Drifting girl,' he said before swinging his long leg over the bench seat and walking towards the kitchen. The other people at the table she'd met also waved her off with smiles and warmth, as they too got up to get on with their day.

At the nest of boots she asked, 'Is everyone always so nice here? All the time?'

'Mostly yes. The people here know.'

'Know what?'

'That there's only one way.'

'And what way is that?'

'Love. It's the only truth. Not money. Not power. Not fame. Not possessions.'

'Love,' Drift echoed, and in a flash, the image of the little girl appeared in her mind's eye.

'Many people in the sleeping world ... the world out there,' Sophia gestured towards the front gate, 'have forgotten they are one with Mother Earth and the Universal laws. They only teach children the law of mankind and economics. That imbalance just creates suffering. There are more forms of capital than money. There's the Earth's natural capital, and spiritual capital as well that feeds our souls.'

As Sophia spoke, Drift felt a tremor of unease. She glanced around.

Sophia sensed her nervousness and laid a hand on her arm. 'I know I use some odd language from time to time, and I can see worry on your face. Are you thinking we're some kind of religious cult?'

'Um ... well, yes,' Drift said, honestly.

Sophia threw her head back, laughing. 'A lot of people would think that! What we do here *is* different. It's done with spirit and a good dose of science and philosophy about human values. Yes, we have in our time inadvertently attracted a few religious nut cases ... but effectively this is just a working farm, and a big laboratory on how we can all live more harmoniously with the Earth and each other,' she said. 'The only difference is that the people who are drawn here here don't come to work in the old sense ... they come to create ... to craft something that is bigger than their own limited selves. They are no longer asleep. They've searched us out because they have woken up. All farms could look like this if humans so choose.'

'What actually do you mean by "asleep"?' Drift asked.

'Well, that's a complex question. There's those who are so plugged into their over-loud thoughts, fed by media, technology and old family and societal belief systems. So much so that they can't hear their intuition and inner guidance any more. Even farmers who are close to the land every day have stopped seeing what they are really doing to it because they've been brainwashed by marketing and blinded by outdated science. By considering ourselves separate from the land, we are destroying not just it, but also our own selves. The people who work here have got past the noise of their egos. They know it's a fact that we all come from the same place and we all go back to the same place. What we do to one person, or one animal, or one soil microbe, we do to ourselves,' she said, pulling on her workboots. 'It sounds woo-woo, but really it's quantum physics.'

Drift stooped to gather her own boots, relishing the conversation, knowing it was along the lines of what Wilma had been saying. Over the course of her travels up and down the country, Drift had also seen how so much of the land had been bullied into producing crop after crop or wool clip after wool clip, and even with the highest inputs of fertilisers and sprays, the soil was now blowing away. Even where irrigation was plentiful, the life of the soil was diminishing and dying, the ecosystem more threadbare than the socks she wore.

'I know exactly what you're saying,' she said. 'My dad and our friend Wilma are teaching me exactly the sort of things you're talking about. Dad says the land is "dead from the weight of human ignorance". And Charlie, another friend, she's like you too — you're all on the same page. Awake.'

'Ah, we soul sisters are everywhere. I could tell by the way you brought the cattle in and handled your horse and dogs that you can see beyond what the world tells you to see. I'm so glad you blew in here, wild girl. There are no chance meetings. You are here for a reason.'

'What reason?'

Sophia shrugged. 'I don't know yet. Let's just trust and go with the flow. C'mon.'

'Where to first?'

'To the temple to meet His Holiness and his fifteen virgin concubines,' Sophia said, deadpan. Drift gave her a concerned glance. Then Sophia burst out laughing. 'No! I'm teasing. Not really. I'll show you our cropping trials.'

Drift was still smiling at Sophia's joke, wishing her dad was here with this extraordinary woman, when she was momentarily distracted by a tall lean man in coveralls and mad-professor hair walking towards them.

'Gizmo!' Sophia called. 'Want to show Drift your baby?'

'Ullo! Yes, sure!' he said in a thick accent as he gestured to a wide double corro door. He rolled it open. Inside lay the most comprehensive machinery workshop Drift had ever seen. It was more like a laboratory with its polished concrete floor and bank of computers on stainless-steel trolleys. There was also an assortment of farm machinery and the coolest of utes, bonnet up, engine exposed.

'Drift, this is Gizmo. He heads up our mechanical engineering division. At present, they're mostly focused on steam weed technology for a partner company, Weedtechnics.'

Drift looked to the alien spray units within.

'Steam?'

'Yes,' explained Sophia. 'Instead of using glyphosate and other herbicides and pesticides, farmers and councils are now looking to use steam and natural treatments to manage unwanted plants. We're refining the machinery for industry. Desperately needed, seeing they're finding those chemicals in breast milk and people's pee.'

Drift felt herself smile from deep within her core, realising what The Planet's work would mean for not just food production, but also for the plants and animals she saw trying to survive on roadsides and watersheds, sickened by council sprays.

'And the ute?' she asked, pointing to the modified Toyota on the hoist.

'Not a ute. A Poot,' corrected Gizmo, who was clearly well named judging from all the gadgets he had in his shed.

'Poot?' Drift asked.

'You're looking at the first farm four-wheel drive to be run on human and animal methane. Poo power — a renewable, inexhaustible resource.'

Drift looked at the vehicle in amazement. 'Methane?'

'We are this close to selling the concept to a major car-manufacturing company and a fuel provider,' Gizmo said, holding his thumb and forefinger a few centimetres apart and squinting his eyes as if looking through a narrow tunnel to an expanded future.

'Wow!' Drift said, amazed all this was happening right here, on remote Pinrush Point.

'But,' Sophia said, putting an index finger up to her lips, 'it's shush.'

'Why?'

Gizmo and Sophia gave each other a knowing look.

'All this wonderful technology that Gizmo and his team are creating will be stopped by the big boys if we're too flashy and noisy about it, so it's quietly, quietly and gently, gently we go.'

'But why?'

Gizmo looked at her with his piercing green eyes and counted the three main reasons on his fingers. 'Greed, unchecked egos and fear of change.'

After a quick explanation as to how the 'Poot' and the bio-digester fuel system worked, Sophia then ushered Drift into another courtyard. More leafy trees circled by stones shaded the ground near greenhouses laid out in a semicircle. Beyond that in the paddocks, mixed broad acre crops overlaid with annual cereal grains thrived behind tall game-proof fencing.

'Multi-species mixed cropping,' Sophia said. 'We sow annual grains with broad-leaf plants like beans and peas all at once into dormant pasture. Then we harvest the grain first, all direct drilled so we have no bare earth. We are creating a diverse root system for the soil. Simple.'

Drift was in seventh heaven to see in action the cropping concepts she'd read about. She was so used to barren single-species crops like wheat in the West that was traditionally burned after harvest. It was uplifting to see the cocktail of cropping before her.

'And these greenhouses?'

'This is where we produce our seed bank. We're collating old varieties of plants that are fast disappearing around the world. Our goal is to distribute this seed freely to communities so they can feed themselves. A basic human right the corporations have tried to take from us.'

'Wow,' Drift said when she saw the size and stretch of the operation. 'This is extraordinary. *Why* are you doing all this?'

'Honey,' Sophia said, 'I'm from Texas, where we were solidly bashed by the Bible. They raised us to believe in the crucifixion, suffering and the vengeance of the Lord. Then, where I came from, if you didn't follow *that* brand of God, you followed the other. The false God of money. My family were right into that God, and the status that comes with it.'

She shook her head.

'Organised religion, modern economics, it's all lies. Now around the world, we're raising kids to either hate those who are different, or to worship money and celebrity more than to love and revere life and the earth itself. Society is sick because of it. I asked what my purpose was, and I heard the answer: to help heal Earth and with it her people. You've got me started with one of my sermons, I'm afraid. Come ...'

She swung open the door of one of the greenhouses; inside the air was warm with moisture and life. Rows of plants in their juvenile stages reached upwards with leafy green potential. Blackboard-paint-dipped sticks marked with chalk were spiked in at the ends of the rows. Avocados, limes, lemons, olives, Japanese plums, figs, nectarines, mulberries, peaches, persimmons, apple trees, pears.

'I realised once we all learn that Earth is truly abundant and we start to feed people with food grown with love, and we honour the feminine energies of the land, society will come back to balance.' She stooped over a plant, lovingly touching it with her elegant fingertips. 'These are our babies. And from here we transplant them out into our orchards or the other greenhouses. Produce is then shipped seasonally to free food hubs.'

'But I've never heard of The Planet or your produce,' Drift said.

'I know. We don't brand it. Much of the produce is a charitable sideline. What the farm is producing is mostly ideas and technology. Methods in how to grow pure food in urban areas, impoverished places, war zones. And also in plush, privileged cities where councils are terrified of dirt, poo and compost. We're trialling systems that can be used in deserts, on shopping-centre rooftops, on the sides of buildings. And we're exporting the ideas under a series of company names. Names that are hard to trace back to here.

'Then there's the renewable-energy component to our operation, like Gizmo's Poot project. We're trialling all kinds of concepts ... some of them crazy, some of them commercial. The people you met at lunch are all going back to their communities to set up their own versions of what we're doing here. Urban and suburban farming, or chemical-free farming on their own land with their own power source — both inner power and outer,' she said, tapping her heart centre.

'But how come no one knows about it?'

Sophia shrugged, and the light in her eyes dimmed for a moment. Her voice altered. 'Quiet, underground grassroots revolutions are the most powerful; plus, I don't want the rest of the world to know I'm here. The Planet is my sanctuary from my past. It's a foundation place, a seedpod of ideas that we need to spread out to the world quietly, without political interference and media hoo-ha. For decades, like Gizmo said, governments and big business have been buying the good ideas and burying them, so the old systems remain. It's time to go underground — get the ideas to such a stage of development and go public before the more rigid corporations even know what's coming.'

Sophia walked towards a stack of wooden pallets and sat upon them, crossing her long legs and patting the seat beside her.

'You see, girl, I've got some big, bad family karma to clean up. I wasn't always this person,' she said gesturing to herself. 'In fact, my name was Eloise Madden. My daddy and granddaddy made a fortune out of oil and tobacco back in Texas and then elsewhere. More money than you can imagine. Our family got fat on two of the most toxic commodities — commodities created by the cruellest of labour to begin with ... slavery.'

Drift could see in her profile the twist of pain as Sophia recalled her past.

'No amount of money coulda dug us outta the ditch of misery our family went through livin life with all those riches. When daddy died and I inherited the lot it went to my head. At first I was gonna be like him. Push it. Grow it bigger. But then, well ...' Her voice faded. She drew in a breath.

'Life taught me different. I suffered the loss of my baby girl. Childhood cancer in her blood. She died right after I found my husband cheatin on me.' Sophia looked skywards, tears pooling in her eyes as if it had happened only yesterday.

'When I was on my knees with misery I saw clearly. I saw I had a lot of redemption to do on behalf of my family. Robbing Earth of Her oil and splashing my power around in property developments and fast cars. Being in the cigarette industry, robbing people of their health. It's just not what a mama should do. I felt I was paying for it.'

She shuddered. Drift instantly settled a comforting hand on her arm. Sophia patted her hand back.

'My girl. She woulda been about your age by now. I never did have the heart to trust a man again nor have another child.'

'I'm sorry,' Drift said, then found herself suddenly blurting out, 'Me, I'm never going to have kids. Or a fella for that matter.'

'Why not?'

Drift shrugged. 'It's not who I am.'

'Really?' Sophia said, not sounding convinced. 'Time will tell, I guess.'

They sat in silence, then Sophia swept her hand towards the pallets. 'So,' she said breathing inwards, 'I've given my life over to this. Finding other ways with renewable energy. Finding other ways with land use and food. Finding ways of water purification. And better ways with animals if we are to ultimately eat them. And better ways with people too.'

She turned to Drift with a smile. 'Enough of me. What about you? What are you going to give your life over to? What lights you up?'

Drift swallowed and looked down to the scuffed toes of her workboots, lifting her shoulders then dropping them. 'I'm not really sure,' she said. 'I love books and art. And nature. And animals. And study. I don't much like people — that's an area I need to work on. I love the beach. And grasslands. Gardens too. Trees, rocks … I could go on and on. But I've no idea where all that will take me.'

'Well, my darling. If you sit still enough in silence, you can hear your inner guide. I'm sure you'll have plenty of time on that horse of yours on the way back to camp.'

She patted Drift on her leg. 'I can tell you're an Earth girl. A do-er. A go-getter. It's just you haven't yet believed it yourself.'

Drift nodded, and words choked in her throat as she began thinking of her brilliant but suicidal father, whose only compass was remaining near the watery grave of her mother and hanging on to the potential of a life they'd never realised as a family.

'If you do find a road, let it be for you to come back now, y'hear,' Sophia said. 'I can always do with a clever, fit young woman, who is clearly a master in stock handling and very, very smart.'

Drift hooked a long strand of hair behind her ear and blushed, feeling the uncertain notion rumble through her that someone like Sophia actually recognised her potential and believed she could do something in the world, something as significant as what Sophia was doing. Wilma and Charlie were always telling her that, but Drift had never really taken the concept in until seeing this place.

Sophia lithely propelled herself off the pallets, her boots thudding on the ground, and led Drift through a side corridor into another greenhouse. There were the same sticks with chalk tags listing crops: rockmelon, tomatoes, corn and capsicum, zucchini, cucumber, pumpkin and watermelon. On some shelving, pots sat beneath small watering nozzles and more tags listed beetroot, leeks, celery, broccoli, kale, lettuce, pak choy, peas, garlic and onions.

Drift was blown away by the variety of edible plants grown beneath the shadecloth. Sophia pushed the back door of the greenhouse open and swung her arm out to the undulating land that was planted with orchards immediately before them and beyond to the paddocks. Drift listened, fascinated as Sophia explained how the green manures were boosting both the cropping and the pasture soils.

'We're not a farm as such. We run this place as an ecosystem. Our job is to support what Mother Nature does and to basically harvest water and sunshine using plants. If this is the foundation of our farming system, then nutrient-dense food will be the end result. And as we produce this kind of food, our pockets fill up too. People all over the world want clean food. This is the way forward.'

Beside them, Sophia pointed out a mobile cold room with a butcher's hook winch, and next to it, a shed where large hides hung in the process of being salted and tanned.

'That's how we process our meat. Many of The Planet people are vegetarians, but those that aren't make the choice to kill the animals out in the paddock, quickly so the animals are none the wiser. Head down eating grass. Then gone. Not like the current abattoir systems.'

She grimaced.

'In our system, before the kill is done quickly in the paddock, we've already moved their herd mates on so there's no distress for them either.' Sophia pressed her palms together and inclined her head in a tiny bow.

'And we always say a blessing, like the ancients did. It was survival back then. Now it's a privilege. So we go about it honourably.' She pointed to the writing on the side of the cool store trailer by Rumi.

After reading it, Drift shuddered. She'd never really confronted her own feelings about the end-of-story for the cows she and her dad cared for. She'd grown up with the quiet knowledge of it and deep down it had unsettled her. Guilt rumbled. Sophia's voice brought her back.

'And over there, we have Gizmo's babies.' Sophia pointed to a line of bio-digester tanks and explained how they collected waste from the houses and from the small dairy effluent pond and the pigs' mobile shaded sheds.

The tanks sat squat and stubby next to silver bullet-shaped canisters that supplied the resulting natural gas to the station's vehicles and kitchen. Sophia explained that the six white tanks had fish in them and that they too were linked into the system.

'We're even trialling growing seaweed and algae commercially too.'

Drift's gaze followed Sophia pointing to the south as she described the web of electric fencing and the strategically placed watering points dotted here and there in the wooded grasslands. She told her how the paddocks were divided into 'woodland walled rooms', through which animals were moved in great numbers for just one day, and then herded on the next.

A swathe of dancing grasses swayed in the wind in paddocks being enjoyed by a mixed herd of cattle, sheep and horses. Behind that, the little movable caravans brought up the rear, the poultry busily scratching through the dung left behind by the bigger animals, and some of the chickens and turkeys making their way up wooden ramps for a rest in the shade.

'But this isn't cropping country!' Drift said, incredulous when she saw beyond the orchard to ground that was vibrant with living edible plants over what looked like a few hundred hectares. In the distance wind turbines turned and a flare of sunlight shone from a bank of solar panels that lay like a deck of playing cards spread under the sky. A windsock drifted lazily beside a runway to the east.

'Where there is soil and water, there is potential to create anything,' Sophia said. 'You just have to know how.'

Suddenly a helicopter appeared and hovered, rustling the trees around them, and began to drop down. Far off the buzz of a plane sliced the air.

'That's odd,' Sophia said. 'We're not expecting anyone.' She turned and set her dark eyes on Drift.

'It's probably something to do with that missing surfer,' Drift said.

Sophia squinted at the aviation invasion in the sky above, nearing. 'Yes. That missing surfer,' she said flatly. 'It's left us wide open to the media poking their noses in. But at least he inadvertently brought you here.'

She rubbed Drift's arm. 'I'd better go sort this. Serge will be about ready for you. Can you find your way back to the yards?' She pointed to the pathway around the far greenhouse.

Drift nodded, noticing a sudden tenseness in Sophia. She clearly didn't like intrusion, even though she'd opened her life up to Drift so readily.

'I'd better go find out what they want,' Sophia said.

On impulse Drift gave Sophia a quick hug. 'Thank you,' she said breathlessly. 'This is amazing. You are amazing.'

As Sophia jogged away and Drift turned towards the yards, she knew her life had just changed forever. It was as if, at last, she had been nudged awake to what was truly possible.

Chapter 16

At The Planet's gateway, Serge got down off his horse and tapped a pin code into a solar-powered security unit while Drift and her dogs held the drought cattle in an orderly herd. A second set of electric side gates beside the ones that guarded the cattle grid whirred to life, opening slowly. She held Bear's lead rope lightly in her hand as the horse's ears flickered towards the unusual sound.

'In some ways, she's a lot like my dad,' Drift called to Serge.

'Who?'

'Sophia.'

'How so?' Serge asked stepping back up into the saddle of his black mare.

'Dad goes to great lengths to avoid people. Especially the types you call sleeping people — even though that's who he works for a lot of the time.'

'Well, in my opinion, sometimes it's not such a good thing. You can only touch the world with light when you touch others. I hope you are braver than both your dad and Sophia. The gates are wide open for you, girl.' He swept his hand back towards the homestead as an invitation.

From astride Minty, Drift cast her dogs out wide with a sharp whistle, Serge's words roaming in her mind. The black cow and the other lead cattle flicked their ears towards the gap that now lay before them. Serge swung around on his classic black stock horse, the mare looking as if she had ambled out of a Tom Roberts painting, with her lean, work-fit body. Serge rode over, pulling up beside Minty's shoulder. Black horse. White horse. Yin horse, yang horse, Drift thought. She actually felt so much more balanced having been here. Standing next to this calm, steady man, she was reluctant to leave.

'You OK to take it from here?' he asked, his sincere eyes shaded by his broad-brimmed hat.

'Sure. Thanks for your help.'

'A pleasure.' Serge tipped his hat at her. 'I need to get back to Sophia,' he said, a glimmer of concern on his face. 'When the outside world pushes in, she gets a little nervous, and the missing surfer storm has certainly unsettled everyone.'

'It sure has. I wonder if he was just a local nobody, would people have made such a fuss,' Drift said.

Serge grimaced. 'I think you know the answer. The world is obsessed with fame. Some people do anything to be part of it. They lose themselves. Don't you do the same.'

He seemed to look right through to Drift's soul. 'I know a young man who was very much like you. He'd been raised the old way, without much of the modern world. So when he met with all the trappings and temptations of it, it got to him. He lost himself in it.' He smiled gently at her. 'Don't be like him. What you have, girl, who you are, is a rare gift. Don't lose what you have.'

'What do you mean, what I have?'

He tapped his temple beneath his hat. 'You have an independent mind. I can see you've escaped the brainwashing that the modern world dishes out to young people. All that Snapchat, Facebook, Twitter, texting. All the bad things technology brings, with its porn, gaming, gambling and the media. It's scrambling young minds. Literally changing the wiring in brains. Technology is a tool but if it's not used with honour it causes such harm ... in the same way a knife can be used to create a carving or a beautiful meal, it can also be used to kill. You are a fortunate young lady. You are rare in the Western world — to have avoided the age of screens and the misuse of technology.'

'And the young man?'

Serge shook his head. 'He fell for it all. He fell deep into the sleeping world, chasing money and the other dark things. Messed his life up … and now his family's …'

His voice faded. There was deep sadness in Serge's tone. Drift wondered if he was speaking of his own son.

'If you ever want to answer your calling — whatever that may be — consider that you may find it here. I hope to see you when you're done with the road, Drifter girl.'

'I hope so too,' she said, meaning it.

She legged her horse around, but then paused and swung about in the saddle.

'Oh, and Serge … as it turns out, *I do*.'

'You do what?' Serge asked.

'Like iced tea.'

He laughed.

As the gates to The Planet swung shut behind her, Drift smiled for a long time as she watched Serge ride away, wishing she could've stayed in there forever. Reluctantly, she turned her horse's head for camp, her dogs at the ready to move the cattle. She was already feeling the needy presence of her father.

Drift had barely got the cattle moving when she heard a car coming up behind her. To slow the driver, she rode right into the middle of the road, as she was prone to do, then turned, surprised to see Simon approaching in a cop car. Tyres crunched on gravel as he fell in pace next to her ambling horse, his face becoming clearer as the window opened. He looked extra handsome today in his police cap, his face slightly shaded with stubble.

'You've neglected to put your stock signs out, young lady,' he said, poker-faced. 'And you ought to be wearing high-visibility safety wear.'

For a moment she felt a flush — not just of attraction for him, but also because she was guilty as charged. She searched his face and wondered for a second if he was serious, then she detected the slightest smirk.

'Well, if it wasn't for those bloody choppers stampeding the cattle through bloody tough fences, I would've done it by now,' she said, sounding as feisty as she dared.

She reined her horse to stop and whistled the lead dog, Molly, to drop to her belly to block up the cattle so they could graze for a bit. Simon braked. He got out of the car.

'Are you going to charge me?' she said, moving her horse over, noticing Simon instantly back away.

'I might.'

'You won't come near me while I'm up on my horse, will you? So you can't inspect my stock permit licence or insist I come quietly or do anything, really. Can you?'

He grinned at her. 'You're right there. So I'm asking you to step away from the horse, ma'am.'

She matched his grin as she swung her leg over Minty's neck and scooted off the saddle on her backside, both feet landing solidly on the ground. She dropped the reins and Bear's lead rope, ground-tying both horses, and walked a little way towards him.

'This far enough for you?' she asked, hand on one cocked hip.

'Nope.' Simon shook his head, a flush arriving on his cheeks.

She took another step. 'This?'

'Nope. A little more.' He stood square on to her, his legs in a wide sexy stance in his solid black police boots.

Drift took another step.

'More,' said Simon. Soon she was standing right there in front of him. Close. She looked up.

'Yes, Constable? What is it you want to reprimand me about?' There was a challenge in her question.

'I came to ask if you'd like to have dinner with me tomorrow night.'

'Dinner?' Drift almost burst out laughing. It sounded so formal. So grown up. And especially out here, in this remote part of the world.

'What? At the nearest fancy restaurant? I think you'll find the only Michelins round here are on the tyre rack at the Widgenup servo.'

Simon laughed. 'Well not exactly that kind of five-star dinner. Maybe a fresh-fish cook-up on the beach? The surfers will be gone by tomorrow. I think their private jet was landing on The Planet just now and we'll escort them out tonight.'

'Under the cover of darkness and intrigue?'

'Something like that. So once the celebs have gone, there'll be an exodus of fans and media too. Tomorrow night is looking like a quiet one … so … dinner?'

Drift smiled. 'Will you be on duty or off?'

'A police officer is never off duty.'

'Really?' She wanted him to kiss her. To prove to herself that she was now twenty-one and she was now an adult and no longer in the shadow of her father. If she had someone like Simon in her life, creeps like Kelvin wouldn't dream of coming near her. Maybe it would even fast-track sorting things out with her dad.

'A stockwoman is never off duty either,' she retorted.

'So, if I want to kiss you, there's no point waiting until both of us are off duty?'

'That's right,' she said, as Simon stooped towards her. She rose to the toes of her boots and swiped her hat off, tilted her head beneath the brim of his cap and pressed her lips to his. They felt warm on hers. Dust and salty sweat mingled with the increasing wetness of the kiss; his arm slid around her waist, drawing her closer. His chest up this close was narrow against her own broad-shouldered strong-girl body, made hard through physical labour. Drift self-consciously wondered if she was too butch and brawny for him, and too sweaty and dusty. Nonetheless he felt nice as the intensity of the kiss deepened. Drift felt the probe of his tongue, and the oddness of having her hands on someone else's body. While her own body was melting with desire, her mind was still noisy with questions, like: is he a good kisser? Am I doing it right? Do I like it? Isn't it funny

I'm being kissed by a policeman on a road? What do the dogs and horses think? Will that sneaky black cow bugger off? Focus, Drift, she told herself. You're receiving your first kiss. Well not your first kiss. Kelvin saw to that.

Desire in her abruptly shut down. She was about to draw away when a tooting VW Beetle full of young surfer-types rolled up.

'Get it onnnn, officer!' shouted one of the cool cats from the back seat. With more whoops, on they rolled, scattering the cattle. Drift stepped back, laughing, flushed, embarrassed. She made a dash for her horse, gathered up her reins and stepped lightly into the saddle. 'Gotta go. Cattle work calls.'

Simon looked at her, eyes ablaze. 'So, dinner?'

'If it gets me out of a fine, then yes,' she said. 'See you tomorrow night ... you won't be able to miss me. I'll be wearing my best hi-vis.'

She left a grinning Simon standing on the road, and put pressure on the cattle to move. As she did, butterflies flew around her stomach. She knew, compared to others, she was old to be experiencing her first meaningful kiss with a man. She also knew she wasn't like other people her age. She hadn't been raised like other girls who had been to school and grown up around boys. She'd seen Shaynene pouncing on boys since the age of fourteen and the remorse, masked by bravado, that had followed when they failed to treat her with any respect. Drift was glad of the isolation the road had given her. But now she'd kissed a man. A man in uniform. She'd felt the stirrings of the wild woman within, and with her awakening, Drift knew the events of today had certainly changed her forever.

Chapter 17

Drift found her father stooped at the base of the repaired fence, twitching the last of the wires. She'd expected him to be finished and back at the caravan by now. Once Drift took the pressure off the herd, tired from being pushed, they dropped their heads immediately to graze. Even the black cow looked spent.

'You took your time,' she said, indicating the fence. Dunston's saddle blanket was spread out on the ground next to what was left of the lunch Wilma had packed for Split before she set off.

'You took yours. I thought you'd been signed up to the sect. Weren't you suited to their leader?'

Maybe not their leader, Drift thought gleefully, but I was suited to the policeman. She felt her cheeks flush.

'Well? What was it like in there?' her father asked.

She breathed in deeply and looked skywards, opening her palms to the Heavens. 'Oh, Dad! You shoulda seen it!' Drift swung a leg over Minty and dropped to the ground. 'It's literally like another planet! But really, it's actually like *this* planet, only properly cared for!' She could still picture the lunch room and the beautiful grounds and workspace. 'It was amazing. Mind-blowingly amazing!' Drift's tone was infectious and her enthusiasm about what she'd seen transfixed her dad. He stopped packing up his tools and leaned on the ute's tray, ready to listen.

Once she began talking, she found she couldn't stop. Trying to tell Split all she'd seen and heard was like attempting to gather the strings from a thousand escaped balloons in a stiff breeze. She was desperate to make the image of the experience whole for him.

'It was a farm, yes,' she said, in a rush, 'but not the sort of farm we've ever seen, Dad ... or would even be able to imagine if I hadn't seen it for myself. The productivity and the different foods and crops they grew! Incredible. And the *people*. There were loads of people! From all over the world. Not hippy woo-woo types. Not naysayer farmer types either. But instead, scientists, cooks, young farmers, inventors, engineers, you name it. I wish Wilma was still here to tell her! And the billionaire lady, Sophia! Oh my God, she was amazing. So down to earth and not up herself at all. And Serge ...'

Her father had inclined his head, a soft smile on his face. He wasn't used to a monologue from her. Normally in shearing shed smoko rooms, or in the yards on a break, Drift mostly sat quietly while the men around her shovelled food into their gobs until they were done. Farm visits never resulted in the mood Drift was now in. When they rattled into farms for contract work branding, drenching or breaking in weaner cattle, it was usually just some old bloke, with a son hanging beside him who was almost as balding or grey. There were rarely many women about either, and hardly ever any children.

Split liked the idea of this Planet place and half wished he'd gone in with her. 'What did they do to you? Give you drugs or something?' he joked. 'You sure they weren't all nutters?'

'Sure as sure. They were sane as sane. Awake!'

'Awake?'

'To life! The people there weren't just doing a job,' Drift continued, 'but living a *life. Creating* a life! They talked and laughed a lot. It wasn't as if they were farming for Sophia as a boss or to just make money ... but they were all farming together, to be better people, healthier, happier, to change the world.'

'So it *is* a cult?' her dad teased.

'Dad! It wasn't. They were so nice ... and *normal*, but *not normal* if you know what I mean.'

'Like us.'

'Mmm. Well, maybe like us. Though Sophia and Serge did ask me not to say too much about what went on there. They don't want the people in power to pry too closely. Or the media to find out all they're about.'

'Ahh, so not a cult, but doomsday conspiracy-theory mob,' Split said solemnly. 'Are they storing food in underground bunkers for the end of the world? And plotting to overthrow the capitalists?'

'No! Dad, stop joking about it! They know things are serious. All the things you tell me about the population exploding, the end of the world — or at least life as we know it — is coming if we don't change how we treat this planet. So they're doing something about it. And now, after meeting them, I think I want to do something about it too.'

She saw her father withdraw a little.

'Life is best for us if we just keep to ourselves,' he said. 'You can't do anything to change the systems. People like us don't have any power.'

'What do you mean? People like us? Don't lump me in with you,' she said, thinking of all the times Wilma had told her that with a disciplined mind, any human was powerful beyond measure and could create immense change. Frustrated, Drift paused on the brink of saying what she knew would hurt him.

'They asked me back to join them. And I think I'm going to.'

Her dad's face shut down to a blank expression. 'I bet they did.' He flung his hat off, tossing it through the open window of the ute onto the seat and yanked the door open.

'Kelv's rolling on in soon,' he said, subject closed. 'The traffic's getting worse so we'd better put the signs out. Your policeman will be on to us if we don't.'

At the mention of Kelvin, dejected again, her hopeful bubble burst, she gathered up her reins and stepped up onto Minty.

'He's already on to us. I'll grab the dog chains, and he's not *my* policeman.'

'Don't you be so sure,' her father mumbled. Drift felt her cheeks burn red, knowing her father knew. Life and the tide of time were about to draw his daughter away.

Chapter 18

At the top of the rise, Drift spun the ute around and cut the engine. The sweeping beach view from over the ridgeline took her breath away. An onshore breeze scuffed up whitecaps on a deep blue ocean. The crescent beach sailed off south into the distance like a curved spinnaker. She framed the view in her fingers, imagining it on a canvas. Dunno leaned into the stiff wind and sniffed the air. He let out a small whine and a woof. Far below, where she'd left the cattle, the other dogs had been set out on the block-up chains on a running wire that crossed the road — their task was to stop the herd continuing on further towards the southern part of the spit and wandering into the search camp. The dogs knew their duty well. The cattle too, having been dogged for most of the day on their Planet journey, were now settled, so Drift relished the time away from it all to think. Dunno barked again.

'What's up, boy?' She knew he could sense something by the way his body quivered and he was whining slightly. As she dragged the heavy metal yellow sign from the ute that read *STOCK NEXT 30 K — SLOW* in bold black letters, she tried to breathe in calmness. Her mind raced with all that had happened. She felt she needed the wise counsel of Wilma or no-nonsense advice from Charlie Weatherbourne. She wondered where on earth Charlie would be on the road now. Instinctively her hand roamed to the thick hand-crafted belt with the knife pouch neatly stitched upon it. She sent her good wishes to Charlie on the wind, along with a call for her to come to her.

With the stock sign in place she went back to the ute. She turned the key, and the ute chugged over but died. Drift tried again. Nothing. She looked at the fuel gauge, which sat just above half full. She tapped the dial and turned the engine again, then with a sinking heart saw the needle falling to below E. The ute, normally reliable, must have a faulty fuel gauge. She was now most certainly out of diesel.

'Bugger,' she said, knowing the jerry can they normally kept on board for emergencies had been ditched to make room for the water tanker, pump and dogs.

'You on channel, Dad?' she said into the handpiece of the radio. Nothing. In her mind flashed the image of the radio handset on the table in the caravan, switched off. Her dad rarely wore the bloody thing anyway.

'There's no more faith in thee than in a stewed prune, Dad. Over and out,' she said, returning the handpiece to its metal clip on the dash. She stood beside Dunno, laying her hand on his alien-shaped cone head. The ute's bonnet ticked in the hot sun.

'Dunno, Dunno, Dunno. Dunno what to do,' she said stroking his ears. Dunno looked at her with his slightly crossed eyes and banged his tail against the ute's tray. She unclipped him and signalled for him to jump off. 'Nothing left to do, buddy ... but walk.'

*

Along the road on foot, Drift disappeared into the internal monologue that she usually ran when reading the world around her, studying the plant mix and soil coverage, the state of the landscape. Analysing the clouds and scent on the breeze. She liked this roadside. It was mostly left untouched by humanity, leaving native species free to grow. On some roadsides she and her dad had travelled, human impact could be seen everywhere in the millions of acres of overgrazing, the burning of monocultures in the paddocks, and the great roadside swathes of plant life nuked by council sprays, the chemicals running directly off into waterways.

On the roads, she saw the flotsam of a careless human race. Ice-block sticks, plastic lid rings, cigarette butts, faded chip packets, soft-drink cans, plastic drinking straws. The same concoction of human thoughtlessness was also to be found tangled in the driftwood piles that were windrowed by waves on the beach or river currents when Drift rode, swam or walked.

Humans, Drift had been taught by her father from very early on in her life, were ugly, careless, selfish, greedy, messy creatures. She realised now, after being on The Planet, maybe he was partly wrong. Her boot clipped a faded crumpled beer can and she thought how The Planet people seemed like a new race of humans. She hoped they would wake more people up. She hoped too she would be brave enough to convince her father it was the place for her to be. And that they did have the power to make change happen. Dunno suddenly stopped and turned. He let out a bark. Drift woke up from her inner musings.

'What?' She followed his gaze back the way they'd come. With a groan Drift noticed the dust rising and Kelvin's big rig coming over the rise. Rotten timing, she thought. Soon, the truck was rolling beside her, the scent of cattle manure heavy in the air. The airbrakes shushed. The window wound down.

'You stranded, little lady?' Kelvin asked.

'Nope,' she said, barely able to look at him.

'I seen the ute back there. Broken down, have ya?'

'Nope,' Drift said.

'C'mon,' Kelvin said in a smooth tone. 'Get in. We'll get you back to Dad.'

'Nope.'

'Don't be silly.'

'Don't reckon I'm the silly one,' Drift muttered under her breath, as she kept on walking.

Kelvin lifted the clutch, rolling the truck on slowly beside her.

'C'mon. I'll take you straight to your dad. I was just mucking with you before. Mates, eh? C'mon, get in.'

Drift thought of the knife that was tucked in the neat pouch of her CW belt on her hip. With her dad less than ten minutes' drive down the road what could Kelvin do? She paused. Should she? Who was he to dominate her? Why should she be the one afraid? She wouldn't let him bully her like this. She called Dunno and going round to the passenger door tugged it open.

'There's a good girl,' he said. 'Sorry about before. I got ahead of meself. Life gets lonely on the road. We are still mates, eh?'

Drift scowled at his meek expression and slammed the door shut.

As they set off, the red hydraulic seat bounced with each pot hole, Kelvin's gut plummeting up and down. He wore an orange hi-vis shirt with a black collar and his name embroidered over his left man-boob. He really is tragic, Drift thought. He kept turning to her and looking at her through narrowed, puffy and weepy blue eyes. Dunno sat on the truck's floor between Drift's legs, gazing at her with a troubled expression, sniffing curiously at the foreign smell of the truck. Sighing, the dog settled his chin on her knee, dozing, but the little light tan blobs above his shut eyes gave the impression he was still on watch.

'You got a boyfriend?' Kelvin asked suddenly.

Drift swallowed and licked her lips, dragging her long hair around over one shoulder and sitting her hat over her bare thighs. 'Nope.'

'Is nope the only word that you say?'

'Nope.'

Kelvin's hand was draped over the gearstick. He poked her thigh with his index finger and looked at her for an uncomfortably long time. She tried her best not to shrink away.

'You're a smartarse. But I like you.' The truck lumbered down the centre of the road, its wing mirrors gobbling up the white roadside guide posts like a video game. His eyes felt like they were burning holes through her clothing, right to her bra and undies … She began to prickle with heat and discomfort despite the air-con, realising she'd made a stupid choice.

'You oughta have a boyfriend,' he leered. 'You're a very pretty girl. You know that? My missus is so dingo ugly. She's a starfish in the sack and never puts out unless I get her drunk. You look like you'd put out for a fella. Wouldn't ya?' He drove on slowly in silence, glancing from the road to Drift. The coastal scrubland and roadside shoulders before her eyes panicked into a bland brown and dull green blur beside the window. The road ahead lay empty and straight. Surely they were getting closer to camp? She'd only set the signs fifteen Ks along the road. But Kelvin was crawling the truck along. As he shifted down to the lowest gear, his hand moved from the gearstick to the front of his shorts and he began rubbing his crotch. 'Ah, girlie, you … you're all young and ripe and wanting it. Aren't ya? Just looking at you gives me a hard-on.'

Drift felt a flush of fear course through her. The smell of his sweat mixed with his supermarket spray-on Brut suddenly made her feel sick. Every fibre in her body told her she was in the wrong place. Instinctively she grabbed for the handle of the truck door, but Kelvin clicked the central lock button.

'Stop,' she said, flashing her fierce blue eyes at him. 'I want to get out.'

Kelvin narrowed his eyes and turned back to watch the road ahead of them. 'You wanna go back to Daddy, little darlin? I'll take you to Daddy.'

Drift shuffled as close to the door as she could. Now Dunno was alert, his expression confused as he glanced from the man to Drift. He licked his lips and shoved his muzzle up under Drift's hand. She thought she'd try her tough-girl talk.

'Stop dicking about, Kelv, mate. Just stop the truck. Dad'll be coming for me. I just radioed him.' Drift's eyes darted to him, but any kind of tough-girl fury in her was quashed when she saw he was inching his shorts down.

'You know what I love about this truck?' Kelvin said in his slimy-toned voice, gaze sliding over her long legs.

Drift didn't answer. She was sweating. Dunno could smell her nerves too and was sitting up tall, ears pointed in alert little triangles, shifting his body.

'The cruise control,' said Kelvin, answering his own question. With fat hands and short fingers, he set the dial and the truck rolled on.

'It means I can get on and play with this.' Drift only caught a glance, but it was enough to sear the repulsive image on her brain. Kelvin had lifted his backside up and drawn the front of his work shorts down, freeing his stubby erect penis from his black underpants.

'Stop!' she said, turning her head and pressing her forehead to the glass. 'Stop! Please.' The curtains of the sleeper cab behind her swayed, the deep blue fake velour fabric making her feel woozy. She caught glimpses of posters of naked women stuck on the wall.

'Ah, don't you like it, little lady? I thought you'd seen plenty of these.' He pumped his penis harder with his fist. 'Little slut. Lucky it still works after the bollocking you gave me yesterday. You need a bit of punishment for that.' He fixed his eyes on her as he moved his hand up and down the shaft. Panic seeped into her.

'You're a fucking creep!' Drift said fearfully through gritted teeth, the truck's engine idling in a low sinister rumble. 'Let me out. Or I'll —'

'Or you'll what?' Kelvin said. 'Go tell Daddy?' His cruel smile faded as he glanced from the road to Drift, his face set in a steely expression.

'You've asked for it, little lady. In your shorty shorts with your pretty young titties popping out in that singlet. Your daddy won't know coz you won't tell him or I'll knife all of your animals one night, just when you aren't expecting it. I'll cut the tendons on those handy horses of yours.'

The sky stretched on endlessly above miles and miles of low tinder-dry scrub. Drift felt tears well in her eyes. He was lying. Wasn't he?

She glanced over at Kelvin. His pathetic stubby cock sat up against his repulsive gut. She hated him and his revolting sense of himself. What gave him the right to be like this? Anger fired in her. She wouldn't be beaten by him. With a surge of fury she began to kick the dash. Her sturdy dogger boots moved in time with her guttural sounding works. 'Let me out of the fucking truck! Let me out now!'

Dunno crouched down, cringing as Drift gave it her all, slamming the dashboard with the heel of her boots and the powerful pump of her legs.

'Oi! Crazy bitch!' Kelvin said as he hit the brakes.

Drift heard the cattle moan in the stock trailers in a sickening, sad tone.

'Quit it, bitch!' he roared. Drift knew she'd found his weak spot. His precious truck. She reached for her hip and the knife that nestled in the pouch on her CW belt. Grabbing it out and splicing open the blade, she held its curved silver point near the seat's upholstery.

'Let me out of the truck, arsehole.' She pressed the knife point onto the seat's fabric. 'Or I'll cut this wanky rig to bits.' She noticed his ugly bare-helmet penis was withering, the skin on it wrinkling in circles like a vol au vent casing. Disgust ran throughout her body, but she kept her blue eyes strongly fixed on his fat-faced profile. He glanced at the knifepoint. He could see she was serious.

'Well, well, well,' he said in a smooth tone, as he held his index finger over the central locking. 'You've got some fire in you. Like your old man. I'm just mucking about with you, little darlin. An old married man like me doesn't get to play much any more,' he said. 'You might wanna walk, honeypot. And take your fugly dog with ya.'

As soon as she heard the click of the central locking system, she shoved the door open. Not caring that the truck was rolling again, she leaped down onto the sloping red dirt beside the highway, hauling Dunno with her by the collar. It was a long drop. The pace surprisingly fast. Her boots slipped and gripped then slipped again. She tumbled over, banging her knee savagely on a rock, the knife in her hand catching on the gravel with a sickening scrape of metal. Dunno yelped as he hit the ground in an ungainly unbalanced way and rolled a few times before he righted himself. Hot air enveloped her and sun blasted her scalp as she spun to see the passenger door still hanging open.

'Prick-teasing bitch!' Kelvin yelled. He braked again, sending the truck lurching, the cattle within bellowing as they hit steel.

Drift watched her hat spinning in the air and the passenger door banging shut. She glanced up at the sun and along the desolate stretch of road. As the truck's trailer rolled past, she saw her reflection in the chrome dust-covered wheels of the rumbling rig. She saw her tanned bare skin and the rise of her breasts above the scoop neck of her bluey. For the first time in her life she truly hated herself for getting in that truck. How could she have been so stupid? She had known he was a creep.

Stifling sobs, she called Dunno to her and tried to crouch down, but the pain in her knee seared. It was swelling already. Bright blood spilled down her leg. She lingered, waiting for the long sheer sides of the stock trailer to move away, but instead she saw brake lights flare. Surely her dad was just over the next undulating rise? Or was it the next? Her thoughts scrambled with panic. The truck had stopped altogether. She began to limp towards a low cluster of boobialla trees on the side of the verge. Her knee caned. Maybe if she hid? She'd barely limped a few metres off the road when from the corner of her eye she caught a glimpse of movement from behind the rear dog trailer. He was there! He was coming for her! His round body rushed at her furiously.

'You think you can do that to me?' he yelled, spittle spraying. 'Huh? Little *whore*.'

She spun around to run, but her knee gave way. He grabbed her wrist, squeezing it so hard the knife fell from her hand.

Turning to him she kicked, she scratched, she screamed. Dunno stood a way off, barking madly, hackles raised, pupils dilated in fear. She swung a punch, but Kelvin caught her arm in a solid grip. He thrust her to the rocky ground, her face pressed to the dirt. Drift caught the stink of sun-warmed cow shit from the truck and smelled her fear saturating her clothing. Every muscle in her body fired. She screamed again as an animal would. Deep and guttural. Swiftly, he rolled her over and cuffed her hard, the shock of the blow silencing her.

He pressed his awful pig-dog face with its slit eyes up to hers in a violent kiss. His stale breath made her want to retch. The disgusting lick of his tongue tasted of rotten meat. The painful press of his mouth turned to a savage bite, and her lip spurted blood. Eyes wide she fought against him, crying out through gritted teeth, every sinew straining. She knew she was strong, but he was stronger. She felt his ugly bare penis pressing hard against her thigh, which prompted her to fight back with renewed energy. He backhanded her again. She tried to roar another scream in the hope her father would hear, but Kelvin's knuckles landed savagely on her cheek. Then again. He lifted her by her shoulders and slammed the back of her head against the rocky ground.

As he positioned himself over her body, Dunno, who'd been edging nearer, dived in, teeth sinking into the back of Kelvin's leg. The man grappled the ground for the knife. Flicking it fully open he lunged at Dunno. The dog yelped a scream, his thick fur sliced open on the shoulder, spilling the surprise of rich blood. Kelvin lunged again, caught the dog with the knife tip, before Dunno scampered crab-like away, yelping, his tail between his legs, rocketing through the fence, the wires making a weird, panicked sound. Kelvin dragged Drift to the bank on the roadside, where there was a softer patch of coastal pig face on which he could kneel.

Drift's body pulsed with pain as she came in and out of consciousness. She caught the flashes of the orange hi-vis, the wobbling red-dotted flesh of his belly. Drift turned her head and scrunched her eyes and all she could do was grit her teeth as she felt his ugly stiff penis probing savagely against her, trying to find its way into her. She could smell crushed plants beneath her, and feel ants biting at her thighs.

She tried to make a sound, but her mouth was filled with blood, and her head thrummed. Floppy like a rag doll, she was pinned down; his thick ham-like arm was over her throat while he struggled to reef open her belt. But the well-worn hobble belt, made by the hands of Charlie Weatherbourne, would not give in. As he cursed the stubborn buckle, Drift felt herself losing her grip, almost willing her mind to wander to another place so she could escape this awful moment.

Suddenly Kelvin cried out in agony. Through blurred vision, Drift saw a flash of blue. Kelvin was being dragged off her and to his feet. His head was flung back in a single punch. A knee to the groin sunk him to the dirt. After an upper cut, Kelvin slumped to the ground, blood and slobber dribbling from his mouth. Before she blacked out Drift saw the figure of a tall man walking over to her. She saw his stockman boots in the gravel. As he bent over, the sun shone like a white fireball behind him. Next she felt his hand on her face and in that one touch she knew instantly she was safe, but she was sinking under. Under the surface into a black sea.

Chapter 19

Through the dark limbs of languid gums, Drift could see stars spinning in the blackness of the sky above her. It felt as if her head would explode. Where was she? From where she lay, she could see a small campfire sending milky-blue wavering threads of smoke up towards a gentler, softer waning moon. She stared at the smoke. Slowly she blinked. It seemed to thicken to white, like mist. Drift peered through the veil. There she made out the brown-skinned face of a little girl. *The* girl. The one in the white dress. She smiled gently at Drift, her eyes holding deep compassion. Drift wanted to ask, 'Who are you?' but no words came. Her lips were swollen and crusted shut with dried blood, her mind sluggish. A gust of wind moved the brown seed heads of grasses that ringed the camp area, so they began whispering too. Drift heard the girl whisper with them. She strained to hear her, but the little girl's words were lost in the breeze dancing through the grasses.

Drift tried to remain focused on the girl, but her eyes kept fluttering shut, no matter how hard she willed herself to keep looking at her. Then she passed out again.

When Drift reopened her eyes, the fire had died down. The smoke had gone. There was no sign of the girl. Cloud now covered the night sky. Drift tried to move, wincing at the pain that shot through her as she shifted her shoulder. She realised she was in a swag, the canvas heavy and noisy. Her fingertips found her knee;

it was bloodied and alarmingly swollen. She could see under dim moonlight a short distance away a white horse sleeping, its back hoof rested upwards and its body glowing in the darkness. She tried to sit up. She murmured in distress as memories of Kelvin raced through her mind, then of Dunno being knifed by him.

'Shhhh,' came a voice. 'It's OK. You're safe.'

Drift's eyes flew open. She tried to turn to look at who was above her, but was overcome by grogginess. She could feel a warm hand on her shoulder. Instantly she felt a pulse of calm run through her. Whoever it was, they were gentle. She knew it innately. Blankets were softly being drawn up around her. Fingertips gently stroked her hair comfortingly.

'Here, can you drink some water?' In the dimness, she could see a tall man squatting next to her. From the sideways frame of the world, the fire lit him enough that she could see it was the bearded stockman in the blue shirt again. She looked at the white enamel mug he was offering her. The deep shadow of his face was masked by a hat, dark beard and shaggy black hair that fell over his shirt collar. He held the cup to her mouth, cradling the back of her head. Drift's eyes gained focus on his hands. Young man's hands. She whimpered when the metal touched the rawness of her split lip.

'Sorry,' he said. She managed a small sip. Tenderly, the man supported the less bruised side of her face and helped her lie back down. Her fingertips gingerly reached up and found a massive swelling over her eyelid. She felt like vomiting.

'Are you warm enough?' The man went to the fire and put a log on it to revive it without waiting for her answer. He came back, kneeling beside her, soothingly putting his hand on her shoulder again. 'I'd say you've got concussion,' he said. 'But you're safe now.' His tone was deep and compassionate, and he had something like an American accent, only different. Something she couldn't quite pick.

'I'm meant to keep you awake I think, but you keep falling asleep. I keep telling you stories, but I must be boring you.' He grinned. 'I keep trying to feed you too, but you mustn't like my food because you keep throwing up.'

She tried to smile but her head hurt too much. She remembered Sophia mentioning the stockman's name. What was it again? Drift tried to speak, to ask. She wanted to ask about the girl? Had he seen her too? Maybe it was his little child? What happened to Kelvin? Where was her dad? And her dog? Had he found her dog?

She could see he had brought her to what must be some kind of stock-camp outpost, judging by the rough shelter she was lying under: a dull green tarp, held up by cut branches. A log served as a seat beside the fire. A slice of a tree trunk had been made into a table on which sat a few cast-iron pots, cans of food and tin plates.

'What's …?'

'Shhh,' he said again. 'Don't speak. Just rest. We can't do anything but that for now. Batteries have died on my two-way and my horse is stone bruised. I'm gunna wait till first light. We'll get you back to Sophia and Serge. For now, you're OK. You're with me. Elijah. Eli for short.'

Eli, Drift thought before she shut her eyes again. That's right. It was Eli.

*

At first light, bird calls roused her. Drift could hear the surge of the sea, waves rolling in, then out. Surely the sea wasn't that close? She knew the timbered country she was in was far enough inland not to hear the sea so loudly. Then she realised the sound was blood pulsing in her ears. The pain in her head hit. She rolled over. More pain raged from her knee. She realised her whole body screamed.

From where she lay long stems of grass reached up to the sky in golden morning summer yellow. She could smell the living, breathing earth beneath her. Although it was beautiful, with

147

a jolt she remembered the ugliness of yesterday and the feeling of Kelvin's half-naked weight upon her. Whimpering, she lifted her hips and tried, with sore arms and shaking claw-like hands, to feel if her underpants and shorts were intact. Had he got to her? The buckle of her CW belt chinked; it was done up, but the prong was not in its normal hole.

Flashing visions of Kelvin on top of her arrived again and again. Surely he hadn't got it in her, had he? She searched her muddled mind. She didn't want him to be her first. She began to cry, the salt of her tears stinging the fresh red welts on her face. With the rising sun so too came the flies, landing on her, drinking the drying blood on her lip with their tiny little suckers. She tried to brush them away. They buzzed in protest, spiralled in the air, but kept coming back. She lay there for a time, wondering where the stockman had gone. Then she remembered Dunno and her heart scrunched in pain. Where was he?

A crow winged its way silently across her vision. She could see the sky above clouding over to the south-east above the scrub line. She wondered if it would rain. A summer shower, to wash away the blood and give her some rest from the flies. Eli? Where was he? She smelled the residue of fear that sheened her skin and clothing in sweat. She rolled over painfully, registering the odour of the swag sheets: men's deodorant and washing powder. Of Eli. She closed her eyes again. Time passed. She tried not to think. Not of her missing dog. Not of what may or may not have happened with Kelvin before Eli came along. As her body trembled she decided to let the earth beneath her hold her like a mother and the sky above her wrap her with his blanket of blue like a father. A mother and father to protect her. She thought of the girl. Drift closed her eyes. She'd had *enough*. Enough of the uncertainty and cruelty of life. Sharp pain stabbed her belly. She shut her eyes to it and crawled into a deep black cave inside herself.

More time passed, and when Drift opened her eyes again the clouds had all gone. Her skin was sizzling hot, and she knew she had to get up. Her blurred vision revealed a cup next to her, filled with water. Beside it was an apple, and some fly repellent. At last she noticed a note Eli had left beneath it.

Gone to get help.

She wanted to drink but she couldn't move. She remained, her eyes glazed, staring at the stems of grasses. An insect made its own wobbling seemingly pointless path to the tip of a seed head, then back down again. Drift blinked. Then she turned her head and saw off in the distance a vehicle coming from the south-east. Soon the engine was rumbling nearby. Next Sophia and Serge were standing above her.

'It's OK, my love,' Sophia said gently, her dark hair falling forward as she kneeled over Drift. 'I'm here.' Her voice was rich and soothing and Drift felt Sophia's hand stroke the top of her head. 'Can you sit up, darling girl? Is anything broken?'

She shook her head. 'Don't know.' Her voice was raspy. Everything hurt.

'Are you OK to walk over to the ute?'

Serge on one side of her was helping her up. She winced at the crunch of torn muscles, bruising and maybe even broken ribs that seemed to grab the breath from her. Searing pain sliced upwards from her knee. Drift's vision blurred in and out. Her head pounded like a jackhammer, thumping in her brain with each painful step. Sophia's hands on her skin felt soothing, as they gently cupped her arms and half carried her over to the waiting vehicle. The caring within their touch unfolded a grief within Drift so powerful she began to cry again. Quietly this time. Great rivers of tears seemed to just keep coming. She leaned into the strong, sturdy body of Serge, but still her body shook.

They said nothing as she limped and listed on the uneven ground towards the twin-cab ute, hot engine chugging, cool air-conditioning waiting for her. Sophia yanked the passenger door open and Serge helped Drift lie down on the back seat. Sophia climbed in and rested Drift's head on her lap. She reached into a bowl and started bathing Drift's wounds with a wet cloth that smelled beautifully of lavender and other oil essences.

'We're not too far from home and our lovely doctor. Sit tight, sweetie,' said Sophia, as Serge slowly pulled away from the campsite.

'Where's Eli?' Drift asked. Serge glanced in the rear-vision mirror at Sophia. They both paused.

'He had to go.'

'Go?'

They remained silent.

'I've lost my dog,' Drift said, tears coming again. 'I thought Eli might have found him.'

Sophia shook her head. 'Sorry, my darling. No sign of him. But Eli will go look for him. Promise.'

Drift sadly whispered to herself, 'Dunno where he's gone.' Then she passed out.

Chapter 20

Drift woke feeling the coolness of crisp sheets on her skin. Hazily she recalled Sophia and another tiny woman with long braided reddish-brown hair washing her down, helping her into a borrowed white singlet top and some pale blue boxers. 'I'm Landy, The Planet's doctor,' the woman had said. 'You're concussed, my dearest, and your knee is badly bunged up. That's a very fancy medical term by the way. But you'll be fine. You're in good hands now.' In a square of vine-filtered sunlight, Drift sat up gingerly, realising she was now alone in a beautiful upstairs bedroom, tranquil and shaded by ornamental grape climbers on the verandah outside.

Inside, the bedroom felt infused with Sophia's loving, serene energy and, like the rest of the place, was built warmly out of natural repurposed materials. Colourful fabrics and simple statues of horses and a lack of clutter made the room feel like a palace to Drift. She realised from the view outside that she was upstairs in The Planet's main homestead. Beside her bed, a timber-framed window revealed an expansive view far off to the south-east. There on a rise the pearl-white wind towers were splicing lean blades through the heat-hazed sky. Stretching beyond them was an endless bracken-green blanket of light scrub and grassland. Nearer the homestead, the rows of black square solar panels mounted on pivoting frames were drizzled in light, slowly turning their faces towards the sun like flowers. The view from up there of the natural-energy systems was spectacular. It distracted Drift from her throbbing head.

She wondered how long she'd been there. Aching, she got up from the bed, shuffling into the bathroom, her knee raging. Rustically crafted woodwork and pretty framed mirrors greeted her, some of the walls washed in soft pastel colours, matching the shells that lined the window sill. Afternoon light spilled through the gentle green and cream stained-glass window — the pattern of which formed a canopy of leaves — giving Drift a sense of peace, until she looked in the mirror. She gasped when she saw the damage Kelvin had done. Cuts and scratches were drying in brown lines on her forehead. Her blonde hairline was still stained red with blood, and her lips were ballooning. Her left eyelid was so swollen it blocked her full vision. The skin beneath her right eyebrow was also blooming deep purple. She inhaled a jagged sob.

In the reflection behind her she noticed a plush towel and a white cotton robe laid out on a chair. She slowly breathed in and out three conscious breaths, the way Wilma had taught her. She told herself she was strong and her inner spirit was always safe out beyond the stars, just as Charlie always mused on the nights they had sat beneath the Milky Way. Turning on the tap, Drift ran the bath. She sat on a small hand-made milking stool as it filled, her eyes staring at nothing, her mind carefully blank, her sore leg stuck out gingerly in front of her. She wondered if her dad knew she was here.

Undressing and then awkwardly easing herself into the bath, she felt the cuts on her body sting as the water touched her skin. She grimaced. Steam rose, smelling of lavender, and the water, softened with Epsom salts, began to gently prompt her to relax and let go. Sophia had lit a candle in the bathroom and it flickered as the vapour rose.

From somewhere in the homestead, Drift could hear gentle, cool folk music playing. She lay back and shut her eyes, the full soreness of her body grabbing at her. She tried to breathe the pain away, but there was a flash in her mind's eye of Kelvin in the truck and his ugly penis beneath his gut. Of the crimson red slash on Dunno's shoulder, blood spilling. Of Kelvin's ugly face above her. Her eyes flew open.

Again she wondered how far Kelvin had got with her. She looked down to the dark hair between her legs … had Kelvin violated her? How soon had Eli come along during the attack? Suddenly she wanted more than anything to see Eli. To ask him what had happened. Surely Kelvin wouldn't be her first? He *couldn't*? She tensed at the thought. The *devastation* of just the idea of it made her want to fold into herself. She wished Eli would come to her soon, perhaps with Dunno. She could still feel Eli's compassionate touch on her shoulder and his gentle hand drawing back her hair from her face where it had stuck in drying blood. She could still picture the kindness and care in his dark eyes. The thoughts of him soothed her.

*

The bathwater had turned pink with residue blood from her hair. Drift stepped out of it, rinsing off in the shower, feeling the water both hurt and heal her. Wrapping herself in the robe, she felt the breeze from the ceiling fan cool her scalp as she trod over the polished floorboards and slid open the upstairs verandah door. From the second storey she took in the flow of the farm below. Through a canopy of green, all the farm dwellings were placed near the hub of the main house and she could see The Planet people moving about. Kids' laughter and squeals floated up from a clear dam surrounded by shaded lawns. Birds flitted about in their clan groups, chattering in trees and darting cheekily in front of her as Drift leaned her forearms on the railing.

As her eyes roamed across the landscape, she could see the web of electric fencing and the watering points dotted here and there amidst the wooded grasslands. She could see the paddock 'rooms' with their swathes of dancing grasses and flowers.

Involuntary tears rose in her eyes as she saturated herself in a sense of relief; she felt here as if she was home, safe. Most of her life had been spent on the road, moving constantly, always with her eyes trained on the sea and the white horses. Longing to find a home. A home with a mother. A garden. This place now gave her hope that a dream like that could be realised.

There was a knock on the door. In came Sophia, looking even more beautiful in a soft pale blue shirt and figure-hugging jeans. She carried a tray laden with food and a small pottery vase with a single red bottlebrush bloom in it.

'Ah, good! You're up and about!' She set the tray on the foot of the bed. 'Here,' she said, lifting up a pottery cup, 'this will make you feel even better. It's what I call Dr Landy's "shocked out of your jocks" remedy. Perfect for the ringers who come off their horses. Or mending lovers' broken hearts. Or for sleeping people when they suddenly wake up. You name it.'

Drift lifted the cup to her mouth and drank the concoction, which tasted like strong tea with a good dose of honey. 'What's in it?'

Sophia grinned. 'A bit of bush medicine, a bit of wise-woman tonic. A bit of witch's brew. A bit of moon juice. And some painkillers from Dr Landy. It'll settle you and help ease the shock. Then we can talk about what happened.'

'I'm not sure I know what happened. But Eli will know,' Drift said. 'Where is he?'

She saw Sophia's expression alter for a moment.

'I don't rightly know. He gets about on the far boundaries mostly, checking water points, so he's probably headed there again now he knows you're safe.'

'And Dad? Have you told him?'

Sophia's brow furrowed. 'Soon. Serge is on his way to him now.'

Drift held the cup still in her hands. 'Soon? But he'll be worrying.'

Sophia looked guiltily at her. 'I know he will. We tried to

get to him sooner,' she said, tensely. 'They've taken the phone tower down so we couldn't call him, or reach him on the UHF, then when Serge was about to go see him, that awful pro-surfer manager turned up at the gate. He was demanding their private plane land here to jet them out. Pushy guy.'

Sophia rolled her eyes. 'After that we had a swarm of media choppers breaching all the aviation rules, flying dangerously close, spooking all the stock. Cattle and chaos everywhere! Media folk in vehicles trying to force the gates. The more clued-in journalists are now trying to break into The Planet to snoop around. They've got drones filming us, even. Just getting out to your dad has been an issue. I'm so sorry. It's been crazy here.'

Sophia's face fell, her normal serene expression gone. 'It's been Hell for another reason too.' She sucked in a breath.

'You see, I know Kai's parents.'

Drift, amazed, replied, 'You do? How?'

'We work together on planetary change projects. Gorgeous people. So full of grace and goodness.' The pain of their loss was written on Sophia's face.

'It was his parents, many years ago, who succeeded in blocking the giant chemical and GMO companies from taking on their home island in Hawaii, Moloka'i. They've been regenerative agricultural pioneers ever since. I've met them many times at conferences and think-tanks in New York. I'd invited them out here next year, to help them mend their relationship with him.' Her eyes teared up. Drift saw the distress in Sophia's eyes. 'It must be so upsetting for them. I think Kai came to Pinrush to find himself. To save himself. So he could go back to them. Personally, he'd been ... on the slide.'

Drift couldn't believe the interwoven connections. She wondered why Sophia hadn't mentioned knowing the missing man and his parents before, when the cattle had strayed on to the property.

Sophia lifted her face to Drift. 'To top it all, last night one of The Planet people went into early labour and Dr Landy —'

'*Last* night?' Drift echoed. 'Have I been here *two* nights?' She felt alarm rise in her.

Sophia nodded. 'I'm sorry. But Serge is on his way to find your dad, *right now*.'

A flash of Kelvin's violence fired in Drift's mind and for a moment she thought Sophia utterly selfish not to tell her father straight away.

'Surely we need to tell the police what happened? And Dad? He'll be worried sick!'

Sophia took the empty cup from Drift's clenched hands. 'I know. *I know*,' she said as she sat down on the bed. For the first time, Drift saw just how stressed Sophia looked. Sophia let out a frustrated groan. 'It's complicated. Really complicated.' She looked to the ceilings and tears pooled in her Cleopatra-like eyes. 'We don't want the police around here, even though I know they really need to investigate what has happened with you, my dear girl.' Tenderly, she lay a sympathetic palm on Drift's arm.

'Why don't you want the cops here?'

Sophia sighed. 'You need to understand, some of the stuff we do here is not fully legal. In terms of council regulations, that sort of thing. One particular cop is like a dog with a bone about you. He's a tall strap of a lad. Thin as a whittled stick. A shy boy, but with police steel within.'

An image of Simon came to Drift. 'Are they on to Kelvin?' Drift asked.

'Yes! We have to get that bastard. We've told the constable you're awake and he can interview you now. He'll be on his way too.'

Drift felt a jolt. To be interviewed by Simon over *this*.

'Only trouble is,' Sophia continued, 'the young policeman said Kelvin is denying it.'

'Kelvin's *lying*!' Drift said.

'I know he is! He said it was one of *our* men who sexually assaulted you. Said he got beat up by our stockman and bitten by your dog when he was trying to help you. He showed them the bruises and bites to prove it and told the police he was on his way in to the Cooperville station to say you'd been kidnapped after he'd dropped the cattle to your dad.'

Drift felt the room swirl around her. 'But can't Eli just tell them none of that's true?' She searched Sophia's face.

'Well … yes,' Sophia said slowly, 'he could. But it's not that simple. He …' She stopped for a moment. 'Like I say, it's complicated.' She lifted her hand onto Drift's forearm.

'But what if Kelvin does it to another girl?' Drift felt tears rise. And her poor father. He'd be distraught. God knows what story Kelvin'd spun to him. How could they have left him hanging so long? She turned to Sophia. 'I have to go to Dad!' Drift said, getting up from the bed.

'Uh-uh. Landy says you're not ready to be up and about yet,' Sophia said firmly. 'So let us care for you one more night, then you can go back to your droving post. Your dad will be here soon. I promise!'

As abruptly as she arrived Sophia stood and left, apologising as she went but taking with her any answers to Drift's many questions. Suddenly the food on the tray looked less appetising. What was going on? She felt the rumble of upset rising again in her, even though the pierce of pain in her head splicing through her thoughts had eased. She went back over to the bed and lay down. She just couldn't keep hold of the threads. The day faded to black and sleep once again claimed her.

*

As the hot afternoon rolled on, Drift found the house was pleasantly cool thanks to the thick stone that faced the west and held the inside temperature steady. Outside, the setting sun was painting the vast sky in a burst of burnt sienna and gold. Below, Drift could see a firepot being lit. The smell of a barbecue was soon wafting tantalisingly through the open verandah doors. Again there was a knock on the door. This time it was Serge with a platter of heat-sizzled meat, salad and the crunchiest of coal-baked roasted potatoes in foil, drooling with butter. Following her was Sophia with Drift's clothes all neatly washed and folded. Her CW belt coiled like a sleepy snake on top of the pile. Behind them came a sheepish-looking Split, his eyes red rimmed.

'Dad!' Drift cried out as she tried to get up from the bed.

'Stay there,' Split said moving to her, taking her in his arms, cradling her as if she were a child again. 'Oh thank God. Thank God,' he murmured as he rocked back and forth with her.

He drew back, pain on his face. 'I thought ... I thought the worst. What happened?'

'Kelvin,' Drift said, but the words choked in her.

'That prick.' Her dad's expressions revealed his fury. 'He told me he found the ute run out of fuel. Said he reckoned a stockman was attacking you. Guy in a blue shirt with a white horse ... Drift, I'm so sorry. He spun such a convincing yarn. Said he'd radioed the police. Sent me off searching in the wrong place.' Her dad's face folded with pain and he held her to him again.

She began to sob. 'He knifed Dunno. He knifed him, Dad. Now he's gone.'

'Shush, we'll find him, hun. Remember the time we thought he was a goner with that snake, and he pulled through at the vet? He's a tough little bugger, that dog. *The miserable have no other medicine. But only hope.*'

Drift felt her spirits rise for a moment with her dad's peppering of Shakespeare.

'He'll come find you if he can.'

'Yes.' She blew her nose on a tissue. 'And we can set the record straight with the police that it was Sophia's stockman Eli who saved me from Kelvin.'

'Eli? I'm getting some crossed wires here.' Split frowned, looking from Drift to Sophia. 'You told me it was Serge who found her.'

Serge and Sophia exchanged glances.

'Doesn't matter how it all happened. As long as Drift's safe, that's all that matters, isn't it?' Serge replied.

'No!' Drift said. 'We have to get the facts straight! What if Kelvin does this to someone else? What if he does what he said he's going to do to my animals? He's already probably killed Dunno.'

'I know,' Sophia said. 'You're right. But for now, eat. We'll deal with it in the morning. The constable said he'll be back from Cooperville tomorrow to help. We'll leave you two alone. When you're ready, Split, come downstairs. Please join us for something to eat. And a word.'

A word about what? Drift wondered as Sophia shut the door.

Split turned to her. His face lit up brightly for the first time. 'You were right,' he said, 'this place is *amazing*. They're good folks, but ...' he hesitated '... they're hiding something.'

Drift gazed levelly at him. 'I know they are.'

They fell silent, the mystery heavy in the quiet room. Drift wished her dad would say he was sorry. For everything. For not recognising Kelvin's predatory intentions in the first place. For scaring the wits out of her with his attempted suicide. Instead he broke the silence by talking cattle. It was the only safe space for him when he wasn't in poetry mode.

'That black bitch cow is sired by an El Toro friggin bull-fighting bull, I swear,' Split said. 'She nearly had me when I was mobbing up the second lot of the herd. Gotta watch her. I need you back. I think you're the only one she trusts.'

Drift watched as her father sat up. He was freshly washed, in a clean shirt, his hair combed.

'*And we must take the road once more, To bring the cattle home,*' he said in his best Banjo Paterson recital voice, then looked at her and smiled. All at once, love for her father swamped her.

Drift joined in. '*And it's "Lads! We'll raise a chorus, there's a pleasant trip before us." And the horses bound beneath us as we start them down the track; And the drovers canter, singing, through the sweet green grasses springing.*'

Together they finished: '*Towards the far-off mountain-land, to bring the cattle back.*'

They smiled. They hugged. Forgiveness folded in on them like a blanket of warmth.

*

In the night, with her father gone, Drift heard the click of the door open and then close. She breathed in suddenly with unease.

'Who is it?'

In the darkness she heard a voice. 'It's OK,' came a whisper. 'You're safe.'

She knew who it was in an instant and her whole body relaxed.

Eli stepped forward into the dull glow of moonlight. 'How are you?'

'Much better,' she said, smiling, sitting up and trying to see him in the shadows. In the darkness he came to sit next to her on the bed. Drift recognised his smell, of earth, horses and outdoor work. She could see how tall he was. Broad shouldered. Lean and fit beneath his work-worn dust-covered clothes. He still had his hat on, as if he'd stepped straight off his horse in broad sunlight. What really struck her, even in the darkness, was his youth. He was such a *young* man. She had thought him old when she'd first seen him amid the trees. Like an ancient spirit. But here he was — all youth and vitality.

'What are you doing here?'

'I had to come see you.' His voice was a whisper. He glanced out the window. The moon and its trajectory told her it was late.

'On the other side of midnight?'

'Yes,' he said, taking his hat from his head, revealing his long mop of hair. It was hard to read his expression in the dark, but she knew concern was knitting his brow over his brown eyes. He didn't seem as calm as he had the other night.

'Are you OK?' she asked him.

'Are you?' he replied.

'I am, thanks to you. You ought to be wearing your undies outside your jeans. You're my superhero.' Drift tried to joke to banish her overwhelming emotion. A virtual stranger. Yet, her saviour.

She saw his teeth flash white in the dimness of the moonlight, a perfect smile hidden by that shaggy bushman beard and moustache. She wondered just how handsome he was.

'It was nothing.'

'But if you hadn't come along ...' Drift's words faded and she felt tears rise.

Eli reached for her hand and held it gently.

'Did he ...' she began in a small voice. She tried again. 'Did he, you know ... get to me?'

She saw Eli straighten his back. 'No,' he said with certainty. 'No he didn't. I got there before that happened.'

Drift was surprised by her own reaction and the sob of relief that escaped her.

He drew her to him and held her.

'I didn't want *him* to be my first,' she said, her less sore cheek pressed against his broad chest.

'Don't think about it. It didn't happen. You're OK.'

She felt his thumb running gently over the back of her hand, the rise and fall of his chest. She drew back, looking up to his face. 'And my dog? Did you find him?'

Eli shook his head sadly. 'No.'

An image of her dear old Dunno dog slowly dying out in the scrub seared in her mind. Eli drew her again into a hug. She laid her cheek on his chest again, and heard his heartbeat.

'How did you know to come — right at that time? Out of all those thousands of acres, why were you right there? Right then?'

Eli paused. 'I can't explain it really. A gut feeling. Like I was led there. I'm just glad I found you.'

'Me too,' Drift said, the image of the little girl emerging in her mind, and goosebumps shivering over her skin.

Chapter 21

The waning moon slid by the bedroom window and sea scent drifted into the room on the breeze, lifting white gauze curtains like spirits. In the darkness Eli was now lying on his back on the bed beside Drift, his boots hanging slightly off the edge, crossed at the ankles, his hands clasped behind his head. They'd been talking for over an hour, with Eli asking Drift question after question about her life, her likes, her dislikes, her self. He was lying so close to her, despite the fact she barely knew him. It was as if their shared trauma of the attack from Kelvin had thrust them together faster than normal meetings between strangers. Drift still couldn't put her finger on what it was about Eli. He had a rare gentleness to him, yet beneath his calm voice she felt a tension. She'd felt safe in his presence that night in his swag, when she'd lain there so defenceless. In his quiet, insular way, she sensed he walked in the world in a similar way to her. How she knew this, she didn't know, but she felt it at some deeper level. But now she could feel an undercurrent beneath his surface calm. She also sensed he was lonely, vulnerable even. He was a strange one, yet, she concluded, it was so nice just to have his quiet, sincere company. It had given her the confidence to tell him about the girl in the white dress she'd seen the night the surfer had gone missing, and again at Eli's campsite. He'd listened in silence, then softly said, 'My mother and grandmother taught me that this life is the dream, and there's a veil between here and our real home. Perhaps she was from there?' Drift lay, comforted that this young man hadn't mocked her, but instead was helping her to find a deeper explanation for what she'd seen.

'Why have you come back to see me in the middle of the night?' she asked bluntly.

Eli turned to her. His gaze was intense; it unsettled her. 'I had to see you again.'

'Why?'

'You saved my life.'

'How? Isn't it the other way around? You saved me.'

'No. You arrived for me at a time when I didn't know if I even had a future … I was thinking of …' He paused, swallowed, ran a hand over his face. 'Of, you know … Of not waking up the next morning.'

Drift felt cold. 'You mean like topping yourself?' Her raw expression hung in the air between them.

'Yes.'

Drift turned to him, feeling the stab of her father's actions. 'Don't you dare even think like that!'

Eli looked surprised.

Drift clenched her jaw. 'Doing that is not fair on the people you leave behind. It's utterly *selfish*.' In her mind flashed images of her father, grey faced, slumped over in the cab of the ute. The ambos had said if Drift had've found him a few minutes later there would've been no bringing him back. There was an awkward silence for a while.

'Have you lost someone that way?' Eli asked as he turned to her.

Drift shook her head, shutting the conversation down with a sharp, 'Almost.' She'd sometimes wondered if her mother, that night, had suicided too. It was a question she never wanted investigated. How could a mother leave her daughter by swimming out to sea? How could anyone take their own life, when life was such a gift?

'I have a friend. She's kind of like a mother to me,' she said, thinking of Charlie. 'She said every one of us has won this big strange Lotto just being here. She said of all the trillions of cells that collide, and of all the long-shot chances of life, we are all walking miracles. And you don't waste miracles. Life is not to be shirked. Or wasted. If you waste your life like that you are inviting Hell, not into your life, but the lives of those you're leaving behind.' Drift pulled up short before she could say, 'My father almost left me to rot in that Hell.'

The silence of the room enveloped them.

'OK,' Eli said soberly. 'I know I won't ever think like that again. Not now I've met you. Especially after tonight.'

'I don't understand.'

He paused. 'This will sound weird but it feels as if I've known you before.'

'What do you mean?'

He looked back up at the timber ceiling in the darkness and let out a long breath. 'I don't know. It was scary, that afternoon I took you back to camp. I didn't want to risk moving you or leave you alone until I knew you'd be OK. I was terrified you wouldn't regain consciousness. It felt unbearable to think it. I already felt I somehow knew you.' He glanced over to her. 'You see, I'd seen you before.'

'Before?'

'Yes, when you were filling your water tank. I was watching you with your dogs. The love you had for them. The joy you had. I thought maybe life was worth living if there were people on the planet like you. People who are just happy because of puddles. And dogs playing. I knew you were someone special.'

Drift propped herself on her elbow to look at him. She recalled seeing him on the horse when she'd filled up the water tank and again in the trees the day the cattle had pushed through the fence. 'That was you? So you've been following me? Spying on me?'

He smiled. 'It was a coincidence, really. I don't stalk girls — that's not cool. It was odd how our paths just kept crossing. Out there in the scrub. It wasn't like I planned it. Time just took me where I needed to be to see you. You have a way about you. With the animals. With the world. It's something I haven't seen in anyone for a long, long time.'

Drift lay back down, puzzled, her head thudding dully.

Eli continued. 'So, when I got you back to camp, as the hours went on and I watched you breathing, I just felt something. *Something*, I don't know … how to put it. Like this was a special meeting.'

Drift felt a shimmer run through her, but she blocked it with a joke. 'There's nothing special about me. You've just been hanging out with cows too long on your own.'

He ignored her quip, holding on to the depth of the moment. 'After that one night with you — willing you to wake up — I felt like I'd somehow known you before … It's crazy, I know, but I felt it so strongly, the moment I saw you at the waterhole with your dogs. And again on your white horse on the road.'

'But you don't even know me.'

'I know … but … Forget it.' He sounded embarrassed.

Drift looked over at him, his face half in shadow, the other lit by the fading moon. 'How can you say stuff like that,' she pressed, 'when we've only just met? How can you know me, when most of the time you spent with me I was unconscious?'

Eli paused and clenched his jaw as he searched for words. He turned his intense dark eyes on her. 'Don't *you* feel it? Feel something? Coming together in such a random way like we have?'

Drift looked at him. Yes. She did feel it. It wasn't just the warm energy of this strange, gentle man. It was something otherworldly. Something deep within her.

'No,' she lied, 'I don't. Besides, I'm not sure I can trust you. From what I can tell, you're hiding something. Tell me what you've been up to and why you, Serge and Sophia are lying to the police and not telling them what really happened.'

Drift felt the shift in his body as he paused before he spoke.

'I can't.'

'Let me guess … It's complicated,' she said, parroting Sophia's words.

'As a matter of fact it is. *Damn* complicated.'

'That's a shame because in my life I like simple,' Drift said with finality. Conversation closed. They lay side by side in silence, Drift, so tired, so confused, her headache back again, and Eli silent and disappointed beside her. Eventually sleep claimed her.

Next, still in darkness, she heard the door open. Her eyes flew open. A soft light spilled in from the landing.

'Eli! C'mon! You must leave! *Now*!' Sophia was whispering urgently. She was shaking Eli awake. 'You're *mad* to come here. I told you to head back to camp. Quickly. He's coming, looking for her!'

'Who?' Eli asked.

'The cop.'

'What's going on?' Drift asked, jolted wide awake now, trying to piece together what was unfolding.

'I'll tell you later,' Sophia said, ushering Eli out. 'I'll bring your breakfast in an hour or so,' she said, shutting the door quickly.

In the empty bedroom, drowsy from sleep, Drift rolled over, feeling the warm space where Eli had been. She couldn't make any sense of what was happening. She'd wished on the now fading January moon for change … and here it was. Confusing, confronting change that made no sense at all. She lay awake, the sky lightening slowly, until a gentle knock brought Sophia back into the room. She carried with her a cup of herbal tea and set it on the bedside table.

'It's not poisoned,' she said jokingly when she saw Drift stare at it.

'That's not funny. I want to go back to Dad. Back to camp.'

'I know.'

'What's going on?'

'I can't say. You're just going to have to trust me on this. The police are coming around and I need you to do something for me. For Eli.'

'What?' Drift replied coldly.

'Could you say you don't know who rescued you? Please.'

'You mean lie? Lie to the police?'

'Yes, I'm afraid. You see Eli ... he's ... it's complicated.'

'You people keep saying that,' Drift said angrily.

'He's done some things ... the police would want to find him. But ... deep inside he's a good man. He needs a little more time here on The Planet so he can bury his past for good and make a fresh start.'

'What kind of things has he done?' Drift asked, her mind racing. Theft, assault, murder even? It was hard to imagine the gentle stockman harming a fly.

'OK,' Sophia said, sucking in a breath, 'I'll tell you. But as long as you swear not to tell a soul.'

Drift nodded. 'I promise.'

Sophia held both Drift's hands. 'Eli is —'

But her words were broken off when they heard Serge stomping unusually heavily up the stairs, talking in a too-loud voice.

'I was lucky to find her when I did, Constable. Right when he was attacking her. If I hadn't stopped him, I hate to think ...'

Sophia squeezed her hands imploringly. 'You've met Eli. You know he's a good man. Please help us. Please help him. Trust us.'

Drift swallowed when she saw Simon standing, tall and slim, in the doorway, so handsome in his uniform.

'Simon!' she said, forcing a painful smile, knowing she was about to dig herself into a very big hole.

Chapter 22

From the window of the police car, Drift watched the scrub blurring past as she and Simon drove towards Widgenup. It seemed like a lifetime since she'd travelled on the same road in the opposite direction with her dad and their stash of birthday supplies, less than a week ago. On this trip, the sea sat off to her left, and to her right the vast expanse of the continent spread out over thousands of kilometres to where the shores met the sea again on the more populated east coast.

Instinctively she kept reaching down to where Dunno normally sat when they travelled this road, only to find her backpack there, and not her dog. Beside her Simon, poker-faced, watched the road ahead. He's so diligent, she thought. So dependable and serious. The secret of Eli sat heavily with her. She hated lying to someone as straightforward as Simon. The kiss they'd shared now seemed like it never happened. He seemed so removed from her. There was no longer any flirtatiousness in him. Drift felt relieved in a way. The mystery of her nights with Eli, of the girl again at his campsite, of Eli's healing touch, it all seemed to seep into her and close her off from Simon.

'So you don't remember?' Simon prompted her again.

Drift shook her head. She dragged sunglasses down over her swollen, blackened eyes. The light hurt. She flexed her knee painfully.

Simon glanced over to her. 'I'm sorry. I'll save the questions for when we're at the station. We'll need to call by the hospital first. It's a little late, but the doctor there will examine you.' He sensed Drift stiffen.

'Simple procedure,' he reassured her.

Drift felt humiliation burn. *Procedure?* She wished Simon would stop talking but he kept on.

'There's so many inconsistencies, but I really want to nail Kelvin if we can. I get the feeling there's more dirt to dig on him, but there're too many questions and conflicting stories to press him further. That Serge fellow. There's something not right in his story. Kelvin swears it wasn't Serge who attacked him. The man who attacked him was bearded, he said.'

Drift turned her face away in a bid to glimpse the sea.

'You're certain it wasn't an employee from The Planet who assaulted you? Are you sure it was Kelvin Waller?'

'Without a doubt it was Kelvin,' Drift said, her voice rising in frustration.

'Sorry,' Simon said again, reaching for the radio and turning up a crackling version of 'Blue Moon'.

We must be nearing Widgenup if we're getting radio signal, Drift thought, relieved she'd soon be out of the stifling atmosphere of the cop car with all its extra equipment and the barking police radio. She knew there was still a couple more hours' travel with Simon before they reached Cooperville Police Station, where the detectives and a detained Kelvin waited for them.

Until the attack, she would've relished time spent with Simon. Now it all just felt too confusing. She decided to feign sleep on that last leg. Poor Simon, she thought, shutting him out like this just because of someone else's lie.

As Simon drove at a neat hundred and ten clicks, Drift tried to focus on the hope of finding Dunno, but her thoughts seemed to jerk about like a startled fish on a line. She'd lose concentration and her mind would catch on the one word. *Eli.* Then the one phrase would hook on repeat. *I felt like I'd somehow known you before.* Eventually she settled her head back on the headrest, shut her dry and painful eyes, and hoped Simon wouldn't start talking. But soon enough he did.

'I thought you'd stood me up on our dinner date.'

She looked over to him. She didn't know if he was being utterly serious or making a joke. 'Well I didn't mean to,' she said.

'I know. I was really worried about you.'

'I was really worried about me.'

'I bet you were,' he said quietly, glancing at her. 'Why didn't you and the people on the property let us know sooner that you'd been found?'

Drift was too scrambled to answer right away. An image of Eli's face in the darkness came to her. 'I don't know.' She shrugged. 'I was mostly out to it. It was a crazy time for them. They said they tried.'

'Yes, but to not tell your father for a couple of *days*? There were police escorts at the property the day the pro-surfers flew out. *After* they'd found you. Surely they would've told us then? What Sophia's telling me isn't adding up either.'

Drift felt heat prickle in her despite the air-con. The same claustrophobic feeling she'd felt in Kelvin's truck cab rose in her. Trapped. The lie twisted in her sternum and she felt she couldn't breathe. Why had Serge and Sophia talked her into this? What on earth had Eli done? She turned away to face the passenger window, guilt and grogginess bringing tears to her eyes. Simon noticed Drift's hunching shoulders, curling her body over.

'Sorry,' he said for the third time, 'but I'm looking out for you. You mustn't lie to police. Whatever it is you're hiding, you could at least tell me.'

'I'm not hiding anything,' Drift said, meaning it. 'I really don't know. All I know is that Kelvin almost … killed me. And I've no idea about the timing of any of it. I feel sick just thinking about it.'

Drift's memory flooded suddenly with an image of a porn poster she'd seen in Kelvin's truck. It made her skin crawl to think of him looking at those women and then looking at her in the same light. The woman on the poster had been lying back, legs spread, revealing the shaven slit between, her mouth pouting in a perfect cock-shaped 'O' for men's pleasure. Drift wondered what possessed women to have their picture taken like that? Why expose yourself like that, just for men like Kelvin to get off on?

Drift only knew Charlie's and Wilma's versions of women and sexuality. According to Wilma, that part of a woman's anatomy was for the miracle of life and for sacred pleasure, which every woman had the right to. And Charlie had told Drift bluntly, when she explained the facts of life to her, that a woman's pleasure was just as important as a man's during sex. So the very aggressive dark energy of porn made no sense at all to Drift. She wondered how men could even like it and not see their sisters or mother belittled by it?

Drift had seen premmie calves slip from the springing pink folds of half-starved cows on the road. She never tired of watching the miracle unfold each time as the calf struggled to take its first breath, to totter and tumble, at last finding its tiny feet and the teat. She was amazed always by the determination of the exhausted, near-dead cows licking their baby dry, nudging her calf to suckle, driven by some kind of powerful mother force. The mystery of birth and of life passed on with blood and fluid and milk felt all-powerful to her. Why then did men like Kelvin turn the business of the passing on of life from one generation to the next into some sort of gritty mindless sex-fest? She was now deeply troubled. In the world she'd recently experienced, men seemed to have had no respect for women. Was that her father's truth when he wasn't being her dad? Was it Simon's? And Eli's? She felt bewilderment and fear swirl in her that she may not know the truth of men. Was her life so tainted now that she ought to be wary of them all? She glanced sideways at Simon.

He too had fallen silent, re-clenching his hands on the wheel and shifting uncomfortably in his seat. Drift was grateful when the radio at last picked up full signal and the comforting sounds of test cricket commentary filled the police car for the rest of the drive.

*

They turned off the Pinrush peninsula dirt road into Widgenup, rolling past the tired-looking double-storey pub and the squat shabby servo. The Widgenup main drag looked the same, but for Drift everything she had thought about life had changed forever, so even the town felt different somehow. Simon pulled the car over opposite the store. The window was cluttered with writing that Shaynene had clearly added herself in bright pens like a kinder kid. *Media crew special: coffee and a toasty $6. Fresh made Surfer Sangers $7.*

'Bit of a pit stop,' Simon said as he switched off the engine. He nodded to the public toilets in the tatty park with its rusting space rocket and dangling chains for one absent swing.

'I might go grab a bite,' Drift said, looking at the Widgenup Store across the road, desperate to get out of the car, and away from him. 'Want anything?'

Simon shook his head and ran his hand over his lean stomach. 'Been eating too much bacon by the beach. Catering is always over the top on police campouts.'

'Suit yourself,' Drift said, wanting to be warmer to him. She wanted to crack jokes to him about bacon and pigs and police. She wanted to be flirting, stirring him up. Seeing him blush. But after all that had happened, Drift felt unhinged. Like she didn't know herself at all. In that space, there was no room for flirting. He waited until she'd slammed the door. The remote-locking system fired.

'Meet you in a minute,' he said, his face blank and businesslike.

*

The shop door jangled. Head Bob let out a screech from where he sat perched on the potato-chip stand, nibbling the corner of a packet of Barbecue Samboys. On the counter Shaynene hastily unwrapped her legs from around the scrawny body of a man who was standing, leaning into her, kissing her neck. When they pulled apart from their snogging, Drift was disappointed to see it was Gup. Shaynene, flushed with lust, took a moment to realise it wasn't just another customer.

'Drift Wood! Holy snap! What the flock are you doin ere? Shit bricks, look at your face!' screeched Shaynene, tugging her denim shorts down and lobbing off the counter.

Gup grinned at her, adjusting the erection in his boardies. 'Hello, Drover girl,' he said in a slimy tone. 'Been bucked off by a bull?'

Drift looked at him with distaste.

'Ha! Just joking! We heard you'd been raped and pillaged and left for dead! Whole town's talking.'

Drift masked her distress, pulling an unimpressed face at him. Shaynene gasped, leaning in to stare at Drift's injuries.

'Just what did you hear?' Drift asked coldly.

'Well,' Shaynene began, 'Kelvin called in here on the way back from unloading your cattle. Said some stockman got to you on the road.'

Drift saw red. 'Kelvin was the arsehole who did it,' she said.

Shaynene recoiled in surprise. 'No, he *never*! I knew he was a sex-crazed old flirt, but I thought he was harmless. Didn't think he'd have it in him! He must've popped a Viagra!'

'Don't joke, please,' Drift said, touching her face. 'He sure does have it in him. If it hadn't been for Eli coming when he did, I —'

'Eli?' Shaynene asked curiously, ever the gossip. 'Who's Eli?'

Drift felt her face tingle pink. She was *hopeless* at lying. She'd never lied in her life. 'Oh nobody,' she said, waving her comments away as if to erase them in the air. 'Just one of the stockmen. He works with the guy, Serge, who found me.'

Shaynene didn't seem concerned about details. She only wanted to hear boy/girl gossip. 'Have you got the hots for him? This Eli fella? Or is it the other one?' She studied Drift's face.

Drift felt a prickle of concern and despair that Shaynene was so caught up in this she didn't seem to see just how banged up and broken she felt.

'You have! I can tell! What happened to your hot cop?'

'He's around.'

'Ooo! Ride one, lead one,' joked Shaynene. 'I like that idea.'

'Oi,' piped up a disgruntled Gup.

Shaynene lunged at him and grabbed his crotch. 'Never you mind, young man. I'm a one-bloke woman,' she lied.

'I thought you'd still be at the beach,' Drift said, trying to change the subject.

'Meh! We bailed,' Shaynene said. 'Those up-themselves pro-surfer bastards ditched poor Gup. Said there wasn't room for him on their private plane. So we hitched home. Didn't we, darls,' she said, glancing up at his dopey-looking red-cheeked face.

Drift would have normally been amused that Shaynene was besotted, flushed and pash-rashed by such an unattractive, shallow marionette of a man. Up close he really was a dead ringer for Pinocchio. Drift suspected he shared the same habit of lying too and his nose ought to be a foot long.

'Wasn't Wilma meant to bring you back?'

Shaynene shrugged, not an ounce of remorse. 'Ol' duck loves me. She'll forgive me. Shit, is that the time? Boss'll be back soon. Been hard to get work done round here lately.'

She winked at Gup, then lugged a box of sports drinks to the fridge and began to throw the bright lime-green plastic bottles into place on the metal racks. She squinted distrustingly at the bottles. 'How can people drink this healthy shit? Looks like friggin anti-freeze. Give me a straightforward no-bullshit cola any day.'

Drift stood at the counter looking at her and almost raised a chuckle over Shaynene thinking sports drinks were healthy. She watched Shay slam the fridge door and stomp on the cardboard box.

'I got something for ya, Drift. Just give me a sec.' Shaynene carried the box out the back of the grimy store, booting the flyscreen open, marching to a big skip bin overflowing with other recyclables. Drift and Gup followed her. Flies in the shade of the shop buzzed.

'That dirty lying old bastard, Kelvin, eh?' Shaynene said, frisbeeing the cardboard up and over. 'He sure made a mess of you. And to *lie* about it. Fuck him. And fuck it's hot out here.' She looked up at the vast sky. 'I need a smoke.' She fished her phone out of her back pocket and looked at the time.

'Fuck,' she said again as they followed her back inside. Walking through the supermarket aisles Shaynene swivelled the front door's sign around so it read *Back in five minutes*. Drift couldn't see Simon at the car yet. She figured he'd know where to find her. She followed Shaynene and Gup into the side room where the staff made their cups of tea and tore the tops from out-of-date newspapers and magazines to send back to the printers. Shaynene flopped down on a chair and thrust the window open with the toe of her sneaker. She lit up a ciggie and dragged on it, puffing out the window, then jabbed her middle finger in the air at the sign on the wall that said *No smoking*.

Gup joined her, pulling a cigarette out of the box that she'd shoved in her top shirt pocket, groping her breast on the way. 'Grrr,' he said to the tiger tat, 'I love your big pussy.'

Drift rolled her eyes.

Shaynene, holding the cigarette half outside with her bright red long plastic nails, nodded to the bench top. 'I kept 'em for ya.'

'Kept what?' Drift asked, following Shaynene's gaze to a microwave piled with magazines and newspapers.

'Us makin the news. Our fifteen minutes of fame!'

Shaynene gave a delighted smile, got up and dumped the stack on the table before Drift.

'I sticky-noted the pictures you can see us in,' she said, pointing excitedly to the images of people gathered at the beach, the long lens probing into the faces of Kai's surf mates, and Drift standing beside Simon. The caption read, *Who is this mystery cowgirl and why is she being interviewed by police? Could this be Kai Kaahea's final fling before his disappearance?*

Drift now looked at Shaynene, who only paused from talking when she was inhaling on her smoke.

'They reckon you bonked him before he went missing! Ha! The shit they make up. But lucky bitch, just them thinking that is rad! He was *so* hot.'

'Oi!' protested Gup.

'But not as hot as you, my sexy man.' She ran her hand up his skinny leg, inside his shorts. 'But you have to admit he was good looking.'

'He was a red-hot mess more like,' Gup said. 'And a snob.'

'More of a mess than you?' Shaynene said pointedly to Gup, who looked instantly sulky. She held up the cover of one of the glossies to show Drift a close-up of the stunningly good-looking Kai Kaahea. The headline read, *Is our Hawaiian Honey gone for good? Exclusive pix!*

Drift took in his shaggy dark hair. Angled cheekbones, cleanshaven jaw, and the lovely deep brown eyes creased slightly by a white-toothed smile. There he was. In full colour. His beautiful face staring up at her. *Eli.*

'Oh my God!' she said, stunned. 'It's *him*!'

'What?' Shaynene asked. She searched Drift's face.

'Yeah? What do you mean?' Gup chimed in, as he took in Drift's shocked expression.

'You look as if you've seen a ghost,' Shaynene said, looking from the magazine to Drift. 'You mean you've seen him? Kai?'

'*No!* It's nothing.' Drift shook her head. 'Nothing. It's just I didn't realise how good looking he was.'

Gup narrowed his eyes at her. 'You sure?'

Heat prickled Drift's neck. 'As if … I've never seen him in my life.'

'Well, he looked like an ape last time I saw him,' Gup snarled. 'He'd grown this wolf-man beard. Pissed his sponsors right off, but he refused to shave it for them. Arrogant bugger.'

'Beard or not, he was still hot.' Shaynene began to lay the magazines out on the bench as Drift's cheeks flamed. She noticed Gup was still staring at her.

'Fuck, look at that body!' Shaynene said, tapping the nail of her index finger on the picture of Kai's bare chest. 'Imagine if you had actually got to do him.'

'Will you give it a rest?' Gup said. 'He's not all he was cracked up to be. He was a total man slut and he was on the way to being drug-fucked. He woulda died from an overdose or herpes anyhow.'

Shaynene sneered at him. 'You're just jealous! You can't die from herpes, and you and I both know you're the biggest pill party boy that ever walked the streets of this busted-arse boring town. But I still loves ya.'

As Shaynene lunged for her fella for another deep kiss, Drift felt the room swirl. Man slut? Drug-fucked? The cigarette smoke was making her feel queasy. She stared at the photos. Pages and pages in all of the major gossip magazines. It was all laid out before her. She saw clearly it was the same man. Kai and Eli. *The same person.* Suddenly Sophia and Serge's secrecy and panic all fell into place.

Just then the shop bell rang out. Shaynene's head dropped back in frustration and she closed her eyes. 'Fuck me!' she said, releasing Gup. 'Arsehole customers.'

She marched out, saying loudly, 'Can't you read? I'm on a break.' There was a pause. 'Well hellooooooo, Officer Simon.'

For a moment Drift's eyes lingered over the image of Kai. She traced her fingertip over his beautiful face, his dark eyes smiling into the camera. Judging from the big gold trophy he was holding, he had just won some kind of world championship.

Despite the smile, Drift knew this was a man holding a sadness within. One so big he must've just staged his own drowning to escape it, and then gone on to think about really taking his own life. She became aware Gup was watching her closely.

'You sure do look like you've seen a ghost,' Gup said.

She shut the magazine hastily. But there Kai was on the cover again. She flipped it over.

'Maybe you know something I don't. Nothing quite adds up with Kai and that morning.' Gup stepped closer to her. Drift's gaze fell to the dirty floor.

'I was the last to see him,' Gup continued. 'He was acting all weird. I told the silly bastard the currents weren't right. But he wouldn't listen to me. He wasn't the type to listen to anyone. He had an ego on him the size of the ocean. But something was fishy about him that morning.'

'Yeah, well I wouldn't know,' Drift said bumping shoulders with him as she limped quickly from the lunchroom, cheeks aflame.

Chapter 23

Chilly air-conditioning pumped from a vented box above Drift's head, making her feel nauseated, while bright artificial lights hurt her eyes. She was not used to being inside for so long, let alone seated in a chair. The ugliness of her assault injuries looked even worse under the harsh tubed lighting. Drift felt like a caged animal, defeated. She traced her finger over yellowing splodges that had begun to shape themselves into fingermarks on her arm. She could tell from his darting eyes that Detective Morgan missed nothing. She didn't know how much longer she could take this questioning. Her time at the hospital had been bad enough as the medical staff took bright flare photographs and probed her with swabs. And then there was the leering suspicion of Gup at the shop and the settling realisation Eli was Kai.

'Who did that to you?' Morgan asked again, his steel-grey eyes holding hers in a strong gaze as he nodded towards the bruising and cuts.

Simon stood behind him with a neutral expression.

'I told you. *Kelvin Waller*,' Drift said wearily for the umpteenth time.

'And who intervened to stop his attack?'

'It was Serge, the manager fella at The Planet.' Drift swallowed. She was putting on her stockman persona the way her dad did.

'Are you sure?'

'Sure as I can be,' Drift said, 'seeing as I was out of it.'

Detective Morgan paused. He let the slow tick of the clock behind her head fill the silence. 'We have witnesses saying Serge was nowhere near you at the estimated time of the attack.'

Drift felt a chill run through her. Where were Sophia and Serge now for her? 'I'm sure it was Serge,' Drift said, sticking to the only story she knew Sophia and Serge had told Simon.

Detective Morgan sighed loudly, running his hand over the back of his military-style haircut. 'Darling. I know you're messing with me.' He perched his backside on the desk, folded his arms and leaned his face close to hers. 'I just can't work out why.' He leaned nearer to her and almost whispered. 'The police escort transporting the surfers out said Serge had been speaking with them from the homestead co-ordinating the plane's departure at the time of your attack. He couldn't have been anywhere near you on the property's boundary at the time you say.'

Fear poured through her as he studied her face. Maybe she ought to just tell them? Just spill the beans that Eli had found her. *That Eli was Kai.* It was all there to be told. She'd then be able to go on back to camp, drove her cattle and be done with all this. She could settle back to life with her dad and forget she'd made any stupid wishes that life would take her on a different road.

She also wanted to make Kelvin pay for what he'd done. No matter how hard she tried to block it from her mind, she had taken in what he'd said about her skimpy shorts and singlet. Now she felt grubby and tarty. She thought of the awful trucker magazines he pored over. How could she let him be right, saying she had asked for it. To be punished for walking alone like that on the road and then to get into his truck? And now here was this detective treating her as if she was in the wrong and it was somehow her doing.

'Remember, your answers are being recorded.' Morgan pointed to the device that sat between them. 'Don't lie to me,

Melody. I've seen physical injuries before on women like you. Was it someone else who did this and you're covering for him? Are you using Mr Waller as a scapegoat?'

Women *like* her? She wondered in horror at his tone. What did he mean *women like her*? And why was it *Mr* Waller?

'Did your dad do this?'

'*No!*' answered Drift quickly, shocked.

'Did you have a fight with him? We've had reports of some odd observations.'

'Like what?' Drift asked, affronted.

'That your father likes to dress up. Like a woman.'

Drift would normally have spluttered laughter, but she half-turned to Simon in horror. He wouldn't meet her eye.

'No! That was a joke. A trick I played on Dad. *It was Kelvin who attacked me!* Can't you do forensic tests or something? Can't you find my hat? My knife? It could have his prints on it. It was *him*!' Her voice was pitching higher in panic. Sweat beaded in the small of her back, despite the air-conditioning.

'Then why are the people on The Planet lying about who found you? Why did they delay reporting the attack?' Simon said, his arms folded across his chest.

She turned to him, incredulous. '*I don't know!*' She stopped and breathed in. 'Surely you can see Kelvin has injuries? Serge reckoned he took a swing at him and I'm hoping I did some damage to him when I was trying to fight him off. Like I said, I was unconscious.'

'If you were unconscious how do you know Kelvin has injuries? How do you know Serge gave them to him?'

Tears pooled in her eyes. She was the one being treated like a criminal.

'Kelvin says he radioed another trucker to say he'd been assaulted,' Simon added. 'The men at the meatworks verify his story.'

She glanced at Simon, hurt. He had *kissed* her. Now he was acting as if she meant nothing to her. 'Those meatworks guys are all in cahoots,' she said, frustrated anger invading her tone. 'They'd lie for Kelvin. They're all the same.'

The detective leaned forwards. His eyes narrowed. 'All the same, are they? Listen here, young lady. We know there's something missing from your story. We know you're withholding information.'

Young lady? What was this? Drift looked desperately to Simon. His eyes slid away from hers. She buried her head in her hands.

'I'm not good with new situations,' she said, almost crying. 'I'm not good with people.'

'Yes, I can see that,' the detective said wearily as he turned his pen on end.

Drift felt another wave of nausea.

'What was his truck like?'

Drift shrugged. 'Awful. And hopefully with a cracked dash where I kicked the shit out of it.' Her head still throbbed and her ears rang. She could remember clearly the blue curtains and the porn stuck up in the sleeper. Ever since she was little she'd known every make and model of truck that flew by on the road, so she would be able to detail every aspect of Kelvin's truck, including the busted electrics on his wanky Christmas lights and the fact it was a twin-stick transmission shift, but she just couldn't find the stamina to deal with this man any longer.

Morgan shook his head slowly and let out a slow breath. 'You are not doing yourself any favours, Melody.' He stood opposite her, arms folded, then he leaned his knuckles on the smooth surface of the table, causing the sinews on his muscled arms to tighten. He pitched towards her so his face was close. She could see the wide pores on his nose and the coarse hair of his eyebrows. 'Don't muck me around. I know you aren't telling me something. Your father is covering something up too.'

Drift looked to her lap. She thought of Eli in the bedroom. The feel of his hand on hers. She remembered the kindness of Sophia and Serge, the energy of The Planet. But despite this,

Drift felt a rumble of disquiet. She recalled the shock of seeing Eli as someone else, a missing pro-surfer world megastar and party playboy plastered all over the magazines and newspapers. Gup's words haunted her. Drug-fucked. Man slut. Surely the Eli she knew couldn't be the same person?

This, she reasoned with herself, was no time to be sentimental about a man who clearly lied big time. She inhaled. She decided she would tell the police now about Eli. Bugger Sophia and Serge. She wanted the pressure off. She looked up. She opened her mouth to speak, but there was a sudden rap on the door and a young policewoman entered. She had a long face and slanted eyes and the menacing air of a Doberman.

'Not being too hard on her, are you, boys?'

Detective Morgan looked daggers at her, yet the woman seemed not to notice his senior-officer stare.

'Remember she's still concussed. The doctor said to go easy. Your time's up with her,' she barked.

Drift searched for eye contact from Simon, hoping he would give her the tiniest of reassuring looks, but instead he was gathering up papers and busying himself with the silver tape-recording device. Next Drift was being ushered out of the bland room by the woman, feeling a sense of vertigo.

'If you don't mind, can I sit outside?' she pleaded.

The young copper looked at Drift's pale peaky face, concerned. The last thing she needed was vomit on the police-station floor. She knew as the only woman on duty she'd be the one made to clean it up.

'Of course.' She spun on her shiny shoes and gestured for Drift to follow. 'It's where the faggers sit,' she said, pushing open a back door that led to a small car park. She blew out a breath at the stifling heat. Drift saw a couple of plastic chairs beneath some straggly gums that sprinkled patchy shade onto the police cars, lined up side by side.

'It'll do for fresh air, I guess,' the officer added. 'He's an arsehole that one.' Drift knew she was referring to Detective

Morgan. 'It seems the old-school boys can still get away with things out here. I'm sorry about him.'

Drift shrugged as she went to sit on one of the grubby chairs while the cop began closing and chaining the high gates of the car park. They were surrounded by a fence fringed at the top with barbed wire. Great, she thought. They've yarded me as if I'm a common criminal.

The policewoman saw her watching. 'Not that I think you're going to do a runner. It's more to keep others out. We get a few dodgy types hanging out by the river. They sometimes come and bum smokes off people who sit out here.'

Drift looked to the closed-off face of the young officer. She wondered if she ought to tell her about Eli. Or Kai. Being in trouble with the police was not something she ever wanted to have happen to her. But something stopped the words coming. The face of Sophia and her genuine pleading came to Drift's mind, along with the face of Eli. His loneliness. And what she knew now was his pain. Confused, Drift put her head in her hands, and flinched when she touched yet another sore spot on her scalp, her mind racing for ways to get herself through this. Ignoring the flies that gathered in lines on the wounds that were now drying and already beginning to heal, she decided she would ask for a miracle of some kind. But all she kept thinking was that the name Eli, when you moved the letters about, also spelled *lie*.

When she looked up, the policewoman was gone.

Time passed. She shut her eyes and let the sunlight fall onto her eyelids. Then she did something she wasn't prone to do. She prayed. She prayed to God, or whatever it was that drove this life. She prayed for help to arrive. She thought of Wilma who had tried to teach her prayer was actually linked with quantum science and there was now data to show how it worked. At the time she hadn't understood, but now she knew she had to reach deep inside to believe she could change the outcomes of her life.

'Thank you,' she said aloud, 'Divine Universe, Goddess, Mother Nature, Holy Spirit, holy shit … whatever you're called. *Thank you already, in advance, for your help.*' A magpie warbled nearby. She sat. More time passed. Then she heard the screen door open. She looked up. It was Simon. Surely he isn't a miracle, she thought, frustrated.

'I bought you a sanger,' he said, dragging up a chair, sitting beside her and handing her the plastic-wrapped sandwich. 'Ham and cheese. Didn't think you'd be a vegetarian.' He smiled gently at her.

Drift took in the way he had slicked his hair back off his high forehead with some kind of gel. She smiled back at him and even though her heart was swollen with guilt and her mind buzzed with anger towards him, she felt a surge of gratitude.

'I'm gunna have to head back soon,' Simon said, hitching his thumb in the direction of the car they'd travelled up in together. 'They're going to let you go now. But they'll probably want you in again tomorrow. Is there anyone you can stay with tonight? Or shall I book one of the motels for you? Your dad said he had no choice, couldn't leave the cattle. Said he was really sorry. Is there any message you want me to give him?'

Drift saw the way his shy brown eyes darted to her face, then away. He was wearing blue police-issue pants that stretched over his long lean legs. His black belt held all the police-business items attached to it. The badge and the neatness of the clothes he wore signed off on the fact he came from a totally different world from her. After seeing his coldness in the interview room, she now wondered what the truth of him really was. Was he a lie too?

Drift bit into the sandwich and looked to her lap as she chewed despondently, thinking over his question. What to tell her dad. Who to call. She looked at the dropped leaves beside her boots. Insects had eaten away the paper-thin flesh so that all that remained of each was an intricate pattern of lace. She thought of Wilma, who lived here in Cooperville. She sometimes stayed home, working at the library, but Drift knew she'd gone north on another run.

The only other people she knew in Cooperville were the dodgy mob from the abattoir and Kelvin. She wondered where Charlie Weatherbourne was. Charlie and Wilma were the only people she wanted right now. They had been the ones who had been there for her when her dad had tried to kill himself, the moment they heard. She *knew* they'd come to her again once the bush telegraph reached them. But *when* was the question.

'I think both my friends are away,' Drift said.

'OK,' Simon said, standing up, 'I'll make a call and drop you off at some accommodation. It won't be flash.'

'You've seen how I live,' Drift said. 'It will be flash by my standards. It'll have reliable power and running water, to start with.'

They smiled at each other. She was already wondering if he had the intention of coming to see her at the motel before he left again for Widgenup and the Point. The thought jangled in her head. But, just then, the screen door at the back of the police station creaked again. This time, when Drift looked up, her face lit with delighted surprise. 'Charlie Weatherbourne!' she said ecstatically. 'Thank God!'

'Yep, here I am, larger than life. Who needs a knight in fucking shining armour when you've got me?' Charlie said drolly, standing in her self-made leather riding boots, well-worn blue-checked western shirt, her long grey plait hanging over her shoulder — a bit like a female version of Willie Nelson.

'Wilma tracked me down. Said you were in a bit of strife. C'mon, girl. I got a truck waiting for you and a ton of rugs need stitching. There's a bed of sorts for ya until we get this sorted.'

Drift glanced at Simon almost apologetically, but Charlie hauled her up by both hands and enveloped her in a warm hug, and Drift knew her prayer had worked. Her miracle had arrived.

Chapter 24

Charlie Weatherbourne parked her saddler's truck beneath a clump of lazy roadside trees.

'Ah, home sweet home,' she said as she climbed down from the cab. Drift jumped down from the passenger side with Charlie's boof-headed blue heeler, Gearbox, following.

The sides of Charlie's solid oblong truck had horses painted on it in swirls of black ink and the renowned CW brand stencilled on the doors. As the sun sank, the Cooperville traffic on the highway towards Perth eased.

'This'll do,' Charlie said, surveying the area and opening up the side door. Gearbox invited himself in first and settled in a fuzzy heap beneath Charlie's wonky chair. On the bench was a strip of leather, a work in progress, half punched with perfectly lined-up holes. A box of tools was nailed to the workbench next to a big stack of books Charlie was always delving into. The timber surface of the bench was scrawled with pencil notes in Charlie's old-style hand. Some of Drift's paintings from earlier days hung pride of place over the workspace, making Drift feel even more sheltered.

Drift always loved happening upon Charlie's truck on her travels, but never had she been so delighted and so utterly relieved to see her friend as today. She settled herself into her normal spot on a stool beside the bench. 'Want to put me to work?'

'Of course. Busy hands will take your mind off what that man's done.'

Charlie noticed how Drift tensed. She moved over and lay her hand on Drift's shoulder. 'Ah, dear girl. Keep reaching your mind out past them stars out there where your spirit is, Drift. Then no one, especially the likes of Kelvin, can touch you down here on Earth.'

Charlie began flipping through her battered notebook containing the names and numbers of people wanting repairs.

'Start with this one,' Charlie said, handing her a saddle blanket. 'Leather banding needs to be restitched. See?'

Drift nodded, glad life felt back in balance for a moment as she began to thread one of the two ancient but solid sewing machines bolted to the bench. As she did, Drift recalled the excitement of seeing Charlie's truck for the first time.

It had been a hellish day, the air heavy with heat. She and her dad had spotted the Hino pulled over at a truck stop under a dappling of gumtree shade. As Drift approached the back of the truck she saw a person bent over their work, with a blue heeler lying at their boots, lip curled in a growl. Drift had gasped in shock when the thin person sat up and turned to her. Charlie Weatherbourne was a *woman*! How could she have not known? For a moment Drift found it impossible to comprehend that the legendary saddler was a woman.

Charlie Weatherbourne called out a greeting with a raspy voice like dust. Lines crinkled her face as she smiled in welcome. Her teeth were worn, and some missing, from decades of biting on thonging as she plaited stock whips, and held fast thick thread in her teeth. Her tannin-stained fingers were bent at odd arthritic angles from the ruthless forcing of needles through thick hide over the years.

'Well, I'll be,' her dad said, taking his hat from his head. 'It's Charlie as in Charlotte, I assume.'

Charlie snorted a laugh. She knew what was what. It wasn't the first time her legendary status had been masked by the wrong gender.

As her father went to their truck to get a saddle and other

gear for repair, Charlie had stooped to Drift's little-girl level. 'What's your name?'

'Melody, but my dad calls me Drift. I thought you were a man.'

Charlie's blue eyes sparkled. 'Is that so, my little cowgirl? Ah … they say it's a man's world. But not in my world. Not in this Charlie's world. I've been looking for an apprentice. Maybe one day, when your dad's done with the road, you might like to make stuff with me in my truck?'

At the time, Drift had felt her heart lift with purpose and potential.

In the truck now, she felt a certainty returning to her as she pedalled the machine into gear and began to stitch. The prospect of work steadied her. Kelvin wouldn't come near her now, not with the police involved, and not whilst she was here with Charlie and Gearbox. She had dreaded the thought of a lonely motel where her thoughts would've run wild. She could see herself lying awake in some bland room that smelled of commercial cleaning products, wondering if Simon would knock on her door. Or not. Or if Kelvin knew she was in town, would try to find her again.

Now, in the cluttered truck, she felt buffered and safe with the familiar surrounds, wrapped up in the rich smell of tanned leather and the sweaty smell of horse gear. What was also present was Charlie's love and concern for her. She saw it in the way Charlie gazed at her fondly and with compassion from over the top of her glasses.

Throughout the years Charlie had taught Drift all she could about life, horses and leather, showing her how to make the best cuts out of one piece of hide, the way to use a needle, and a block to punch holes easily and how to prep the heavy-duty sewing machine.

'The thing about life and work is,' Charlie had begun, one afternoon, dragging her old bent glasses down over her long elegant nose to look at Drift, 'we're meant to follow the seasons.

Particularly us girls. Work is good, but understand there's a rhythm to it. Sap in the trees slows in winter for a reason. You don't wanna work flat out in the darker months. It goes against nature. That's the problem with people now. They don't realise they're out of rhythm. Forever chasing the money god. That's why most of them drug 'emselves on telly or their dumb phones, or pop their pills to make emselves numb to their pain. It's coz they don't live by the seasons, or by the sunlight. You 'n me, girl, we're the lucky ones. We get up with the sun and go to bed with the moon on the rise. When you do what you love at the pace you need, life just rolls on. Ain't nothin out there in the world outside yourself that can make you feel truly alive. You gotta stoke up that big campfire inside yourself and don't let no one dim your flame.'

As Drift now recalled Charlie's lesson from long ago she again wondered why she'd wished her life to change. Grass is always greener, she thought as she looked to the comfort of the familiar tools secured to shadow boards with leather thonging so they wouldn't be jolted out as Charlie drove to remote stations for repair work and saddle fittings.

'When I was little,' Drift said to Charlie now, as she threaded a needle, 'I heard all about you from other people, but for about a year Dad and I could never find you on the road. I thought people had made you up. I used to think you were some kind of Saddle Santa who turned up, fixed stuff in the night and went away again with no one seeing you.'

From her wonky office chair cobbled together many times with baling twin and thonging and covered in a wool pack, old Charlie spluttered her mirth. 'Ha!' she said. 'Saddle Santa, eh? Well I'll be.'

'I was so excited to know you were real. Even better to discover you were a woman. And that you're here now, right at the moment I need you most. You really are my Saddle Santa, Charlie! I don't know what I would've done if you hadn't turned up today. Thank you.'

Charlie looked at her with her clear blue eyes that seemed ageless and wise. 'It wasn't my doing. It was yours. You *believed* I would show up. Most folks say seeing is believing, but the world actually works the other way around. What you believe will always come to you one way or another. Good or bad. Do you believe you are alone and the world is against you? Or do you believe you are supported and the world wants you here? Either belief is true. It's up to you to decide which story to live by. You done good in knowing I would turn up.'

'I prayed you would.'

'The trick with praying is to be grateful for it already happening, even when it hasn't. So, here I am. Now you see me!' Charlie said with a smile. With a deft swing of a rubber hammer on a wooden-handled punch, she stamped her CW mark into the rich brown hide she was crafting into a stirrup leather. It was like a full stop to her lesson, so Drift continued on with her mending in silence.

After a while, Charlie pointed at Drift's belt. 'Is that old thing seeing you through OK?'

Drift looked down to the belt and shuddered. If it hadn't been for her CW belt, Kelvin would've surely got his ugly penis inside her. It was a thought too horrible to bear. 'Yep. It sure is.'

'Want a new one?'

'Nope, I love this one,' Drift said, hooking her thumb under it.

'Need any more holes in it to expand it a bit?'

'Nope.'

'You ain't eatin enough then, girl. A woman ought to have an appetite like a wolf. Live voraciously like a wolf.'

'Really?' Drift said, thinking of Shaynene's constant diets and judging herself against the weight of other women, and whether men would like her based on how many kilos she was.

'Really. And if you ask me for more advice — which I'll give you anyway whether you want it or not — it's always remember it's ol' Charlie hitching up yer daks. When you're past this business with Kelvin and get your eye on the blokes, don't drop yer daks for just any old dickhead. He's gotta be a good man. Respect ya.'

Charlie saw the cloud of pain cross Drift's face.

'I know you've got off to a rough start with men who behave more like wild bloody animals,' Charlie said gently. 'Rougher than most, but you have to believe with all your heart in what you want. Believe it and you'll see it. Works with attracting good men as well as it does with attracting good horses or good dogs.'

Drift's fingers again roamed to the belt. She'd used it many times as a hobble on a drove to set aside a horse that wouldn't ground-tie. She wore the leather strap about her waist every day, loving the feel of it with its metal rings and brass buckle. She loved the way how, over the years, Charlie had had to alter it because she was growing up. How it began to fit snuggly above the new curve of her hips, the buckle lying comfortably against her stomach like it was part of her. She considered for a moment telling her about the surfer masquerading as a stockman. Or about the policeman who had kissed her. But Charlie was on a roll.

'That bloody Kelvin. He once even had a crack at me!' Charlie said, lifting an eyebrow and delivering a wry smile. 'Fancy that, wanting to violate an old chook like me.' She snorted. 'He's a devil of a man. If it weren't for ole Gearbox here, he would've got me.' At the sound of his own name Gearbox flopped his tail in a lazy wag from where he dozed.

Drift felt her skin prickle at the thought of Kelvin.

'I just have to keep reminding myself, old Kelvin is a sad old bastard who thinks he's entitled over women just because he has a set of nuts. Poor old bugger has forgotten about love with a capital L. He's got a soul full of fear, and it's fed by a world that is powered by hate.'

'So are you saying I should forgive him?'

'Yes. Absolutely. Forgive his soul, but don't accept his actions. Did he get his old fella into you?' Charlie asked. She looked at Drift with such sympathetic eyes Drift felt emotion escalate in her again. She shook her head.

'No. Thank God,' Drift said. 'Though if it wasn't for your belt, he would've. It held me safe. And if it wasn't for —' She thought of Eli's surprise arrival. Kai, she corrected herself.

Charlie's perceptive eyes didn't miss a trick. She hitched her chair closer. 'Tell me, Drift,' she said, reading her face, 'what's the matter? What really happened?'

Drift looked levelly at Charlie and drew up her courage within. It was time to tell all. She knew she could trust Charlie. With a deep breath, Drift began her story. Charlie didn't react how she had imagined. There was no response of amazement that the missing surfer was not missing at all but hiding. She seemed to accept Drift had been rescued by Eli who was really Kai, and that Sophia was covering for him and that she'd seen a ghost girl in the dune grasses, as if she were hearing news about the everyday. Instead, when Drift was done, with slow deliberate action, Charlie stood up. She went to the long cupboard that ran above the area in the truck where she slept.

'I know it was your twenty-first recently,' Charlie said.

Drift wondered how this was in any way relevant to what she'd just said but then Charlie continued.

'I've kept something for you. To give to you when the time was right.' Charlie reached into the top cupboard and pulled down a beautiful hand-made wooden box the size of a shoebox, with a curved lid and tapered sides.

'Here,' she said.

Drift received the box between both hands, but wondered why Charlie was giving this to her now. She looked at the warm tones of the wood and the artful dovetail joinery. 'It's beautiful.'

'It's rosewood. I made it years ago. For another girl.' Charlie's voice was unusually soft. Drift opened the lid that was hinged with delicate silver chains. As she did, Charlie kept speaking.

'I was going to wait until a time in your life when you were settled and maybe had a bloke and even a little one on the way, but I figure you need to believe it before you see it. You need to see, after Kelvin, that you'll get past your experience with that awful man. You need to *see* yourself, *believe yourself*, in a future with a loving partner. Don't let bad men taint your future. A family is your calling. I've seen you with animals. You'll be a good mother. A good, wonderful, aware mother. The most powerful, important work a woman can have. This I know.'

Drift searched Charlie's face. She'd never heard Charlie sound so warm and tender. Her wisdom was often delivered with rough dollops of dry wit and humour. But not today.

Drift opened the lid of the box, intrigued but also rattled by Charlie's words. She'd often told herself she would never have children. There was always that cloud she'd turn out like her own mother. What if, when she had a baby, she ran wild and mad in her mind like her mother had? What if she grew cruel and taunting towards the man she settled with, like her mum had been with her dad? She held her breath as she lifted up the tissue-wrapped parcel within, undoing it carefully. Folding back the paper she saw a beautiful white cotton dress with delicate white stitching. She held it up. It was a child's size. Drift gasped. It was *so* familiar. As if she'd seen it before. It was *just like* the dress the girl had been wearing. She felt goosebumps rise on her skin.

'It was Rose's,' Charlie said quietly.

'Rose?'

'My daughter.'

Drift felt a jolt of surprise. She hadn't known Charlie had any children. She'd never mentioned her past. 'I didn't know you had … that you were a mother?'

'Yes, once, I was a mother. I had a daughter.' Her voice cracked a little. 'She died. A horse kicked her.'

'Oh, Charlie, I'm sorry. I had no idea,' Drift said, tears springing to her eyes.

'Oh, my dear, it's just life.' She waved her hand, but her eyes held deep grief. 'We're born into this crazy dream we call life and we walk our road and then, eventually, we return home. She just went home before me. I'll see her again. I'll see them both.' Charlie, eyes moist, reined in her emotion with a sigh.

Both? Drift wondered.

'I wanted to show you this ...' Charlie pulled out a worn old photograph from a drawer beside her bed. 'That's us.'

Drift looked at the photo. She saw a young Charlie with long blonde hair cuddling up to an Indigenous man with cool '60s Elvis-style sunnies and groovy sideburns. Between them stood a little dark-haired girl in the dress from the rosewood box.

Charlie tapped the photo. 'That's Rose. That was our girl.'

Drift sucked in a breath. She peered at the photograph and realised the life Charlie could've had, if she'd been dealt a different hand.

'She died when she was just six, but she's still here with me. I feel her. I feel them both.' She placed her palm on her chest. 'Lionel went too a few years after. Car accident. But he and she are here. This I know. They say we come back, over and over, to learn the one lesson.'

'And what's that?' asked Drift.

'That love is all there is,' said Charlie simply.

After refolding the dress reverently and setting the box aside, the women began cooking their meal together in silence, the gas burner hissing steadily as the steaks sizzled.

'Charlie?'

'Mmm?'

'Why is it, even though I have love, that I still feel I don't belong in this world?'

Charlie set down the fork she was holding and looked at Drift. 'What makes you say that?'

Drift shrugged. 'It's just lately. Like, that cop today, the detective questioning me, he treated me as if I were ... somehow, *dirty*. He made me feel like there was something wrong with me.'

Charlie snorted. 'Darling girl, it's a white man's world, and he's one of 'em. He doesn't see you as a person because he doesn't know how. Same as Kelvin. Think about it. All those fellas have grown up being taught a man's version of a women. They've had men at the front of churches in their long frocks, tellin us all that women are sinners cause we lust out of wedlock and bleed every month. And for years the fellas have sat there and listened and believed it too. And then they've had all them teachers and parents tellin them that girls are sugar and spice and all that, yet on the telly and movies it's tellin men that women are sluts and objects. Then there's the fancy-pants educated medical doctors telling the world there's something wrong with women's bodies just because we're female. That there's something to be scared of just coz we have tits. That cop you saw today is no different to Kelvin and a lot of blokes. He's shaped by a sick culture. It's no wonder you don't feel you fit here, Drift. How can a woman truly fit in a world like this one?'

Drift felt a rumbling. Charlie stood square to her.

'You have to create your own world, girl. Don't believe any of their bullshit. If you're open to the world that you want, and you read the signs, hear the spirits, hear what the Earth is saying to you, you can make a good life. You're already on your way. You're already open to what it is to be a woman, on your own, away from the hype. But you gotta be brave. Make a whole new world. Head high, and fuck 'em all!'

Charlie's blue eyes flared. 'Trust me, I've had to be brave, especially without my Lionel and my Rose. The number of times I've been called a lezzo or an old maid for living on my own. Or a witch for healing a horse with plants! I'd always turn up just at the right time for someone when they're in need, and they'd get creeped out by it. As if there was something wrong with me. I was only following signs and living with my loved ones who no one else can see or feel. But say that sort of thing out loud and people look at you all funny. It's been a dangerous thing for a woman to talk honestly and follow her instincts. We remember the stonings and the burnings. The men do too. They know they are afraid of our power. So, often we women don't say nothin. We shut ourselves down.'

'So you think I should tell the cops tomorrow about Eli?

196

Um … Kai? Or will they somehow pin it on me? Like they did with Kelvin?'

Charlie thought for a moment. 'Why should you protect this Kai person? He's some bigwig surfer with more money than sense, isn't he? So why should you keep his secret for him?'

Drift pushed her plate away. 'Mmmm.' She twisted her mouth in thought.

'What does your heart say?' Charlie pressed.

'My heart?'

'Yes,' Charlie said. 'Your heart. Not your head.'

Drift watched as Charlie stood and arched her back. She gathered up the plates and went to the sink of the tiny truck. An image of Eli's face lit by firelight flared in Drift's mind. 'My heart says keep the secret. Don't tell.'

'It does?'

'Yes.'

'Why?'

Drift paused. 'Just because,' she said, remembering the safety and calm she'd felt with Eli and his comforting touch that first night in his swag. 'I guess it's not my secret to tell. And I think, that first night, I saw the truth of him. I *felt* his truth. And it was good.'

Suddenly Gearbox was on his feet barking, his hackles up, and then there was a jarring knock on the door. Charlie, grabbing up Gearbox's fancy leather collar, swung the door open. There stood Simon looking utterly different in jeans and a neat striped shirt. His polished RM Williams boots shone in the feeble light that spilled from the truck.

'Hello,' he said. 'I'm here to see Drift, um, Melody Wood.'

He glanced nervously at the dog, who was curling his lip. Charlie eyed the young man, recognising him from the cop station that afternoon. She caught the scent of his deodorant, laid on a little too thickly for her liking. She saw how buttoned-up and nervous he was, so she put him out of his misery straight away.

'Sure. She's here,' she said in a friendly tone.

Drift came to the door. She wasn't sure how to react. He looked so different from the night of her birthday, when he'd shown up at her caravan door. Maybe it was his uniform that made him extra good looking? Now in his civvies he looked a little bland and biteless. Not like Gearbox, who was still having to be restrained, baring his yellow teeth, barking. Drift saw how the old heeler would've been a match for Kelvin. He was famous for taking chunks out of horny old station workers who came calling on Charlie in the dead of night once they'd sunk enough rum for courage.

'Oh, stop it,' Charlie said to Gearbox. 'I'll just take him up to the sleeper and tie him near his basket. He's always in gear, this bloody dog.'

With Charlie and Gearbox gone to the front of the truck's interior, Simon looked up to Drift.

'I'm off duty at last,' he said.

'I can see that,' Drift said, feeling resentment rise in her for his behaviour today at the station.

'Would you mind if we had a word?' he asked softly, nerves colouring his cheeks red.

'I think he means in private,' Charlie called out from the sleeper, pulling a 'go on' face and waving them away.

Reluctantly Drift, barefoot, stepped out onto the gravel, hoping he wouldn't start asking her all the same questions over again. A lone car travelled past, its headlights glancing off the white guide posts.

'I'm so sorry it's turned out like this,' he said.

'Turned out like what?'

'Well … you know. I was hoping to ask you not just for one dinner, but lots.'

Drift saw the vulnerability in his face and felt empathy rise. 'Why can't you still ask me?'

'I can and I can't. Not while there's an investigation.'

'Investigation? You're treating me like I'm the one at fault.'

'You're not … It's just things aren't adding up.'

'I'm done with talking about it,' Drift said, hurt. 'It's not fair you come here at night to question me. Can't it wait until tomorrow?'

Simon looked at her apologetically. 'I'm not here to question you. I came to see you. And to tell you I've pulled a few strings. I've talked to the detective. He was way out of line with you this afternoon. He knows it. He's going to question Kelvin again. I'm headed back down the peninsula to get some more evidence. We're impounding Kelvin's truck and instructing him to stay in Cooperville and most importantly stay away from you.'

Drift felt a chill run through her.

'They've agreed to let you go back to camp in the morning so you don't have to go into the station again. We'll keep investigating, but I've asked them to leave you out of it for the most part.'

Drift didn't know whether to feel grateful or angry. 'For the most part? What do you mean?'

'I know you're hiding something. Information.'

Drift looked deep into his eyes and tried to hold an innocent face. 'I'm not,' she said, thinking of surfer Kai, or the stockman Eli, or whoever, whichever, he was. *The lie.*

'OK,' Simon said, 'I trust you.'

Stepping forwards, he reached for her hands. She could feel his palms sweating. She could feel her guilt making *her* palms sweat.

'I really like you,' he whispered, 'and I'm sorry this has got messed up and mixed up.'

Drift wanted to say back to him that it didn't seem like he really liked her today in the police interview. But she refrained. Part of her wanted to fall into his arms and to shut out the rest. Part of her knew it was guilt that kept her from holding his hands back with any feeling.

Even though her lips were sore and still puffy, and her eye swollen and black, Simon stooped over and gave her a warm, hesitant, nervous kiss.

'Ouch,' she said, pulling back and touching her fingertips to her split lip. She smiled shyly at him, but inside was furious with herself. This was not the time to be starting anything with Simon. She was *lying* to him. All because of dumb surfer boy.

'I'm sorry,' she said, looking to the ground, 'I don't think I can do this. Not with everything. You know ...' She indicated her facial injuries.

'Of course, I understand,' he said, squeezing her hand gently. 'We'll take it slow. I still think you're beautiful, despite all that.'

Drift's mind swam, searching for some kind of anchor of thought. If it hadn't been for Kai/Eli she'd be bursting at the seams with excitement over this lovely, stable, sensible local cop, even with her awful experience with Kelvin so fresh in her life. Damn you, Kai Kaahea, Drift thought, as she turned away from Simon.

'Good night,' Simon said, looking at her as she climbed into the truck.

'Goodbye, Simon,' she replied a little coldly before shutting the door.

Chapter 25

Almost a month later, Drift sat on old Bear watching the land on Pinrush Point fall to flat grey tones, the sun sinking into the sea. A February full moon was on the rise, gently doming over the scrubby horizon. In the muted light, Drift set the dogs on the long chain to block up the cattle for the night, and as she did pain scrunched her heart that Dunno was absent from the team. The cattle, full and fat from a day on fresh coastal scrub and grasses, were mostly camped, chewing their cud, so Hamlet and Molly wouldn't have much work to do. The herd was now into the groove and the routine, comforted that water and tucker were plentiful and the leadership from the humans was kind and consistent.

As Drift ambled back towards camp, Bear began snorting down for the day, dropping his head, drooping his ears, knowing his work was done. Apart from Simon taking her to the site where Kelvin had attacked her, she'd spoken to no one but her dad for weeks. Wilma and Charlie were off on their trails again, and Drift's visit to The Planet seemed like a past dream. As she rode she looked at the property stretching out beautifully beyond the fence. Sophia and Serge had called into camp once with a giant basket of fresh vegetables and the thickest cuts of NY steak, apologising for all Drift'd had to go through with the police on Kai's and their behalf. Then they'd left, saying they'd be away travelling for a few weeks. More global regenerative farming work, this time in New Mexico. She'd accepted their apology and decided to just get on with her life.

Drift was still ever hopeful that her Dunno dog would come running out of the scrub to greet her, or she might glimpse the blue-shirted surfer stockman amidst the trees.

The memories of the surfer stockman were constantly in her mind to be wrangled and roped and pushed away. Eli, she felt drawn to. Kai, she felt repelled from. To her they were separate men. Neither truly real. The man on the white horse in a blue shirt had been a mirage after all.

Her trail of thoughts led her to Simon. Unlike Kai/Eli, Simon was *real*. But Drift had seen two versions of him too: one as a potential nice boyfriend, the other as a rigid, cold policeman. The stress of the questioning room rushed over her again. Bear's hooves clopped along steadily as Drift realised she'd thought this way every day for the past weeks. A tangle of what felt like three men. It was time for a new mental track, she vowed. Drift twined her fingers through Bear's mane and concluded it was best she simply stuck to her animals. The rest seemed like too much trouble.

Another few weeks and the herd would be fattened enough to truck out. There was new contract work after that and they'd need to find a new working dog, but Drift knew she would miss the rhythm of the drove — up before daybreak, breakfast scoffed, horses saddled, cattle bellowing happily for their calves to follow them onto fresh feed. Her dad too was buoyant again, for now, busy with stock water runs on sections of the route where there were no waterholes, bringing tucker and tea for Drift, delivered cheerfully. She hadn't mentioned leaving him again. She hadn't dared. In a way, the past few weeks had been nice. After the recent turmoil, Drift loved the fact the only sign of human activity lately had been planes flying off in the distance and container ships, like tiny floating Lego blocks, far out to sea.

As the campsite came into view, Bear picked up his pace. Drift frowned when she saw a car was parked next to the van. Her father was talking to a group of people. Five in all. As Drift rode up, Shaynene gave a hesitant wave. This time she had turquoise hair and wore jeggings that burgeoned over her thighs like two blue jellybeans. Next to her, in the usual brand-name over-sized boardies that highlighted his matchstick legs stood Gup, his face determined. Then Drift noticed the fury in her father just as a cameraman swung his lens her way, filming her arrival.

'This is a load of shit, Shaynene,' Split blurted, irritated. 'You're not only invading our privacy but also contributing to the mindlessness of the masses. Will you get those scum-dogs to stop filming!'

A shiver ran through Drift. She knew what this would be about. She breathed in deeply to gain control of her expression. She rode right up to the guy with the camera, forcing him to back away from the giant Bear, almost walking over the top of him. Bear, curious to see if the boom mike the other man held might be tasty, stretched out his thick neck and with his big boxy head and his inquisitive lip began to nuzzle the fuzzy cover. The men retreated from the imposing horse.

'What's going on?' Drift asked in a matter-of-fact voice.

Shaynene stepped forwards, gushing, 'Hey hot chick.'

Drift looked at her coldly. 'What is going on?' she asked again.

Shaynene put her hands on her hips. 'I know you know something.' Her eyes narrowed accusingly.

'Yes. We know,' Gup quickly added, sneering like a primary-school kid.

'Know something about what?' Drift said as she swung off the horse, loosened his girth and took up one of his reins.

'That you're hiding something.'

'Hiding what?'

The interviewer, a middle-aged man in an open-neck white shirt that stretched over the makings of a beer belly, came forwards, proffering a business card.

'Michael Delang, Channel Seventy-Six. *What's the Truth?*'

'What do you mean, what's the truth? What's the truth about what?'

'No. That's the name of the show. *What's the Truth?*'

'Oh,' Drift said, looking at him as if she'd discovered dog crap on her boots. She was utterly furious Shaynene was creating her own soap opera in their stock camp. 'The truth? My truth is I'm tired, I'm sore, I'm thirsty and I'm sure my horse is the same. Dad? Are you right to run water and tucker down to the dogs? I'll do hay.'

Her dad looked up at her with a grin. She had even surprised herself. She decided she would be the unbendable Drift. The Drift who would not be swayed from the road that she wanted to take. Sometimes she knew that woman was in her. Sometimes that version of her shrank. But today she was out in full force, her emotions swelling with the moon. She was over this drama. Head up and fuck 'em all, as Charlie had said. Seeing the predatory narrow eyes of the so-called journalist, his arrogance and unease, she felt a simmering rage that he was invading this place and their camp.

She glanced at Shaynene, for the first time seeing she was more than just a harmless local gossip. She really was putting negativity into the world, even if it was under the guise of bawdy humour. As for Gup, he was like the ticks on her dogs. A parasite. She walked quickly past them, leading Bear as her dad saluted her.

'Roger that, Captain,' Split said, making for the dog dishes and biscuits stored at the truck.

Drift walked purposefully to the horse line and the hay bales. The horses whickered. The camera operator followed her closely. She swung Bear about, his big disced hoof catching the sound guy's shoe so he stumbled.

'Oops,' Drift said. She began to take off Bear's bridle and draw his halter over his head.

Michael Delang stood a wary distance from the giant horse. 'Your friends here suspect Kai Kaahea has staged his own

204

disappearance and you know he's hiding on the property known as The Planet owned by oil baroness Eloise Madden, or who we now know as Sophia Gaier,' he said in news-interview tones as the man with the mike recorded him, then swung the boom to Drift for her response.

Drift glared at Shaynene, but remained tight-lipped. The boom swung over Delang again.

'We also know it was Kai who saved you from being attacked by a local truck driver. Where is Kai now?'

Drift cast him a sarcastic look. 'Are you bonkers?'

The journalist looked over to Shaynene, who rushed forwards.

'Gup and I seen the look on your face when I showed you them magazines at the shop,' she said with an urgency. 'We seen you recognised him!'

Drift looked at Shaynene. The camera zoomed in, capturing the exchange. 'Has he put you up to this?' Drift indicated Gup.

'I knew something was up,' Gup said. 'Kai had been acting odd the whole trip, and it was him who insisted we come here. Here where he knew Sophia.' Gup was loving that the camera had now swung his way. 'You know he has connections with The Planet and I'd say they've planned the whole thing.'

He pointed accusingly at Drift, so his leather bands jiggled around his skinny wrists. His expensive brand-name sunnies pushed his dark red curly hair up in a ridiculous way. Drift noticed Shay's new bling cowgirl boots and salon nails of glittering turquoise to match her hair. Shaynene only ever had her nails done like that in Cooperville if she came across money.

'You've sold your story, haven't you?' Drift said.

There was an awkward pause.

'So, what if we have?' Shaynene blustered. 'Head Bob wanted a new cage,' she tried to joke.

Drift wasn't taking any of it. She swung Bear's rump around again so he almost wiped out the cameraman, clipping the horse to the nightline. If she ignored them like flies, they could stay all they liked, but they just couldn't rumble her. She dumped her saddle in the storage beneath the stock truck and began filling the hay nets.

The journalist persisted, but Drift just kept brushing his questions off as she got on with her evening routine. She was not going to cave. She was not going to reveal anything. These were the sleeping people Sophia had talked about. She could feel Shaynene's energy waning and doubt creeping in. Maybe she was thinking they'd have to pay their money back if there was no story. But Gup followed her about, egging her on.

'Will you just go?' Drift eventually said.

The cameraman closed in on her.

'Or what?' Shaynene replied. 'You'll call the cops? *Your* cop?'

'Don't be ridiculous,' Drift said. 'There's no need for cops. It's all just a big drama in your head, Shaynene.'

Shaynene's round cheeks flushed pink. 'Well it's too late. Your cop is coming already. They're going to do a raid at The Planet tonight.'

Gup stepped in front of Shaynene. 'Shush, babe. She doesn't need to know that.'

'Well, what can she do? You'll be able to watch both your cop and your surfer boyfriend on the news,' Shaynene said, baiting her. 'Oh, no, but that's right. You don't have a telly. You're a homeless bum who thinks she's above everyone else because of your brainy father and all them books.'

Was she that hungry for attention? Drift wondered. She tried to reach for Charlie's wisdom about forgiving others who are in pain or fear, but nothing came. All Drift felt was fury and Shay's betrayal. Then a radio crackled to life in the four-wheel drive.

'Delang, you copy?' a voice said.

The journo dived inside the vehicle. 'Yep. Go ahead.'

'Cops will be there in ten with a search warrant. They've gotta open the gates.'

The journo turned to her. 'We'll catch up with you later.'

'I don't think you will,' she said and watched as they all scrambled for the car. Shaynene shot her a glance that held no warmth and no apology. No wonder her dad had kept them in such a reclusive life. Most people were dickheads.

Her dad, arriving back in the LandCruiser from feeding and watering the dogs, nodded towards the departing car. 'What now with those clowns?'

Drift shrugged, trying to remain nonchalant. 'They reckon they're going to bust the missing surfer on The Planet.'

'Really? *A fool doth think he is wise, but the wise man knows himself to be a fool.*'

'This is not the time for Shakespeare, Dad,' Drift said, frustrated. 'C'mon. Let's crank up Gerald and go find some tea.'

As she opened the door of the caravan, Drift felt her stomach turn. Ought she go warn Sophia and Serge? Were they back from their overseas trip, even? Should she cut the fence and ride her horse in ahead of them? It would be a dead giveaway if she did. Kai or Eli or whoever he really was could be miles away by now. What was he to her anyway? She looked up as her dad walked in. Despite her resolve she asked, 'What should we do, Dad?'

He looked at her sympathetically before answering. 'When in doubt, do nothing. Do absolutely nothing. Let go and let good.'

Chapter 26

An unbearably hot night and a blindingly bright full moon had Drift in a tangle of sheets, unable to sleep. The chainsaw snoring of her father in his bed behind the hanging curtain didn't help. Nor did the knowledge that at The Planet tonight Sophia and Serge had been invaded by Shaynene and her media pack, along with Simon and his colleagues. She wondered if they'd uncover Kai, camped somewhere in the bush. Or was he far away now, somewhere else in the world? Even home with his parents? Drift drew back the curtain to look at the silver-glow view from the caravan window above her bed. Outside, the moon was lighting up the whitecaps. The dunes glowed luminescent. Silver grasses wavered. Drift thought she saw a flash of white, off on the beach at the water's edge, and sat up, straining to see. Was it the girl again?

Sudden wind shook the van and Drift drew in a sharp breath. She got up and made her way outside. The sea breeze felt pleasant on her skin. Barefoot, she walked over the gravelly sand towards the beach. She stopped at the edge of the dunes when she noticed the horses on the nightline. They were standing, heads raised, ears alert, all looking in the direction of the stock truck. She turned to it. In the shadows, a dog began whining frantically … not in distress but in joy. Like a rocket, it ran towards her in the darkness. At first she thought it was Molly or Hamlet who had got off the running line where the cattle were camped, but as it dived out of the shadows into moonlight Drift let out a cry. 'Dunno!'

His entire bean-shaped body danced in a wag as he leaped before her.

Drift sank to her knees, receiving him into her arms. 'Oh my God,' she cried. Burying her face in his fur she felt a wash of joy and relief. As she stroked his barrel side, her hands met with a coarse line of stitches that ran in a long row, puckering on shaven skin. She winced and pulled away and in the dimness tried to look closely at the healing wound, puzzled as to who had stitched him so neatly.

A voice came from the shadows. 'He's one lucky dog.'

Drift looked up and there, framed by the full moon, was a tall slim figure. She had to stand up and move sideways to see him properly, but she knew already who it was.

'You!' she said, not sure if she was meant to be overjoyed or angry with him. Kai. Eli. *The lie.*

'I thought he was a goner when I first found him,' Kai continued, 'but The Planet's vet, Daisy, is a genius.'

Drift searched his bearded face in the moon's glow.

'Were you ever going to tell me the truth?' she asked.

He fell silent. He hung his head.

'About who you really are?'

'I'm sorry. I wanted to bring your dog back to you first, so you might forgive me for being such a mixed-up idiot,' Kai said, his eyes pleading.

The images from the magazines raced in her mind, of him caught by flash bulbs stumbling out of nightclubs, with women hanging off his arms, bottles in his hands, looking bombed out …

Kai squatted down next to Drift. She felt his nearness as if butterflies fluttered over her skin. Dunno shoved his nose under Kai's hand for a pat. Drift could see by the way the dog leaned into him that they had formed a solid bond. The doubts she'd had about this man's character wavered momentarily as she watched her dog's connection to him. Drift knew her animals could read people better than she could. She felt confusion roam within, not knowing if she ought to open up to him or not. He'd brought her dog back, hadn't he?

'I wanted to tell you sooner,' Kai said.

'What? About the fact you found my dog? Or the fact you're a famous pro-surfer who's turned the world upside down by staging your own death?'

Kai looked downcast.

Drift felt the living warmth of Dunno beneath her hands and relented. 'I'm not used to talking to celebs, and I'm not used to lying to police on their behalf.'

Kai grimaced. 'Look, I'm sorry about the police, but that's just it, isn't it. Celeb. I never wanted that other shit that surfing came with. I just wanted to ride waves and see the world.'

'Really?' Drift challenged him. 'Did you hate that surf life so much? You were forced to party and do drugs and sleep around and lie? I saw the papers.'

Kai closed his eyes. She saw his jaw clench. 'I know what it looks like. Some of it's lies. But the part that's not, I carry that shame every day.' He opened his eyes and looked directly at her. 'You know where that shame took me. How I almost —'

Drift remembered something Charlie had said after Split's suicide attempt. 'Let's get this straight,' she had said. 'There is no past. There's only *your memory* of the past. Don't hold on to that dark moment with your dad any longer. Otherwise you'll punish him forever. Meet him in this moment, like you would a horse.'

'A horse? What do you mean?' Drift had asked.

'You only give a horse a chance when you forget his history. If you meet your horse in the moment, then you're no longer thinking of the time he bucked you clean off, or swung round to bite you. If you do saddle him up with those past crimes, then you'll always be wary of him and he'll be wary of you.'

Drift had nodded. 'Makes sense.'

'Horse sense is the same with people. Treat them like they have no history — especially when it's history that's hurt you, and let them be by not bringing the past into the moment of now. Then life moves forward more easily for you.'

Drift sighed, knowing that to live by Charlie's ways was challenging, but the old lady was right. Kai clearly had been in so much pain and so lost in the past, but in this moment, right here, right now, he was making amends. Wasn't he? She decided to trust Charlie's wisdom and reached out and laid her hand on his forearm.

'I'm so grateful to you for finding Dunno, and if I'm truly honest with myself I'm really glad to see you. But, you, this whole situation, scares the shit out of me. I can see how you're desperate to start again.'

Kai looked suddenly hopeful, vulnerable too, as a small smile arrived on his face.

Drift looked down at Dunno, sitting between them. Meet him in the moment, she thought. 'So where'd you find him?'

'I borrowed one of the dogs from The Planet. We followed a blood trail and sniffed him out. We weren't sure he'd pull through … and then, well, he did and I wanted to tell you. But … you know now how I'm lying low … things have got a little crazy. It's —'

'I know,' Drift interrupted. '*Complicated.*'

He smiled at her, grateful she was making a joke.

She was struck again by how farm-boy beautiful he was. This time he wore a khaki workshirt and dusty denims. He looked every part the stockman and nothing like the cleanshaven pin-up whose image was splashed all over Shaynene's magazines.

'You shoulda heard the jokes though when they were patching him up!' he said, his face lighting up at the memory. '*Dunno* if he'll live or die. *Dunno* how Drift will go without him. *Dunno* how we can get a message to her without raising suspicion.' He massaged behind Dunno's ears. 'All The Planet people have been spoiling him rotten. Eh boy?'

Dunno thumped his tail in the dust and Drift saw how Kai's strong but slender brown hands touched the dog. In an instant she was reminded again of the feeling of his hands when she'd been lying in his swag. There was truth in his touch. She could read he wasn't what the media had made him out to be, and even if he was, it was now his past. Suddenly she wanted to touch him.

'Thank you,' Drift said, laying her hand over his. Something in her fired. She looked deep into his eyes.

'It was my privilege,' Kai said. 'He's a beautiful soul of a dog.'

'He's a lifesaver,' she said softly.

Kai looked at her hopefully.

'Hey, speaking of lifesaver … I could use a huge favour.'

He paused. Drift waited.

'Could you take me on … here … in your camp, as Eli?'

'What do you mean? Take you on? You mean hide you?'

He inclined his head in the direction of The Planet homestead that lay to their north-east. 'The hype has started to die down, but there's been media drones and spotters all over the place nosing into what goes on at The Planet now. Sophia has had enough. Just having me about stresses her out, so I thought maybe you could use a hand … you and your dad. By way of an apology. Just till the dust settles. Would that be OK?'

He watched Drift's face as she absorbed his question.

'So you do mean we hide you and hide the truth from the police? *Again.*'

She watched a muscle in his jaw flex.

'Look I know I've been an asshole. To a lot of people, including Sophia and Serge. Including you. If you want me to stay, I'll help — I'm here. If you don't then that's fine too. It's just your dad told Sophia how low he'd been lately … more than you might know. I thought …' His words faded.

Drift closed her eyes knowing deep inside she wanted someone else around because of her dad.

'I want to make it up to you. Prove to at least one person on this planet that I'm not a completely selfish ass.' He looked pleadingly at her.

Drift frowned as she took in the full extent of what he was asking. 'But what if they come looking for you here again?'

He grimaced. 'I know. I don't want to land you in it again with the police but they're monitoring every plane that's coming and going, so I can't fly out just yet. But if you aren't prepared to risk it, I can leave, right away, now.'

Drift looked at his sincere expression as she weighed up her options, thinking out loud, 'They've already hounded me and I guess, now we're this far down the spit, they'll be less likely to go off road and come back to hassle us again —'

Kai butted in. 'I'll work like a dog for you and your dad. I promise.'

She smiled at him, the decision to allow him to stay settling in her like warm rain.

'Like a dog, eh? I hope you'll work harder than this dog,' she said, scratching Dunno's ruff. 'He's got a reputation for being lazy.'

Kai chuckled, patting Dunno affectionately.

With the silent stars above, and in the stillness, save for the wash of waves, excitement rose in Drift. She could spend time with him. Get to know him better. She knew her father's answer would be the same too. Split would be eager to pay him back after the business with Kelvin, and for bringing her little mate back.

'And just one other thing,' he said, taking hold of her hand and shaking it up and down. 'From now on, I'm Eli. OK? I'm done with the other.' His vulnerability was laid bare in his face and Drift squeezed his hand back.

'Of course,' she said, 'Eli. C'mon, let's get you settled in.' She hauled him up.

'I'll just grab my stuff.'

'Stuff?'

She followed him to the stock truck, where he dragged out a saddle bag. Then he reached inside again for a bedroll.

'You knew I'd say yes,' she said, giving him a friendly shove.

He grinned back at her. 'Well no, I didn't, but I kinda hoped you might.'

*

Later, with Eli settled under the stock truck on his grass-matting bedroll and the added comfort of Drift's swag, she lay back down in her caravan bed. Unsurprisingly, sleep would not come. Drift looked to the moon that was sliding through the night sky. She felt her body aching all over. She checked in with herself, wondering if she was stressed, or sore from long days in the saddle, but then she realised the ache she felt was for one thing. For Eli.

Her dad rolled over, his snoring interrupted for now. As she felt the hot sheets grip her skin, she swore under her breath at the longing she felt. The sweat beneath her breasts trickled over her torso. She tried to force the window open further to get some respite from the heat. The illuminated numbers on the clock ticked over. It was almost midnight. The breeze had dropped altogether and the seas had calmed. It wouldn't hurt to cool off in the water on Minty, would it? On hot nights like this she normally dragged out the swag, but she knew that perfectly gorgeous boy, the stockman Eli, would be lying on hers right now. Quietly, she got up, telling Dunno to stay where he slept at the foot of her bed on a saddle blanket. She couldn't wait to surprise her father with him in the morning. And then again surprise him with Eli. Drift opened the van door, stepping out onto the earth.

Barefoot, she went to the tether line and unhitched Minty, drawing the rope over her neck and fastening it to her halter for reins. She led her away towards the dunes and the water beyond, the grey moonlit beach still warm from the heat of the February day. Soft sand squelched as she and Minty made their way over a small rise, the view of the ocean spreading out in an inky black swathe. It sparkled with the light of the moon. With relief, she walked into the inviting water, leading the mare. Phosphorescence on seaweed had her hypnotised as she trailed her fingertips through the dark water. Small waves broke rhythmically. She breathed in the beauty of the night and the knowledge he was *here*. And would be for a while, if he wasn't discovered. She waded in, Minty snorting happily, relaxing down into the cooling water. Waist deep, Drift dragged herself up onto the mare's back and out they swam, the white horse plunging forwards and striking her legs out when her hooves lost touch with the sandy bottom. Drift felt power course through her. As she turned for shore, she looked back at the glow of the milky white beach. There he stood.

She smiled at the strong figure, bare chested, wearing only board shorts. She swam Minty to him, riding up to him, halting before him. He laid his palm on Minty's dripping shoulder and looked up at her with his deep brown eyes.

They held each other's gaze, a current running between them.

'Can't sleep?' he asked.

Drift shook her head.

'Same. So … aren't you going to offer me a dink?' he asked, not taking his eyes from her. He took the rope and guided Minty over to the bleached carcass of a driftwood log. Suddenly his bare foot was stepping up on the limb and he was slinging his leg over Minty's back, up behind Drift. She felt his hands slip about her waist, the warmth of his body pressing against her spine. She melted into him, into the moment. Then she told herself to get a grip, to not rush things with this complicated man and his complicated recent history. On an impulse, she whorled the mare around in a hindquarter spin, then whipped her the other way so Eli, laughing, had to grip both Drift and his legs to stay seated.

She caught the flash of Eli's white smile as she half turned. She saw how he sat astride the horse and knew he would stick, no matter which way she bent the mare.

'How do you know she won't buck you off?' Drift said, laughing too, trying to break the intense feeling his closeness was triggering in her body.

He reached round to stroke Minty's rump with his divine brown hand. 'Because you love me, don't you, girl,' he cooed to the mare.

Minty, as if in answer, stopped and half turned her head, nodding into the rhythm of his massaging scratches.

Drift smiled. 'First you win my dog's heart. Then my horse's ...' She left the rest of the words unspoken, knowing that over the passing of the days, he was about to win hers, no matter how hard her head tried to steer her away from him. She turned Minty back towards the water and they waded in up to the mare's knees.

'I thought I saw the little girl tonight. Just before you arrived,' Drift said.

He leaned towards her ear and breathed a warm whisper. 'She's drawing us together. Like the moon draws the tide. Because without each other, we are both lost at sea.'

There was a jokiness to his tone, yet he looked serious. His breath was warm in the seashell turn of her ear. Momentarily she sensed the genuine energy of his pain and his loneliness.

'Ready?' he asked as she felt him fold his arms more firmly about her waist. Despite herself, Drift felt a throb of desire at his warm breath on her neck, and the weight of his body against her back. He nodded towards the far end of the beach-crescent.

'I'm ready,' she answered.

With that, Drift sprang the mare into a canter and soon they were gaining speed, galloping over the beach, the grey disc of the moon above them, laughter trailing behind them on the marble-like sheen of the sand.

*

Later, with Minty's breath pushing their legs out rhythmically, they walked back to the caravan. Drift halted the mare on the line. They slid from her and waited for her to roll. Eli helped Drift give each horse a handful of hay, the moonlight now casting long shadows in the hillocking sand.

'That boy there, he'll do you nicely,' Drift said, indicating the tall lanky white horse, Roger. 'I tend not to use him as much as the others. He's not my type. A bit hyped for me. But he could be yours.'

Eli went to the horse and spoke softly to him, running his hand over his neck. Roger responded instantly, drooping his ears and leaning into Eli's palm. Drift found herself wishing the caresses were over her body. She thought of the swag beneath the stock truck and a craving settled inside her. As Eli moved over to straighten the noseband on Minty's halter, he stood near Drift. She looked up at him. He looked down at her. She willed him to kiss her. For a moment, she thought he would, but a glimmer of uncertainty crossed his face.

'Well, I'll see you in a few hours for work,' Eli said, friendly but a bit cool again — like a mate. 'Thanks for the midnight ride. Wouldn't want to wear out my welcome before I've been welcomed though.' He indicated the caravan where her bear-like father rumbled. 'I'd better not keep his head-drover awake a moment longer.'

'Good idea. Good night,' Drift said, half disappointed but mostly grateful he was taking all the pressure away. 'Welcome to the exclusive Pinrush Point droving team. Where free poetry and verse and black comedy is provided.'

Chapter 27

The days merged into a rhythm that made time seem irrelevant. All there was for the droving crew of three was *the present*. The rising of the sun, the grazing of the cattle, the motion of the horses beneath them. The endless comedy of the dogs, the humour and community of the horses, cows and calves. The tick and hum of summer-happy insects. The setting of the sun. The blooming of the stars. The cooking of shared meals between Eli, Drift and Split. The sighing of tired bodies into bed at night. The crashing of midnight waves.

In the first few days, their watchfulness for the police and media had kept the three of them in a tense silence. Eli stuck to jobs with the machinery and equipment near the truck, in case he had to hide. But as the days passed, there had been no sign of anyone else on the far tip of the meadow flats of the furthest section of the long-forgotten droving route. Even Simon hadn't shown up, so Drift assumed he was back to his normal duties in Cooperville. As they sat behind the cattle, he on Roger, she on Minty, stories from Eli's childhood emerged, bringing with them the vibrancy of island life and featuring ancient stories that absorbed Drift for hours.

As the days stretched to weeks, and the dogs working now for both of them, they made a steady, efficient team with as much stirring between them as she and her dad had once shared. The days were so long and hot, the workload so consistent, her dad so near, any sweep of romantic feelings from the first night had eased to companionship. There were moments, though, when Eli and Drift held each other's gaze for a fraction of a second too long. Drift was cautious. Eli was still battered by his recent past. Both were hesitant at crossing the line of friendship that lay clearly between them.

For Split, he could see the tension between the two, but he could also see the perfect fit. The sight of his daughter and the quiet strapping Islander lad tailing the cattle on two white horses had given him an extra boost. Having someone as hardworking and steady as Eli in his camp meant Split could at last tackle Gerald the generator and get him running less ragged. He had time too to service the ute a bit with the engine oil, grease gun and spare parts he had on hand. He swept out the caravan. Hand washed a few things and set them to dry on lines strung between wind-slanted gums.

In the evenings Split enjoyed Eli's company, questioning him about his family and his life on the island of Moloka'i. When Split heard he had parents who spent most of their time teaching regenerative agriculture on farms in America and travelling the world speaking, his interest and liking for the young man deepened.

It seemed to Drift that her father's visit to The Planet and Eli's stay had shifted him out of his slump. He barely stopped talking about Sophia and what he had seen there. It was as if he were waking up from a deep dark slumber. He wanted to share in Eli's knowledge of his parents' life work. To hear about the healing work his grandfather and grandmother did with humans and horses on their ranch. And he wanted to find out exactly what Sophia had done to turn a run-down, walked-off station into a thriving ecosystem and profitable food production and energy-source think-tank.

'It's what I've been looking for with Drift for all these years,' Split would say, on hearing more of the methods. 'Common sense. Wisdom. Integrous business acumen. There is a God!' Split would clap his hands together and pick up a magazine or a book and read out a quote that would round off and sum up their discussion perfectly.

'There's set to be eight billion people on the planet by 2024 and most of them live in cities,' Split said, 'and the people who are going to be in trouble aren't the poor ones in rural areas that the charities make the fuss over. Those are people who know how to feed themselves. It's the rich in the city who'll be stuffed when all the systems crash. They've forgotten how to feed themselves. They don't know one end of a spud from the other.'

Their talks were held over shared meals of slow-cooked camp-oven roo and baked potatoes. Bought supplies were getting low, but none of them wanted to burst the happy bubble they had found themselves in. It was too risky to go into The Planet to get fresh produce or up to Widgenup Store. Having run out of dog pellets, they simply shot the occasional roo for the dogs, and ate some themselves, Split teaching Eli how to prepare the meat. With the sea beside them, fresh-caught food was abundant. As Split kept saying, 'There are feasts to be found in nature if you know where to look.' Drift at last was relieved her dad was back. No more supermarket-packaged plastic crap. He was back to his self-sufficient self, making their food stretch as far as he could.

Today, as the cattle slowly grazed and Drift looked across to Eli, who was leaning on his saddle, deep in his own thoughts, she felt her heart swell. Their conversations led them to fascinating places and sometimes funny ones, and their silence filled her with a companionship so complete.

Earlier, they'd come up over a rise on the track and found an extra lush section of coastal meadow spread out before them. By mid-morning the cattle had settled to lie down and digest, chewing their cud lazily, reluctant to move anywhere. With the cows and calves in this full state, the workload eased. The expansive native grassland meadow would likely sustain the cattle for the next few days, so Eli dropped his reins and let Roger graze. Drift did the same with Minty.

Drift asked, 'What was life like?'

Eli glanced at her, a cloud across his face. 'When?'

'As an elite surfer.'

His jaw clenched. 'It was … OK.'

Drift could tell there was more to come, and she sensed him struggling with how to tell it.

'You know,' he said suddenly, the words coming in a rush, 'it was amazing at first. I was travelling the world, riding these fantastic waves, living how I wanted, and winning all these tournaments. And the more I won, the faster life got. Amazing hotels, room service for anything and everything you ever wanted … grog, drugs, like … lines of cocaine on tables when you'd get back to your room, and girls just … everywhere. Anywhere. They could be ordered like freakin pillow menus.'

Drift flushed and looked away, taking up Minty's reins, but Eli seemed to read her mind and grabbed them to stop her moving away.

'No, I mean … it was a shock to start with — for a farm boy like me. Exciting but awful at the same time, you know? Like I could have everything I wanted and more, but I knew there was a huge price to pay. My grandparents … they taught me well. I mean, they're so old school. They just about raised me because my parents were away so much, doing their work with Sophia and the rest of the regen network. For a time I stayed on the outside of it all, but then … I just … forgot everything they taught me. Especially their lessons about greed … and about respecting … respecting women.'

Guilt clouded his face. 'It was a journey that I took. I was very young when I began it. Too young.'

For a moment Drift thought Eli might cry. He laid his hands on Roger's neck, as if steadying himself.

'Mom called me when she heard some of the older surfers were busted with some underage girls. She said I was complicit in a male culture that was shameful. That being part of it but not doing anything about it made me culpable. It was one of the worst moments of my life. For my mother to see that.'

His voice softened. 'The truth hurts. I'm relieved it's over. I just miss home now. Miss them.'

His sincerity and pain were evident, but the party-boy photos reared themselves in Drift's memory as did photos she'd seen in the magazines of his beautiful grace-filled mother, and she felt the old tug of unease about him. 'Will you go back home soon?'

'I don't know. I don't think I can face my parents, especially my mother and grandmother.' He sighed.

'What are they like, your grandparents?' Drift asked.

He smiled. 'Puna and Tutu set up Horseheart Ranch on Moloka'i when my mom was young, after one of her teenage friends got caught up in drugs and overdosed. Horseheart is a place of healing for people. Ironic, really, given my stupid choices in life.'

Drift took in his words, visualising the images she'd seen in Wilma's books of Hawaii and how the verdant green plants seemed to slide right down to the impossibly blue Pacific Ocean.

'I know what you're thinking,' Eli said. 'That they run a rehab centre using horses as therapy and yet here's their own grandson, who ought to know better, shaming them.'

Drift shifted in her saddle and looked at him. 'No, I was thinking how beautiful it must be. The island. Paradise.'

'It is. It's a beautiful place.'

Drift wondered what it was about being young and not being satisfied with paradise, and always wanting *more*. She saw she too was in a wild paradise on Pinrush Point and yet she'd been yearning for *more*, just like Kai had.

'It's only stayed beautiful because my parents and Puna and Tutu were part of the island group who fought to keep tourism from ruining the place. My family, my community, stopped the big seed and chemical companies from taking hold of our farming there too. GMOs are banned. Chemicals, pesticides, herbicides — banned. They even have their own community seedbank. And they limit tourism so it doesn't trash the place.'

'It sounds amazing! They must miss you.'

A muscle flinched in Eli's jaw. 'I think I've let them down too much to go back.'

'No,' said Drift insistently. 'You're wrong. You must go. They'll forgive you.'

Eli looked out across the meadow, his eyes distant.

'I've shamed them.'

'But even still ...'

'My parents and grandparents didn't want the ugliness of the modern world to reach me,' he said quietly, 'so they were quite controlling when I was younger. I guess I pushed against that. Stupidly, I see now.'

Drift thought of her own father and nodded. 'I think my dad's the same as your family. I get it, what they wanted to protect you from.'

'As a teenager I guess I rebelled,' Eli continued. 'I began to take myself off to surf each night after school. I stopped doing my ranch chores. I started to hate my parents' fight — they were fighting these big legal cases against all kinds of companies, always speaking out against them, and it seemed crazy to me. Like they were wasting their time. Getting crucified by powerful people for no gain.'

Drift brushed away a fly. She could hear the frustration in his voice.

'I began to see money as the only way to have a say. I didn't want to live poor and powerless like my family did, scraping together donations for their campaigns. I saw how the big-name surfers who came to Hawaii with their sponsors had so much kudos. I believed it was my only ticket off the island. And then they offered me a big ad campaign for a soft drink ...' His mouth twisted. 'My grandfather was angry, so angry. Said the sea gods would be angry too. Surfing Mother Nature's waves for money was a crime to him. Selling sugar addiction to people was a crime also.'

Eli fell silent, and then Drift could see him make an effort to shake off thoughts of the past. 'Fancy a swim after work?'

he suggested suddenly. 'And maybe a fish in the ocean? Then if we're any good at catching one, can I cook you and your dad up some dinner on the beach?'

Drift glanced down to where Minty was picking at a green spray of lush plants in a ditch. She was suddenly reminded uncomfortably of Simon and his unfulfilled request for a dinner date in such a remote spot. She looked across at Eli, at his now familiar face. She told herself they were just friends. Good friends. There would be no future with him, not with a sordid past like his, despite how hard she tried to cling to the present of now.

She knew life's ocean would wash him away anyway, in time. He was a global guy. He was worldly, well travelled and well loved by women. Yes, he was in hiding, but he couldn't stay hidden here forever like she could. Time would move him on, perhaps to his old ways. To women who were more suited to him. Simon, on the other hand, fitted with her, she reasoned with herself. He had no deep, dark past. He liked being a local cop. He liked being in the region. Simon made sense. Kai didn't. She looked away across the ocean, narrowing her eyes at the glare, her heart beating a little too fast for her liking. Just friends, she told herself sternly, but then she heard herself say, 'Dinner? Yes, that would be nice.'

Chapter 28

Warm water fell from the bush shower onto Drift's wild-girl hair, causing her dusty, salty twists to unravel into silk. She frothed shampoo, massaging her scalp. From behind the blue tarp, strung from a gum, that served as a shower curtain, Drift peeked through the gap. She hoped Eli was still busy trying to resurrect the old fishing rods he'd taken out of the truck.

Normally, standing naked in the bush washing behind a tarp didn't bother her, but what if he could see her? She quickly rinsed her hair and slathered conditioner through it. She wondered why she was taking this much trouble when she knew she would be swimming in the sea later on.

Just friends, she said to herself sternly again.

As the last of the water trickled out of the solar bag, Drift stepped onto the wooden draining board, reached for her towel and dried off, putting on the new blue bikini Wilma had given her. Next she grabbed the denim shorts and singlet draped over an acacia. She pulled them on, looping her wide hobble belt though the keepers, grasping the supple leather in her fist to tighten it one more hole. She smiled, thinking of Charlie. Would Charlie consider Eli worth 'dropping her daks for'?

Drift felt a flush of embarrassment. Such keen anticipation flowed within her that trying to contain her thoughts was like trying to hold a beach ball underwater.

She began to drag an old plastic gappy-toothed brush through her hair, which took on the quality of spun gold as it began to dry, lifting in the breeze from her bare shoulders, the straps of her pale-blue tank top highlighting her tan. Gathering up her toiletries and stepping back into her boots, she almost skipped to the van, reefing open the door. A fly buzzed past her ear.

In the too-hot van she pushed open a window and went to her tiny single bed. The curtains hung for privacy across her bed had been freshly washed and re-hung. Her dad had even washed her bedsheets and put them back on, propping one of her old teddy bears up on a pillow. She smiled for a moment. The caravan had never looked so neat and clean. Good on him, she thought. He was trying. He was re-emerging. Again she thanked the blessing of having Eli with them. This change in her dad and their campsite was all due to having him around, and his quiet, steady ways. She'd watched how Eli and Split had sat, side by side one night, rubbing glistening oil into thirsty saddlery, talking.

'When I was young I just wanted to run away,' Split had said, recalling his Tasmanian childhood. 'I thought we lived dirt-poor out there in the scrub beside the sea, making sawdust for a living. Now, when I see these suburbs and cities, turns out *we* were the rich ones, tucked away from the world like that. I was a fool not to see it. Must be like that for you now? Looking back at your island?'

Drift had seen Eli's eyes glisten at the memory, Moloka'i — a place he'd described to Drift as a 'she', describing her with love; the island wrapped in her blue twisting currents in the channels.

'Yes. I've certainly been a fool,' Eli said hanging his head, 'and I do see it now.'

'Ahh, son. Don't wait for time to heal things. We all make mistakes. Forgive yourself instantly. I have to … over and over!' Then Split had put on his best King Lear voice. '*When we are born, we cry that we have come to this stage of fools.*' The men had resumed their cleaning in silence, one thinking of an island down in the southern seas, the other, a dot in the vast

Pacific. Drift had glowed within, being in the presence of her two favourite island men.

Now with her younger island man waiting for her, Drift tugged open a drawer, and rummaged through her things to find a tube of gloss that she smeared over her lips with her index finger. The shiny foil condom packet Shaynene had given her caught her eye. She picked it up and turned it over in her hand, before putting it back and shutting the drawer.

She opened the skinny cupboard door so she could see how she looked in the mirror. Checking her reflection was something she rarely had any need for. Drift noticed her father had wiped away the film of dust that normally draped itself, like mist, over the glass. In the clarity of light, she puzzled at her reflection. She recalled the magazine images of Kai with the most beautiful of women ... models, actresses and party girls in groovy micro skirts and done up to perfection like brand-new Barbies. The bold letters of the headlines shouting *MISSING SURFER PLAYBOY BREAKS HEARTS ALL OVER THE WORLD*. The collection of images of women he'd been reported as 'dating', including film stars so famous even Drift had heard of them, made her head spin. Doubt clutched her.

She looked at her freshly washed hair, shining in the light, and her full lips. Her long, tanned limbs gleamed with some moisturiser Wilma had recently given her. Did she look OK? She ran her fingers through her hair.

'You're so skinny you rattle,' Shaynene had once told her.

But how did others see her? In Drift's world, beauty came from the landscape around her, in the sheen of blue silver in a black-coated cow, the frozen jagged crystals of ice on a log, the intricacies of a spider's web made visible by gentle dew. Too often she thought of humans as ugly because of their ugly actions, like the unloved ugly houses she saw on the outskirts of towns, junk-filled yards and industrial landscapes that gave way to inflexible hard-lined cities and roads. Signs of human ugliness were everywhere once she left nature and the countryside behind. She

227

even found society's 'beautiful people' ugly as she looked at them in the magazines. They seemed to live from a place of narcissism.

She couldn't help thinking of Kelvin. He had seen her in a way she had despised, and it had made her feel she should wear baggy shirts and cover up her body so as not to draw that kind of ugly male attention to herself. But how did *Eli* see her? Drift felt another surge of uncertainty. She was determined not to let herself get swept away by comparing herself to other girls. Instead she told herself it didn't matter how she looked. As Charlie often said to her, it only mattered that she carried joy and gratitude in her heart.

As she opened the door to the most golden of evenings, there stood Eli on the brown soil, looking lean and tanned in denim shorts and a singlet. Barefoot, bucket in hand, rods held upright.

'Ready?' He smiled at her.

There, Drift thought, momentarily breathless, was something to be grateful for. Him. Now.

'Just a sec.' She half closed the door, swore under her breath, then dived for the drawer, grabbing the condom, shoving it in her pocket.

When she stepped out, she saw he must have found Split's and Harmony's old surfboards in the truck. Drift looked at them leaning against the trailer, surprised. The surfboards had been carted about all these years, and never ridden. They were banged-up bits of history, but her father had always resisted throwing them out. Her mother's board, once a gentle cream, was now vintage yellow, wearing fins from another era. The board's presence unnerved her a bit. It pushed Eli away, and brought Kai front and centre.

'Your dad lent them to me,' Eli said, sensing her focus on the boards. 'I'm kind of getting wave withdrawals. I hope you don't mind.'

Drift shook her head. 'Not at all,' she said, but something inside her tumbled. Her distrust of surfers, linked to her mother's disappearance, flared. Eli seemed so unlike those guys, she thought, trying hard not to compare him to the awful cluster of his teammates and the types her mother had hung with. He seemed so mild. Old fashioned even. Surely, after weeks working with her night and day, he couldn't *fake* that. Could he? A cold feeling ran through her.

As he took up the boards, he turned to her. 'You look beautiful, by the way.'

Heat burned her cheeks. 'Thanks,' she said, though in her mind she thought, *Liar.*

Chapter 29

The ocean sighed in and out, wrapping its constantly moving energy around Drift's and Eli's legs as they cast their lines out beyond the breakers. Behind them, above the tide mark, a red plastic bucket slowly filled with good-sized silver-grey tailor fish and mulloway as the hour passed. The waves were too loud for conversation, so Drift and Eli stood in silence, exchanging the occasional smile — or a whoop when the line jerked in a bow shape. Drift realised her internal monologue of uncertainty had evaporated the moment she'd stood near Eli on the beach. They had clicked back into being easy with one another, like friends would be.

As she inhaled the sea air, happy to be fishing, she thought how ridiculous she was being, comparing herself to the more worldly, glamorous girls Kai had hung with. Both Charlie and Wilma had told her she was beautiful and that her beauty came from within. Sometimes that was hard to believe, but on a day like today, she felt it. Standing there on the beach with a mate, fishing in the ocean. It felt good. As she watched the gulls dip and bob in the strong breeze, Drift concluded she loved her life. Every long, hard, natural day of it, especially now with fishing and good company like Eli's to balance the work. For the first time she realised she wasn't looking out at the water with that ache for her mother. In an a-ha moment, she saw that her mother's memory held an energy as restless as the sea. Not like Eli's solid, grounded company. Like the land beneath her boots when she walked the road beside Minty on long droving days. He seemed to be earthing himself in life too as the droving days passed. She looked over to him. He was staring at her. She smiled. He returned her smile. They held each other's gaze for a time. As the sun slid close to the doming horizon Eli flicked his head in the direction of shore.

'Shall we go?' he called during the momentary quiet of a wave's in breath.

Drift nodded, winding her line in, then wading for shore. In the bubble and fizz of the shallows she took knives and an old wooden chopping board from another bucket. She and Eli cleaned the blank-eyed fish, the gulls circling, keen for tossed knots of innards. Drift watched Eli's beautiful hands wash the blade of the knife in the bucket's salty water, the scales glistening like coins. He seemed at home by the sea, his bare legs washed an even darker brown, his feet slippered by sand. Again and again in each action, she saw his beauty. There was an inner beauty there too — maybe that dark shadow within him no longer lingered.

'Did you want a quick surf before we go?' He nodded at the boards. The disquiet in Drift rumbled. She looked at her mother's board sitting next to her father's. The old wetsuits lying in the sand like shadows. A wave boomed in the pause before Drift spoke, trying to hide the tension in her voice. 'OK. Why not?'

*

Surf crashed around Drift as the board popped out from the froth of a breaking barrel. The buzz from riding another wave until its last sigh made her laugh uproariously, the sound rising into the dusky pink and golden sunset fanning out above them. Eli arrived beside her in the tumble wash of bubbling water.

'You're a natural,' he said, laughing, flashing perfect coral-white teeth. He hauled the board back to her by the leg rope. There was the touch of his thigh in the water. A zing ran through her.

'Yeah, a natural at falling off! I haven't tried to surf since I was little,' she said, her mind casting back to summer sunshine-filtered memories of days at the beach with her mum and dad. She grabbed the board with her strong tanned hands and both of them hauled their wetsuit-clad bellies flat against the lumpy wax surfaces and together dived through the wall of another breaking wave.

'This one,' Eli said, nodding to an oncoming skimmer wave. It gathered itself up, and Drift moved forwards in a strong-armed paddle before propelling herself to her feet. Steering the board with a sure-footed grip and strong legs she flipped up onto the perfect lip of the wave. Wobbly and unsteady though she was, she had a brief moment of pure-bliss surfing, hearing Eli crying out his encouragement and celebration, before she sank into the water with a wide smile.

On shore, Drift swiped her hair back, licking the salty taste of seawater from her lips. Eli stooped to release the strap from his ankle before undoing hers. She tingled at the intimacy of the moment, with him crouched at her feet. She looked down at the top of his dark head, droplets of water falling over the seal-like covering of his wetsuit. Suddenly he looked up at her with a gaze so clear it stole her breath. She fell into the beauty and the sadness in his eyes. As he stood up near her, the wall of his chest wide and certain, Drift was reminded of the physical perfection of a superhero. Could a man's body be any more beautiful?

He paused. As if about to say something. As if, maybe, about to kiss her ... but instead he slung their towels and clothes over his shoulder, then picked up both his board and the buckets. 'C'mon, before it gets too dark. I'm starving.'

Drift took up her board and the rods, following Eli, trudging in the sand away from the camp.

'Where are you going?'

'You'll see,' he called over his shoulder. The grin returned. A few hundred metres down the beach, they rounded the curve of a dune.

'Here will do,' he said. Drift looked in wonderment at what was before her: a beautiful tepee structure of driftwood, tied with sea-faded flotsam ropes where the bleached limbs leaned on each other at the top, had been draped in a couple of Eli's sarongs that now billowed gently in colours of seascape blue and green. Eli had also taken the time and trouble to string sea shells that tinkled together in a light breeze from the structure's apex.

On the sand beneath it, he had set down his seagrass sleeping mats and anchored them with round grey beach stones. An unlit fire, set with newspaper, grasses and driftwood, had been prepared a small way off from the sarong tent. The battered camp Esky sat beside it. A stone pathway leading to the dunes had been laid out and circled the tepee too.

'It's beautiful,' Drift said. 'What's it for?'

'It's for you,' Eli replied.

Apprehension clouded Drift's face. Alarm bells rang. She set down her mother's board. Surfers were dangerous.

'Here,' he said gently. 'Let me help you.' He grabbed the cord of the wetsuit zip and tugged it down her back. She peeled the suit from her clammy arms, feeling cold droplets of seawater from her wet hair trickling over her warm bare skin, catching in her bikini top in her cleavage. She caught glimpses of Eli skinning the wetsuit from his body, his nakedness making every zing of fear and desire sheen over her.

He stooped for the towels, handing her one. She took it from him.

He discreetly turned his back as she got dressed, while he pulled on shorts and a T-shirt. The night was impossibly warm and now still.

'Eli,' she began in a low voice, 'what is all this?'

'I wish I could take all the credit, but it was your dad who suggested it. Said all you do is work. That you needed time out. Away from him. So, welcome to our beachside retreat!'

'He did?' Tears sprang to her eyes. For so long the weight of her father's neediness had hung heavy on her. But somehow, in the past weeks, Split's dependency had slowly but surely melted away with Eli's presence.

'Here,' Eli said, inviting her to sit. He went to the Esky and pulled out a couple of mineral waters. 'Sorry they're not that cold,' he said opening one and handing it to her. 'Unfortunately the only other thing on the menu, aside from catch of the day, is more two-minute noodles and a box of Jatz biscuits.'

Drift laughed and saw the way he was looking at her. She felt as if a million silver baby fish were swimming inside her belly.

'Come on,' she said, trying to stem the tide of feeling. 'Let's cook! I'm starving.'

*

Drift and Eli squatted together beside the cooking fire, shoulder to shoulder, the only sound the searing fish and crackling salt-dried wood. The heat of the flames warmed Drift's face as she felt the invisible sparks flying between them. It was tangible now. The flames turning the skeleton-dry bones of driftwood to coals evoked the ancient, and each time their eyes met or their hands touched in the action of their cooking, Drift felt the mysterious pull of energy between them. The only thing that weighed on her was Eli's secret. His masquerade. The lie of his death.

The fish cooked, light white flakes of buttery flesh melted on Drift's tongue. She closed her eyes, savouring the clean, pure taste, listening to the roll of the waves and thinking about the world from which the fish had come, hooked out of all that expansive water. When they'd eaten most of it down to hair-comb bones, saving some for Split, the March moon was waxing to full as it revealed itself from over the dunes. Reviving the fire with more crackling driftwood, Eli took Drift by the hand and without words invited her to lie beside him under the shelter. Moonlight revealed the colourful hibiscus on the gently drifting fabric. The ocean delivered a soundscape of watery music as waves broke and clapped on a low-tide beach, now strewn with brown shells and seaweed.

Drift looked across to Eli's dark eyes. She smiled at him. 'This has been so much fun. I never want you to leave,' she said suddenly. 'Life will feel so different after you go.'

Eli propped himself up on one elbow. 'Who said I'm going?'

'Everyone leaves eventually,' Drift said sadly. Lying on her back, her hair spread out on the matting, she pointed to a constellation. 'That's the one I look at when I think of Mum, after she left me,' she said.

Eli reached out, laying his hand over hers. A fire ran through her as their fingers entwined.

'Our loved ones never leave us,' he said finally. 'It's impossible. All our ancestors are with us, always. It's what I was taught.'

His words and his touch gave her the courage to speak.

'Mum did keep leaving us, though. She was a bit of a gypsy. She kept Dad wandering, following her. I guess she still does,' she said. 'Dad gave up everything to keep in step with her and even now we never stay still.'

Eli remained silent, as if wanting her to talk further.

'She was a bit of a tree hugger and one day she turned up in Dad's tiny timber town in Tassie. I guess she blew into his small life and made it bright. She told him how clever he was and that he didn't belong there. His family hated her. It made him determined to love her, I think. He never went back.'

Drift looked up at the blinking stars and paused for a long time. When her words next came, they were slow and reluctant.

'She got him hitching up the east coast and surfing all over the place. Then, when I was on the way, Dad wanted to settle so they could raise me in one place. They hitched over the Nullarbor and bought a cheap run-down place to raise me, and that was when Mum lost herself a bit I think — you know how some women can with babies? She was always picking fights with him, like she was trying to find an excuse to go for good. She did go one night. Forever. And we've never settled since.' Drift fell silent.

'Do you know what happened?'

Drift fingered the fringes on her shorts and shook her head. 'All Dad told me was she went out one night partying with the surfers. She used to go in a few amateur comps, so she was always hanging around them. Dad said she was using and that giving someone like Mum drugs was a disaster waiting to happen; she was already pretty wild. I see now she wanted to be free in a selfish kind of way. All Dad said was while the rest of them partied, she took herself off on her board and went into the water. And they never found her. I think really she'd had a fight with her lover. I get the sense she was cheating on Dad. They didn't even notice she was gone till Dad came looking for her the next morning.'

'I'm sorry,' Eli said.

'Don't be. It was years ago.' Drift roamed a fingertip through the sand, sketching whitecaps. 'I remember it so clearly, though. I was in our old ute. There were cops on the beach. Dad was screaming, the cops dragging him off some guy. Her lover, I suppose. I remember looking everywhere for Mum on the beach and in the surf, but I just saw empty bottles thrown around in the sand and some scraggy people hanging around. So you see, it's why I don't like surfers. They took my mum. Hurt my dad. And you … I guess, what you did … it's triggered a lot of memories for me … so I'm … it's …'

Eli swallowed. '*Complicated.*'

Drift smiled at the pitiful joke.

'I get that,' he said. 'It explains so much about you.' Illuminated by the leaping flames of the fire, his eyes looked soft and kind. 'So because I'm a surfer, you don't like me?'

'Pretty much,' Drift said bluntly. 'I like Eli, the horseman. But Kai the surfer, no. I don't think I like him. I don't know if I can trust him.'

A flash of pain crossed Eli's face. 'I can understand that too, I guess.' He lay back down, staring above him. 'I don't like him either. But he's gone now,' he said in a whisper. 'That man has gone. He died the day he found you. But how do I convince you of that?'

He moved closer to her and she saw the intense gleam of the firelight in his eyes. She turned away.

'I don't know,' she said flatly. They lay in silence for a time, with just the crack of the fire. Drift felt herself shrinking away from him inside. It *was* all too complicated.

Suddenly Eli broke the silence. 'Can I tell you a story?'

'Sure,' she said, unsure where this was leading.

'It's my puna's, my grandmother's, story. She'd retell it to me when my tutu, my grandfather, was being difficult. As if to remind herself that she still loved him, no matter what, even after fifty years of marriage.'

Eli's voice had a thread of sadness running through it and Drift couldn't help but feel it tug at her heart. He cleared his throat and began.

'It's a legend, a mo'olelo. And it's a love story. It begins with two lovers who were separated because the high priest, the kahuna, wouldn't sanctify their union,' Eli said. 'The man was sent away, up to the mountains, and the girl was sent to live by the sea. But, as Puna said, it was too late … their hearts and minds were united forever in love.'

Drift now really wondered where on Earth all this was leading.

Eli continued, 'Just before they said goodbye forever the maiden removed a flower from her hair and tore it down the middle, giving half of it to her soon-to-be-lost love. She kept the other half of the flower.' In the dim light, Eli's face took on an expression of sadness. 'It's an actual flower where I come from. The naupaka flower. On Tutu's farm, when we would take the young horses out on the trail he would point out the flower in the bushes on the mountainside. It's a beautiful white half-blossom that seems to lean down towards the sea. On the shores of the ocean, the other half of the flower grows and it seems to lean up towards the mountains. Puna said the flower is symbolic of the

237

couple's inseparable, eternal love despite their physical distance from each other.'

Drift remained silent, absorbing the tale.

'Each half-blossom is stained with the faint purple tears of the maiden,' Eli continued, 'because even though they were apart, they are forever joined as one in their hearts and minds, as kakou. The legend's moral is that love's unity takes us beyond time and space to be united forever in aloha. It's a belief where I come from. Love is eternal. Not in the diamond ring, forever in time, sense of the Western world, but in the sense that the energy of life and love that runs through all living things can't be stopped. When two people unite with pure hearts, it's a powerful union. Eternal.'

Drift turned to him. 'That's a beautiful story, but my friend Charlie would say our screwy beliefs around romantic love cause the greatest suffering. No one outside our selves can "complete" us, as the romance novels would have us believe.'

Eli laughed gently. 'I like the sound of your friend Charlie. She has the same take on the world that my grandmother and grandfather have. Their love is not a romantic relationship. It's a holy one. They choose to serve one another and offer their best selves to each other. Every day. They make it their priority to pleasure each other. Grandma often jokes she's still on her honeymoon with Grandfather and he plans on dying with her that way. If you know what I mean ...'

Drift smiled, trying to picture Puna and Tutu. Then she frowned. 'Why are you telling me this story?'

Eli cleared his throat. Then he spoke in the faintest of whispers. 'Because, I feel something ... something deeper when I'm with you. Something I've never felt before.'

Drift looked to him, and saw his vulnerability and his truth, and instantly she wanted him more than anything. She rolled towards him and he reached for her. Suddenly they were swimming in the warmest of kisses. Desire flooded her system, they pulled each other close, the kissing stronger, the passion building as their hearts pressed close, their fingers, toes, limbs, feet entwining. A clamouring to be close. His fingers in her hair, hers in his. The taste of the sea between them, the sound of the waves in their ears. Stars above and within them burning brightly. Drift felt the press of his desire hard against her. The surge of wanting in her felt more compelling and intense than any massive wave she'd ever seen. She wanted to drown in him. Eli tugged on the leather of her hobble belt, the belt sighing open, zip sliding down, his hands reaching around to cup her backside. His other hand moved up under her tank top and gently moved aside the small triangle of bikini that covered her. His warm palm cupping her breast sent another wave of wanting through her.

Frantically now, she kissed him harder, faster, reaching for the button of his shorts. Her hand slid within and met with his desire. He felt as hard as wood and yet his skin was as soft as velvet. Her drover-girl hands were strong and her virgin grip had not an ounce of tentativeness to it. She was too overcome with wanting, to be self-conscious. She was driven, like she had been most of her life, by instinct. Raw womanly instinct. He too felt her readiness and gently slid her shorts down. When his fingers trailed over her inner thighs slowly and eventually met with her warm wet sex within her bikini, they both groaned with desire. He whispered her beauty to her. She murmured her pleasure. The Heavens heard. With deft and gentle, yet strong and rhythmic, strokes he brought her to her first orgasm shared with a man. She cried out and her head rolled back so her face turned upwards to the stars. When she shut her eyes, she saw the stars too within, and the swathe of the Universe rolling on for eternity. Breathing hard, still wanting more, she began to shove her clothing down and away, and guided Eli to lie above her.

'In my pocket,' she said, breathlessly, 'there's a condom.'

He pulled back from her and found it. She watched avidly as he rolled it onto his magnificent cock. When he came to lie upon her, he stroked her hair and looked into her eyes in the darkness. 'Are you sure?'

'Yes,' she said.

Next he gently, slowly, lovingly, eased himself inside her, concern in his eyes as he studied her face. Smiling, she arched upwards to meet him and felt the joy of receiving him as her first. A small tear of pain barely even registered as he pushed fully inside her, such was her readiness for this man. With the roll of the waves serenading them, the lovers joined forever.

When they were spent and sweating, breath shared, caresses continuing, Eli whispered to her, 'Aloha wau ia 'oe.'

'What does that mean?' Drift asked.

'You will feel it in here,' he said, placing his palm on her heart space.

She smiled and pulled him close. 'Something about love?'

'Yes,' he said.

Drift at gazed the stars and the moon above. She felt his love in every cell of her body, and in her heart, but in her mind she heard a little whisper that he was a smooth one, this one. This surfer boy was a player.

Chapter 30

Drift woke, her eyes blinking open, her gaze falling on Eli's sleeping face. She lay on the seagrass mats, studying the divine perfection of him. She wanted to run her fingertips across his high cheekbones, his smooth eyelids and long dark lashes, but she didn't want to wake him. She didn't want this night to ever end. In the semi-darkness over on the spent campfire that was now just grey coals, her father's fish lay wrapped in foil. Embarrassment swamped her: Split would know they'd stayed out all night, and were most likely now lovers.

Over the dunes the sky was blushing in russet tones and the moon was sinking like a cloud into the sea. The sun would rise soon. If she left now, taking Split's share of the fish to the kitchen table and sneaking back into her bed, her father would be none the wiser. Would he? He hadn't been drinking lately, so even though he slept just as heavily, she was aware he was getting up earlier, switching on his solar torch and reading his books before dawn. Maybe he'd been keeping one eye out for them already this morning.

When Drift looked back from the pre-dawn sky to Eli, his eyes were open, locked on her. He reached out and stroked her hair, clearing a strand gently from her face.

'Is it almost morning?'

'Yes.' One lone cry from a gull in the darkness confirmed her answer.

'Is it time to go?'

'I think so.'

Eli rolled over and propped himself up on his elbow, his bare chest deliciously ripped with fit-boy muscles. Drift felt herself melt just laying the palm of her hand on his warm skin.

'I wanted to give you this,' he said, reaching under the woven mat. In his palm he held a small white beach stone, and in the muted light Drift saw the stone was shaped exactly like a love heart.

'I'm giving you my heart,' he said, grinning and placing the stone on the place where her own heart beat.

She took it and held it above her, turning it over, her fingertips taking in its perfect, smooth form. 'It's amazing. Mother Nature made that? All by herself?'

'She did. I found it the day I first saw you.'

'Thank you.'

'My pleasure.' He began to kiss her again, and Drift felt his desire growing. She looked at the sun rising, and guilt pulled her away.

'Maybe I should get back to Dad.'

Eli frowned.

'You're an adult,' he said, nuzzling into her neck. 'He'll be fine. It was almost as if he was giving us permission, the way he was saying I ought to give you a night off and a fish cook-up on the beach.'

Drift looked at him. 'I know, but —'

He stopped her sentence with a lingering kiss. 'Stay a little while. Please?'

Uncertainty niggled Drift.

Eli pulled back from her and studied her face. 'I don't want this to change us,' he said.

'What do you mean, *this*?'

'Becoming more than just mates,' he said. He looked skywards, beyond the shield of the sarongs. 'These past few weeks on the drove with you have been the best days of my life. I've never felt so certain about anything. Anyone. *You*.' He turned his eyes to her. 'I believe we are part of that legend of the naupaka flower. That we are kakou — united forever as one and have been before in kakou aloha.'

As Drift began to let his words sink in, another bird called. It was a crow. The jarring, jagged sound unsettled her. In her mind rushed the teachings of Wilma and Charlie. She knew not to trust romantic love. She and Wilma had spent hours reading and talking together about the myths and realities behind fairy tales, and how they had been twisted to lure women into thinking they had to be rescued by a prince. Red shoes and princess dresses. Drift didn't trust knights in shining armour. She felt the wild woman within her stir and rise against the notion that a man was going to save her, even own part of her, particularly a man as mystifying as Eli. She said the words before she could stop herself. 'So, you've seen the light and now, despite all you've done, you want some pure girl like me to save you?'

'What?' He pulled away from her.

'It's OK for you to sample women all over the world, but now you're done with that, you're saying you're going to be satisfied with me?'

Eli propped himself up on his elbow again. 'Women all over the world? What are you talking about?'

'I've seen the magazine photos of you.'

Eli's jaw clenched.

'You're my first,' she said, 'whereas you've had hundreds of women. Isn't it a bit soon to be talking about together forevers?'

He frowned. 'I wouldn't say hundreds. Don't believe that stuff they write. Most of it's bullshit.'

Drift could see him flush. She felt a winged bird of fear flutter darkly in her mind.

The road train of negative thoughts about surfers was back in her head. You don't know him, she thought. You know nothing about this man. And he lies ... Eli the lie.

'*Most* of it, you reckon?' she said.

Eli drew further away from her, clearly hurt. She thought for a moment he was about to get angry. Instead his voice was gentle.

'Hey,' Eli soothed, running his fingertips over her arms, 'I can understand how vulnerable you feel right now. I have a heavy past, I know, but I'm now free of that. All I'm saying is that I hope there's time ahead for you and me. Us. That we have a future. Together.'

There was that word, Drift thought … *us*. Suddenly she felt as if she were being caged. Like the way Simon had made her feel. She didn't want to be anybody's 'us'. She liked her freedom. She loved her solitude. Mistrust of men fired in her, particularly of Eli, who had led her into such a turbulent situation.

'How can we plan anything as "us" when the world thinks you're dead?' she asked.

He looked beseechingly at her. 'We just have to trust that time will move us on from here.'

'But none of it is true. Your life and my life just don't fit.'

He looked pained. 'How can you say this isn't true?' He touched his palm from his heart to hers, the stone pressing warmly into her palm. 'This is truth,' he said. 'What I feel is truth.'

Reluctantly, she felt it too and, with his butterfly kisses resuming, she felt a powerful surge of connection. Maybe I'm tangling all this in my head too much, Drift thought. She ought to simply forgive and follow her heart. She relaxed onto the sand, falling into his kiss, cupping his hip with her hand, guiding him on top of her.

'I don't have protection,' he said breathlessly as he rested his forehead on hers, Drift feeling the press of his cock near her. She wanted him in her. More than anything. She lifted her hips, craving him.

Eli propped himself above her, looking down at her. 'No,' he said, 'we can't. Safety first. Plus, what if I got you pregnant?'

Drift turned her head and breathed in heavily then let out a frustrated sigh. He was right. It was irresponsible. She tried to shake some sense back into her lust-filled mind. She drew his head down to her chest and began to run her fingers through his thick hair.

'OK.' She laughed. 'The last thing I'd want is a baby. I've seen enough calvings to know I'm not going there yet!'

Eli laughed and Drift felt the desire dissipate from them both, but their connection remained.

'At least I know your mum will like me when she meets me,' Drift said, 'going on what you've told me about her. When things settle, we could go to your island and I could get to know her.'

'My mother?' Eli said, his voice tight. He rolled off her.

'Yes,' said Drift tentatively, 'and your father and grandparents.' She noticed shame twinge in his jaw.

He turned his face away as if holding back tears.

She sat up suddenly, drawing up a sarong to cover her nakedness. A terrible thought dawned on her. She studied his face closely. 'Your mother. *She doesn't know?* And your father? They don't know you're still alive?'

Eli sat up, dragging his shorts on, then hugging his knees to his chest. He didn't answer.

'They think you're dead? Drowned? You haven't contacted them?'

She saw how he winced. She reached for his face and turned it towards her, but he looked fiercely back out to the darkened sea.

'I'm not ready to face them,' he said in an expressionless voice. 'Not yet.'

Drift felt her skin crawl in horror. 'Your grandparents? They think you're missing or dead too?'

He was silent for a time, jaw muscles flickering. 'Yes.'

Drift sat for a while, trying to control her breath. Childhood pain over the agony of her mother's disappearance swamped her. How could he do that to his own family? How selfish he must be! She'd given herself over to Eli last night, only to be greeted in the morning by the type of man she'd wanted to avoid. Kai, the liar. The party boy, rich kid, the womaniser, the narcissist.

'Do you know how selfish that is?' she burst out.

He seemed slapped by her words. Across the dull ocean, dark bands of a swell could just be seen forming and moving slowly towards the shore. Beyond the headland Drift watched the white horses gleaming in the pre-dawn darkness, scuffed up by a surprise wind. The waves were gaining height.

'Do you have any idea what it's *like*?' Drift said, the years of agony rumbling in her.

She began to reach for her clothes, speaking as she quickly dressed. 'To spend a lifetime always looking out to sea for a mother who may or may not have drowned? To wake in the night wondering who is crying out, then realising it's you? Reliving what it must've been like, lungs filling with water. The pain. And to drag Sophia and Serge into it too. Colluding with them to hide things from your family!'

'But —'

She stood up, rage firing in her. 'For years and years, I've watched.' She pointed to the sea. 'Watched those white horses. Searched the horizon, walked the sand. Looking for her. Waiting for her. Living with the question: would she come back? Did she really drown? Or was she just trying to get away from Dad and me?'

'But —' Kai began again.

'But what? That's *unforgivable*. To let them think you are dead! Even for a second!'

He ran his hands through his hair, anger on his face. 'You don't understand. I just need a bit of time … to get myself together, then —'

'Time! That's so dumb! You're so dumb! Young and dumb. The agony you're putting them through is awful. It's not their fault you trashed your life!'

His expression told Drift he'd taken another slap. 'That's a bit harsh.' He ran his hands over his face.

'A bit harsh? Where's your sense of responsibility? You're just like the rest of the selfish idiots out there in the world. Caught up in yourself. I thought you were somebody different,' Drift said. 'Somebody better. But to put your family through this even for an instant … and for Serge and Sophia to be drawn into your dramas … it's just not *right*!'

'I thought you were somebody different too,' he fired at her.

'Who? A groupie girl who idolises you? And never questions you? And never challenges you?'

Drift pushed past the breeze-carried sarong, its exotic touch making her feel foolish. Staring at the extinguished fire and the bones of the fish, she wrapped her arms around herself. Her mind raced. The voice of Shaynene came into her mind.

'Bloody men only want one thing,' Shaynene had said. 'They just want to hump you and dump you.'

The gentle in-out breath of fallen waves did nothing to calm her. The rising sun painted the landscape in rust. She could feel Eli come up behind her, placing a tentative hand on her shoulder. She shrugged it away.

'You're not Eli. You're just *a lie*.' There. She had said it out loud. 'And I want you gone.' She stepped out of the circle of rocks and ran back towards her father in the stock camp. Back to her life.

Chapter 31

The sun burned, but clouds of cold air rose in frighteningly tall columns above a darkening sea. Swirling pockets of hot air wilted the dogs, horses and cattle and then rushes of cold air chilled them to a nervous restlessness.

'Not again,' Drift said, looking up at the change racing across the water. Split turned to watch the broody build-up of angry clouds coming from the north.

'Where's that lad?' he asked.

Drift had shrugged, but inside she could feel a squall of panic rising. Split sensed her turmoil but shut his mouth in a line.

By ten am, when the weather fully hit, the seething energy of the storm sent Drift and Split scrambling even faster to secure all their camp gear and re-tether the horses so they at least had some shelter on the lee of the truck. The cattle bellowed as the rain slung itself in sheets sideways. The ground was instantly mud, the camp tarpaulins ballooning from the deluge. The dogs cowered, ears flattened, tails tucked, Dunno trembling from the boom of thunder. Split opened the door of the Cruiser, inviting the dogs to nestle inside.

Normally Drift relished the excitement generated by a storm, but there was something sinister about this one. It was so odd to experience one in the morning. It was like it had come from an otherworldly place, whorled up by the gods of the sea. Her mind kept being drawn to Eli. *Where was he?* All morning she'd battled with herself over whether to return to the beach. To apologise. No one ought to be judged on their past over and over, and if anyone needed help now to right his wrongs, it was him. She'd been so self-righteous with him, about how unforgivable his actions were. Now she just felt sick with guilt after he'd reached out to her. What did she know? What right did she have to judge him so harshly when he was so clearly trying to escape the mess that he'd made for himself?

Right before retreating to the caravan Drift yelled to her father, 'I'm just going to take a look on the beach. I'm going to find Eli.' Her words were whisked away. Hoping she wouldn't be hit by the shatterings of lightning getting nearer by the minute across the water, she pushed herself into the ferocious gale, tilted forwards, head bowed, shielding herself from the onslaught of the torrential rain.

Over the dunes the sky above the shuddering sea was black with ghoul-shaped clouds. The sea itself was a fearsome sight of black and grey wave-mountains beyond the breakers. The boomers were so loud and so enormous it seemed as if the whole landmass would be consumed by their frothing fury. Monster waves were haphazardly hammering the beach and dragging out tons of sand with every lurch. Along the beach a lagoon was already spilling out to sea and carving a deep channel, again severing the beach in two. The wrath felt so savage Drift wondered if they'd need to move the camp and the cattle to higher ground above the dune area of the spit if the sea might not be contained. It was fearsome to behold.

She ran to the previous night's beach camp. Bucketing rain was making ash soup of the dead campfire. A thunder boom crashed inside her and around her. It made her flinch and she felt the power of it in her belly. Frowning, hair plastered to her face, she looked about frantically for a sign of Eli. Anything. But all that was left was scuffed sand where they had lain surrounded by the stones he'd set out. The sarongs and the mats had gone, along with her mother's surfboard. Her father's board lay all alone beside the old Esky, now covered in the sticks, blown over in a pile as if about to be burned.

Drift stood at the place where Eli had held her the night before. She watched as black coal rivulets washed into the white sand. About a hundred metres offshore lightning flashed, splicing the air with a loud crack. The air pockets ran hot then icily over Drift's face. *Where was he?* She was about to turn away and go back to the caravan, confused, defeated, when something caught her eye. Drift, shivering now from the cold, ran along the beach. There, being dragged in and out by the waves, she saw a jagged broken section of her mother's surfboard turning over and over in the frothy chop, the pointed nose like a shark's.

'Oh God. Please God. No,' she said, wading into the terrifying water and gathering up her mother's board.

'Eli? Kai?' She screamed to the buffeting wind and waves, scanning the sea and the beach. Where was he?

She'd ridden roughshod over Charlie's advice about meeting a person in the moment and forgiving them their past. She'd convicted him of the crimes she'd kept record of all these years against the surfers her mother had fallen in with. She'd poured onto him all the anger she'd been trying not to feel for her mum. Surely he hadn't been swallowed by the sea, this time for real? So his lie to his parents would now be the truth? Turning back towards camp, she looked to the place they had been just a few hours before. She stooped to look for the heart-shaped stone, but rain blinded her sight. A lightning crack jolted her and she turned and ran, leaving the heart stone lost in the sand.

*

That afternoon, after the wild weather had passed, Drift and Split came to stand once more on the dune, surveying the aftermath of the storm. Drift turned to what was left of the camp. She glanced at her father. Bleak-faced they walked towards it.

'Do you think he was in the water at the time?' Drift asked.

'Surely he wouldn't be so stupid?'

Drift thought of their parting words. Her wanting him gone. Would Eli really have thrown himself into the sea because of her words? To save himself from people judging him, including herself?

Her dad's voice startled her out of her thoughts. 'If something has happened to him how can we tell the police?' Split said. 'They think he's out there anyway.'

He turned to her, pain in his eyes, memories stirred of his lost wife. Both of them looked at the remainder of the surfboard she'd propped up on the stones of the campfire. She stooped to retrieve it and turned to collect her father's board too.

'No,' Split said too loudly. 'Leave them. I'm done with dragging them about with us.'

Drift hugged her arms about her body, trying to swallow the tears that were threatening to overcome her. She felt hysteria rising in her so she dug her fingernails into the palms of her hands to quash it.

There was nothing to do but to turn their backs to the sea and focus their attention on the cattle, who were now trapped on a high point on the road, the estuaries bursting around them. It was time to saddle the horses and wade the herd through the floodplains onto higher ground.

'There's not enough tucker for them down here now,' her dad said as they trudged through wet sand. 'We'll be hard pressed to move them through some sections. I think we're gunna have to truck 'em out to the abattoir early. That's if we can get a bloody truck in.'

'So soon?'

'They're fat enough as they are, and the calves are looking good for on-sell. Or the abattoir will take them and feed-lot them, I reckon. I'll radio for a truck.'

Drift felt devastation rise in her. 'And Eli?'

Her father's face flashed anguish. He shook his head. 'We'll let them know at The Planet now ... He might have gone back there. Let's just hope he has.'

'And if he hasn't?'

Split looked at her. 'Well, like I've said, we can't exactly call the police, can we?'

'But —'

'What would Eli want us to do? That's what we need to ask ourselves.'

Drift didn't answer. On the crest of the dune, Split looked at his daughter for some time. 'Ah Drift,' he sighed. 'You sure made mincemeat of that, didn't you?'

'Of what?' she flashed back at him.

'Your first date. Your brand-new boyfriend. To offend him so much he runs off. Haven't I taught you anything about livestock handling? Pressure on. Pressure off. You must've kept far too much pressure on the poor bugger. *Lovers and madmen have such seething brains!*'

Drift heard her father trying to joke her out of the dreadful situation they were in, with his clever reference to *A Midsummer Night's Dream*, but she wasn't finding anything remotely funny about what was happening. Her father hadn't been there. What if Eli had in fact now drowned, for real?

'C'mon,' urged Split. 'He'll be fine. You'll be fine. It's time you and I both moved on. I'll start packing the gear. You head on up to The Planet, see if you can get through Sophia's fortress and see that Eli of ours.'

'OK,' Drift said, looking at her father, feeling at last comforted by his words. Eli of ours, she thought fondly. Wiping her windblown hair from her face, she made her way to the ute.

As she drove down the puddled, rutted road towards The Planet gates with Dunno resting his head in comfort on her lap, sobs stuck jagged inside her chest. It had been a heavenly night, followed swiftly by their argument. Her judgement and fear and his betrayal of his parents had washed their love-making away like sentimental words written in then wiped from the sand. As she saw The Planet gates come into view she held on to the hope Eli would be already on his way home there.

She couldn't yet face the fact the time had suddenly come and they were leaving Pinrush Point, and losing her cattle to the markets. For an instant, panic gripped her. She didn't want to leave. She didn't want to betray her herd of cattle, her girls. She remembered the state of the cattle when they'd first arrived. The near-dead eyes of the weaker cows. The dark brindle one with the swollen ulcered udder and another so thin her hips looked like coat hangers draped with a coat. She remembered the different girl she'd been back then, a young girl, unloading her cows, not knowing anything about what was about to happen. She had, in the space of three moons, become a woman. Drift realised she had utterly changed.

Chapter 32

At the gateway to The Planet, Drift jabbed the intercom insistently over and over. In the speaker box a spider shrugged itself out of the way of her finger. She looked skywards. Why should Sophia make it so hard to get into her place? Surely they had provisions for an emergency like this? She pressed the button again. At last Drift heard a scuffling sound.

'Hello?' she said hopefully into the metal mesh of the speaker.

'Yellow?' came a crackling voice. The voice of a child.

'Is Sophia there?'

'No. I'm here.'

'Who is it?'

'Me.'

'Who are you?'

'Me, me, me, me, *me*!'

'Can I speak to Sophia or Serge, *please*,' Drift said trying to retain her patience. There was a giggle. And another. Two children.

'Please. *It's urgent*. Can you open the gates?'

'We're not allowed.'

'Can you get an adult to open the gates? Where is a grown-up? This is really important.'

Drift rolled her eyes as she heard the kids blowing raspberries into the speaker, then the intercom raged static and cut to silence. Behind her the Cruiser rumbled in neutral. The gate remained shut. She buzzed a few times more. She looked up to the camera that was angled her way and waved. She waited. Silence.

Eventually, after a few more tries, with a heavy heart she drove back down the peninsula road through large watersheds and shallow creek crossings. Luckily the sandy soil meant the country dried fast. She hoped there'd be no trouble with the trucks. Before she'd left, her dad had got on the two-way radio, the bush telegraph working well over the UHF all the way up to Cooperville. Drift had overheard her dad say, 'Anyone other than that fuckwit Kelvin Waller,' when it came to sending in a transporter. Drift had felt a tension within her ease, knowing he'd been banned from travelling out of Cooperville anyway, thanks to Simon.

When she arrived back at camp, Drift saw her dad had made good progress resetting the yards on a high dry knoll. The cattle bellowed nearby from where they were stuck on the rise, sensing something was shifting. A sweat was on his brow, his cheeks red from exertion as he paused to watch his daughter arrive.

'I can't bloody raise them at The Planet!' Drift said to him, holding a wide stance in her boots, frustration creasing her brow. 'What should we do? Cut the fence in? Radio the police?'

She thought of Eli's mother and shuddered. Mrs Kaahea's and the whole family's grief could now be for real. Anger towards him stirred, but with it sympathy. She'd opened up enough to trust him. To sleep with him. To fall for him. Now this. She vowed she'd never go near men again. She'd stick with what she knew: horses, dogs, cattle, sheep and solitude.

'Like before, I guess the only thing to do is ask yourself what Eli would want,' Split said.

'How would I know that?' Drift replied angrily.

'I think we both know.'

Drift looked infuriated. She opened her palms as if to say, 'What?'

'He would want his secret kept.'

'Why is this all about him? He's cocked up this trip for you and me. He's made it Hell down here for us and for so many others. Just because he can surf better than anyone else. So what. He's a selfish arse.'

'Drift,' her father said. 'Yes, his actions may say that ... but you and I both know that away from that storm he's a good guy. He treated you —'

'Why does it matter how he treated me, when he's treated his family so badly?'

'He treated you well and that's what counts,' Split said firmly.

'Are you taking sides?'

'No ... it's just I know what I saw. He handled the animals magnificently, all of them. Their response to him showed us he is a good person. He seemed different from other blokes I've seen around you. It was like he really saw you. The Drift I know.'

Drift was taken aback. Maybe the experience of thinking he'd lost her after Kelvin's attack had opened Split up. Sobered him up. Settled him. And Sophia's influence too, and then sharing their camp and their lives with Eli. Morning and night. The quiet times, the jokes, the conversation. He had been steady, always making himself useful. So kind and humble.

'Really? Do you think?' Drift's face crumpled. Tears formed. She felt the swell of his betrayal. Of his loyalty. She shook her head in confusion. 'But his family? Shouldn't they know he's alive? If he is now alive? Oh God! This is so ... so ... fucking ridiculous.'

It was rare Drift ever swore, but emotion overcame her. Split moved to her, his thick patchy-haired legs in tradie shorts marching over so he could catch her. He gathered her up in his big arms, the way he had when she was a child. Gratefully, Drift pressed her face to his broad hot chest. Split shushed her and stroked her head. For once he didn't reach for a poem or a quote to cope with the emotions of the moment. Instead, he spoke again from his heart.

'We know he's a good man — on the inside. He may have made some bad decisions, and acted like a brat, but being young and dumb is not a crime. It shouldn't be a life sentence.

Remember what Charlie says about the past? It doesn't actually exist. All that exists really is the here and now. You know that. But he's bringing his guilt with him to the now. Wherever he goes. If only I could learn that lesson too,' her father said. 'I'm so sorry. For the past. It's not here now.'

Drift felt a fresh swell of tears. She had been one of the people not to forgive both her father's and Eli's pasts. Maybe in forgiving Eli and helping save himself from his own judgement, she could've, in some way, saved herself? She knew they had both been hot-headed and hurt. But now there was no other option but to turn away from the sea and follow her father. Now, it would be unbearable torture to always be searching that great changeable stretch of ocean for him, right after she'd made the choice to stop searching for her mum.

On calm days, in the past she'd found rays of hope that her mother would simply walk back into their lives one day, the happy imaginings piercing through her mind like sun through gauze rain curtains over a mellow sea. But on stormy days, the knowledge that Harmony was lost to her forever was like a churning grey sea, washing despair right through her. She'd sometimes wished they'd found her mother's body washed up on the sand. Now she found herself picturing Eli discovered in a slumped heap on the beach, ragged fish-sucked flesh on bones, or skeletal shards sliced by the jaws of sharks. She didn't know if Eli had walked away by choice, propelled away from her by her judgement, or if he had finally been taken by the sea, but either way, it was too awful to comprehend.

Her dad was about to speak when the UHF barked itself alive inside the ute. A couple of trucks were on their way. There was no time for emotion now. There was work to be done. First the horses had to be saddled and the cattle moved from their island through shallows and yarded. Then there was the packing-up.

Later, with the animals settled on the last of the sodden hay, the steady regimented way Drift and Split normally packed camp was this time done in agonising silence and back-breaking haste.

Drift knew it would take several hours before they'd set up a makeshift loading ramp, packed the stock truck and sorted all the gear, but she was grateful for the busyness. She wanted to revisit the dreamy place of falling asleep in Eli's arms and making love to him, but instead her body felt taut, as if electrified wire ran beneath her skin. As she dropped the pins in the portable panels and pulled up for a breather she glanced at her father. He looked at her sympathetically.

'You know, I think I'm done with drinking,' he said. '*Why, sir, for my part I say the gentleman had drunk himself out of his five senses*. I've found some sense. After we haul camp I'm giving the grog away.'

'Is that so?' Drift replied, her head inclined, hope swelling her heart.

'Yep. And, I reckon I'm done with coastal living,' he said out of nowhere. He leaned his elbow on the rail. 'I reckon after we deliver these cattle, we head inland. You 'n me. Whaddya say?'

Drift smiled at her father, her heart in painful knots. Then she nodded. 'I reckon inland would be good.'

Chapter 33

The next day, Drift watched the dust-covered indicator lights of the rumbling old stock truck and trailer flash on–off as her father readied himself to pull over. Drift groaned. Her dad was going to stop at the bloody Widgenup Store. She'd been following him in the Cruiser, towing the caravan, and had hoped he'd roll right on past the store to the petrol station instead.

With the cattle gone yesterday evening, this morning they had completed filling the first section of the truck with all their gear. Water tank, pump, fuel drums, hay ring and toolboxes. Next Gerald the generator was hoisted on and forced in so the divider door of the stock truck could swing shut. Last on were the horses and the little feed trailer, hitched on like a dinghy.

Drift and her dad had then turned their attention to finishing loading up the Cruiser and hitching the caravan on. As they'd set off from their beachside camp Drift saw how they had erased themselves from the landscape almost completely. She looked to the scuffed place where Eli had last slept in her swag beneath the truck. There was not a trace of those weeks with him, save for the ring of stones around campfire ash. A tear escaped and rolled down Drift's cheek. Angrily she had swiped it away and kept her eyes set straight on the road ahead, focusing on the tailgate of the truck. She didn't want to see the view to her left, where the wide stretch of wind-ruffled sea and beach lay, holding so many memories. Holding so many mysteries.

To her right spread the rich ecosystem of The Planet behind Sophia and Serge's impenetrable fence. She felt suddenly an outcast. Like she wanted to be there, but the tangle of Kai's lies and their repercussions had fenced her out of a future there. Every now and then a flash image of Eli came to her. The polish of his smooth skin. A shimmer of his remembered touch. Again and again, she pushed the memories away. Instead, she let her body be jolted for hours over the slow-going Pinrush Point Road, churned up by the rains, made worse by the departing cattle trucks. Every now and then her hand reached for Dunno's side as he lay with his head on her lap, her fingertips running over the puckered scars slowly being covered by his fur. She felt her own face too, feeling for the faint scars left by Kelvin. Her heart was heavy, especially when she remembered the stone Eli had given her, now lost on the vast stretch of beach forever, her one token of his presence in her life.

Now, as the horses heard the climb-down of gears at Widgenup, they lifted their ears, hopeful they'd be let off the truck. Drift knew they had another long slow slog up the coast to Cooperville before they would touch their hooves on the ground again. She saw her dad get out, kick the tyres, cast his eye over the horses angled in the rear pen. Underneath the truck's tray, the dogs banged their tails on the metal sides of the dog boxes and pressed their noses to the wire, hoping too for a run.

She knew the dogs and horses were excited to be on the move, but frustrated by their containment. On longer hauls it was Drift's job to climb in to the horses, shovel manure from beneath them, water them as best she could with a bucket and rehang the hay nets. Today she was hoping it could all wait until Cooperville. She had never felt such tiredness and distress when leaving a place. Eli was never out of her mind. Nor had she ever felt such a pull of hope that her dad was ready to change.

Split motioned to her and pointed to the shop. She rolled her eyes. The last place Drift wanted to go was the Widgenup

Store. She dreaded seeing Shaynene, but she knew her dad would be itching for a coffee — even if it was crappy black soup that squeezed itself out of a press-button machine.

The Cruiser was so loaded up it seemed to sigh when Drift cut the engine. She stretched her neck and felt her whole body ache. Yesterday's task of lifting the big heavy metal panels onto brackets on the sides of the truck could be felt in her shoulders. She'd heard her father make declarations of sobriety before, but now with the situation with Eli weighing heavily on him too, she felt her unease returning. She looked over to Dunno.

'And what of you, faithful hound? I can trust you, right? Can I trust him?' She invited Dunno out of the cab too. On the road, sweat on her back cooled as her pale pink workshirt unpeeled from her skin.

'Hot chocolate?' her dad asked from where he stood at the back of the truck, brushing flies away.

She shook her head.

'Comin?'

From his demeanour, and the way he was glancing at his phone, she could tell he'd got his own head into a tangle on the drive. The neediness was there again. His resolution would've started to slide last night after the tubby young truckie who had loaded the cattle with the now leggy and healthy little calves and rotund cows had gossiped about the trouble the meatworks were in. Drift could tell the driver wasn't even telling them the worst of it.

'Reckon they're about to go belly-up,' the truckie'd said, 'but they're guaranteeing the transport and your lot first.' His equally overweight older mate driving in the second truck had made it worse by not saying much but responding, 'Too right. Too right. True. True,' to everything the young truck driver said.

After the trucks had geared up and driven away in convoy with the cattle bellowing, her dad had become fixated on the situation, saying over and over there'd be Hell to pay if the meatworks did fold before the payment went through. She watched her father, seeing how the strain of Eli going missing, the impenetrable Planet gates, and the packing-up had begun stacking up on him and weighing him down. She could see he was doing his best to control himself, but she hoped by Cooperville that he wouldn't be back on the hunt for the bottle shop. Reluctantly Drift followed him over to the shade of the shop awning. There, to their surprise, the doors slid open. Her dad stepped backwards and forwards across the threshold a few times. Dunno slunk away to sit beneath a rubbish bin, fearful of the strange sound and movement.

'Automatic doors! Widgenup has made the big time,' he said, then whistled. 'The world is truly an insane place.'

A voice came from inside the blast of too-cool air-con: 'Get yourselves in quick or he'll escape!'

Drift's eyes scanned for the owner of the unfamiliar voice. Out from behind the biscuit aisle stepped a thin girl, almost as orange as Twisties thanks to a slathering of fake tan gone wrong. She pointed to the till on the counter. There, a bedraggled-looking Head Bob sat, his eyes dull, pink patches of bare skin revealed on his pale yellow and grey chest.

'He's depressed,' the weedy girl said. 'Shaynene cleared out with that awful bloke of hers. Whole town couldn't believe she'd abandon Head Bob. For *him*.' She stroked the bird. 'And those bloody doors. He keeps going to look for her. I've already had to go get him from the pub twice!'

'What's with those doors?' Drift asked, looking at them distastefully.

The girl rolled her eyes. 'That bloody missing surfer. Shop made so much money from all the weirdos comin and goin, the boss's put in new flash doors and new air-con. When the friggin power goes out, which it does fifty times a week, I gotta send people round the side near the skip bins to get in and out. Doors won't budge. It's a bugger. So we're either roasting as they get stuck shut and I can't let air in, or I'm freakin freezing coz the size of the unit he bought is for a friggin plaza, not here! Place is always filled with flies too. Rotten.'

'That's progress for ya,' Split said.

The girl turned to Drift. 'I heard about you,' she said, her pale eyelashes closing in a squint. 'You're the one who got it on with that Kai fella before he went missing. Shaynene told me. Well, she told everyone actually. The whole freakin world in fact. What was he like?'

Split glanced cautiously at Drift. Drift tried to mask the distress she was carrying within. Her dad stepped up.

'No idea what you're talking about,' he said. 'One thing you oughta learn working in this job is not to believe rumours. Especially ones started by Shaynene. And who might you be?'

She looked him up and down. 'I'm Cartier.'

'Fancy name.'

'Fancy girl,' she said, twirling her long red-blonde hair and grinning. 'I'm Maude Cordwell's youngest.'

Drift and Split recognised the Widgenup family name, and the scrawny likeness of the undernourished batch of kids. 'What are you? Number seven?'

'Eight. Different dad, but. What can I get youse?'

'Large cap thanks.'

As Cartier went to the coffee machine, Drift wandered the aisles, her mind racing as she listened in to the girl's conversation, before taking a few things up to the counter to buy.

'Of course I told Shaynene he was no good, but they had all this money, see, from the story they sold. She's let all this stuff go to her head. Got too big for her boots, I reckon. Seeing herself on the telly and in all the mags turned her into a right bee-arch.' Her eyes flashed in Split's direction, checking in that he was on her side with the whole fiasco. He was nodding. It encouraged her to continue.

'Gup told her he'd take her up to Perth and introduce her to all his professional surf friends, take her to all these parties.

I can understand her wanting to get out of this shit-hole, but I can't understand how she could leave Head Bob.'

On hearing his name, the bird murmured a *chirrup* and shuffled closer to her. She invited him up onto her shoulder by holding out her hand. As he slowly edged his way up her arm she rang up Drift's groceries on the till.

'We oughta name you Hung Head Bob, you're so down, aren't ya, matey? He won't even talk. Bag? We got these new enviro-ones since the journos got their knickers in a knot about the plastics, and that. Save the planet, y'know.'

'Thanks love, yes. Polypropylene bags are absolutely the solution,' Split said cynically. 'I'll do my bit.'

'Yes!' Cartier missed his tone.

'We got them KeepCups here now too. They're only $9.95.'

As Split began his spiel to Cartier about the bonkersness of green marketing, corruption and meaningful consumer choice, Drift roamed away from the counter. She saw the pinboard in the lunch room. There, plastered all over it, were clippings of Kai's disappearance. A magazine photo of Gup and Shaynene with their arms about each other, beachside, with over-the-top serious expressions. Her eyes fell on Kai's beardless face and her heart lurched. She wished her dad would hurry up. Now he was buying a KeepCup.

'Well, nice chat. I'll be seein ya,' Cartier said as she pushed the bag towards him.

'Nah,' Split said. 'Don't reckon you will. Me 'n me girl are headed inland. Don't reckon we'll come this way again. Not with the meatworks the way they are. Waste of time. Send any mail on to Cooperville Library, will ya? Wilma'll get it from there.'

Drift felt a shimmer of deep regret and sadness rise in her. There would be no more droving here beside the fresh blast of salty wind. No more days of seeing just her animals and the turn of the sky. No more gazing into The Planet to see what was possible on a holistically run farm. Then there was *that night* she would have to farewell forever. The one night with Eli. Her first.

She was leaving this place with two questions in her head, not just one. What had happened to her mother? And now, what had happened to her Eli?

She told herself she just wanted to get their money for the cattle in Cooperville, then get the Hell out of there. She was glad to be turning east, to be absorbed by the wide brown expanse of dry land, so huge it would be easy to get lost, as far away from the sea and the recent past as she could get.

Chapter 34

The stern steel gates to the Cooperville abattoir were locked, firmly fastened by a snaking chain as thick as a man-eating anaconda. A few hundred metres away, through the diamond mesh fence, laced on top with round coils of barb, Drift could hear distressed bellows from her cows and calves as they milled about a large barren yard.

In the stock truck, unsettled by the overpowering greasy stench of the meatworks, the horses shuffled restlessly, Minty pinning her ears back at Dunston and baring her teeth, Roger kicking at the metal sides with a foul-tempered clang. Even Dunno was not keen on getting up off the floor where he huddled in the Cruiser's cab. Her dad was pacing back and forth before the high gates. Again, he used his battered old flip phone to try the office staff, slamming it shut in frustration each time the call went to message bank.

An hour earlier, when he'd come into range driving towards Cooperville, the phone had buzzed with messages from his clients coming in in a rush. He'd steered the ramshackle truck with his knee, holding the phone to one ear, listening to them. His clients talked in stammering sentences, or had exceedingly abrupt voices. All held the same message. They were cancelling his services. One after another.

At first Split thought it was the drought that was starting to bite and farmers selling off large numbers. But then he thought of Kelvin Waller. Kelvin and his bullshit-artist talk. Was he behind it? Had Kelvin been spreading rumours? Undermining him? After listening to all the messages, Split had hung up the phone, angry not just about the lost work, but also the fact there wasn't a message from the farmer who had contracted them to take the cattle down the peninsula. Did he know something was up with the abattoir? His square hands had formed fists around the steering wheel and he'd rattled it in fury as he passed the thirty-kilometre sign advertising Cooperville Bakery, pitted with bullet and buckshot holes.

Now, at the abattoir, Drift looked at the grim face of her father, knowing things were spiralling worse than she'd suspected. He jabbed at his phone with his thick index finger again. At last someone must've picked up, and she heard Split's irritated tones as he talked to someone inside the gates. Soon a heavyset bald man in green hi-vis with grey hair that tufted above his ears like a koala was striding across from the work buildings and unlocking the big chain on the gates.

'Sorry bout that,' he called. 'Shirl was laid off so we don't hear the phones when we're on the killing floor.' He bent, lifting up a metal pin to widen the entrance for the truck by opening the second gate.

Drift and her dad fired up the vehicles and drove in, the man swinging the high gates shut behind them. Drift swallowed down upset as she neared the yards and glimpsed her cattle. She could see the black cow, fear back in her eyes, and the old toffee-coloured slow-walking girl nudging nervously at her calf. They pulled up outside the shoebox office, her dad getting out of the truck, speaking to the man for a moment, Split and the man standing side by side. The man threw his arms in the air in an 'I give up' gesture. Then Split came over to her.

'Mal reckons it's going to take a bit of time to sort this mess out,' her dad said to her through the open window of the ute. 'But we can unload the horses and camp here for the night. Boss isn't back from Perth till morning.'

'*Here?*' Drift echoed incredulously. 'I'm not sleeping at the friggin abattoir.'

'Well I'm not leaving until I get my money. Now we're inside the gates I'm not goin anywhere.' His face was held in a firm expression of suppressed fury. Clearly the worker had done his best to reassure him, but it was also clear from the state of the place that things were dire.

There were broken windows, busted fences and yards, and weeds growing in the car park as if the staff had been annihilated months earlier in some kind of apocalyptic event. The place looked virtually abandoned. Drift felt a prickle of fear and resentment. She felt like a child being bossed by her father again. The mad version of him was back. Disquiet rumbled in her. She didn't even want her cattle here. Technically they were never *her* cattle — they were simply the cockies'. Even so, she now felt treacherous in bringing them here and more compromised than ever before.

Her girls, fattened and quietened on coastal scrub and grasses, were now penned behind high yards, bellowing in fear from the death-smell that lingered over everything. Drift felt like letting the cattle out. She didn't want to think what went on behind the high white walls of the slaughterhouse with big-gutted, thick-armed men like the one she'd seen. She knew this was where the animals she handled came to ... but she'd never faced the reality of the human-created space or its lack of honour or heart. She'd read books by livestock-handling revolutionary Temple Grandin, but clearly her practices hadn't made it to this bleak place.

For a moment she thought of the mobile meat cool room on The Planet that Sophia had shown her. It was hard to believe that this other extreme still existed.

Drift remembered Sophia showing her the writings of poet Rumi, written in swirling calligraphy on the side of the mobile chiller. Sophia had remained silent, allowing Drift to read it and for its meaning to sink in:

'We began as mineral. We emerged into plant life, and into
the animal state, and then into being human, and always we
have forgotten our former states, except in early spring when we
slightly recall being green again.'

'It's gruesome for some, but most folks don't understand the
basic laws of energy. Those who object to it have never been
truly hungry,' Sophia said, 'so it's easy to judge when you live
a life of luxury and always have a full belly and vast choices.
I love my animals, I do, but when you see it clearly, eating is
simply energy transference — that's all life is. I eat a carrot; the
energy is transferred to me. I eat a steak; the animal's energy
is transferred to me. That animal's energy has come from the
energy of the grasses, which has come from the energy of the
sun and the life in the soil, which in turn is transferred to me.
When I die I've asked to be buried here in the soil so my energy
is transferred into soil. One day sunlight will grow me into a
plant.

'In the sleeping world, people can't see themselves. They aren't
aware that being an angry animal activist who is aggressive and
strongly opinionated against others is just as destructive as the
people who profit from the factory systems where some can be
aggressive and mindless towards the animals they process. Some
people are too asleep to see that their angry energy is equally
disruptive to the world, no matter what form. It's a trend now to
eat only plants or plants made to look like animal products, but
what the good-intentioned consumers don't know is that most of
those plants are farmed as brutally and soullessly as the animals.

'At The Planet, we teach peacefulness along with humane
slaughter ... if that makes sense. It means the food you ingest
is actually better for you. Food that comes from a place of love.
Not profit or dominance.'

Drift looked now at the desolate Cooperville abattoir and she
could feel the distress of the cows and calves she knew so well.
She felt a chill run through her at the thought of the beautiful
kind-eyed cows meeting their end here at this dismal place.

Most of the cows had a few good breeding years ahead of them, but there had been very little rain in the wider region, and few farmers knew how to manage their grass in the way Sophia and her team did. No one would buy them after a season like this one. She wished more than anything she had land and money herself, so she could buy the lot. Drift realised it had been a mistake not to face where her girls went before now.

Drift walked over to her dad. 'I don't want to leave them here. Can't we load them up and take them back? Buy them off the cocky?'

'With what? And run them where?'

'But … I can't have them end their lives here. Sophia says —'

Split interrupted his daughter, incredulous. 'Where else do they end their lives? In a retirement home? What do you think we've been doing each time we fatten cattle?'

'I know,' Drift said, feeling defeated. 'But Sophia said —'

He cut her off again, irritated. 'Sophia's not here, is she? Sophia lives in her own world. And we're not part of it. At least these guys opened the gates for us. You get the horses off. Put them in a yard. Set the caravan up. We're staying.'

Drift looked at her father. Tears welled.

'I'm goin in to see what I can find out from Mal and the boys.'

'Suit yourself,' she said.

She slid the bolts on the dog box beneath the truck and Molly and Hamlet leaped out, shaking themselves, stretching, dancing around her. Unsettled by the overpowering stench of the meatworks, Drift called the dogs to her. She slumped down on a scraggly patch of grass, her back pressed against the warm truck tyre, holding the dogs to her, ignoring the pungent smell that came from them being too long in the dusty hot boxes. She swiped her eyes and nose on the sleeve of her workshirt and shut her eyes. The horses in the truck whinnied.

'All right!' she said, knowing that she'd struggle to find a yard that wasn't hard concrete. Frustration with her father burned in her.

The yards were all empty, so she picked the largest one with the cleanest trough and led the horses in. They snorted nervously at the grooved concrete beneath their hooves. She hated putting her horses on such a hard surface, even if it was just for one night. She thought about setting up the electrics under a straggly tree across the car park instead but felt too exhausted to even get the gear out, knowing it was jammed under the heavy canvas tarp. She'd need her dad's help to get it out and he was nowhere to be found. Again she cursed Split. Her arms still ached from the day before's manoeuvring of the big squares of steel panels, and a bruise was blooming on her shin where one had skidded sideways and collected her.

Later, with the horses a bit more settled with hay nets, she looked at the caravan. Why unhitch it and set it all out if it was just for one night? She found an extension lead and ran it to an outside power unit on one of the meatworks walls. She looked at the row of humming chillers as she walked past the stacks of wooden pallets, blue plastic drums and giant skip bins. What an awful place, she thought as she unfolded the steps of the caravan.

Inside, she righted a few objects that had been jolted loose on the trip then grabbed a rug from her bed, surprised by how tired she felt. On the shady side of the truck, Drift spread the blanket and lay down, the dogs settling beside her. Dozing, trying to shut out the smell and the irritation of the flies landing on her skin, she also battled to shut out thoughts of Eli. The bleak mooing from her cattle in the holding yard was a sad soundtrack as thoughts of Simon elbowed their way in. Again she pushed them away.

The hours passed. Flies buzzed by. The sun moved and the shadows lengthened. She got up, feeling dehydrated and slightly dizzy. Where was her father?

She put Hamlet and Molly away in their boxes, feeding them pellets, topping up their water, then watched Dunno at her boots as he scoffed his dinner. 'Where do you reckon he is, eh?'

Dunno looked up at her and licked his lips, hoping for a second serve.

'Bugger this,' Drift said to him. 'Let's go find him. Let's get his phone and see if Wilma's home. She might come get us.'

Dunno wagged his tail and followed her as she turned towards the sign that said *Office*, with a finger pointing along a pathway.

'Wait there, mate,' she said to Dunno.

When she opened the door, Drift heard laughter and tinny music. She stood before an abandoned desk, a computer with no keyboard, piles of messy paperwork and bills on a spike. The phone was ringing. And ringing. Drift pushed open a door and followed the sound of the music down a hallway to an adjoining building. There she found her father in the staff lunch room. Mal and another man were laughing and pushing shot glasses about like chess pieces. Her dad, pink-faced, was whooping with them as he joined in the drinking game. Their revelry died when they saw Drift standing in the doorway.

'Dad?'

Her father's eyes slid to her.

'It's gunna be like getting blood out of a stone, my friends here tell me,' he slurred, 'so we've found the boss's best drop. Might be all we get.'

Drift was devastated. The bottle was almost empty and Split's head was wobbling. He hadn't been this drunk since the night he'd tried to top himself.

'Come, girl,' said the bald man who sat at the head of the table. He had a thick Russian accent and a friendly red face. 'Sit down. Have a nip yourself. I know where boss keeps wodka.' He gave Drift a wink.

'No thanks. I don't drink.'

'Suuuuure you don't.' Mal chuckled, grabbing up a glass. 'Just one glass …'

*

Over an hour later the clear spirits burned inside Drift's belly as she ricocheted off the grey walls of the workers' canteen, bursting through the doors and vomiting violently, hands on her knees, bent over double in the Cooperville meatworks car park. The world spinning. She placed her palm on the Colorbond shed to steady herself. It was her first time drunk, and above her the swathe of stars was so thick it seemed to form an eddying mist. She felt as if the planet revolving in the night sky had sped up and she had to hang on harder to the shed. Dunno hovered near, his ears flattened. How did her father do this to his body? She hated the feeling of being drunk, yet in the lead-up to getting pissed it *had* felt like a relief … to not be thinking about Eli. Or Simon. Or the dark shadow that lingered from Kelvin's attack. Even her dad had seemed fine and funny.

She propelled herself away from the wall. On wobbly legs she wove unsteadily towards the stock truck, cooing affectionately to her dogs. The horses called to her, their hay nets empty. She was about to climb into the caravan when she heard shouting. Then a crashing sound. As she ran in a weaving unsteady path back into the canteen, she banged the door open to find Mal wedging Split up against the wall, his forearm to her father's throat.

'Arsehole,' Split was saying as blood oozed from a swelling split lip. A purple shiner was ballooning too over his right eye and the bridge of his nose was fattening, seeping blood from another gash.

'Hey, hey, hey,' soothed Vlad as he tried to drag the men apart.

'You think a night on the grog is gunna sweeten me up? You knew they're sunk and can't pay me!' Split shouted.

'I'm likely not getting any fucking money, neither,' said Mal angrily, spittle spraying from his clenched teeth.

'If you fucking knew it, why'd you open the gates to the trucks and take the cattle? You shoulda just sent them on back to the cocky!'

'I don't call the shots around here,' said Mal as Split tried again to reef himself free and swing another punch.

'Stop it!' Drift cried out. *'Dad!'*

Mal saw Split's eyes slide to his daughter, and his body soften. He relinquished his grip.

'We're all on the same side here,' Vlad said. 'We're all getting screwed. It's time to chill out, Split. You too, Mal. Just chill out! We are up to our eyebrows in alkie. Na brovyakh!'

Drift grabbed up a blue checked tea towel and went to her father, thrusting it in his face to stem the bleeding. She hauled him off the wall where he leaned.

'C'mon, Dad, let's go to the van.'

The night air outside was unbearable. Heat radiated from the concrete yards. Insects thronged around the lone light illuminating the tatty empty car park. Her father and Drift staggered their way to the van. He hauled himself up the small steps and inside.

'Hungry,' he said. 'Fucking hungry.' Like a drunk bear he bashed and crashed the deep-fryer out of the cupboard and rummaged in the Esky for the chips and dim sims he'd bought earlier from the Widgenup Store.

'You don't care, do you?' Drift said, alcohol fuelling her anger as she watched him, noticing the way his eyes and mouth turned downwards, the bitterness of his life revealed on his face. Tonight she hated him. And she hated the town they were in. She wanted to be with anyone but him. Or anywhere but here.

'You don't care about the cattle and what's going to happen to them,' she found herself shouting at him. 'You don't care about yourself. Look at how you pour grog inside yourself when things go wrong and then chow down on fatty foods so you won't make old bones. You don't even care about me. This is no kinda life.'

He swung around, pointing a slotted fryer spoon at her. 'You? *I don't care about you? I've given up my life to raise you!'*

'Bullshit!' Drift exploded. 'You gave up your life the moment you decided never to let the idea of Mum go. Never to move on from her!'

'Leave your mother out of it,' he growled.

'How can I, Dad? I've been paying for your anger about her leaving ever since the night she disappeared!'

'How can you say that? After all I've done for you?'

In the doorway of the caravan Drift could see Dunno cowering in the shadows, his ears now pinned to his head in distress. 'You've used me as an excuse not to get on with your life. You've used me as an excuse not to be somebody better.'

'Somebody better? What's that supposed to mean?' her dad said angrily. 'You ungrateful little —'

He paused, but Drift knew the next word he was going to say was 'bitch'. To be called a bitch again by my own father, she thought, devastated and enraged at the same time.

'That's it. I'm going!' she said.

'Where?'

'Dunno,' she said. 'Anywhere but here! I'm done with you.'

Drift spun from him and jumped from the caravan into the darkness. She jogged over to the gate, rattling it angrily, swearing at the lock that held it fast. She turned to the office, where the lights were still on. Inside Mal and Vlad were nowhere to be seen. She knew there was a door directly on to the back street, so she propelled herself through the building, Dunno trotting after her. On the street, gaining her bearings, she set off hell-bent on walking into Cooperville and out the other side to Wilma's house. She just couldn't be around her dad any more, nor the stench of death.

Chapter 35

The next morning, Drift woke with a pounding head, curled up on the padded floral porch seat at Number Seven White Swan Drive, Wilma's house. Dunno was nesting in the crook of her legs, a warm brown ball of snores. Drift sat up, her heart sinking when she realised there was no car in the pristine concrete carport attached to the neat coffee-coloured brick home.

Drift recalled how she'd rung the doorbell over and over the previous night, even though she knew Wilma would be somewhere up country. In the harsh morning light, she looked over to the unimaginative cul-de-sac of new houses, interspersed with vacant blocks, just waiting for the developers to mushroom more same-same eco-blind housing. Each time she'd come here, she'd found it hard to fit Wilma into living in this neat house. It was all so sterile, compared to Wilma's rambling life on the road in the dusty bus. The path leading up to the house was lined with blooming yellow rosebushes staked as straight as soldiers. The small front porch where Drift had slept was ringed with potted flowers, giving a rather forced cheery welcome, along with a doormat that read *Home Sweet Home*. A blue metal ornamental cat grinned up at her.

'You shouldn't be on Wilma's couch,' Drift said, pushing Dunno off, thinking this was no place for a working dog, particularly one who smelled like Dunno. She regretted coming here and cursed herself again for getting drunk. Her head ached.

She looked at the screen security door and wondered when Wilma would be back. No time soon, she surmised. There was nothing left to do but to walk back across town to the abattoir.

The day was already hot and the sun wasn't even fully up. Drift berated herself again. Split would be furious with her. And she knew he'd be hurt. She stood and staggered slightly to the corner of the house, taking a long drink from the end of a neatly curled hose before setting off down the path, Dunno at her boots.

After winding her way on to the main highway into town, she heard a car coming. It slowed. The window wound down. A piercing wolf whistle from a young guy lifted Dunno's ears before the white Commodore revved away.

'Wanker,' muttered Drift, watching it go, her nerves jangling at the memory of Kelvin. She ran her fingers over her CW belt. She fixed her eyes on the wide sweep of blue sky ahead of her, brushstroked with fine wisps of white cloud above the low skyline of Cooperville. Charlie Weatherbourne had travelled alone for years, Drift thought. Why shouldn't she? She ought to just leave her dad, and go. To become like Charlie – old, weathered, wise, and above all, *free*. In contrast, Drift knew she was taking stupid risks, even after what had happened with Kelvin, just by walking alone at night, and in the dawn hours now. Was she *that* young and dumb? According to what she'd discovered lately, thought Drift bitterly, yes, she was.

But then a voice inside her rebutted with a deep resounding, 'No.' She wasn't stupid and realised she resented the world she found herself in. Why *shouldn't* women be able to walk the streets safely on their own? Drift wound her long hair in a thick twirl like a rope and jammed its beacon blondeness up under her large pale hat. She pulled the hat down over the crown of her head in the stiff hot breeze and kept walking along the highway's edge.

Tiny thistle seedheads blew by, some nestling inside her long-top workboots. She looked down to them as she trudged, thinking of Mother Nature's insistence that the seeds make the trip with her. Mother Nature sure was tough and persistent. She resolved to be more like her.

As she walked past the ugliness of the BP, KFC and Macca's, her mind ran to The Planet and Eli. She sighed at the long stretch of road ahead flanked by industrial estates and tried to resist the deep pull within her to go back down to Pinrush Point and hide herself away from the mindless world. She knew for her dad's sake she had to stay in Cooperville and drag him from the abattoir then get him back on the road. She knew she needed to nurse the silly bugger through his current slump and help him nut out their financial problems and find a future. But like the moon's pull there was something still drawing her away from him. She could feel it. Her heart ached for Eli, as much as she wished it didn't. But her anger flared at Kai. She hastened her pace as she remembered her horses, longing to get them out of the hard yards. The dogs too would be bursting for a run by the time she got there. How could she have left them? As a hangover swamped her system, she vowed never to drink again.

Even walking at a brisk pace, it took her over an hour to make it back. She stopped suddenly, shocked to see the gates swung wide open, the chains cut, and a gathering of cop cars and fire trucks. A stench worse than before filled the air and she gasped when she saw the stock truck, Cruiser and caravan, burned-out, black, unrecognisable wrecks. Running between police cars and fire trucks Drift sprinted towards the caravan.

'*Dad?*' she screamed in a voice that seemed not her own.

She barely registered someone's strong arms holding her back. Her whole life and home lay scattered before her, black and smoking — the van and vehicles, charred skeletons, the dirt and dried grass around them torched.

'Drift ... Oh thank *God* you're OK ...'

It was Simon holding her.

'My dogs!' she screamed. Simon tried to spin her about and face her away from the chaos, but not before she saw the burned-out dog boxes and sickening black remains within.

'No! Please no! Not my dogs!' Drift sobbed. 'And Dad?' Her voice rose into a horrified whisper. 'Where is he?' She looked wildly at Simon, her fingers clasping his arms.

'We can't find him,' Simon said, holding her just as tightly by the upper arms, his voice punchy and urgent. 'The firefighters say he's not in either of the vehicles, nor the van.'

'Are you sure?' Panic seized her mind. She thought she would go mad. Her dogs! *Burned.* Her dad missing. Dunno hovered near, sniffing the air nervously, his tail curled between his legs.

'Yes. We're sure. We're searching for him.'

'And are you sure about the dogs?'

Simon looked at her grimly. 'Sorry,' he said. 'They were locked in their boxes. They didn't make it.'

Drift felt her legs threaten to give way as she looked again at the undercarriage of the truck and spied a black lump. Molly dog.

'Oh God! Please, no!' The words tore at her throat. 'It's my fault! I should never have left them! What's happened?' She broke away from Simon, running to look at the wreckage of their life: the water tank melted in its aluminium frame, the caravan windows in shards on the ground, smoke oozing still from the blackened wreck. Firies stood, still spraying the scene with white foam retardant. She glimpsed Gerald in the front of the stock truck, cooked.

She turned to Simon. '*Where is he? What's he done?*'

'We think ...' Simon fumbled for words. 'The deep-fryer was left on. It ignited the curtains. Then that sparked a fire in the hay on the truck, from what we can tell.'

'And Dad?'

Simon shrugged his shoulders. 'He certainly wasn't in the vehicles. We're trying to find out more from the workers.'

Drift scanned the scene in desperation. Mal and Vlad were standing with slumped shoulders, being questioned by police, their heads hanging low. Simon led her over. They looked at her bleakly then continued talking to Detective Morgan, who glanced disapprovingly at Drift.

'We left out the front entrance through the office,' Mal said. 'As far as we knew, he'd gone to bed.'

'And how did you come by that fat lip?' the detective asked, indicating Mal's swollen mouth and bruised cheekbone.

Vlad piped up. 'We were pretty full. It was just piss talk. Mal and Split had a bit of grog, a bit of biffo. But they parted company as mates. Didn't they? No problem.'

Mal nodded. They both looked at Drift.

'Didn't we, darlin?' Mal said to her. 'Mates.'

Simon looked at her.

'I don't know,' she said.

'I told your dad to chill out, didn't I?' Vlad said. 'And he did. He went to bed fine.'

Drift nodded, but wondered if the men were telling the truth.

'Where were you when all this was happening?' Simon asked her, his blank police face back on.

Drift looked to her boots. 'After they had a fight I got mad with Dad. So I left.'

'Where did you go?' Simon pressed.

'I walked to Wilma's.'

'Can Wilma vouch for that?'

Drift shook her head. 'No, she wasn't home.'

Just then a silver Prado swung into the car park. Out stepped a man in neat beige trousers and a blue and white checked Rodd and Gunn shirt.

'What the Hell is going on here?'

'Steven Dennison?' Simon asked. 'Are you the owner here?'

'Not strictly speaking no more. Not right now. The bank is. Tell me what the fuck is going on!'

'Please sir, language in front of the lady,' Simon warned.

Drift glanced at him. *Lady? Language?* As if she gave a fuck about language at this point, with her father missing and her whole life up in smoke! Simon didn't seem to notice her rising frustration.

'It seems there's been an accidental fire and Dennis Wood's plant and equipment were burned overnight.'

The meatworks man glared at his staff. 'What the fuck is Wood's droving plant doing in here?'

Mal and Vlad stood still, as if trying to suddenly become invisible.

'That's a question for later,' Simon continued. 'Mr Wood is still missing, sir. And there're a few further questions we will need to ask your men.'

Just as Mr Dennison was about to bluster on with more protests, a cry came up from the searchers. '*Here!* We've found him!'

A pimply policeman motioned from behind a set of shipping containers.

Drift ran with the men, weaving through the containers to a large white chiller box, air-conditioner rumbling on its side. She pushed her way past the men gathering in the doorway and barged into the chiller. Inside, under the hanging beef carcasses, the ambo officers were already crouched over Split, dragging out a silver thermo blanket to cover him.

'Dad!' she cried out as she saw his large body slumped inside on the floor beneath butcher's hooked sides of beef, all pink with yellow fat marbling around the ribcages.

Was he dead? Drift could see his skin was a ghostly white and his lips shockingly blue. After fixing an oxygen mask over his face and pressing stethoscopes to him, the ambos motioned to the firies to help lift the large man out of the ice-cold room. His head lolled back for a moment and Drift let out a cry. Surely he wasn't dead? She couldn't think of life without him. She'd already faced the possibility of that once. She couldn't bear to go through it for real. Drift watched in horror as the men loaded him onto a trolley. As they began to get to work on him in the ambulance, she felt an arm circle about her shoulders.

'Don't worry,' Simon said, drawing her near. 'I'm here for you. All the way.'

Chapter 36

On the way to the hospital in the police car with Dunno at her feet, Simon glanced over to Drift, sympathy on his face. They were following the ambulance the short distance to the Cooperville hospital. Shock had rendered her still.

He reached for her limp hand and squeezed her fingers gently. She looked at him bleakly. All she kept hearing in her head, over and over, were the words, 'We've found a pulse,' coming from the ambulance officer right before they'd closed the door. The words were a life buoy of hope she now clung to as Simon swung the car into the hospital car park.

He settled her into the waiting room near a too-loud clock with hands that moved too slowly. At some point, Simon disappeared. She sat in a fog as doctors came and went, as did nurses, all of them with looks of concern and care. They offered paper cups of tea in hushed tones. Drift could feel both alcohol poisoning and shock invading her body as she lifted the tea to her lips with trembling hands.

After a time, the faces blurred and Drift was grateful Simon was there to deal with it all. They were discussing whether to transfer Split to Perth or not. As he liaised with the doctors, it was decided her dad was best left where he was.

Once Split was stabilised, they led her into his room and she sat beside him, holding his big square hand, thinking of the night she'd painted his nails, the night when this had all begun.

His hands were ice cold, the staff coming in from time to time to check the electric blanket that was slowly warming him back to a normal body temperature. Drift was hopeful that as the warmth returned to his fingers he'd wake, but then the doctors came and wheeled him away for more tests.

More waiting. And praying. She realised that in these past few months she'd never prayed so much in her life. As she slumped in a blue moulded-plastic hospital chair, exhausted, she prayed with grateful intention for her wise-women posse to arrive. She pictured Charlie or Wilma turning up. She'd tried reaching both on her dad's phone — they'd found it in the abattoir crib room, battery nearly dead, lying on the table beside his final glass of neat vodka. Frustratingly both Wilma's and Charlie's phones went straight to message bank. She knew her gypsy women would be in remote regions, doing their thing. She vowed to summon them by other means. She closed her eyes and willed them to appear, imagining them walking into the ward in great detail. Eyes shut, she also imagined her father awake and well, sitting up in bed, quoting Shakespeare.

All the hateful thoughts she'd had about her dad bubbled up in her mind. Now all she wanted to do was to take back the angry, ungrateful words she'd said. Hearing footsteps, she opened her eyes. Simon stood before her, offering her a cup of water in a flimsy plastic cup. The TV above his head was advertising funeral services. She hoped it wasn't a sign. She pushed the grim thought away and smiled gratefully at him, taking the cup. He looked handsome in his creased uniform, sympathy again written openly on his face.

'The doctor said it could be hours before they know more,' he said gently, 'but he's stable now. He's breathing by himself. Still not conscious, but scans show his brain function is fine. And his ticker is good.'

Drift looked to his face, thankful but guilty that she couldn't let him in more. She felt her night with Eli burn on her cheeks in a blush. She looked back at the toes of her scuffed, dry leather workboots.

'Drift. I think you're in shock. You need to lie down somewhere and get some sleep.'

Drift massaged her temples. 'I know.'

'Would you be up to coming to my house?' he offered gently. 'If you thought it appropriate?'

'But ... my horses.'

'I can swing by and check on them after I've settled you in. I'll arrange some hay for them.'

She looked at him and frowned. 'I ought to do it. They're my horses.' Then she felt panic rise. The hay was all burned. All the gear. All her clothes. She had no money. They weren't insured, she didn't think. It was all gone. She suddenly remembered the photo of her mother. Destroyed. The realisation hit her that her life truly had changed forever. She'd been so focused on her dad she had only just now seen how helpless and alone she was. And trapped. Tears rose up.

'It's OK,' Simon said, sitting down next to her, rubbing his hand over her back. She looked at him. He was being wonderful. She'd seen how he'd taken charge of Dunno and the way he'd tied him up outside the Cooperville hospital in the shade of some trees under a bench seat, where Dunno was happily wooing all the smokers for pats. Simon seemed to read Drift's mind.

'Dunno is welcome at my place. And I've spoken to my mum and my sister about clothes for you. They're there now, making up the spare room. It's yours if you like.'

Drift noticed how his hair had been recently cut, revealing less tanned skin on his neck. She felt tears spill onto her cheeks. He was being so kind. So sincere. And the fact he'd asked the women in his family for help on her behalf made her want to cry all over again. Then once more she felt the wrench of Eli. Of the lie. No, she couldn't involve herself with Simon. Not now. But, she reasoned, what else was she to do? Where else could she go, unless she found her wise women?

'No pressure,' he added. 'It's just it would be more comfortable than a hotel.'

'OK,' she said in a small voice. If she thought about it, she felt uncomfortable going to his place, but on the other hand, she knew she had no other choice. The van was gone. All her books. Her dictionary, paints and sketchbooks. Charlie's rosewood box and the dress, destroyed. The one remaining photo of her mother, gone. Her dogs, dead. The cattle impounded. Her horses locked in a concrete yard. No money for the job coming. No funds to replace the stock contracting plant. Her dad, nearly dead … again. There was nothing more to lose. And he was being so very nice to her. She was silent for a moment.

'I guess he thought Vlad meant it for real,' she said with a half smile.

'Meant what?'

'He told dad to chill out. He must've taken it literally.' She chuckled and rolled her eyes. 'So he went to chill out, in the chiller.'

She saw a confused expression pass over Simon's face. She and her dad's shared black sense of humour bubbled out. It was humour Eli had got so readily, joining in on their family pranks, but clearly Simon wasn't within range of her sad attempt at lightening the situation.

'I'm joking,' she said. 'Him being in the chiller. What was he thinking?'

Simon looked terse, as if it wasn't a time to make jokes. He's probably right, Drift thought.

'I'm sorry. I'm not in my right mind. I guess it was such a hot night. Do you think he just went in there to cool down and got trapped? You don't think it's anything else, do you?'

Simon ran his hands through his black hair and frowned, his police face on again. 'I don't know. I can't say. But time will tell. We're treating it as suspicious until we clear the men who were there.'

'Suspicious?' Drift shook her head. Surely the men at the abattoir wouldn't have done anything like that to her father? 'Do you think Dad will wake and tell us?'

She wanted Simon to say, 'Yes, yes he will,' but instead he answered, 'We'll just have to wait until the doctors know more.'

'Can I go see him again?'

Simon shook his head. 'They're still running tests. They said it's best to wait until morning. I'll bring you back in then.'

She felt a surge of distress.

Simon took her hand in his. 'Melody, we just have to have faith,' he said. 'C'mon. You're tired.'

Gently he took her by the elbow, inviting her to stand, then he guided her past the green glowing exit sign on the wall. 'I know it's under really terrible circumstances, but I'm so glad to see you again,' he said as he pressed the button for the elevator and the down arrow illuminated.

'Yes,' Drift said, 'me too,' not certain at all that she felt the same way.

*

Drift looked at the spartan spare room: there was a print of a pale pink lily above the bed, echoing the tones of the walls and bedspread. Outside Dunno was sniffing around on the end of a chain, where a newly bought plastic kennel had been set up. She glanced at Simon, trying to look grateful, but she was a little shocked by the fact his mother and sister had *bought* a kennel just for her dog.

'I hope it's comfortable enough for you,' he said, as they stood in the doorway of the spare room. Behind them was the brown-toned lounge room of his police-issue house, square and bland, both inside and out. She turned to what was now 'her room' and Drift noticed the tightly tucked rose-print sheets and the frilled-edged pink satin pillow.

'Yes, it's lovely,' she lied, her heart breaking for her old tumbled bed in the caravan with its views of the sea and her horses. She berated herself for being ungrateful and forced a smile. Maybe it would do her good to be normal for a change.

Stay under a normal roof. Eat in a normal fashion at a dining table with food dished up from a normal kitchen. Simon noticed Drift's glance at the minimalist kitchen with the canisters set out in a row on the bench from little to biggest, all labelled neatly.

'Mum and Teena helped do the bed,' he said, 'and they've even left us a casserole.'

Us. Even the word *casserole* was making Drift want to run for it, but she held her ground. She told herself to stop being silly. She just wasn't used to such kindness from virtual strangers. Until her dad came round from his coma or until Wilma and Charlie came back, she had no option but to accept where she was. She looked up at his deep brown eyes and felt his attentiveness almost burn her. If only she didn't hold that secret about Eli. Simon seemed to be leaning nearer her, maybe angling in for a kiss. She swallowed at the thought of kissing him again after her night with Eli. Just as he was about to press his lips to hers, his pager fired. He tightened his lips impatiently, let out a tense breath and walked over to the kitchen bench to retrieve it.

'The sergeant needs me. It's a domestic.' He smiled apologetically at her. 'Sorry. I'll be as quick as I can.' He grabbed up his keys, reached for his cap and strode from the room. She heard the screen security door click shut and Simon turn the lock.

The fridge buzzed as Drift looked about the sterile environment. She moved the sheer curtain aside and watched Simon drive away. A man across the road was firing up a lawn mower to cut a lawn that didn't need mowing. She tried to settle herself on the couch, flipping her bare toes over the edges of the stack of *Home Beautiful*s Simon's mother must've left for her. She suddenly wished for her dad's *New Philosopher* magazine, but with the wish came thoughts of losing her home. She couldn't bear that, so she got up and went to the sink and drank a glass of water. She needed fresh air … not this chilled air-conditioned ice. She turned the key to the security screen of the back door and stepped out onto the hot concrete path.

'Give me a sign,' she said, looking out to the cobalt wash that blanketed the sky beyond the clothesline. There was not a breath of wind. Not a cloud in sight. The back lawn was framed by the same-same green Colorbond fence. There was a neatly concreted and edged path to a Hills Hoist from which Simon's uniform shirts hung in the stillness. A hose was curled up neatly like a snake on the back fence.

She turned to the plastic green kennel shaped like an igloo. 'Dunno, you look ridiculous in that thing.'

The dog knew he was being mocked. Such was his humiliation at being tied to a plastic kennel in a backyard he practically turned his back on her.

Drift went over to consult her old mate. 'Any idea what to do, Dunno?' She crouched down at his kennel to pat his hunched back, feeling a surge of grief for her other dogs. 'What do you think?' She sighed. 'You dunno, do you, Dunno?'

She'd asked Simon to find a phone charger for her if he could. That way she could at least keep trying Wilma and Charlie on her dad's phone. She stood and went inside. She knew she should eat and sleep, but the hours ticked by. Drift let the pain come. She hugged her knees to her chest on the couch and wept.

In the corner a phone startled her when it began to ring loudly. She wiped her eyes and hesitated before she picked it up. 'Hello?'

'Ah! I hoped you'd answer,' came Simon's voice. 'Look, I've been held up. Heat yourself up some dinner. I'll be as quick as I can.'

Drift wanted to make jokes with Simon about being 'held up' — did he mean as in late or as in cop-style held up? She now knew he probably wouldn't get the fact she wanted to make jokes at a time like this.

Drift listlessly picked at her microwaved chicken that swam in some kind of apricot sauce. She tried as best she could to return the kitchen to its pristine state and do her dishes tidily. She looked at the blank black square of the large television that dominated the room. She hated TV. She flipped through the magazines, not taking in anything she saw. Her mind returned again and again to her father, to her poor horses at the abattoir and to Eli. Soon she heard a car. From the window she saw Simon getting out, carrying a bouquet of plastic-wrapped supermarket flowers. Drift hastily made a dash for the spare room and shut the door. If she was quiet enough, he'd think she was asleep.

Chapter 37

The next day Simon, neat as a pin in a fresh police uniform, ushered Drift into the hospital. She found herself at the door of her father's room with Simon pecking her on the cheek, quietly saying goodbye, heading off to his work. What was going on? Drift wondered, as he strode away along the corridor. Did Simon think he'd fallen into a relationship with her? Was she giving him that impression? Under her circumstances, at least she had *someone* to care for her during this storm, but she was still uncertain about him. It was hard to stifle her wild-girl ways in his fastidious home. His perfection-focused mother had phoned him three times the night before. Despite the order and routine of their lives, Drift felt the undercurrent of tension and obligation Simon lived by under her wing.

And always on her mind were the questions of Eli. Had he truly drowned? Was he on the run again? She was getting mad at him, again. Where was he, after all his talk of bloody flowers-together-forever sentimental stories?

She sucked in a breath and stepped into Split's room. There he lay, looking normal enough, but not. His mouth was dragged down on one side with a tube and the back of his hand was taped with a drip. A monitor on his index finger linked him to a machine on wheels beside his bed. She shuddered and tentatively went over to him, laying her cool hand on his arm.

'Dad,' she said, her voice cracking, feeling the warmth of his skin, 'what should I do?'

Drift stood in the dim light of the ward remembering Charlie's words years back. It was on the day she'd found Drift crying over the death of her dad's old kelpie, Min. Charlie had taken Drift by her shoulders and stooped to look her in the eye. 'You just have to accept this is all part of a bigger plan than you and I can ever understand. Sad though it is, trust that the big old Universe knows exactly what it's doing. Trust with a capital T that death is not really death at all.'

Drift tried to channel some trust with a capital T in the unnervingly quiet early-morning hospital. She wished Simon hadn't talked the nurses into allowing her in before visiting hours. She should have held her resolve to walk from his place later, but Simon would have none of that. He wanted to help her. Sighing, she dragged a chair near to the bed and plonked down in it. She stared at her father, wishing she could talk to him about Simon and the rest.

'I've never seen you so silent,' she said. 'You're not even snoring like a chainsaw any more.'

Her dad remained motionless. She searched her mind for one of his Shakespeare lines. '*Be checked for silence. But never taxed for speech.*'

Three days later, she found herself saying the same phrase over and over, shutting her eyes and letting her forehead fall on the super-clean sheets, reaching out, laying her palm on her father's hulking chest, which lifted and fell with each gentle breath.

Drift felt her own breath fall into rhythm with his. In, out. In, out. She didn't know how long she remained there, but her mantra that he would wake up and all would be well was interrupted when she felt the pressure of a gentle hand on her shoulder. She looked up at the slack face of her father, thinking her prayer had worked, but he hadn't moved. Instead she turned — and sobbed to see Wilma standing beside her. Her hair was in its usual grey-brown halo of curls, there was dust from the road on her Cat boots and her dress was crumpled from driving the long stretch home.

'I came as soon as I was in range and got your message,' she said. 'I'm so sorry, my girl.'

Drift, who had been holding in her emotions, unravelled instantly. She felt the tension swell and burst outwards. Tears slid over her cheeks as she stood stiffly and leaned into Wilma's soft bosomy hug. 'He won't wake up, Wilma.'

Wilma cupped Drift's face in her hands and looked her directly in the eye. 'He will. He will. Give him time. We can't give up on him. Plus I know he can hear us. So let's just enjoy his silence. You can't backchat us now, can you, Split?' she said, squeezing his forearm and leaning over him. 'C'mon, mate ... we know you're just being sulky. Your girl needs you, so you just come back to us when you're ready. You hear?'

Drift looked at the hopeful tears in Wilma's eyes.

'Just have faith,' she said, looking back at Drift, echoing the same sentiment as Simon.

'Yes,' Drift said. 'Faith. It must be all part of a bigger plan.'

'Never a truer word spoken,' Wilma said, stroking Drift's hair back over her shoulder. 'We sometimes perceive change as a frightening thing but we forget there's *always* one constant everyone can hold on to, no matter what.'

'And what would that be?' Drift asked with a reluctant grin, knowing the answer already.

'That constant is love with a capital L. You can feel it when you are still and silent. What better chance for both of you? You can't get more still and silent in life than this. In silence, we truly hear. I bet your dad is having a lovely time where he is.'

Drift looked at Wilma gratefully.

Throughout the rest of the morning, true to her name, Wilma the Wondrous stepped in with her brilliant bedside manner. She tidied the room, spoke kindly but briskly to the nurses, set about combing Split's hair and asked the carers to give him a shave and another body wash. She instructed Drift to massage her father's feet, gnarly old things that they were.

'Do his hands too,' Wilma said. Just holding them and rubbing the oil into them reminded Drift of the night she'd painted his nails. It felt so long ago. That same night she'd wished for change. Well, she thought, *here change was*!

'Shall I do your nails in a nice blue this time, to match your gown?' she said to her dad.

'That's the way,' Wilma encouraged. 'Give him so much lip, he'll wake up ready to whop your backside!' She grinned at Drift.

Drift grinned back. With Wilma here, she found her footing. Love was in the room with a capital L. Drift realised suddenly it had been there all along. She just had to remember to reach for it and everything would be fine.

'What on Earth was he doing in the chiller anyway?' Wilma asked.

Drift shrugged and turned to Split. *'Thou sodden-witted lord! Thou hast no more brains than I have in mine elbows!'*

Wilma giggled. 'Now, tell me … where have you been staying these past few nights?' she asked. 'The nurses told me you lost everything in the fire.'

Drift's cheeks coloured when she thought of the sleepless nights she'd been spending at Simon's. He had been infinitely kind, setting the table, sharing meals his mother had cooked. Even lighting candles. Each night he'd held her hands and told her he thought she was lovely, then pecked her on the cheek, leaving her to go to her room.

In the night, she wondered if he'd come to her, tapping his knuckles tentatively on her door. She wondered if she'd let him. To feel a man's body close to hers and to be held might help, she thought as she lay alone, grieving her cattle and her dogs, and her father's health, their life forever gone as she knew it. But he never did come. Part of her was relieved. Part of her was confused.

'I've been staying at Simon's. The policeman's.'

Wilma titled her head inquisitively, a cheeky look passing across her face.

'It's not what you think. At least I don't think it is.'

'And how's that going for you?'

Drift looked heavenwards to the ugly panelled ceiling. 'I don't want to hurt his feelings, but ... can I come stay with you? Please?' she blurted.

Wilma looked at her, amused.

'Dunno is bored out of his brain there. And, I, I just don't think I can handle any more nights of watching game shows with Simon on the couch! And the constant vacuuming and wiping. I'm going nuts. He won't take me to see my horses at the abattoir because he thinks it will upset me too much. Plus I'm over wearing his sister's clothes!' She looked down at herself. 'Look at me.'

'Yes, well, I didn't like to mention that,' Wilma said taking in the long navy skirt and the bluebell long-sleeved blouse.

Drift kicked out her workboots from underneath the skirt. 'I drew a line at the sandals. They were too small anyway. And with my white feet it looked like I was wearing socks.'

'You look lovely,' Wilma said, tugging at the skirt, grinning at her.

'I feel as if I'm being crucified in this get-up. His sister and his mum are *very* religious,' Drift confessed, feeling guilty she was judging the women who had been so good to her.

'It looks as if you *are* being crucified ... by someone else's expectations. I think you'd better come back to my place. Simon will understand, I'm sure.'

'Thank you,' Drift said, the tension leaving her body.

She held back from telling Wilma about Eli. It just didn't feel like the right time. Particularly with her dad right there, and Wilma saying Split could hear everything they said even if he was out to it. Drift knew she would tell her everything once they got settled at Wilma's place. She had to, otherwise she thought she might go mad. Then there was the issue of the cattle and her horses, still stuck in the abattoir. Plus, there would be time for Drift to cry properly with Wilma about dear Hamlet and Molly dog. Sadness swamped her.

'We'll finish up here with Split and head around to collect your things and we'll get you back on track. I promise,' Wilma said.

*

Later that evening, Drift stared at the flames in the tiny firepot as she sat in Wilma's leafy brick-paved courtyard under a ceiling of crimson bougainvillea. The flames licked and crackled, and Drift found it odd to see fire trapped within steel bars. It also felt odd to be sitting on such a padded outdoor couch. She was used to the metal bite of wonky old camp chairs and a fire that was simply ringed by stones and rose freely into the air.

The streetlights dampened the impact of the night sky, so Drift couldn't see stars or feel the certainty of life within the dirt beneath her feet. The flowering garden plants surrounding her were all contained within matching pots. She felt disconnected, as if she were in a foreign world, but at the same time the order of the house gave a kind of comfort and certainty. She felt an unwavering current of love towards Wilma.

Earlier that day, they had tracked Simon down at the police station. When they'd told him about Drift spending some time with Wilma, she saw a shadow cross his face momentarily before he beamed a smile.

'Sure!' he said, the muscle in his jaw twitching slightly. 'Great idea. I totally understand,' he said, looking at them in turn.

'It's not that I don't ...' Drift began. 'It's just — the garden is better set up for dogs. Y'know,' she said, feeling dreadful.

Simon waved her explanation away. 'It's a good idea. It's more appropriate anyway. Mum was already starting to make a few comments,' he said, his eyes sliding to the floor. 'It will be better for us in the long run. You take your time.'

Drift felt herself flinch when she heard the words *appropriate*, and *us*. His very formal mother, Mrs Swain, towered even higher with her dominating presence due to grey culvert-pipe hair styled high on her head. She was terrifying in an aggressive, surly cat kind of way, and had already dropped hints about avoiding even the appearance of 'living in sin'. Bible verses spilled from her lips routinely.

The first time she handed Drift a pile of clothes, she said, 'Women should adorn themselves in respectable apparel, with modesty and self-control.' When Drift had looked startled, Mrs Swain had said to her as if she was slow, 'The first letter of St Paul to Timothy, chapter two, verses nine to fourteen.'

Drift shuddered a little now, feeling the sting of her judgement still.

'That policeman's pretty sweet on you,' Wilma said as she threw more wood in the firepot.

'Yes, he is, but ...'

'But what?'

'I don't know. I think his family are pretty, you know ... They seem a bit ... Oh I don't know.'

'They've been kind to you? Yes?'

'Yes,' she said, 'they have.'

'Then that's all that needs acknowledgement. He's very handsome, isn't he? In a neat-boy way.'

Drift could tell Wilma was trying to steer the conversation in a direction she wasn't ready to face. If she spoke about Simon's feelings for her, she would need to speak about Eli, and then out it would all come ... about the night of the storm. And Eli's leaving. Dunno rescued her by letting off a stinking fart from where he lay at her feet.

'Oh God,' said Drift, waving her hand before her nose, 'I'm so sorry, Wilma. I told you not to give him fresh mince!'

Wilma laughed. 'He's fine. It's been years since we've had a dog in the place. He's more than welcome. I was used to it at one time. Our dog Beans was named Beans for a reason, you know!'

Drift laughed. 'He might need a bath.'

'We can do that,' Wilma said. 'When my Bob was alive we used to bath Beans. He was a little cocker. But then Beans died. His kidneys. And then Bob died. His heart. I was on the road too much with the books after that to get another one. Dog that is, not husband.'

Wilma chuckled at her own joke. She sat down in the chair and sighed, then suddenly slapped one of her bare upper arms so it wobbled. 'Bloody mozzies! Do those silly citronella candles actually work?' She waved one of the candles in the air. 'Bugger off!' She delivered a cheeky look to Drift, her brown hair frizz backlit by the light like a Botticelli painting.

Drift smiled at her. She helped Wilma with the cutlery and setting the plates out on the glass table. Drift looked down at the clothes Wilma had bought her, feeling guilty she had no means of paying her back, but she liked the fact she was in her standard dress of denim shorts and tank top and out of Simon's sister's clothes. 'Thanks, Wilma — for everything.'

'Oh that's all right, dear,' she said, placing a chicken salad in front of her. 'Mention it not.'

As Drift reached for the salad servers, Wilma laid her hand on hers. 'Dear girl, don't for a minute think you are putting me out. I'm so glad you're here ... although not the circumstances of course ... but look ...' She swept her hand around the picture-perfect home. 'My life is boooooring! Without Bob and Beans, it's ...' she paused and sighed '... it's empty. Don't get me wrong: I'm grateful every day, and my life is full when I'm at work. But my home life is made up of stuff I never intended. You know? It's empty of the important stuff, but full of the daily living stuff. Bob and I used to like to travel. We had so many, many plans and places we wanted to go. He was going to retire and fish for the rest of his life, and I was going to write the whole way on our trips. This was only ever going to be a temporary base ... an investment for the future. But the world turns and life changes, sometimes not in the way you want it to.'

She looked about and laughed. 'That's why I took on the bus after he died. I love the bus. I get to go into the wilds — the wilds where you live, my dear. But it's been ten years now! I've been begging for a change, and I reckon you're it.'

'Me?' Drift said, her damp hair drying in soft spirals.

'Everything is part of a big puzzle. You being here is my gift. You're a special girl, my dear. Most young people your age are …' She hesitated, trying to find the right words, '… I don't know, *tainted*? Tainted by technology and advertising and marketing — even the food they give kids these days is tainted. By money. By greed. The poor things don't know which way up to butter their gluten-free bread when it comes to walking in the world. You do. Thanks to your dad raising you the way he has, you do.'

Drift blinked.

'I'm not saying the old ways were better — God knows every generation says that — but I'm saying with modern living, we've all lost our balance. But you, my dear girl, you're connected to the earth. Even though you've lost everything, you're still grounded, here. Present.'

She sighed and for the first time Drift saw the sadness and the age around her.

'I'll shut up now. Our salad's getting cold,' Wilma joked, her eyes creasing. 'But just know, you are welcome to stay here for as long as you need. We'll get you on your feet, and I'll be very, very glad of the company. Both of you,' she said, looking down to Dunno and raising her glass of water at him. 'But maybe less mince for you, dear man.'

They ate their meal and afterwards sat on the couch staring at the fire.

'I know it's too warm a night for a fire,' Wilma said eventually. 'But I need a fire. It reminds me.'

Drift cocked her head in a question and shifted her feet to lightly rest on Dunno's snoozing body as he lay stretched out in a deep sleep. 'Reminds you?'

'Yes. That all possibilities and probabilities may exist in the future and it's not my business to limit them. It's up to me to stay still long enough to look into the flames and see that this moment *now* is connected to all the ancient moments that have happened, and all the moments that will happen, and so really I'm not to be fussed about anything. What's the point? Life's not to be taken so seriously and sadly. Plus you can't ever feel lonely with a fire.'

Drift looked at the flames and realised she was right. Fires gave her a sense of comfort too. Wilma dropped another few bits of thin kindling into the iron basket and vibrant orange sparks rose up, then disappeared from vision as they burned out.

'Sad really,' Wilma said, 'that we've replaced fireside living with televisions. Another disconnect from ourselves.'

Drift nodded.

'Tell me,' Wilma went on, turning to her, eyes probing, 'what has happened to you? I can read a change in you.'

So Drift began to tell Wilma all about Eli. Kai. And the days they had become friends on the drove, then the one night they had spent as lovers. Then his disappearance — for a second time. Like Charlie, Wilma sat with the information for a while in silence.

'I'm sorry your surfer stockman boy is lost and your dad has gone to sleep. It's tough. You know, I wouldn't have been born but for the war and the prison camps. Mum would never have met my father otherwise. Good came, eventually, from their time of horror. Every encounter we have with every person we meet is a lesson and a chance to grow. Remember that.'

Drift thought of the images etched in her mind of the burnt-out equipment, the horses back at the meatworks yard, despondent and confused. She thought of the last herd of cattle she'd been able to care for, destined to have their heads chopped off prematurely. Her dad in a meat chiller, passed out. The light in Eli's eyes. The long thick mane of her giant slab-of-chocolate horse Bear, dear angel grey Roger, and soft and gentle ever-faithful Minty. Her dad's Dunston, possibly never to be ridden by him again. It hurt too much to think too long of the dogs. She remembered the child's dress Charlie had given her. That was also gone, and any sense of a certain future. She folded her arms about herself in comfort. Wilma sensed her slump.

'I know it feels insurmountable right now, but in the morning I'm going to call that wretched meatworks for you and see what we can do about getting the ponies back. Now it's time to sleep. To reset your self,' Wilma said.

Wilma took Drift by her hand and invited her to stand. Drift's body felt battle weary and bruised as she shuffled inside like a ninety-year-old woman. Dunno padded after them, moving his stiff body as if he were just as old.

Wilma led Drift to a spare room done out in blooming roses.

'It's funny you know. This house,' she said as she pulled back a floral quilt edged in gold. 'I've done the garden out in Bob's taste and the interior is done in my mother's taste. It's as if I've built a shrine to them inside and out.' She shook her head. 'You being here, Drift, with the wildness of Mother Nature radiating from you, you help me see it. So thank you. It's time for me to make some changes. Let go of the past. You are the one helping me. Not the other way around.'

'No really,' Drift said, and emotion clutched her throat, 'God knows where I'd be if not for you … and Charlie.' They gathered each other up in an embrace and Drift, who was so over crying, just closed her eyes and allowed herself to be held. At the same time she gave all she could in the form of love and gratitude back to spongey loving Wilma, who had come, yet again, to her rescue.

In the corner, Dunno circled three times in Beans's well-chewed cane basket and slumped down with a heavy sigh. Life had altered forever for them both, and he seemed done with the day.

Chapter 38

Drift stood again outside the gates of the gloomy abattoir and shuddered at the blackened area shadowing where the truck, ute and caravan had been. She said again to Steve Dennison through the wire, '*But the horses are ours!*'

She could hear distress rising in her voice, and realised she had to stay calm in dealing with the likes of Mr Dennison, the arrogant but bankrupt businessman who had owned the struggling abattoir.

Wilma stood her ground beside Drift, bringing her older-woman authority to the situation, and in her best stern-librarian voice said, 'Now, listen here, young man.' Her words were draped in sarcasm. He was far from young. But Wilma was older. 'Keeping the cattle for financial reasons I can understand, but *not taking her horses! It's her droving team. Her livelihood!*'

The man looked at Wilma with distaste. Drift could see older women didn't rate with him. She despised him and what he represented. Steven Dennison may have been better dressed, but he held the same entitled, misogynistic energy as Kelvin Waller, she thought.

'The cattle are impounded with us as part of your father's debts,' he said, jaw jutting out. Today he wore yet another designer shirt, this time in red gingham, with polished RM Williams boots and neatly ironed chinos.

'What do you mean, my father's debts?' Drift said in a growl.

'Weeeell,' he explained, in a fake breathy voice as if he was offering her his benevolence and patience, 'there's the money we've spent on feeding both the cattle and the horses —'

Drift quickly cut him short. 'But Constable Swain has been dropping horse feed in, and the cattle's feed isn't our debt to carry.'

'Your father is the contractor. It's not the cattle owner's cost,' he said, irritated.

'If you'd bought and processed them as agreed ... and given us time to reach the cocky for permission to wean and on-sell the calves ... You should never have —' Drift began.

But Steven held up his hand and shut his eyes as if summoning strength to deal with the tiresome women in front of him. 'Allow me to continue please, young lady.'

'Oh please,' said Wilma, rolling her eyes.

He drew in a breath, then spoke in a quiet, vinegary tone. 'Then there was the cost of moving all your father's burnt-out crap from the yard. That wasn't cheap. He never ought to have been here in the first place. I ought to sue him. He almost burned the place down.'

'This place?' Drift said, casting her eye around the virtually worthless facility.

He ignored her. 'So the horses stay. They'll be sold so I at least get a tiny percentage of my money back. It's what my lawyer has advised and if you disagree I suggest you engage your own lawyer. And if you come around here again like this, I'll be getting a restraining order. This is nothing short of harassment.'

Wilma made a scoffing noise. Drift clutched the wire as she looked over to her animals milling about dejectedly. 'No,' she breathed. 'No! Please, not my horses. Please don't do this! This is not about money.' She shook the fence. '*Please!*' Her voice was loud now, desperate.

'Calm down, miss,' he said. 'This *is* about money. It's always about money. Nothing more.'

Her horses had heard her voice and were now lifting their heads to spy her over the high railing. She wanted to run to Minty and hug her, burying her face in the white-sand neck, entwining her fingers in the mare's mane. A memory of Eli came flooding back — just thinking about the mare brought back the feeling of their bodies pressed together as they dinked. He'd ridden Roger each day of the drove, a horse–man match made in Heaven. With such oneness in their movement, at times Drift could imagine Eli and his horse as a centaur. She'd painted a quick watercolour of him that way once on a sleepless night as he lay outside the van in her swag. Magical and mystical. The memory of him flared. Her beside him, their two white horses moving through the landscape. A man and a woman together. She could see Roger now, his ears pricked in her direction. He looked far from magical in that yard. Miserable was the only word to describe him now.

'At least let me see them!'

Minty whinnied.

'Please,' she said again to Dennison, '*please*.' Her face crumpled in pain, but he was already turning his back, walking away.

'Surely there's something we can do, sir,' Wilma called after him. 'I'll pay for the horses. Good money.'

But the man, clearly holding a grudge against Split Wood, life in general, and, in particular, against women like Wilma and Drift, entered the abattoir office, the door slamming at his back.

'Good luck living with yourself. You cruel, cruel man,' Wilma called after him. She took Drift by the shoulders, and waited for her to uncurl her fingers from the wire. 'Come on, my darling,' she said with such tenderness.

'But they are my home,' said Drift brokenly. 'Those horses are home. They're all I have left.'

'I know, my dear. I know.'

In the car Drift pressed her forehead to the glass, gazing numbly out the window, breath stuttering in a silent cry.

Wilma angrily clicked on her seatbelt. 'We'll get Simon on to this. But for the time being, just remember, for whatever reason this is happening, you must, if you can, see it all as a lesson. It's all learning. A chance to grow.'

Wilma's words burned and hurt her, and Drift wanted to rail against them. She felt like kicking the floor of the car in fury, but she held it in. She knew Wilma meant well, but with her dogs and horses taken, her entire life felt lost.

*

The next day, Drift woke in an emotional black hole. At first she didn't know where she was. But as her mind cleared from the fog of sleep, she remembered it all, cold, sharp and painful. Her horses. Her beautiful horses, stolen. Her dogs burned. Her home gone. Her father, floating in the ether somewhere else as his body wilted in a hospital. Eli missing or dead or simply avoiding her. She dragged the covers over her head, finding their crispness and washing-powder smell no comfort. This surely could not be her life now?

She was used to waking in the crumpled bed in the caravan as soon as the night sky glowed with sun and birds began to harmonise. Drift wondered what time it was. Shifting the curtains beside the bed, she could see bright sunlight hitting the high wooden fence outside. Her gaze travelled upwards and met with the brick wall and frosted bathroom window of the neighbours' place. Blue sky beyond was cut away by the sharp angle of a crinkled roof. She knew from the shadows and the depths of the sky's blue that it was mid-morning. She wondered how she could've slept so long.

Rolling over she checked her memory for dreams, as she always did, but nothing came. For the first time, she'd lost track of the cycle of the moon too. It unhinged her. Like she was drifting in space. Somewhere in the house a phone was ringing, shrill and insistent. Dunno lifted his head and flattened his ears, looking at Drift for some kind of cue. Both listened to Wilma's footfalls in the house as she went to answer it. The ringing stopped. Wilma said something, sounding tight and frustrated.

Drift peeled back the covers and, with Dunno stretching and yawning then following her, padded out to the kitchen, where Wilma, dressed in her usual floral frock, was standing with pink cheeks, looking at Drift with concern. She'd hung up the phone.

'Sleep OK?'

Drift nodded and said, 'Yes, thanks,' slumping down at the kitchen table. Dunno pressed his nose on the glass sliding door and Wilma opened it for him, letting him out into the dappled shade of the courtyard. He disappeared through it and out to the expanse of lawn beyond.

'That was Simon,' Wilma said. She drew up a chair. 'I want to protect you from any more trauma, but it's got to come out.'

Drift looked at her, her mind in a panic.

'The cattle have been on-sold to another grazier. There's no hope of getting the money out of the farmer who originally owned them. Simon chased him up. He's walked off the land.'

Wilma laced her hands together and looked down.

'But don't worry about the money side, dear. I can lend you some so you can pay off your truckers and any other people you owe.'

'And the horses? Minty? Roger? Dunston? Bear?' Drift urged.

Wilma swallowed and shook her head. 'I'm sorry,' she said, 'they've gone.'

'Gone? Gone?' Drift sat back, shocked. 'You mean as in *killed*?'

Wilma's thin brown eyebrows knitted together. 'I don't know,' she said morosely, 'I don't know. They've shut up shop there now. The bank has locked it up. Simon just said they weren't in the yard any more. And Steven Dennison has cleared out.'

'Can't we find him?'

'Simon's trying,' Wilma said.

Drift felt her body begin to shake, her face scrunched in pain.

Wilma went to her and rubbed her back soothingly. 'I've got a shift at the library,' Wilma said eventually. 'I'm sorry, but I've got to run. But I'll call by the abattoir and find out what I can on my way. I'll go back in to see Simon too. Then, after work, we can visit your father.'

The horrible to-do list hung in the air. Drift blew her nose on a tissue and nodded mutely. She gave Wilma a look of gratitude.

'Simon also passed on his best to you. Said he'd like to take you out for a proper dinner some time soon,' Wilma said gently.

Drift grimaced.

'Come, we don't have to think about that right now,' Wilma said gently, shaking her by the shoulders. 'I've made you a pot of tea. Have some breakfast, then take yourself off back to bed, or go for a walk. The beach is only five minutes away.'

The beach, Drift thought. She never wanted to go to another beach again.

'Once I've gone to work, would you mind watering my plants? Just a squirt here and there. You'll know.'

Drift nodded, then shut her eyes and tried to stop the panicky sensation that was overtaking her body.

'Are you sure you'll be OK?' Wilma hovered, hitching her handbag over her shoulder.

Drift nodded.

'You can come sit in the library if you'd prefer. I'm just doing catalogue orders for the next trip. We're headed up Broome way for a special writers' festival. When I say we, I mean you, me and Dunno.'

Drift smiled a little at the prospect.

'Are you sure you don't want to just come with me now? I don't like leaving you alone?'

'No. I'm fine. Really.'

The moment she heard the front door click shut, Drift felt a dark cloud swallow her whole. She went to the bedroom. The house, the garden, the street, were ridiculously quiet. She longed for the thrum of Gerald, the rattle of the wind, the call of birds on the wing, and of calves and their mothers mooing to each other as they grazed the long paddock, the constant motion of the sea, but all she heard was a door slam and a car start up as another person shot out of their drive. Dunno sighed. Drift shut her eyes. She must've fallen asleep again because some time later, the sound of the doorbell chimed her awake.

Through the gauze of Wilma's security screen door there stood Simon in full uniform. The police car was parked on the street; his partner, a little blonde woman she hadn't seen before, sat inside it, busy on her phone. An involuntary smile came to Drift's face when she saw him. He was as handsome as the first evening they met. She didn't think she'd be this glad to see him. But she was.

'Thanks for helping with the horses,' she said. 'Any word?'

'No,' he said, as Drift stepped out onto the porch, shy at being caught in her little striped boxer shorts and singlet Wilma had bought her, bed hair falling wildly over her tanned shoulders.

'That's not why I'm here,' he said. He held an envelope.

'Is Wilma about?' he asked, glancing in beyond the screen door.

'Work.'

'Oh. That's not ideal.'

'What?'

Drift took in his grim expression. Police business.

'I'm sorry to tell you, your friend Charlie Weatherbourne has passed away.'

Drift felt the punch. '*What?* Charlie?' Her hand flew to her mouth. Her guardian, gone. Numb, she sat down on the porch couch.

Simon stood before her, one thumb hitched in his police belt.

'You OK? Can I get you a drink of water?' he asked.

'No. Thanks. How? When?'

'The people at the last station where she worked said she was on her way back to you. We think she simply died in her sleep, about a day's drive from here. She was camped on the roadside. The farmer noticed her truck and her dog barking constantly.'

'Gearbox? Where is he?'

Simon looked over to the police car. 'He's at the station, along with something else that involves you.'

Simon sat down beside her and passed her the envelope. Drift felt the weight of it. Puzzled, she opened it. A set of keys with a round leather CW key ring fell into her palm. Unfolding the letter she saw Charlie's familiar writing, which she'd seen so often on invoices and on brown cardboard tags that she used to label clients' saddlery for repair. Drift began to read.

This is the last Will and Testament of me, Charlotte Anita Weatherbourne. I give all of my worldly possessions, my business operation and my financial earnings to my beneficiary, Melody Wood (aka Drift). And my dog, Gearbox, is left in her care. Instructions are filed with Wilson Preston of Preston, Walker and Barnett, Cooperville solicitors.

The paper had been witnessed, signed and dated by two other people, whose names Drift didn't recognise, but she saw they lived on Gullberong Station further north up the coast. She sat staring at the letter, the weight of the keys sitting in her palm.

Charlie? Dead?

She thought back to the time after they buried Split's dog Min, when Charlie had said to her, 'Don't grieve your guts out, girl. Dogs know when to come and know when to go in our lives. We oughta be more like 'em. We're only in these old meatbag bodies of ours for a walk around this place for a laugh, a bit of fun, a bit of life's rodeo ... then we return to where we really come from. Home. So don't be so sad about death.'

Drift had swiped her runny nose with her sleeve, taking in Charlie's words.

'We'll all be with each other again ... it's just we can't remember or see it from inside these funny suits they give our spirits to try on for a bit.'

Drift had looked at Charlie sceptically.

'Believe me,' Charlie insisted, 'there is no end at death.'

'Then where's Min gone?'

Charlie softened. 'She's around, love. Always remember this is all one big fancy dream. Might as well not turn it into a nightmare in your head.' She tapped her temple.

'Once my body is done with, I'll be still with you, like Min,' Charlie had said.

Simon's voice cut across Drift's thoughts.

'Of course it'll all have to go through probate and these legal things take time,' he said, 'but if you come help us with that damn dog now, I'll pull some strings and you can take the truck sooner. I know you're in a tight spot money-wise. The truck is at least a start. The dog thinks it's his kennel anyhow. I know my fellow police officers will agree to it.'

'Thanks, Simon,' she said softly and wiped away a tear with the back of her hand.

'You sure you're OK?'

She nodded numbly.

'Are you right to get yourself dressed and come with us? No one can get near the bloody dog. He's already taken a chunk out of Morgan's leg — he's at the GP getting a shot and stitched up.'

Drift looked at Simon, trying to absorb the news, but chuckling a little on the inside about Gearbox's excellent sense of who to bite.

*

'Left a bit, keep coming,' Wilma called out later that day, as Drift let out the clutch and swung the wheel of the boxy saddlery repair truck.

'That's it. Half a metre more! Stop!'

The truck was now parked perfectly beside the shed in Wilma's backyard. On the lawn Dunno lay on his back, his long tongue lolling as Gearbox chewed playfully on his neck, tails wagging.

Wilma shook her head at them, smiling. Together she and Drift went to the back of the truck and unlocked it, swinging the back door open. There it was, all laid out, as if Charlie would be back any second to begin work. The rich smell of tanned leather hit her full force and suddenly the old woman with the long grey hair was there with her again.

'Oh, Charlie,' she sighed. She dropped the step and climbed in, fingering the tools on the shadow boards, tears prickling her eyes. 'I can't believe she's gone.'

'I can. The Universe wishes it. Charlie wishes it.'

Drift looked at Wilma. There was no drama around death with either Wilma or Charlie. They shared the same stance. When your time was up, it was up. Life was to be grateful for and celebrated, even when it transitioned into another realm.

Gearbox leaped up the steps, jumping onto Charlie's work chair, sniffing the air a little in search of his mistress. Wilma and Drift glanced at each other.

Drift opened cupboard doors above the workbench, finding more neatly stored tools. She peeled back a curtain and there was her sleeper. The quilt was rumpled, the patterns of beautiful Indigenous designs swirling in greens and rust tones. Drift slumped down on the bed, feeling abruptly like she'd lost a mother. This time, a solid one.

'Let it sink in slowly, dear,' Wilma said, patting her hand. 'Absorb what it means for you now. But thanks to dear Charlie and her foresight and love for you, your life is suddenly now your own.'

Chapter 39

With the truck settled in Wilma's leafy backyard, Drift could lie on the bed and look up through the skylight to a canopy of iridescent sliver-thin green leaves and the pastel froth of blushing pink gum flowers. Beyond, cotton puff clouds floated in a forever-blue sky. At night, with the beetles, bugs and moths kept at bay by a clever retractable screen Charlie had fixed on the rear door, Drift found herself falling asleep in her new home of fresh air, never needing to return to Wilma's tiny air-conditioned spare room again.

In her first few nights in the truck, Charlie Weatherbourne's presence hovered near and she swore she could hear the whir of a far-off sewing machine. Eli's face came drifting to her in her dreams too. He had a half flower tucked behind his ear. He was cleanshaven and smiling. From the tiny white and gently purpled flower stepped a girl onto the stamen of the bloom. Drift peered at her. It was the girl in the dress with the long dark hair. Then, in the dream-space her father arrived, floating like a corpse on a still river of black, causing Drift to toss and turn in her half-sleep. A dog barked and Drift woke with a start.

The beauty of the April moon, soft fairy-floss yellow, gave Drift a sense that she needed to trust the miracle of landing herself with this truck, along with Charlie's estate, which the solicitor, Wilson Preston, had told her would be released to her in full when she turned twenty-four. Drift had sat in the solicitor's squelchy leather chair thinking how Charlie's bush-woman ways and humble dress and lifestyle had belied the sharp businesswoman she was.

Charlie's long-time Cooperville solicitor had looked every part the small-town lawyer with his scruffy hair, unshaven jaw and ill-fitting brown suit. He'd studied the estate figures and had whistled. Charlie had lived cheaply and earned good money for her sought-after leather goods. Her constant work of repairs and sales had flowed into her estate over a period of thirty years, and she'd astutely managed her money. So much so that her account was bursting at the seams.

'If you manage this right, Melody,' Mr Preston said, 'Charlie's pretty much made sure you have a solid financial future.'

Mr Preston had shunted his glasses back up his long narrow nose and beamed at her, passing her the file. Wilma and Drift had looked at the documents, then at each other incredulously.

'You do know it's possible that with all this, one day, you could buy your own land ... a farm?' Wilma had said.

'It's early days,' Wilson Preston said, 'and it's too soon for someone as young as Miss Melody to decide. But be assured Charlie's finances will be working away earning themselves interest and dividends until Miss Wood is of age.'

Drift and Wilma had glanced at each other again, knowing the seeds of the dream were well and truly sown. But for now, Drift had a father in a hospital bed. She had a policeman suitor who doted on her, even though she wasn't sure she liked it. And she had a secret lover who might or might not be missing at sea. In Charlie's bed, watching the gentle butter moon, Drift began to laugh at the ridiculousness of her circumstances and the outlandish chain of events. Soon she was laughing so much the truck began to shake. Dunno and Gearbox at the foot of the bed lifted their heads and looked at her, puzzled. A neighbour's dog three houses away heard her mirth and began to bark in the night.

'Sorry,' she said, to them, still chuckling a little to herself. 'Go back to sleep.'

*

By the time the moon of May had slid into a black sky, with her father still in his dark sleep, Drift found herself searching in the silence and private space of the truck for ideas on where to go next in life. Money or no money, she wanted *purpose*. Those long nights of silence in the truck, nights where Charlie seemed ever present, gave Drift enough of a compass to make her swing her legs out of bed each morning, kick back the quilt covers and say resolutely, 'Thank you for my life,' no matter what shape it was in.

Beyond the truck window, the rising sun illuminated the sky in a flourish of crimson. As the nights passed in the truck and another moon arrived, Drift was soon waking to beautiful winter mornings with clear pale blue skies. When the June moon slid past, growing bigger and bigger with its pale blood light, her father was still in his sleeping world. She still felt the tug of missing her horses, her dogs and her life, but each time the river of worrisome thoughts burdened her, she would hear Charlie's power-packed voice telling her: 'Have faith in yourself, Drift. Find and follow your own road. But make the road a good and interesting one. Choice is yours. It's up to us to make Heaven on Earth, remember? Just look into the eyes of that horse of yours and you'll find it.'

But, as Drift argued back at the invisible Charlie, her horses were gone.

Still she set about her days with determination.

In the truck, Drift distracted and disciplined her mind by gorging on books. Books of all kinds, fed to her by Wilma. There were books on leatherwork and saddlery. Fiction, non-fiction, pictorials, biographies. She would take the books to the hospital and read aloud to her father. Or sit beside him and quietly paint the vistas she conjured from memories of Pinrush Point, humming as she did. He was steadily losing weight and with it muscle tone, but oddly that meant Drift was witnessing the father of her childhood returning to her as the heaviness of his previous life melted away. His face was less marred by worries and his body was slimming down to the frame of his younger days. He looked well enough to suddenly wake and drench a race of sheep, and even bowl the cricket ball again to her on the beach as he had done when she was little.

With Wilma by her side they'd turned his hospital visits into special trips and mini celebrations. Instead of focusing on the bed sores that troubled them more than him, they chose to look on the bright side. They'd stuck a party hat on his head for his fiftieth birthday and blew paper whistles into his ears.

They played him Toby Keith songs with titles like 'I Wanna Talk About Me', 'I'm Just Talking About Tonight' and 'A Little Less Talk and a Lot More Action', culminating in telling him to shut up, tears of laughter streaming down their faces, their bellies tight from hysterically guffawing at their own silliness. They talked to Split as if he'd just put more logs on the campfire and they were settling in for another round of jokes.

Sometimes, so engaging was their energy, the hospital staff and even the patients joined in their fun, turning up in Split's room, all of them commenting how he was slimming down ... and, weirdly, looking younger.

'He's nearly hot enough to pull a nurse,' Drift had said as she surveyed his cleanly shaven jaw, razor in her hand. There wasn't time to be glum around him with Wilma there. She taught Drift that he still had life, and where there was life there was also joy to be found with him, no matter what the circumstances.

On the day they'd discovered Split could breathe perfectly well on his own, the hospital board gave them special dispensation so that Split could stay as long as he needed.

With Wilma's counselling, Drift had also stopped thinking of Eli in agonising terms. Instead of reliving that one night of love-making on the beach with a kind of painful regret that he'd disappeared, she remembered her droving time with him with a fondness. She re-conjured the love-making tenderly, now knowing it was a memory to treasure.

'It's all about perception,' Wilma had coached.

'Seeing Heaven on Earth,' Drift had answered, like the good student of life that she was.

Despite her midnight dreams of Eli, she had Simon to dote on her. He was rock-solid and real and he had become part of her weekly routine. Gently, slowly, he'd wound his way into her life, picking her up from Wilma's to take her to the movies on a Friday when his shifts allowed, or out for Chinese. He was old fashioned in his ways and would kiss her goodnight on Wilma's porch, holding her near but always stepping back when their kissing got too heated.

She knew now he was run by the religious dogma of his mother and his raising. She also knew that sex out of wedlock was taboo in his world. This was a comfort on one hand, but guilt rumbled in her that maybe, deep down, she was stringing him along for her own gains — to stop herself feeling so utterly lonely.

Since Eli, she lived with a secret but full bloom of desire. Sometimes the furnace of longing within her was physically hard to bear. On the beach that night, months ago now, the wild woman in her had been woken. However, with Simon, she found herself stuffing that woman back down inside.

There was still so much uncertainty elsewhere in her life, so over time she'd come to know him and to like his predictable ways. She now knew from being around people her age in Cooperville that a man like him was a rare find, which drew her closer to him.

Her father, she realised, had been right to keep her away from boys her own age. Most in Cooperville seemed to be addicted to casual hook-ups on Tinder and didn't care genuinely one bit for the women they messed about with. Same for the girls too. It didn't make sense to Drift, not after her time with Eli. And not after being raised by Wilma and Charlie, who had drummed into her that sex was a sacred act and that if it was for ego or involved a money exchange it hooked into a person's soul negatively. It was a reason Drift was happy to tell the wild woman in her to settle and be patient.

Drift found she also loved the library work Wilma had led her into. She was now officially 'on work experience' with the library and had a plastic ID card that hung about her neck on a red cotton-weave ribbon. Drift barely recognised the photo on the card of the lean, blonde girl with a gentle smile on her tanned heart-shaped face, hair brushed back in a ponytail, in a light blue cotton summer dress. Drift could now almost see her natural beauty when she looked at the photo. She was beginning to understand why there was an increasing number of young men taking books out of the library. The staff, Tilly, Doreen and Anne, had commented on it, teasing her gently.

'Loans have never been so good in the books aimed at young males,' Anne said. Anne, who always wore long and numerous strands of different coloured beads each day, had rolled her heavily made-up eyes to the ceiling. 'In fact loans have never been better with our oldies either. You're a master with the senior citizens. A special girl.'

Drift had slowly got used to making polite conversation with Wilma's library staff and enjoyed listening to members of the public talking about subjects other than livestock, soils and plants. She'd even got better at dressing herself daily for work as if she cared about how she looked.

Then there was technology to deal with, though it baffled her and frightened her. The closest she'd come to the information age was her dad's flip phone, and that had been as dinged up as the old ute. She felt no interest in the gadgets that everyone seemed to be locked on to, and was even wary of them.

In the early days of walking through the library, she would often put a shelf or two between herself and the computer section, using the books as a buffer from the strange energy the computers emitted. She reminded herself of a skittish horse scuttling past a flapping flag. She'd laugh at her backwardness, but then find herself laughing more at the young people her age walking down the steps of the Cooperville library, noses so glued to their phones that they sometimes came a cropper. Their heads were so bent over, intent on their phones, it was as if their necks were permanently shaped that way. None of them seemed to know the others were there. None of them seemed to *see anything*.

Drift wondered at it all. Then she would shrug it off and gaze at the clouds of white horses in the sky, waiting patiently for the next road trip on the bookmobile schedule. On those precious trips with Wilma she could once again glimpse wide open spaces and feel the comfort and adventure of the white lines darting beneath rolling tyres.

Wilma had dedicated a special cupboard in the library bus for a selection of leatherwork tools so Drift could keep practising the art. There was a calico bag of leather thonging, and she would spend hours learning to plait, making first a dog lead for Dunno out of thin strips of roo hide, and then trying to create a stock whip that never quite found the balance to crack properly. On the sewing side, Wilma encouraged her to thread up a sewing machine and keep stitching. Soon her fingers were stained with leather tannins, and calluses had developed on her fingers and hands. For the more complex leather workmanship, Wilma knew Drift would have to teach herself using YouTube at the library and books.

'At least you're having a crack,' Wilma had joked, fingering Drift's snakelike stockwhip, which looked like it had swallowed a rat.

'Very funny. Punning again, are you?'

'Always.'

'It's a dog's breakfast,' Drift said, chucking it down on the floor of the bus.

'It's a first attempt,' Wilma had countered, picking it up again and handing it back to her.

Some nights, Wilma sat next to Drift and coached her in her writing, giving her nice pens with which to loop words in pretty notebooks. They also spent many days telling each other stories as they drove hundreds of kilometres to the next school or cattle station.

As time passed, no amount of digging by Wilma, Drift and Simon could uncover the fate of Minty and the other horses. Wilma and Drift had called the meatworks daily for weeks, but one day the line to the office was cut off, dead. When they drove past, the gates had been locked and spiders had already set about building their webs in the chains. The ombudsman and the police were still chasing Steven Dennison, but he was nowhere to be found.

As she and Wilma drove the library route north, new landscapes viewed through the bug-splattered windscreen reminded Drift of places she had travelled with her dad, and the sight of the beaches reminded her constantly of Eli. Once, a squadron formation of ducks, flying as if in a regatta display, swooped over the glassy mirror of a lagoon. The vision evoked a clear memory of The Planet and the coastal lagoons they had ridden past. She and Eli, side by side on the road.

A sudden breath-catching view of the ocean over the crest of a hill would remind Drift that he was potentially still out there in that sea with her mother, lost for all time. Or was he? Was he somewhere on the other side of the world making a life for himself? If he was, she hoped he would remember his time with her, her horses and the herd fondly.

The windswept water cast with white horses spurred on by a stiff onshore breeze caused Drift to turn her eyes away. There was nothing more to seek, she told herself. They had spent the droving time together and had become firm friends and they had spent one night together as lovers. Her first. He had simply been her first crush, and she had to let him go. He was gone now anyway, possibly into the water. Possibly not. What did it matter? As Charlie had said, this life is but a dream anyway.

She let the deep sigh of the bus brakes soothe her, announcing their arrival at another rural primary school in the middle of seemingly nowhere. The bus door would swing open on its hydraulic hinges, set in motion with the flick of a lever by Wilma.

'It's showtime!' she would call gleefully.

Each day, the shrill of children's voices spilled into the bus. As each class was brought in, youngest to oldest, Drift smiled at the bookish kids, eager to satisfy their cravings. She also noticed the way the non-readers gradually caught the buzz from the other children. They were soon lured into the curious space with its colourful decor and dangling mobiles and wallpapering of beautiful books. The fold-out display and teardrop banners set outside gave it an air of carnival, particularly on still, sunny days. Dunno had become central to the show. Like a not-so-majestic stone lion sitting beside the steps, he allowed the kids to ooh and ahh over him with a big kelpie bitser mongrel grin on his ugly face. Gearbox was a little more aloof, preferring to sleep on the driver's seat when kids were around.

As she and Wilma drove through the countryside, Drift's knowledge and passion for the landscape also grew. She pointed out cattle on barren land and the way the gullies were washing and hillsides eroding, sparking long conversations about water, soil and grazing management. Drift was constantly fed by Wilma's orders for more books on soil regeneration, water conservation and managed grazing. Bit by bit, she learned the science behind it all. She became an informal student of The Savory Institute and learned the story of its founder, ecologist Allan Savory, and read all she could on the Mulloon Institute over east.

As a girl watching nature unfurl itself against the seasons, and now with regular access to education and the internet, lights turned on in her mind with such ease, like stars coming to life on a frost-filled night. She now understood how Sophia and the team had achieved the thriving ecology of The Planet. She came to see the way each farm reflected the climate of the mind of the landowner, knowing it was the manager's mindset that determined how healthy the landscape would be.

'Some of the biggest landholders Dad and I used to work for would think they were poor,' she said to Wilma as they drove. 'They couldn't see the riches all around them. All they did was moan about money and drought. Sit in their big tractors, or on their big verandahs, and believe things were all wrong. They'd made their environment harsh and deadened. And they too were going the same way. Why take out bank loan after bank loan and bust your gut overgrazing and spraying your place into oblivion when there are other ways?'

'I don't know,' Wilma said. 'Is it ego? Is it a lack of knowledge? Is it trying to compete with your neighbour?'

Drift shrugged. 'I never figured it out, but I wish I could have a go on my own place,' she said suddenly as she watched the land whizz by.

'One day you will,' Wilma said. 'God willing. You know how to run sheep and cattle, work a dog, graze animals to health. Now all you need to do is figure out how to make it happen. So start focusing on what you truly want, feeling it with all your heart. Visualise it not just in your mind, but also feel it in your heart girl, *your heart. It will happen.*'

Drift watched the country blurring past and goosebumps shimmered on her skin. She saw herself on a horse again, in wavering, rich grassland. She tried to visualise it over and over, but always, in rode the image of Eli upon a white horse beside her. He kept muscling into her vision. She grimaced at herself. She wasn't going to be fooled again. She knew she didn't want some bloke on a white horse riding up to save her. She thrust the memory of Eli out of her head. She would do this by herself. By herself and for herself.

Chapter 40

'Visitor!' Drift heard Wilma call from the house. The sound caused the chattering pink galahs to take flight from the White Swan Drive powerlines, screeching away in the afternoon light. In the truck, Gearbox raised his hackles and gave a gruff bark. Drift looked up from her work and told him to pull his head in. Meekly he laid his chin down over his paws and sighed.

The dog had taken some re-training on Drift's part, but it was paying off. His rudeness in jumping up on people and his tendency to ankle-bite had now stopped. At the sound of someone coming out of Wilma's back door the forever friendly Dunno began to thump his tail on the truck's floor, lifting particles of dust in the sunshine. Drift and the dogs watched Simon walking across the lawn towards them. At the workbench, she set down the hand-stamped dog collar she'd been oiling. Wiping her hands on a cloth, in her tattered old jeans, she stood and stretched. She pulled her hair up in a loose ponytail and in bare feet stepped out onto the grass.

'Hi,' she said, looking at him as evening glow illuminated his smile.

'Hi.' He stooped to kiss her on the cheek. She noticed his freshly cut hair had been spiked up at the front with product and he smelled strongly of aftershave, his jaw paler than his cheeks from being shaved so closely. He was wearing a neat navy polo shirt, olive pants and boat shoes. He looked like he could walk into a men's catalogue photo shoot and give the models a run for their money.

'Where are you off to all dolled up?' she asked.

'Hopefully out with you? I thought it's a nice mildish night for fish and chips down near the beach. Are you up for it?'

Drift looked down at her ratty jeans and Charlie's old green-checked western shirt stained in blotches with leather dressing, tied at her waist in a knot. 'Do I need to change?'

'It might be best,' he said, looking her over and grinning.

She grinned back at him, thinking they were chalk and cheese, but she liked the way he encouraged her to dress up and go out to do normal things. 'Just give me a moment.'

Fifteen minutes later Drift was sitting next to Simon in his little green Kia. He held a small paper ticket and was waiting for their number to be called from the wharfside fish punt. A warm winter breeze was rattling the wires on the masts of the nearby yachts, while a young family argued over the last few chips at a picnic table under a wind-bent coastal pine, giving the seagulls stiff competition in the squabbling stakes. Drift arranged her denim dress a little more neatly. She'd grabbed it from the foot of the bed, where it had lain, all scrunched and creased. She was now feeling self-conscious that it was extremely crumpled. Looking down to her cowgirl boots, she lamented that she ought to have made more effort and put on the strappy shoes Wilma had bought her for library shifts.

Simon, who normally reported snippets of his police work to her, or talked about what his sister's children were up to, was unusually quiet. He seemed relieved when the number was called through a tinny speaker, and he was able to get out of the car to get their paper-wrapped packet of fish and chips. Drift frowned, wondering what was up with him tonight. He got back into the car, handed her the parcel of fish and chips and turned the keys over, so the Kia purred. She sat their meal on her lap, the heat turning the tops of her thighs pink.

'I thought we'd have a picnic down on the sand by the water. It's still enough.'

'OK,' Drift said, not really wanting to, but too put off by his strange mood to say she'd prefer the park.

On the beach, Simon spread out a blue-striped picnic blanket and settled himself on it. He indicated Drift to sit beside him, opening up the fish and chips. They ate in silence, watching the waves crash on the beach. Without a breath of wind, the surf seemed louder than normal. A bird hung in the sky, joined by another, and then another. Seagulls gathering like clouds above, hopeful for some tossed scraps. Soon they began to land nearby to chatter and bicker. Simon offered Drift some bottled water.

'Drink?'

'Thanks,' she said, trying to think what small talk she could make. She'd been turning the letters of Simon's make of car around in her mind: Kia. Swivelled around the letters spelled Kai. She shut the thought out. Maybe comment on the seagulls? There was one that stood on one red leg; the other had been chewed off. She turned her face to him about to point it out, but before she knew it, Simon was leaning in to her, kissing her with his salty chip lips. At the same time, his hand was fumbling in his pocket. He pulled back from her, his eyes intense.

'Melody, I've brought you here to ask you a question.'

Drift felt a wave coming and there was no stopping it as Simon moved onto one knee to finish what he had to say.

'Will you marry me?'

She looked into his brown eyes, then followed his gaze to what he was holding. There in a small black box was a diamond ring, stones delicately set in a flower shape on a thin band of gold.

An involuntary smile sprang to her face when she saw the ring. Then she looked up at Simon, intrigued and even amused that a man would ask her to marry him, but then she saw the deep seriousness of his expression. Her mind raced. It was as if time slowed. Would she *marry* him? *Could* she marry him? Simon kept his dark eyes fixed on her. Before she could even think, she heard a voice deep within her say, 'No,' but as she looked at his pleading face, and she weighed up how kind and predictable he'd been, out came the words, 'Yes. Yes, Simon, I will marry you.'

The smile that crossed his face was like the sun rising. He pulled her to him and buried his face in her neck. She could feel his surge of relief and the waves of emotion he'd held on to so tightly by the way he laughed against her skin, almost like a sob. It was wonderful to be so wanted, so cherished, by a man who was so stable. She felt joy run through her. There would be no more wandering. No more wondering. About where the road would take her, about Eli, about where she was meant to be, and if she'd be all alone forever as her father lay as silent and still as a corpse. No. She was *here. Now.* With Simon.

'Oh!' Simon said joyfully. 'I can't wait to tell Mum.'

*

That night in the truck, unable to sleep, Drift sat up. Again and again the doubt prodded at her, like an insistent finger tapping her on the shoulder. *Why did she say yes?* Was it because her dad wasn't around? Maybe. Even though she had a life with Wilma, did she feel stuck? Simon's family had welcomed her in, but did she fit? Did she crave a family that much? Most importantly, did *she love him enough*? She asked herself so many questions, over and over. Sometimes she found a glimmer that, yes, possibly, she could love Simon — in a comfortable, safe way. He was *so* dependable and polite. Kind. *But what was missing?* No matter how many times she tried to lasso her thoughts, her mind kept roaming back to Eli ... or at least to the Eli version of Kai.

She saw his eyes so clearly. Memories of their jokiness together brought a smile to her lips. She could recall the sensation of his hands on her body so easily. When she thought of the moment he'd entered her sacred space, she felt she'd almost pass out with desire, but with that desire came a depth of feeling she couldn't explain. She'd never felt that level of attraction and connection with Simon. She wondered if she ever would.

Drift lay down and rolled over, groaning, and shoved the pillow over her head to block out the gleam of the July moon. She thought of all the Cooperville creeps who had been smutty and disrespectful as they clumsily chatted her up outside the library while she tried to eat her lunch in peace, all of them not so subtly angling for casual sex with her. Calling her a 'hottie', offering 'friendship with benefits'. When she wouldn't flirt back or 'put out', they called her frigid. Uptight. A prick tease.

As she lay back down on Charlie's bed, she sighed. Simon was nothing like that. He was a great catch. In terms of looks he was a total spunk, as Shaynene would say. And he had real principles. She knew as well, because of her sheltered life, with adults at the centre of it and never mixing with people her own age, she too was old fashioned like Simon. Maybe they made a good pair. She was quiet, hardworking and liked solitude. He was the same. He came with a pure past. *Not like Eli.*

As she lay on her back, her thoughts swirling like the turning tide, Drift's fingers ran along the edge of the picture frame that hung beside the bed. The print was an Albert Namatjira of a white-trunked gum emerging out of red desert rocks in pastel tones. It made her think of the road. Her life of open skies. She realised if she married Simon she had to let that old life go. Her plans with her dad, to go inland, never realised. Maybe even her dream of having a regenerated farm and a big garden gone too. She wanted a life surrounded by animals, but Simon didn't even like horses and he barely paid any attention to Dunno. She turned away from the picture. Suddenly in the moon's glow, it slid from its hook with a thud, hitting her on the back.

'Damn,' she said, sitting up and flicking on the light. As Drift went to set the picture back on the wall she saw the wire had broken on the back. The frame was old, and from the looks of it, the print was too. She'd have to fix it in the morning. She put the picture down beside the bed. Settling back down to stare at the blank space where it had hung, she noticed the wooden-panel seams of the wall. There was a crack between them. She swept her fingers in the join. The panel moved slightly. She hooked an index finger in and the entire panel came away.

'Sorry, Charlie,' Drift said, trying to push it back, 'I don't mean to be busting up your truck.'

She'd have to glue or nail it back on later. As she tried to put it back, she felt the whole panel flex. Frowning, she lifted it away, revealing a secret set of shelving in a false wall.

'Wow, Charlie! How many surprises do you have for me?' she asked as she peered inside. It was too dark to see. She reached for a torch beside the bed and shone the light. Drift gasped. Inside she could see all manner of things. There was a box filled with turquoise stones and silver. Drift recognised the canvas-wrap kit of jewellery-making tools. She remembered how Charlie had often said, when the leather work died down, she'd set time aside to make jewellery. That day had never come. Drift looked further into the shelves. There was a collection of old hand-bound books, diaries by the look of them, and a cash tin. But it was something else, something extraordinary, that caught her eye.

'No?' she breathed nervously as she dragged a roll of fabric out onto her lap and her skin prickled. *Eli's sarongs!* An image of their lovers' tepee flashed in her mind.

'Eli!' she said, tears coming to her. She re-shone the torch into the secret shelves and saw the seagrass sleeping mats she and Eli had made love on. Beside them lay a pile of clothing. She reached in and pulled out his stockman's blue shirt and his green one too. She held them to her nose. The scent was unmistakeable. Inhaling the balm of him fired her brain. Instantly she was being held by him. *Eli.* He was alive! He *must* be alive!

She unfolded the sarongs and more of Eli's clothing, intrigued at how and why they were hidden in Charlie's truck.

Drift clutched his belongings to her chest, her mind swirling back to the night he'd left and the madness of the storm. Eli must've found Charlie on the road somewhere and camped with her. But for how long? And when? Had he been there when Charlie died? Where was he now? And what were these things doing hidden in Charlie's truck? She inhaled deeply, holding his clothes to her.

The important thing was he was alive! But why hadn't he let her know in some way? She felt hurt rise in her. She put the shirts to her nose again and breathed in as much of the familiar scent as she could. It was still there, her instinctive connection with him. Eli. She looked again inside the cupboard. The last thing there was an old cigar box. She took it in her hands and opened the hinged lid. Inside piled neatly and wrapped in rubber bands were wads of green one hundred- and yellow fifty-dollar notes. More money.

Was it Charlie's or Eli's? Who could know? Drift put the money back and replaced it on the shelf.

'Damn it, Eli! Or Kai! Or whoever the Hell you are!' she said aloud. Frustrated that he was still causing her confusion and heartache, she lay down on the bed, holding the shirts to her chest with the sarongs draped over her.

'Eli, Eli, Eli,' she whispered. He came to her in her vision. The beauty of him. The perfection of him. The love she felt swelled in her when she pictured his gentle hands on her horses. On her thighs. On her back, her shoulders, his fingertips reaching for her face. The surge of energy he exuded. She felt as if she were again swimming in the warmest ocean of love, just from holding his things close. Holding his memory close. Then with a jolt she remembered Simon. The man she'd said yes to marrying.

Chapter 41

More than a year rolled on after Drift found Eli's things. Her life settled on the surface, but alone in the truck in Wilma's backyard, she found herself thinking of her father, her horses and Eli. The August blue moon rolled into view, the late-winter sun setting over Wilma's garden. Drift breathed in the vibrancy of the new green leaves, feeling them heal her soul a little. She'd told Wilma about finding Eli's things behind the false wall, and all Wilma had said, in her calm steady voice, was, 'Time will tell, my darling. Time will tell. Just let it go. Let *him* go.'

With the approach of warmer weather, Drift tried to feel the flush of the new season, but she was restless.

The saddlery truck began to feel uselessly idle parked in the garden. Library funding cuts meant Wilma's book bus was also stranded until the admin staff could plunder an already stretched budget next financial quarter. To keep her from going stir-crazy, Wilma encouraged Drift to take the truck out for a run and a rumble every week or so. Drift would drive past the outskirts of town, looking longingly at the horses in the semi-rural bare-dirt paddocks there. Each time she saw any horses shaped and coloured like her droving team, she would look again with hope, the hope always fading when she realised it wasn't one of hers.

She and Wilma had found a good mechanic in the next small town north, who flirted unashamedly with Drift each time she took the truck in, checking out not just the engine, but also Drift's legs when she swung down from the cab.

'When are ya gunna marry that fella?' he'd ask, pointing his oil-stained finger at the engagement ring on hers. 'He's a copper, isn't he? If he doesn't do it soon, someone else might snaffle you up. Someone who's good with motors. Someone like me. Eh? Whaddya say?' He'd make clicking sounds in his cheek and wink at her. Drift would laugh him off, but then think of Simon and his urgency over setting a wedding date. Always she'd use the excuse, 'I want my father to give me away. I want him to wake up first and for you to ask him for his permission.'

She'd see the same cloud cross Simon's face each time he raised the issue, feeling the current of his sexual frustration swirl within him, but she knew, given the way he was brought up, he saw it as a fair request. And part of it was true — she did want her father to be part of the decision — but she also wanted, as Wilma said, *time to tell.*

Despite the routine of work and the good company of Wilma along with enjoyable times with Simon and his family, more and more Drift felt anchored in Cooperville, not in a safe-harbour kind of way, but more like a run-aground ship. Her father still lay where they left him in the hospital, flat on his back, looking younger than ever, if not a bit pasty, but just not conscious. Because of his treatments to keep his muscles toned and his body well nourished, the bills kept mounting. Drift wanted the best for him, as he would've done for her, so she spared no expense. She missed him dreadfully.

She committed herself to earning money to pay for his extra treatments with her library and saddlery work. She also chipped in towards food and board for Wilma, even though Wilma insisted she didn't want any money. Drift knew that in the secret wall there was enough cash to practically buy her father a room at the hospital, but she just didn't feel right touching it, even though she knew Charlie would insist she spend it. It seemed an age away until she could access the money Charlie left her when she turned twenty-four, but for the moment she was a little afraid of what possibilities it could bring her. She now felt that wishing for change could be a dangerous thing.

For the past year she'd been dropping flyers in mailboxes to build her horse saddlery repair work. She would watch for messages from clients on a new phone Wilma had insisted she get, texting them back, realising she had to move into her life as a working adult independent from her father. Despite Wilma's protests, she'd set her prices low to start with — bargain basement rates for her saddlery and rug repairs. She figured her inexperience meant she couldn't charge full prices just yet, but soon customers were actually offering her more money and more work. And she found herself guiding and advising her clients on how to rest their paddocks and grow more natural, rough grasses, more suited to horses than expensive feed scooped out of bags morning and night. She even began to encourage a few to try her bitless bridles, freeing the horses from the hard pressure of cold steel on their tongues. Increasingly her clients came to love her and seek her animal wisdom.

Wilma had helped her with the CW graphics of her cards and brochures, and together they'd designed a new range of simple but stylish leather goods like wristbands, necklaces made of thonging and stones and other unique pieces that spoke of the beauty of nature and the gift of simplicity. Drift didn't feel right using the turquoise stones she'd found in the wall, but in quiet moments in the library she'd begun studying silversmithing online. Clients were soon dropping rugs off at the back gate and taking time to buy a few things and ask for more grazing information, or solutions to their problems with their horses. Drift loved that side of her work and was adding to the spare-cash stash in the wall: it was growing substantially. Not that Drift cared much for money. She like receiving it because it meant taking off the secret panel and again drawing Eli's clothes close to her chest.

Now, well into September, as she was putting another three hundred dollars into the hidden wall cavity, she glanced at the clock. She groaned when she saw the time. Gearbox lifted an ear at the sound of her voice, while Dunno snoozed on. Simon would be here in half an hour. He was taking both her and Wilma out for Chinese with his mum, Mrs Swain. Joining them were his sister, Teena, her husband, Rob, and their two kids.

As she began to change, Simon's mother's voice echoed in her head. 'Oh Melody, you look so lovely in a dress. I don't know why you don't wear them more often.' She thought of Simon's sister, Teena, who always joined in, agreeing with her mother's opinions on Drift. This past year, Teena had been flourishingly kind to her, although with a matronly air that made her bossy beyond her age. Lately she'd been putting bridal magazines under Drift's nose, marked with sticky notes.

'This dress,' she'd say, tapping her fake fingernail on an image, 'would suit your figure.'

Drift sometimes stood in one of her simple library work dresses, looking at herself in the small mirror, failing to imagine herself in a wedding dress and wondering where on Earth her real self had gone.

A little later, as they settled into the garishly lit Wok'n'Woll restaurant, Drift knew for sure Simon was up to something as he hovered at the too-big round table, impatiently waiting for them all to sit. Wilma gave Drift a wink and a wry smile as Teena wrenched the chopsticks from her kids, who were already sword fighting with them loudly. Drift had sometimes confessed to Wilma, 'If those kids were dogs, they'd need a good brain-schnapping to wake them up to a few manners!'

Wilma, forever the diplomat, said very little, but deep inside her, Drift knew her friend thought the same. Drift also knew Wilma thought she was too young to be diving into an engagement with Simon, and that the Swains walked too much of a different path from hers. But like everything, Wilma always gave Drift the space to learn her life lessons. Some days Drift wished she wouldn't. She wished her father was around.

She knew, unlike Wilma, he never gave her enough rope and would've been clear cut about them from the start.

As she looked at Teena's kids poking their tongues out at their mother, Drift felt a shiver as her mind flashed forwards a few years. Would she too be in this very same Cooperville restaurant, possibly with her own children, sired by Simon?

She remembered Charlie saying she'd make a great mother and to visualise the life she wanted. Could she picture this? She was sure her kids wouldn't be as unruly as Teena's, but as she looked at the flushed face of Teena and that of her husband, Rob, who sat impotently in the furthest seat against the wall, she felt again the weight of that heavy anchor. Rob was failing to notice the hints and dark looks from Mrs Swain, who believed 'children should be seen but not heard'. Her disappointment in her son-in-law was barely disguised.

'I'd hate to cross her,' Drift had once said of Mrs Swain to Wilma.

'Often the religious types are the most judgemental, but there's judgement just in saying that.' Wilma had smiled mildly at her. 'The lesson of "judge not others" is the least heard. I think the Swains would test anyone.'

Wilma was watching Simon now as he at last took his place at the table between Drift and his mother.

'Do order for all of us,' Mrs Swain said, patting her son's hand. Drift pictured golden light like a religious painting of a halo radiating from his head, such was his mother's one-eyed pride in him. She sipped her water and looked at her lap. Soon plates of spring rolls, dim sims and prawn crackers were arriving, at last quietening the children.

Simon picked up a glass and dinged it with a knife. All faces turned to him as he stood, clearing his throat, clenching his jaw. 'As you know, Melody and I have been engaged for a while now.'

His comment was met with a small cheer from his sister.

'I have something to announce. Melody, Mum, I've spoken to Father Peter and we've booked the church. We have a date.'

'Oh! Well you two took your time!' cried Mrs Swain as she clapped her hands and leaped up, hugging and kissing her son. 'When, Simon? *When?*'

Drift felt her cheeks burn. He hadn't even discussed it with her! She cast a 'help me' glance Wilma's way, but Wilma was looking up at a Chinese lantern with gold trim.

'Mum, *Mum*,' soothed Simon, 'before we go on, I have to let Melody know something.'

He turned to Drift. 'I've heard what you've said about your dad, and I want you to know ...' he sucked in a breath and puffed out his chest, 'your father will be there. At the ceremony. I've been into the hospital and asked the staff. They're going to arrange an ambulance and a trolley bed, so your father *will* be there to walk you down the aisle. Or at least wheel you.' He beamed at her as if he'd done the most amazing thing.

Drift felt tears rise in her eyes. She looked from face to face at the table around her and the room blurred. Heat rose in her. She felt her body shake. 'No, Simon! *No!* He'd hate that. That would be humiliating for him!'

She stood, pushing her chair back too loudly on the ugly tiles of the restaurant. Other people were looking at her. Even the bustling waiter paused as he passed with a sizzling dish of beef and black bean sauce. Simon's face was crestfallen. Mrs Swain's cheeks were colouring with a mix of embarrassment and fury. Wilma was looking sympathetically at Drift, but remained anchored in her chair as Drift propelled herself from the restaurant and out into the street. She turned and ran, cursing her silly strappy shoes. She knew Simon would follow her, so she darted down a side street and into the shadows of a narrow lane between Centrelink and a locksmith's. She slowed to a walk. She needed to think. To buy some time before she made her way back to Wilma's. She kept walking. She wanted her dad.

A short while later, Drift arrived at the low, well-lit hospital. The nurses, seeing her face, let her in, even though visiting hours were well and truly over. Inside, the corridors were eerily quiet. In her father's room, she drew up a chair and sat beside Split, taking up his hand and holding it. It looked as if he were ready to wake and saddle up.

'Dad,' she said, 'I'm in a tight spot. Please wake up. Please help me. I need you. Dad?' She leaned her head on his chest, which was covered with a light blue blanket, and began to whisper to him. She told him about the wedding date set by Simon. And how she felt pressure, not just from him, but also his family. Then, she spoke of Eli.

'I can't forget him. I think I love him. Even though I don't even really know the truth of him. But I do. It's hopeless.' She began to cry. Sniffling, and hating the fact she was so often crying these days, she looked up for a tissue, and noticed a tear sliding down her father's cheek.

'Dad?' she urged, squeezing his hand. She glanced to the doorway. Ought she get the nurse? It wasn't uncommon for her father's eyes to run but Drift wondered if he'd actually heard what she was saying. She squeezed his hand again.

'Dad?' She willed him to squeeze her hand back, but no response. She noticed there was no tissue box beside the bed where they were normally kept, so she reached for the bedside drawer, where she knew the nurses kept a few supplies. As she removed the box, her fingertips also met with a small hard smooth object. Drawing it out, her eyes widened when she saw what it was. In the palm of her hand lay a stone. A beach pebble, smooth, white, and shaped exactly like a heart. It was *the* stone. Her and Eli's stone from the beach that night.

She gasped.

'Dad,' she whispered with urgency now, 'has Eli been here? Dad?' Another tear ran from his closed eyes. She mopped it with a tissue, composing herself.

At the nurses' station she held up the stone.

'Abigail,' she said to the red-haired older nurse, 'do you know where this came from?'

'Ah! I wondered where that got to!' Abigail said, coming to her. 'I've been meaning to ask you about it for months now. Where was it?'

'In the drawer beside his bed.'

Abigail made a clucking noise. 'One of the other nurses must've tidied it into the drawer. Sorry I didn't mention it earlier.'

'But how did it get there?'

The nurse shook her head in puzzlement. 'I have no idea. It was so odd. I found it sitting on your father's chest on one of my early shifts one morning. At first I thought it was you, but I remembered you were away on a library run with Wilma. So I had security check their footage, but nothing. In fact that was the night the system went on the blink. Very strange.'

'Very, very strange,' Drift said, holding the stone so tightly it made a heart-shaped indent in the palm of her hand.

*

Late that night, back in the truck, she heard Wilma knock briefly on the door.

'I won't come in. I know you need your space. I'm just seeing if you're OK.'

Drift held the stone over her heart, lying on her back, tears sliding down into the shells of her ears. 'I'm fine,' she lied.

'Don't worry, my dear. Just sleep on it. I'll come see you in the morning.'

When she was gone, Drift edged her fingertips around the wooden panel. She took out the clothing and laid it out on the bed to make the shape of Eli. His blue workshirt and worn jeans. Then she lay nestled in under the arm, pretending he was holding her, clutching the heart stone.

Drift shut her eyes and surrendered up her past. She knew if she was to realise her dreams of the future she had to let go of what other people believed. She had to forget the things that had hurt her. She knew she needed to feel a new future of her own bloom within, and visualise it as if it had come true already. She cast her mind back to the things she had wished for as a scraggly-haired child on the road, in the wilds, perched up high on the back of plodding old Bear, listening to the wind whisper and weave those dreams through grasslands. As a fingernail moon came into view Drift knew if she was to have a better future she needed to take her life into her own hands and recall those early dreams when she was little, before life had become dark and motherless. She'd always seen her life lived out in her own natural paradise, with animals and nature around her. Just like Sophia had created. She saw now how she'd been drifting along in life. First in the wake of her father, and now, bobbing along behind Simon and what he wanted. But she didn't want to do that any more. She didn't want to wait any more either. She couldn't afford to sit around until her dad woke up. It was time to do something, to start her life. Before she fell asleep, she wished on the stone, giving all of her troubles over to the Universe, surrendering them utterly. Then she began to see herself, on a white horse, on land teeming with life, with the breeze on her face, the sun on her back and a smile in her heart.

*

The next morning Gearbox let out a sudden bark, setting Dunno off too. Drift sat up in bed. She looked at the old clock nailed to the wall above the sewing bench. It was just after seven. There was a knock on the truck door. Before she had time to get up Simon was already calling out his greeting.

'Can I come in?'

'Just a minute!' Hastily Drift bundled the sarong and Eli's clothes back into the hidden cupboard, shoved the heart stone under her pillow and propped the board back up, covering it with the Albert Namatjira print.

'OK,' she said, dragging her robe around her. The door opened and he stepped up into the truck. Simon filled the space with his handsome man-in-uniform presence, his face beaming.

'Good morning, beautiful,' he said, holding plastic-sheathed supermarket roses in his hand. 'Are you OK? I'm so, so sorry about last night. I didn't mean to shock you.' He came to her and sat on the bed, the plastic around the roses rustling as he laid them beside her. 'It was thoughtless of me. I ought to have discussed it with you before. I was just trying to be helpful, you know, about your dad. Do you forgive me?'

He stroked her gently over her neck and kissed her there. Drift didn't want her body to respond to his touch, but just that one action caused her own desire to flush intensely. It flooded her system. The red-blooded woman within her awoke. Her nipples rose, and feelings fluttered between her legs. As she let him kiss her more deeply her mind ran to Eli.

Simon laid her down, and she let him, even though all the while her mind was screaming that this was the wrong guy. As he kissed her more deeply, Simon took her hand and placed it on his police pants, over his erection.

'See what you do to me?' he said in a husky voice. Drift's eyes sprang open wide. Simon had never been this forward before. For a moment she was reminded of Kelvin's violating, invasive touch. As he kissed her harder, mouth open, tongue probing, she at last found her voice.

'No,' she said, pushing him away.

He frowned, his cheeks red. 'I know,' he said, pressing his lips together determinedly. 'I can't wait to have you after we're married. It will be so worth the wait, I promise. I promise I'll be gentle.'

His words raised the memory of her exquisite night with Eli, and her cheeks coloured.

'But we do have to wait until you are Mrs Swain,' he said, reaching out and brushing the hair from her exposed shoulder.

Drift shrunk away from his touch, drawing the covers up over herself. Beside her, Eli's belongings seemed to burn a hole in the wall.

'What's the matter?' Simon asked.

'We need to talk.'

'Yes, we do! Mum told me women need to talk,' he said, 'so talk away.'

They both sat in silence, Drift not sure what to say.

Simon decided to fill up the space. 'Father Peter says we'll need you to join our church, of course, before we marry. It's a simple ceremony. It's something Mum is really keen for. She's been asking questions about you.'

Drift wondered, as she listened to him, where his mother had got the notion women like to talk. It was the same as Mrs Swain's notion that all women liked to shop.

'Questions? What questions?' Drift asked, her skin prickling.

'You know.' He cleared his throat. 'About your past.'

'Pardon?' Drift stiffened. '*My past?*'

'Your parents' religion. Other boyfriends and stuff.'

'What? Why?'

'You know.'

'No, I'm not sure I do,' Drift said, frowning.

He inclined his head and looked at her with an apologetic face. 'As Christians we are supposed to be sinless before we marry.'

'Sinless? What do you mean?'

Simon looked upwards, to the ceiling. 'Virgins. Particularly the girls.'

Drift pulled an 'are you kidding?' face. '*Sinless,*' she scoffed.

Simon patted her hand. 'Don't worry, I told Mum she didn't need to worry about you being a tart or anything.'

'A tart?'

'Yes. You see, I looked at the doctor's records.'

'What records?'

'The police file. You know. After Kelvin Waller attacked you,' he said quietly.

Drift felt a chill run through her. 'You did *what*?'

'Yes, I saw his report. That you were a virgin. I'm sorry, but I had to be certain.'

Drift's heart froze. An image of beautiful Eli lying upon her, pulsing into her, flashed in her mind. She sucked in a breath, steeling her resolve. 'Simon,' she said coldly, 'I think you'd better leave.'

He looked as if he was suddenly jolted. And insulted. 'Why?' he asked, a surprised look on his face. 'What's the matter? I thought you'd be pleased I knew how pure you were.'

'Pure?' Drift's voice came out as a growl. A wild-woman growl. 'Leave, Simon. *Now.*'

Chapter 42

The truck gears took some getting used to, but after many months on the road, Drift could now drive the clunky beast as if by instinct. She thundered over single-lane bitumen roads, weaving around wandering camels, dodging docile cattle, braking intuitively as huge red roos bounded past her bull bar. The colours and scenery of the Namatjira print came alive before her eyes as she entered red dirt and rock country. White gums. Salt bush. Spinifex. It was mostly fenceless land apart from the occasional cattle grid or a bedraggled rabbit or dingo fence. There was not a whiff on the wind of sea air, anywhere. And Drift liked it that way.

Drift roamed from town to town, gaining work through word of mouth as she called into a pub, a store or a petrol station. With Blu-Tack in hand, she'd stick up flyers at the local roadhouses or independent grocers to drum up a bit of business. Enough to keep her busy, but not enough to keep her anchored in one place for more than a few weeks. Time taught her the truck's inner workings and idiosyncrasies. Thankfully it had a mechanical energy that was much kinder and easier to get along with than Gerald the generator had been. Still, Drift had been discovering surprises in the vehicle ever since she'd found the secret cupboard.

There were little hidden nooks everywhere behind false walls, most times empty, but some filled with old photos, letters and keepsakes. The letters were mostly from Rose's father, Lionel, clearly a man deeply in love with Charlie. Drift stared at the faded tatty photos and saw the same man looking adoringly at young versions of her old friend. Once Drift gleaned the personal tone of the love letters, she hadn't read them and instead wrapped them in the leather satchel in which she'd found them and put them back reverently.

'Love with a capital L, Lionel,' she said.

She wondered if her life would play out the same as Charlie's. Alone, having met a man she'd loved, but who had now left for an unreachable place. Then she'd chide herself for being a drama queen like Shaynene. Charlie had coached her that a person was never alone, especially when there was a good dog at your boots, or like Wilma said, if you had a good fire.

'Y'know, girlie,' Charlie said one day, 'you're made of the same stuff that stars are made of, and so is everyone and every living thing. We're all one big flock. Loneliness is simply an undisciplined mindset. When you start to feel sorry for y'self, pull them weeds out of your head and grow some better thoughts in your mind garden.'

'Yes, Charlie,' Drift said, smiling, shaking her head. 'I hear you.' Night and day, it was as if Charlie's spirit infused her. Whenever she felt the pull back to Cooperville to see her dad, for whatever reason the road, or instinct, kept on calling her.

If she was honest with herself, the thing she missed most was the sea air and a saddle. There was an ache in her that longed for her horses, for Pinrush Point and The Planet. But she couldn't go back. Especially each time she thought about Simon. She couldn't face him.

She'd felt dreadful leaving only a note for Wilma under the cyclamen plant her friend kept on the kitchen counter. She'd also left a letter for Wilma to read to her dad, peppering it with jokes, funny poems, and a suggested playlist with songs such as Wham's 'Wake Me Up Before You Go-Go', and Green Day's 'Wake Me Up when September Ends', throwing in The Wiggles'

'Wake up Jeff!' It had taken her an hour and several drafts to pen a letter to Simon. It took all her self-control not to let her anger spill into the phrasing.

Instead she explained how grateful she was to him, and how kind he'd been to both her and Dunno. But in the final paragraph she told him she just wasn't ready. As she'd written it, she knew it wasn't her truth. A collective, ancient female fury had burned in her the last time she'd seen him. Kelvin had wanted to hurt her, which obviously put him in a different category, but like Simon he had set out to dominate her. Simon wanted her to conform to his religious ideals of a woman, to dial down her wild-woman inside, to limit her right to experience pleasure where and when she wanted.

She knew the night she'd lain with Eli, under his considerate touch, her body had taken her sky high and beyond. She saw now how her pleasure and sense of safety had been Eli's priority. Because of that one experience, she now knew Simon's priority was all about protecting her in the way he saw fit, and even possessing her. Certainly not pleasuring her. He *and* his mother wanted a 'pure' virgin. It made her feel sick, still, to think of it. How could she have said yes in the first place? She had almost married him! Drift noticed her knuckles clenching the steering wheel tighter, so she told herself to stop dwelling on it.

She turned to the wide blue sky that domed before her through the truck's windscreen. Reaching for the dial on the CD player, she turned up The Wolfe Brothers, 'Ain't Even Close to Gone'. She soon found herself singing and smiling again, within twenty minutes of the next town, ruffling the thick double coat of Gearbox and running her palm over Dunno's wonky head as the dogs lay beside her on the bench seat.

At her next stop, she stood under the whir of the fan in the local store, the balding man with the comb-over and the big gut telling her of the big Campdraft event coming up on a nearby station in a month. He said if she hung about there'd be a line-up of 'horse nuts' needing her services. She glanced across the main drag to the caravan park that nestled beneath a group of white-trunked gums. One tree looked just like the gum in the Namatjira print that hung over the false wall; she knew it was a sign that she should stay.

'Reckon I'll stick about, then,' she said to the shopkeeper. 'Who do I see about booking a spot at the caravan park?'

'That'd be me,' the man said, thumping a blowfly flat with a rolled-up magazine. Judging from the gunk on the end of it, the magazine had served that purpose for some time. As she left the shop, Drift sent a thank you to the Heavens. She loved the fact her life was like following a path of stepping stones — except the stones only appeared after she'd already lifted her foot to take the next step. If she was open to reading the signs, she knew the path would take her where she was meant to go. There was a certainty to her choices now.

She knew her dream was not to stay forever in the truck, like Charlie had until her last breath, but to keep walking towards the day when she could establish a place much like The Planet. She knew she was no billionaire heiress, like Sophia, but Drift could see that she could make it happen over time. She'd been amassing wads of cash in the false wall since setting off, and had only a few overheads to cover. Other than that, her expenses of fuel, more leatherwork supplies and food for her and the dogs were low. She visualised creating a multi-layered farm that fed the soil and fed the community. Even if only in a small way. She tried not to be impatient to get her own dirt under her feet, and have horses and livestock in her life again — and it would take time to do it properly. Plus she was not yet twenty-four. She knew she ought to be guided by the stillness within and trust it would unfold in time.

As the months passed, with those dreams firmly replaying in her head, she kept landing her boots solidly on those stepping stones. The Campdraft led her to another competition, then another, then on to a large company-owned station. Then via the bush telegraph she was sent on her way to another station owned by the same company. At every step of the way, she was building her skills and her reputation. She had learned that synergies were to be cultivated, trusted and expected. The more she honed her focus and opened her heart, believed in herself, the more life unfolded her way.

Dixon Station was a famous beef property and quarter horse stud and as she drove into the station she was greeted by the cheery overseer, Owen Cuthbert, who was walking over to her from his ute.

'Heard you were on your way. We've got a full day's work lined up for you to fix.'

He'd taken off his hat, revealing a balding head, and was looking up at her where she sat in the truck.

He gestured to the squat building behind him. 'Jackaroo's quarters. Hook up for power there. Feel free to use the toilet and shower.'

'Luxury!' She beamed at him. As she glanced at the horizontal corro building, she was looking forward to a proper wash, even with the rather stinky bore water that was common out this way. Her solar bush shower was good when it was warm, but lately the cloudy July weather had meant the shower was often colder than was comfortable, and on some nights, she was just too done in to bother.

The next morning, she stretched and lobbed out of bed, her bare feet landing on a circular leather woven rug. She invited Dunno and Gearbox to hop out from their nest in a shared basket at the foot of her bed. Still in her sleep shorts and singlet, she grabbed up her standard onroad wear of denim shorts, new pale pink, CW logo collared T-shirt that Wilma had posted her for her twenty-third birthday, gathered up her scuffed dogger workboots, a towel and toiletry bag. Opening the little side door and folding down the steps, Drift took in the view of the early sunlight landing on the steel rails of the Dixon Station cattleyards. Beneath the squawk of cockatoos taking flight overhead, she made her way towards the abandoned-looking jackaroo quarters, treading over red gravel.

With winter keeping a chill over the ground, the horses that were destined for a big quarter horse futurity in Perth were being rugged from ears to tail. Yesterday evening, Owen had loaded her up with eight torn rugs and a number of summer undersheets to repair. They sat ready for her in the stables.

'Don't go too far,' she said to Dunno and Gearbox as they sniffed at tufts of grass in the barren backyard. At the rear of the quarters under a clump of gumtrees, three working dogs emerged from their kennels to sniff at the air at the sight of the strangers, but didn't bark. Well trained, Drift thought. She was looking forward to her day. Just being near horses gave her both a lift of comfort and a yearning for her beloved Minty, Roger, Bear and Dunston. She pushed the sad thoughts away and tried to find the happy place in her heart again by looking to the burning gold flame of light that was draping itself over the landscape. Off in the distance some Santa Gertrudis cattle were lit to glowing as they grazed over wintry pasture sheened silver from dew.

Humming to herself, she tugged open the screen door. The hallway was painted a rather grimy lemon colour. She noticed a frosted glass door and a small sign tacked above it saying *Bathroom*. Drift backed her way through the doorway, using her arse, thinly covered by her boxer shorts, to push it open. When she spun around in the tiny room she realised it was already steamy from use.

She let out a small gasp. Before her, a young man stood naked in a waft of warm mist, drying himself with a towel. His blue eyes sparkled.

'Why hello,' he said, not seeming to care in the least he was not wearing a stitch of clothing. Even though he was holding a towel, he didn't seem in any hurry to cover himself, the towel hanging casually in front of his crotch. 'I wasn't expecting company … but I'm glad you're here.'

His eyes travelled over her legs and bra-less breasts in her singlet, his full lips twisting to the side in a wry smile. Her face flaming red, Drift turned her back. Even in the briefest of glimpses her eyes had taken him in. He had a firm young body and a tanned triangular torso, with pecs that looked as solid as the peak-trained quarter horses she'd seen in the day yards. Although his hair was wet she could see it was dark brown, cut short at the sides and wavy on top. A drip of water from a curl had been threatening to fall onto his perfectly proportioned nose. His biceps rounded out on each arm and gentle blue veins ran beneath his smooth tanned skin, blood stirred by the heat of the shower. It was all there already, etched in her mind.

'I'm sorry,' Drift breathed, shutting her eyes as if it would block out the vision seared on her brain. 'Owen didn't tell me there'd be anyone in here. I'll come back later.'

The young man stepped towards her as if to pass, but he didn't leave right away. Instead he stood very near her bare shoulder, smiling down at her. He smelled of fresh soap, shampoo and a recent blast of deodorant. Drift glanced at him and saw a smile and cheeky eyes that were taking her in and teasing her at the same time.

'It's OK. I'm all done. Your turn.' He brushed past her, clipping her arm with his bare chest. Drift hugged her bundle of clothes to herself, biting her lip. He sauntered down the corridor, not bothering to drape the towel around his waist so she got the full picture of his tight naked backside.

'I'm Jack,' he said, calling over his shoulder wickedly as he disappeared into a bedroom. 'Jack, the jackaroo.'

'More like jackass,' Drift called after him, before she could stop the taunt coming out. She cupped her hand to her mouth as if she might be able to scoop the words back in, scrunching her eyes in a cringe. Then she giggled. She was glad to see the return of the old Drift, who had been buried down deep while she was with Simon. It was the smartarse, smart-mouthed Drift from the droving days with her dad, before grief and life had nearly swallowed her whole. She was glad to know the confident stirring girl she had been had erupted back up in her. She snickered at herself as she shut the door, turning the shower on full. As she soaped up her naked body, she was surprised to find her thoughts wandering back to the bold young man who'd just showed himself off to her as if he were a randy peacock. She smiled, thinking suddenly her day of mending rugs on Dixon Station was looking a little more interesting than she'd anticipated.

Chapter 43

Looking into the bathroom mirror, Drift wound her hair into a fishbone braid so it lay over her shoulder. It was Wilma who had taught her the style, recounting stories of her childhood when she would wear her long frizzy hair in the same plait.

'It was so thick, my mother said I could tie a warship up with it,' Wilma had said. Drift realised she hadn't written to Wilma this month, like she usually did at the start of each new moon. She found it was a good time to set her wishes for her life down on paper and share them with her friend. Sometimes, if she was staying in a place for a long time, or she roughly knew where she was headed, she'd send Wilma an address. She wondered how many of Wilma's letters never found her. Each week Wilma would call with news of her father, which was usually no news at all. On the night she'd turned twenty-three, alone under the bright-starred inky sky, Drift knew she ought to go see him, but Wilma had said Split was as happy as Larry, off in his dream world, hearing news from her letters, and she was best to just keep going.

She looked in the mirror knowing she ought not to feel guilty about Wilma or her dad — they would want her adventuring at her age, given the circumstances. Weaving an elastic around the end of her plait, she told herself that the attention she was paying to her hair wasn't vanity, or because there was a good-looking (and naked) jackaroo in the house. It was because her hair got in the way when she stooped over her sewing and rug repairs. It was a safety issue, and tying it back was a necessity and the plait fitted better under her hat. At least she told herself that. *Right?* Still she found herself checking her face in the mirror.

Emerging from the bathroom, excitement wafting with the dispersing steam, Drift told herself to get a grip. Still she felt the flush of longing, making her heart beat faster. It wasn't that she needed a man. It was more that she wanted to rediscover that feeling she'd had when she was with Eli. That raw physical desire she'd felt when lying with him. Could that same feeling be found with another man?

Instead of heading back out to the work truck, she followed strange noises along the hallway. It sounded as if someone was being throttled. In the kitchen Jack stood at the chipped laminate bench beside a grease-splattered old stove in his work jeans and a plaid shirt, collar up. The lemon and orange paint on the cupboards was grimed with years of workers' comings and goings, their finger marks on the edges, handles missing and replaced by loops of bale twine. The one stand-out thing, apart from tall Jack, was the big shiny red coffee machine that sat on the bench making the noise Drift had heard.

He turned to her briefly. 'This is Carlos,' he said, waving his hand at the machine. 'I'm making myself a skinny latte. Want one?'

Drift looked momentarily puzzled at the strapping young man and the coffee machine.

'A what?'

'A latte,' he said as he busied himself with frothing and heating the milk. 'I've got almond milk, soy or skinny.'

'Are you serious?'

'Very,' he said with a grin.

'You have a coffee machine called Carlos? With an assortment of milk choices? Out here?'

'Well I wasn't going to call him Jim or Barry, was I? Too ordinary a name for something as magnificent as this. Coffee?' he asked again.

'No thanks,' she said.

He spun about to face her, and that blue-eyed gaze hit her, making her heart flutter instantly.

'You sure? Carlos and I make a wicked cappuccino,' he tempted.

'I don't drink coffee.'

'You don't? Well that's weird.'

He smiled charmingly at her with his model-boy looks as he swirled the warmed milk in a silver jug before pouring it into a coffee glass. Then he set about wiping the machine lovingly, as if it were a child with a dirty face.

'Brought it all the way from Sydney,' he said. 'My swag and my coffee machine. That might make me a bit of a wanker!' Then he laughed and Drift saw how even his teeth were, like a movie star's.

'You said it,' she countered. He paused, taking her in, post shower and clothed.

'And who is this tetchy yet beautiful young woman invading my shower and now my pop-up coffee palace this morning?'

Jack lifted his latte to his mouth and sipped, waiting for her answer. Drift saw the flirtatious way he narrowed his eyes at her. Her own eyes seemed to have taken on a life of their own, looking over his gym-sculpted arms again. As they did, her heart lurched instantly back to Eli.

She told herself to let go. This man had an edge to his energy that seemed to fill the entire room with a buzz. She was drawn to it, but she felt like a horse bent to his will. With Eli, she had been drawn towards him with trust like Minty had. With Eli she had still felt safe, despite his mystery and secrets, and his past. This man made her feel like she could be his prey. But while she felt threatened, she also felt a thrill.

'I'm Drift,' she said, trying to sound nonchalant. Jack simply smiled and nodded, like he was satisfied with something. He continued looking at her as he sipped at his coffee.

'Well,' Drift said, to fill what felt like an awkward silence, 'I'd better get going. Get to work.'

'Me too,' Jack said, sipping his coffee as if he was in no hurry at all. 'See you round, Drift, darling. Happy stitching.'

She frowned at him. 'Yep. See you round, Jackaroo Jackass. Happy … whatever you do,' she said trying to sound cool and failing.

When she stepped out of the back door to find Dunno and Gearbox waiting for her, she heard Jack call out to her, his voice following her down the hall. 'We're headed to the pub tonight. You're welcome to tag along.'

A faint smile arrived on Drift's face as she let the door swing shut behind her without giving him an answer.

*

As Drift sat sewing in the back of the truck beside the shady corro stables, she cursed how her head wrestled with the same question over and over. *Should I go to the pub?* The repetitive loop in her brain made her irritable, and the thought of Jack and his rich-boy Sydney arrogance made her cross but excited at the same time. She felt like a snorty horse, whose curiosity was winning the battle to approach the thing it feared.

Drift was so used to just keeping to herself and focusing on her work that she was annoyed a bloke had got to her. God knows, in her travels there'd been so many who'd tried. Why this one? She stood, arched her back, stretching her neck, interlacing her fingers and flexing her hands. She grabbed the rug she was working on and checked it was all fixed and functioning, then clipped the leg straps and folded it neatly, stepping down from the truck and carrying it into the airy stables. She set it on the growing pile of mended items.

A handsome quarter horse with a chestnut coat and wide paintbrush stripe down his nose looked out from the stall, ears cast forwards, chewing on hay that hung from his muzzle. The horse reminded her of Sophia's stallion Alphie. More irritation rose in her.

'What are you looking at?' she said to him. She reached out to pat him, taking in his steady energy for a moment, worshipping him for his purity, and grateful just to be back in the presence of a horse. Humans are so complex compared to horses, she thought. Horses were clear. Humans masked things, they contained secrets. She leaned against the timber wall beside the beautiful animal, picking at the hard calluses that had formed on her hands from the tough machining needed to work the thick material of horse blankets. The question came again. *Should I go to the pub?*

If she went, she would be tired for the drive tomorrow. She'd planned to be in the next town for their country show over the long weekend. She had to be in the gates and set up by eight am, so a late night would make it all so much harder. She ran the movie in her head of her evening here on Dixon, if there was no Jack. She would take a luxury second shower for the day, falling into bed early after a slap-up meal of pasta. The silent time spent with just the hiss of the small gas stove in the tiny kitchen section of the truck, and the peaceful company of the dogs. Books to read on the bed before she fell asleep not long after sundown.

'That's it,' she said to the chestnut horse, 'I'm not going.' Satisfied, she went back to the truck and recorded the most recent rug repair on to the invoice for Owen. Picking up the next rug, she settled herself down at the machine. The belly strap had come away and the fabric was perishing in a right-angle tear. She was just about to cut a patch when her phone buzzed with a text message. She picked it up and frowned. The message simply read, *Well? You coming?*

She looked about the work yard. There was no sign of anyone. She smiled, knowing it was Jack.

She texted back, *How'd you know my number?* Then she threw the phone down as if it were hot in her hands, and set to work again, but instantly a reply came.

Take a look at your truck door Blondie.

Drift rolled her eyes. Of course! Her mobile number was painted there in large font. She felt her face flush red and her body prickle at both her stupidity and Jack's implication that she was a dumb blonde. She looked at his message again and conceded it had been pretty dumb of her, but why would he even think to have got her number from the truck door?

Don't you have work to do? she texted back, wishing he would just go away and leave her alone.

Well? You coming? his text came again. She threw the phone down and let out a sigh. About ten minutes passed. Then another text arrived from him: *Pick you up at seven.*

Chapter 44

Jack Hawkins swung the Landcruiser wagon into line with the other vehicles along the main street of Gunnington. During the hour-long trip to the single hotel town, sitting up front next to Jack, Drift tried to tell herself it was a good decision to come out for the night, but her stomach still twisted with nerves. She wasn't used to hanging with a gang of young people, and yet there she was with a crew of brand-new 'friends' in the form of other ringers they'd collected from the big station of Cobworth along the way. An hour earlier she'd swivelled in the front seat to meet the young workers, all scrubbed clean and ready for a big night as they clambered into the Cruiser with their six-pack of roadies already half drunk. Jack introduced Connor, Adele and Wal, and the fun and bulldust had begun.

At Gunnington, they now spilled out of the vehicle, stretching and tugging down their clothing, ready to roll. Drift noticed Adele was wearing a little black dress teamed with Durango boots and her blonde hair was hitched high in a classic ponytail. Only her square strong hands and grimed fingers gave away she wasn't all glamour girl. Drift was relieved she wasn't the only girl with rough hands not in jeans.

Back in the truck, she'd agonised over her outfit, at one stage wishing she could wear a bloody horse rug. She only had one pair of 'good' jeans, and they were stained on the thigh where she'd dropped a greasy piece of chicken on the road to Dixon

Station from the last roadhouse. She only had cheap T-shirts, and her best collared shirts were the logo ones Wilma'd given her for the saddlery work. She didn't want to bother talking about her business tonight so they wouldn't do. The library dresses just didn't seem right, so she'd taken out the light cotton cowgirl-style dress that Wilma had sent her as another birthday gift. Why not give herself a belated twenty-third tonight?

As she slipped it from the hanger, she slid the material, printed with pretty little green-stemmed cherries on white, through her fingers. The dress was a bit short in Drift's book, not good for climbing through fences, but she liked the look of it when she put it on.

'Wilma the Wondrous,' she said as she ran her hands over the perfectly fitting dress. She had no choice but to drag on her best workboots, as the sandals Wilma had bought her had long given up the ghost and the only other footwear she had was thongs. The cuban heels and fancy stitching of her boots gave the pretty little dress some extra grunt. Satisfied, Drift turned and walked away from the mirror.

Now outside the Gunnington Hotel she felt nothing but vulnerable in the dress, as the rabble sounds of a raucous country crowd overflowed from the open windows. The single-storey pub had a slumpy sideways lean to it, but coloured footy flags hanging from the verandah gave it some cheer. She looked up and down the main street noting it was the *only* street in Gunnington. Dwarfed beneath the evening blush of a vast sky, Drift concluded Gunnington was *less* than a two-horse town. Less than a blink. Smaller even than a pin dot on a map. All the place had to keep its faint heart beating, as far as Drift could tell, was the pub. Across the street a defunct church was falling down. A community hall barely managed to echo its lost dance-hall days. The people who had built the once pretty hall would be rolling in their graves to see the broken windows, the rotting bare boards, and unreadable sign that was threatening to fall over altogether at the slumping fence. Any other houses in the place had long since crumbled to ruins. Drift looked at the square fenced block they'd parked near, chewed short by a pair of dull-eyed bay horses so the soil revealed the cornerstone foundations of old buildings long since forgotten.

Despite that, about fifty utes and farm vehicles surrounded the pub. Some had the footy-team streamers of blue and white draped from aerials.

'This place is the hub,' Jack said, as he saw Drift looking about. 'Friday-night raffles, SES meetings, farmer group get-togethers, but there's no night bigger than a footy fundraising night. C'mon,' he said. They followed the three other ringers and walked up the shallow steps onto the wonky verandah.

Inside, ceiling fans turned fast overhead in a futile attempt to blast some cool into the crowded bar and a cheer went up from around the pool table when Jack and his friends arrived. The other ringers were enveloped into the fold, but Jack hung back with Drift. She was partly grateful but also unsettled to find Jack hovering near as if they were on some kind of date.

'You like?' he asked, stooping down to her and having to shout over the top of the pub noise. Drift nodded, but this kind of environment was not one she'd ever really liked. Nor willingly experienced. When she was underage, her dad had most times left her locked in the caravan on his bender nights, though he'd never left her alone for long, even if he was rolling drunk when he came back. Even when she turned eighteen, she never went, preferring to comfort herself with a book. She associated pubs like this with losing her dad to booze.

A rush of movement caught her eye and suddenly a boy was up on the bar. He was a bulky dark-haired footy player, sculling beer from a trophy while everyone about him cheered and people shoved notes down his daks. Money for the club if he drank the lot. Then as the roo-cha-cha footy songs started, Drift's eyes travelled beyond the gulping boy to the collection of hundreds of stubby holders nailed to the walls and stuffed crocodile above the bar, holding a beer and grinning down at the drinkers. Drift knew they were miles from croc country, so she wondered what its story was.

Jack saw where she was looking and smiled at her. 'Like the decor?' he shouted to her over the din.

'What's with that?' Drift asked, pointing to the crocodile.

Jack just shrugged, smiled and made the motion with his hand as if having a drink.

Drift shook her head. 'Just a water, thanks.'

'A *what*?' he shouted.

'Water.'

Jack pulled a 'you're kidding' face at her, and held out the palms of his hands, as if pleading with her.

'*C'mon*. No coffee? No grog? Jeez, live a little, woman!'

He shouldered his way to the bar, Drift taking in how the neat cornflower-blue shirt hugged his broad shoulders. As she waited for him to return, Drift felt a shimmer of regret. She shouldn't have come. She remembered the last drinking bender she'd had with her dad at the abattoir. She was *never* doing that again. Standing alone in the crush of the pub, she began to notice male eyes upon her, and boys at the bar glancing at her and making comments to each other. Nausea rose in her belly and she felt the crowd around her spin a bit. The CD machine in the corner kicked into action and a Luke Bryan song crashed over the sound of raised voices and filled the room with a burst of country rock sexiness. A bunch of girls squealed in delight and grabbed each other for a dance just as Jack returned.

'I got you a water,' he said with a wink, offering her a glass with brown liquid in it.

'That's not water,' Drift said, frowning up at him.

'Yes it is,' Jack shouted, raising his own glass to hers and chinking it. 'Water with a little bit of whisky. Makes you frisky.'

Drift looked at the drink, then back to Jack. 'Noooo,' she said, pushing it away.

'C'mon,' he cooed, 'don't look at me like that. Cheers.' He raised his glass and sculled it, offering her the glass again.

'I don't drink,' she said firmly.

Jack looked at her, a tiny movement in his eyebrow and a glimmer of disapproval on his face. He shrugged. 'Oh well, more for me. You only live once,' he said, downing the other. He bent towards her ear, his breath like fire. 'I'll get you a water.'

Drift didn't answer him. Instead she nodded and looked about her as he disappeared into the crowd for the bar again. She watched the girls bump and grind. The men leaning on pool cues whooped when someone sank a shot. She looked at the TV flashing news up on the wall in the corner. An earthquake. A war. A car crash. She saw the sweep of eyes turning at once to see the footy results blink up on the screen.

Drift knew that Jack was wrong ... you didn't only live once. After hearing Charlie talk, she knew you were around forever, but you were only ever here on this Earth with your heart beating fleetingly, so it was best to live awake to the world, and to peacefulness and nature and love. Not masking it with alcohol or distractions. Yet here she was in a bash and crash bar with someone she barely knew. Suddenly her adventuring felt wearisome. She wondered, if the room were filled with people from The Planet, how different would the vibe be? She knew, as intrigued by Jack as she was, he was no Eli. During their time on the road together, Ei had been so mindful of her. Never egotistical or pushy, like this bloke.

In the hubbub of the pub she felt as if she were in a bubble, her desolation and isolation made even more apparent in the crush and the noise. Sleeping people, she thought, hearing Sophia's words in her head, before instantly trying to push her feelings of judgement away. Jack and his mates were being friendly. But Sophia had been right, Drift thought as she watched them cluster at the bar for more grog. These people were asleep. The planet was imploding all around them with overpopulation and greed. The landscape outside was virtually a desert and the rural town in ruins. Surely that was a neon sign that things were really crook, but in here, no one seemed concerned.

She wanted to be asleep too. If she were asleep like them, then she wouldn't have to feel the pain of the world as intensely as she did. She wouldn't have to bear witness to the violence humans measured out to each other and to Mother Nature. She was just so *over* the world and herself.

Drift forced a smile at Jack when he returned. She made herself take in just how ridiculously good looking he was as he passed her a glass. She frowned. It was brown liquid — this time with bubbles in it.

He smiled. 'It's ginger beer. They're out of bottled water. And trust me, you don't want to drink the tap water round here.' He looked at her with an open honest face as she sipped it cautiously. Get over your deep, tortured self, she heard her inner critic say. Then she chinked her glass with his and smiled.

'Cheers. To sleeping,' she said, then she took a gulp, the bubbles fizzing her eyes so they watered.

'*To what?*' Jack shouted.

Drift shook her head. 'Nothing.'

As Luke Bryan sang lustily of tan lines, tailgates and getting it on down in the creek, Drift took Jack's hand and dragged him over to the dancers. She'd barely shimmied one hip left and right before a girl with early-days Nicole Kidman hair and a body shaped like the women at the front end of ships dashed up.

'Dance with me, Jack!' she said, her eyes bright with booze, her breasts bouncing.

'I'm right, Imogen,' Jack said.

Drift glimpsed his harshness and wished again she hadn't come. The girl ran her eyes coldly over Drift but Jack ignored her and took up Drift's hand, then began again moving with the boot-stomping dancers. Drift did her best to fall into the world. A world she'd avoided for most of her life.

*

Three hours later, Drift was poured into the back seat of the Cruiser around closing time wondering why she felt so odd, like the world was blurred and tilted. Sound bubbled like it did underwater. What had been in the ginger beer? Was it something she ate? She was sheened with sweat from dancing and the world was spinning. Her words arrived from her lips as if they were strung together in some kind of gloopy glue. Jack charmingly gave the impression to the others that he was looking after the young saddlery repairer, who'd 'had a few too many', but she'd not touched one drop of alcohol, as far as she knew.

Drift felt Jack's hands brush too far down the back of her dress, cupping her backside when he caught her in a stumble. She wanted to be afraid, but she couldn't quite hold on to the emotion before it slipped away again.

'You'd better drive, Del,' he said, throwing Adele the keys. She looked with concern at Drift.

'You sure you're not bringing your fucked-up drugs from Sydney out here again, Jack Hawkins, you wanker?' Adele said crossly. 'She's rooted.'

'Shut your mouth,' Jack said, as he got in the back with Drift. 'You can't pin that on me again. She's just pissed.'

Adele looked at him in the rear-vision mirror. 'We don't do your shit out here. It's for city dicks. If I find out you've spiked her drink ...'

'Shut it,' he said as he leaned over Drift, brushing the back of his hand over the round curve of her breast as he put her seatbelt on for her. He made sure Adele was watching as he did. She averted her eyes.

'Wal!' Adele yelled out the window. 'Hurry the fuck up.'

As the car travelled on to Cobworth, Drift's head kept lolling towards Jack's chest, her eyelids heavy. She was too bombed to take much of it in but she felt Jack's whisky breath on her skin, and his lips pressing firmly on hers, his hands running up her dress along her inner thigh.

The headlights swept along the country road with Adele at the wheel as she swore at Connor, who was for some reason wearing a bra on his head. Drift barely registered the other ringer, Wal, wedged next to her in the back seat. She woke with a sudden jolt to find his pudgy hand travelling up under her light cotton dress too, his fat fingers pressing firmly on the soft flesh of her inner thigh.

'Hey,' she heard Jack say from beyond the fog. 'Quit it, Wal. She's mine. You shoulda got your own.'

'Jack!' came an aggressive protest from Adele.

Drift wanted to tell them both to piss off, but her system was awash with whatever it was Jack had put in her drink, the tide of which kept dragging her out to a black place. When she did open her eyes, a sickness swamped her and the stars beyond the window of the moving vehicle spun. She shut her eyes again.

'She'd be up for a threesome. She's some kind of hottie,' Wal said.

'Not sharing,' was all Jack had said, and then Drift was out for the count.

*

Drift could feel someone beside her in the bed. There was the smell of stale alcohol and a hand wandering over her skin, travelling up the front of her leg, then cupping her in between her legs. A finger found its way inside her knickers and probed her with increasing roughness. She tried to protest. As she did, the person got rougher in his touch. She felt her knickers being dragged down and scooped over her feet. Drift lay on her back, her head pressed against a smelly pillow. She murmured her fear, but she was so lost at sea, her limbs felt like lead. When her eyes opened momentarily she saw she was in a worker's bedroom. She remembered vaguely being half carried into the Cobworth Station quarters by the boys. Above her Jack shushed her by pressing his mouth to hers aggressively, his wet tongue penetrating her mouth, his rough kisses travelling down over her neck and onto her cleavage. He bit her nipples hard. The pain brought her back momentarily.

'No,' she mumbled, turning her head away, trying to push him off.

'C'mon baby,' Jack said through gritted teeth as he pinned her wrists to the mattress.

She tried to get up, but Jack held her firm. She began to cry, fading in and out of consciousness.

'Shh, shh,' he said clambering over her. 'It's all right. You're gunna love it.'

Drift was so out of it, all she could do was succumb to what was happening. Her mind wouldn't work. Her limbs were paralysed. Next, Jack was above her, drool almost escaping from his hungry mouth as he parted her legs wide. He positioned himself above her and slipped his large cock inside her. The pain of his first dry thrust made her cry out. It seemed to excite him more. He pumped with an ever-increasing vigour, Drift lolling her head from side to side, her eyes clasped tightly.

'No, no,' she murmured, over and over. Soon she heard Jack cry out. She felt his dead weight over her. Then he pulled out of her, rolled off, and lay beside her, breathing heavily. He slapped her on the rump, covered her roughly with a grimy blanket and kissed her on her shoulder.

'A dead root, darling,' he said to her. 'You're a dead fucken root. But man, you've got a body to die for. Can I get you a drink of water, baby? Or a bucket?'

Drift rolled towards the wall, hugging her knees up to her chest, scrunching her eyes tight, trying to black out again, to stop the room spinning and her heart breaking.

*

The next morning, Drift woke to laughter coming from the kitchen. She found her dress on the floor and got dressed unsteadily. She wandered out, lost and disoriented. She had to find a bathroom. She wanted to wash away the stench of semen that stuck clammy between her aching legs, and she needed a drink of water desperately so as to evict the acid taste of whatever drug Jack had given her. She found the grottiest of bathrooms and ran the tap. Tepid water spluttered out. A moment later she staggered into the kitchen, placing her hand on the wall to steady herself.

'Ah! There you are, beautiful,' Jack said from where he sat at the ringers' quarters table, tucking into bacon and eggs, looking only slightly ruffled from the late night. 'All set to have some brekky, then we can head back to Dixon? I'll make you a proper coffee there with Carlos.'

'God, Jack,' Adele said. 'You and your bloody coffee. You wanker.'

Drift looked at the normality of the scene before her, her head pounding. The fog about what happened last night hazed in and out of vision. He was acting as if he'd done nothing wrong.

Adele proffered a plate of baked beans, eggs, bacon and toast under Drift's nose. 'Hungry?' she asked. The sight and smell of the meal sitting greasily before her was enough to propel Drift to the sink.

'Oh no you don't,' Jack said steering her out to the hallway. 'Toilet's this way. I think you might have overdone it last night, little lady.'

As she stooped over the bowl, Jack holding back her hair, she wanted to turn on him and rage at him. He had raped her. *Drugged* her and *raped* her. Her mind raced. She thought of Eli, and his talk of their bloom of true love in two half flowers joined. Where was the fucker now? Drift raged inside. Eli was full of shit. Men were full of shit.

Deep inside her shame bubbled. She shouldn't have gone with Jack. She'd read him as dangerous, but then she'd gone ahead and ignored her gut. Like she'd ignored her gut about Kelvin. She shouldn't have got in the truck with Kelvin that day. Maybe it *was* all her fault. She had been so stupid. And where was the support of the sisterhood that Charlie had spoken of? Why had Adele not stopped them? Where was she in all this?

Suddenly the pain of being a woman in this ugly, aggressive world swamped her. She felt like dying.

On the drive back, Drift sat in silence, pain burning between her legs, looking out to the red-dirt country that whirred by.

'You're very quiet,' Jack said. 'Bit hungover, are we?' He reached over and tried to place his hand upon her knee.

'Don't,' Drift blurted out, hitting his hand away.

'What are you so antsy about?'

'What do you think?' Drift said savagely, wrapping her arms around herself.

'Darling girl, you don't dance like that, dress like that and flirt like you did without putting out to a fella.'

'But I —'

'But you what? You want me to fall in love with you? Take you out to dinner on a second date? You want me to marry you now? Have babies with you? Get a grip. It was just sex.'

Drift cast him a furious look, but he just kept his eyes on the road. God knows what diseases he might have given her, not to mention the fact she could fall pregnant. Rage simmered in her again.

'It was a bit of fun. That's all,' Jack said. 'A bit of fun for us *both*. You were hot for me. Now we have some nice memories, you go your way, I go mine.'

He tried to pat her knee again. She shrank from his touch.

'I'll make you a coffee before you head off this morning, and I'll see you next time you patch a rug on Dixon. That's if Carlos and I are still here.'

'Like Hell you will,' Drift spat.

He opened his hands on the steering wheel for emphasis. 'What? I'm not sure why you're so cut up about it. Didn't you have a good time?' Jack turned his eyes to hers. 'C'mon, babe, it was only a little party drug. Loosen you up a bit. You sure as Hell needed it,' he said as smoothly as warm milk offered to a child. 'I'll make you a cappuccino. We can have a kiss and cuddle before you go.'

Drift shut her eyes and sucked air into her lungs. There was no kick and fight left in her any more — not like there had been in the truck with Kelvin. She thought about going to the police but just couldn't face that experience again. Instead, she turned her face to the window and wished for change all over again.

Chapter 45

Drift packed the truck up in record time, still in her dress and boots from the night before, revolted by Jack's rank smell on her skin, but there was no way she was going near the shower in the jackaroos' quarters. Misery rose in her. She couldn't bring herself to stay here any longer. The dogs hovered nervously, sensing her distress. Dunno — following her every jolting, frenzied move, Gearbox sniffing at the strange new scents on her.

As she yanked open the truck door to put a water canister in for her and the dogs, she was relieved to see an envelope sitting on the seat of the truck. Owen had paid the repairs invoice she'd given him before she left for the pub. She fingered the edges of the cash he'd placed there, along with a thank you note. She wondered if she ought to tell him about Jack. Catching sight of herself in the oblong side mirror, her hair wild, her face drawn and pale, she decided against it.

She saw from her reflection she had been crying silently without even realising it. Tears were spilling out of her eyes, over her cheeks and yet she felt nothing but a blankness. The memory of the grimy bed rose in her, along with the shame of her naivety. She ought to have wised up that Jack was untrustworthy.

Right now, her instinct was to run to the sea. She wanted the purity of the saltwater to wash the tainted sex from her and a beach to walk out her pain, but she was days' and days' drive from the coast. Lost on the inland sea, but mostly lost now inside herself, Drift tried to cling to memories of Eli and his kindness as if they were a buoy. Did she want to keep trucking east, veering north where she could be swallowed up in the isolation of desert country, never to be found again? Hang the repairs route, she thought. Hang the business. Drift decided she couldn't go on. Not this way. Who was she to think she was capable of running her own business on her own, anyway? She was just a stupid, naive and sheltered stock contractor's daughter who'd never even been to school. A weirdo. All it seemed she was good at was being used and abused by men.

She summoned the dogs up onto the passenger seat and fired the old girl up so the engine rumbled, missing a little. She drove quickly past the quarters.

'Bastard,' Drift said through gritted teeth as she caught the image of Jack's quarters in the side mirror. As she passed the big open skillion machinery shed she saw a stack of paint tins sitting next to one of the uprights and braked suddenly. Mouth set in a firm line, Drift got out of the truck. She found a half-full tin, the wire handle biting into her palm as she lifted it, and grabbed an old chisel and prised open the glugged-up lid. With a wide brush, she stomped to the truck and swathed paint over the doors and sides, blanking out the lettering she and Wilma had put on the truck. She whitewashed her number in thick, drooling paint. Hidden now from the world.

As she painted, traumatic memories of the night before kept bubbling up. Images would flash through her mind of Jack taking pleasure from her body, while she lay partially unconscious. She froze, the paintbrush raised and dripping, remembering Wal there too, in the shadows of her mind. Waiting his turn. Her vagina burned with pain. Jack had let Wal rape her too. Then Kelvin's face flashed in her mind. The men's faces kept floating towards her.

As she climbed into the truck and rumbled away, she wiped away tears of distress and frustration. What was the lesson this experience was meant to teach her, like Wilma always said experiences were supposed to do? Why was this happening to her? And how did she reach the part of herself so it never happened again? Her hands on the wheel began to shake even more as she rattled the truck over the bone-jarring drive that led out of Dixon Station.

*

About two hundred clicks further on, heading north on a dirt link road, Drift eventually found a ribbon thread of single bitumen. At the turn-off Drift spied a group of small trees near a turkey's nest dam. She hauled the truck over beside the steep wall of the nest and checked her phone. A text had come in.

Thanks for last night, Blondie. Followed by a row of Xs.

A lump in Drift's throat rose up and a noise like a wounded, trapped animal escaped her. Fury ignited, Drift saw how she was turning her anger towards her own self, instead of the men who had attacked her.

She wrenched open the door, and threw herself out of the cab, going into the workspace of the truck. At the workbench Drift picked up a large pair of scissors. She sat on the truck step, hacking her long blonde hair off. As the threads of gold landed in the dirt, Drift dragged the toe of her boot over and over them, sobbing. The dogs hunkered down in the shadows, eyes looking nervously away until her storm passed.

Eventually she slipped through the dam's fence, her dress catching on a twisted join of wire. With clenched teeth, she tugged at the dress so it tore. Clambering up the sparsely grassed bank of rubbled dirt, she looked from the top to see a patchwork square of brown water. The level was low. A barren denuded landscape spread out before her. Overgrazing. *Everywhere I go,* she thought, *Mother Nature, stripped bare. Raped. Just like me.* She looked again at Jack's message through stinging tears, then hurled her phone into the water.

Running down the steep cowshit-splattered bank she threw herself in a belly flop into the chilly water. Gritting her teeth, she let the syrupy muck swallow her. She stayed under for as long as she could, hoping she could somehow wash the horrible creepy feeling of Jack and Wal, Kelvin and even Simon from her. In the water she rolled over and floated on her back, hearing the thud of her heart within her ears. Above her there was not a cloud in the sky. Dunno was standing up to his hocks in mud, whining at her, like he knew she'd lost her mind.

'Well I have,' she shouted at him. 'I have lost my mind! Go away, Dunno! Go back home!'

He licked his greying muzzle and with flattened ears and his tail between his legs skulked off to the truck. Then Drift began to scream. Guttural screams that crashed with anger and hurt and fury. Screams dredged up from the past, beyond her life, of other women who had suffered the same way. She reached behind her for the zip of her dress and dragged it off, wanting to be rid of the hateful memories it now held. Stumbling forwards in the thick oozing clay bank, she fell to her knees. She pounded the dress with fistfuls of mud and stones. She dragged off her knickers and bra and threw them onto the dress. Naked, she began to wipe her body all over with mud. She covered her jagged hair, her breasts, between her legs. Bathed in mud and the stale outback water, she lay back on the bank and let the cold earth hold her weight. Blood pulsed in her body, pain seared her brain, the back of her throat burned and between her legs stung.

'Help me,' she wept. 'Help me.' Drift wasn't sure who she was calling to. God? Her mother? Charlie? Her sleeping father? The goddesses Wilma referred to? Sophia's Mother Earth?

Deep within her, the voices of her wise women arrived, like whispers on the wind.

'Surrender,' came Wilma's gentle tones. 'Life is about making peace with any situation you find yourself in. What you resist persists. What you fight, you strengthen. Surrender, Drift, surrender to the bigger plan.'

Charlie's voice arrived as if she too were in the water and *of* the water, and within Drift herself.

'Where thoughts go, energy flows, so don't rest your thoughts on people who have hurt you. If you're going through Hell, you don't pitch a tent there and camp! No! You keep heading towards the light. You keep heading home. Home to Love, right where I am.'

As her breathing returned to normal and she became aware of the solidity of the ground beneath her, she realised it was her own self she was seeking … the larger, future version of herself. The inner self who knew the map in the stars towards home. She began to feel her … her future self, where these awful lessons had been turned to wisdom, the future her who knew that surrender was more powerful than striving. With stillness, suddenly, she felt her. Her own, beautiful, powerful, grown woman self, way out there in the future days.

With that realisation, her crying subsided. Calm came to her. Dunno settled beside her, his paws wetly caked in mud as if he were wearing tall brown-top boots. Gearbox sat on the high bank as if keeping watch. Drift shut her eyes and the sunlight warmed her eyelids. She wanted to sink into the earth. Be swallowed by it. Then she remembered lying on the ground like this at The Planet in Eli's swag, the night he'd saved her. And again on the beach in his arms. She remembered how beautiful life could be. The miracle of life.

In the shimmer of the sun on the dam water, a breeze lifted ripples of mottled silver and rust on the dam's surface. And through her half-closed eyelids, she thought she saw, against the haze and glare, the girl. It was as if she were standing in the water, her dress white, but muddying brown where the water seeped into its fabric.

Drift blinked and the vision was gone. A calm sigh escaped her, and she lay with her arm over her face. A blast of sudden sunlight comforted her, until the mud dried and the sun had warmed her bones.

To her mind's eye came a picture of the thick lush grasses of The Planet, the coastal sweep of Pinrush Point. The smell and taste of the salty air, and the comfort of dust and horse sweat blending on her palms. The way Wilma's eyes creased in a smile as she stepped from her bus. Her father's grin when he'd pranked her. She saw the cattle, scudding excitedly onto the beach to chew on seaweed tendrils and paw their front hooves in the sand. She saw Sophia and Serge in grasslands so beautiful her heart swelled.

'Home,' Drift whispered, realising that what she most needed was the comfort of a familiar place, and her family around her. Even if family meant an unconscious father, an elderly librarian and a visionary billionaire recluse. At that moment, Dunno sat on his haunches and lifted his chin, and began to bark. Drift turned to him and saw the light in his eyes. The spunk of him. He play bounced, encouraging her to play too. He wagged his tail. He danced. He made comical noises. He smiled. He coaxed her. He invited her. Gearbox, on the bank, began to bark too. Soon the dogs were skitting about in the mud, playing and leaping in the joy of life around her. Skylarking without a care in the world.

'Home, eh, you reckon,' Drift said, propping herself up and smiling at her dogs. *Home.*

*

Back in the truck, Drift slept for hours. When she woke, it was getting dark. She went out and set a campfire. She could hear last-minute lizards, still warm from the sun, busy searching the scrub for a meal of insects. The fire crackled as it consumed the sun-bleached sticks she'd gathered. She waited until the stars arrived one by one, draped under a blanket as the cold came in, and then she saw the fingernail sliver of a moon emerge from the tumbling clouds. The July moon, ending its phase, making way for next month.

At a small eucalyptus tree, she snapped off a branch of young green leaves, then set to burning it. It fizzed with moisture within its thin curved leaves and began to smoke. She waved the smoking branch around her, closing her eyes, swaying her hips, inhaling the smell of eucalyptus and smoke. Above her a big cloud of towering black loomed and she felt a big fat droplet land on her skin. The unseasonal warmth of the day was about to burst. The drop trickled down over her arm in a gentle caress. More plump drops fell. Her skin was soon sheened with warm outback rain and the perfume of wet earth was enveloping her senses. She shut her eyes, heard the sigh of the fire, held out her arms and imagined the droplets kissing her body. They were like kisses from Heaven. She was suddenly filled with a sense of love so powerful it was inexplicable. There were no words. Love with a capital L for Life and for simply Living. She felt beyond time. Beyond space. Beyond her own body. Beyond the circumstances she was in. She felt whole.

When she opened her eyes, she drank in the sight of the moon rimmed with an aura of colours like a rainbow. She marvelled at the light prisms in the droplets on the vegetation around her. Upon the moon she thought she could imagine the translucent image of the little girl in the white dress.

'I really don't get you,' she said to the girl sitting on the moon's hook, swinging her legs and smiling, 'but I'm glad you're still with me.'

Drift felt as if she was being given the chance to see the world anew. I get it now, Charlie, Drift said to her in her head. I don't have to hate myself for anything. I don't have to take on other people's views of the world, either. I can create my own life. I can see the past is gone and it just is what it is. And I'm not a victim to men, or to anyone, or anything. From now on, Drift thought, if I just focus on the kind of world I want in the future, and live in the precious moment being grateful for all life's gifts, everything is gunna be OK. She smiled, looking up at the stars. Even if life dished up more lessons, Drift knew she'd be strong enough to handle it.

'Right, Charlie?' she said aloud. The brightest star seemed to wink at her.

The next morning Drift settled the dogs in beside her on the bench seat and turned the truck around. She back-tracked through cattle country, where the grids were set miles and miles apart through sections of bedrock and sections of bulldust, knowing that in this direction she'd eventually find the sea. Eventually, she would arrive *home*.

Chapter 46

Drift walked along the hospital corridor, running her fingers through the jagged ends of her short hair. Her scalp still felt odd, like a chick fallen from the nest with few feathers. She wondered what her dad would say about her 'new do' if he could talk. She rounded the corner and walked into his room.

The bed was empty. Shocked, Drift's mind ran straight to catastrophe. Had he died? Surely they would've sent word? Then again, if he'd woken up, they would've sent word. Wouldn't they? She told herself to calm down. They'd probably just moved him to a new room. Or Wilma would have him outside, propped up on a trolley bed getting some sun in the patients' garden. She looked in the nurses' station. No one was about. The clock showed it was almost noon. She could hear a television in another room. A patient elsewhere coughed. Suddenly a nurse was standing at her shoulder, staring too at the vacant bed, his hands clicking a pen. It was a nurse she didn't know.

Drift introduced herself, then asked, 'Where's Dad?'

'He woke up,' the man said.

'When?'

'About a week ago now. On a Monday morning. Time flies. I can find out exactly when on the file, but from memory it was about eleven am. Doctors have no idea why he woke. Without being rude, some of us wished he was still asleep. Woke up as

374

cranky as a bear after hibernation, raging to see you. Sorry ...'
He shrugged his angular shoulders.

Tears sprang to her eyes.

The nurse saw her distress. 'Sorry, love. We've been trying to reach you. Your phone wouldn't ring through.'

Drift thought of it in the murky depths of the turkey's nest the morning after the rape, the very same morning she had surrendered. The very same time her father had woken. She shivered.

'Where is he?'

There was that shrug again. 'We couldn't keep him here. He wouldn't have a bar of it. Not when he found out you were missing in action. So his friend took him.'

'His friend? Was it a woman?'

'Look, I don't know. Best to ask Nat at the front desk.'

'Nat?'

'She's new too.'

Drift muttered her thanks before hurrying down the corridor. The woman there looked up with a smile.

'I've no idea, dear,' she said after Drift asked about her father.

'Can you tell me who took him?'

Nat began tapping on the keyboard. 'Yes, love, it seems it was a Wilma Schnitzerling who discharged him.'

'Did they say where they were going?'

The woman shook her head. 'Can't help you on that one. Maybe she took him home to her place. Woulda thought he'd have more doctors' appointments, but there's nothing scheduled. A mystery.'

*

Looking out from the truck's window to Wilma's house, Drift noticed the roses had been pruned back. There was no car in the driveway, and the house looked deserted. Disappointed, she kept rolling and turned in the cul-de-sac, heading towards the library.

Maybe Wilma was there? As she lumbered along Cooperville's main street, changing down a gear around the war memorial in the centre of the town's crossroads, she could see the library off in the distance. Wilma's bus wasn't there, which meant she would be on a book run somewhere. The truck wheels bumped over the kerb as she pulled up in the car park. She wound the windows down for the dogs and dashed into the library, eager to find out more.

The women behind the counter didn't recognise her at first, but then rushed to her, cooing when they did.

'You're *back*!' called out Anne.

'Your hair!' said Tilly.

'It … it looks cool!' Doreen added, not sounding convincing at all.

They huddled around her, Drift feeling a little mobbed and self-conscious. Drift knew they would be too polite to mention the bruising flaring on her body from Jack's rough handling.

Anne was gripping her arm a little tightly, just where he had. 'Oh my darling! We are so relieved to see you. Where have you been? We've all been so worried,' she said, her dark brows knitting together. Anne began hugging her repeatedly while the others clustered about, waiting to hug her too.

'Dad — he's not at the hospital,' Drift said, pulling away from Tilly's embrace. 'The nurses said he woke up, and Wilma took him.'

'Oh my dear.' Anne tugged anxiously at the string of red beads around her neck.

'I'm sorry no one's been able to get in touch with you! When he came to, Wilma took leave to get him up and about. Once we couldn't reach you there was no keeping him in there. You're the only one Wilma says who can boss him. He needed rehabilitation and they wanted to do more testing, but he was like a bull at a gate to get out. Wilma tells us he's not the sort of man you can coop up. If she didn't open the gate for him, he was going to jump it anyway.'

Drift smiled at Anne's words.

'Wilma made him compromise and negotiated with the hospital. She's taken him down to that property on Pinrush Point. You know, The Planet. Wilma said they have doctors there who can look after him. It was the only way the hospital would agree to let him go. He's staying there, and they're keeping an eye on him. Wilma said you'd head there.'

'The Planet?' echoed Drift.

'Yes. Best place for him, according to Wilma.'

'And Wilma, where is she?'

'She's off again in the bus. Just a short hop this time. She'll be back.'

Drift's face fell.

'Don't worry, dear,' said Doreen. 'He's in good hands. Wilma called in to see us after she dropped him down there. She says apart from being anxious to find you, he's as well as he could be.'

'Thanks,' Drift said gratefully.

'Can we get you a cuppa or anything? Bikkie? You must be in such shock,' Tilly asked, concern on her kindly angled little face.

'No, thank you. I'd better go straight to him,' Drift said.

'Travel safe, and be mindful, dear,' Anne began. 'Wilma said he's changed. A lot.'

*

As Drift rumbled Charlie's truck out of Cooperville, her mind raced with elation that her father was conscious. What kind of change did Anne mean, though? She told herself it didn't matter. All that mattered was he was awake and walking and talking. It was *a miracle*. About thirty kilometres out of town, headed for the Widgenup turn-off, Drift noticed an unmarked police car flashing its lights as it hovered in her side mirror. She looked down to the speedo. She was doing eighty in a sixty zone.

'Shit bricks,' she said, Dunno flattening his ears as if embarrassed to hear her swear. She saw a lay-by a little way ahead with a set of picnic benches and a public toilet. She pulled over. As the car pulled in front of her, she watched the brake lights blaze then go out. Drift wound down the window and rummaged in the glove box for her truck licence. When she turned back, she was surprised to see a familiar tall figure standing there.

'Simon!' she said, a little stunned.

'Hi.'

He looked well. Incredibly well, in fact. Instantly, she felt guilty as she remembered the note she'd left him. The engagement ring placed upon it. The secret knowledge she'd hidden from him about Eli being alive. She swallowed and got out of the truck.

'We've been looking for you all over,' he said, his eyes examining her face.

'So they say,' Drift said. Her fingertips flew to her neck, where she knew Jack had left marks.

'Are you OK?' he asked suddenly, looking at her with a tilt of his head. His police mind was running at high speed, she could tell.

She drew in a breath. 'I'm fine,' she replied, but she could tell he knew she was lying.

'You cut your hair.'

She saw him noting her vulnerable gestures, the way she touched her throat and fingered the jagged ends of her hair.

'Did someone do something to you?' he asked bluntly, seeing the bruising on her arms and collarbone.

'Like what?' Drift said, a little defensively.

Simon's eyes narrowed at her.

She shook her head. 'No. It doesn't matter. I'm on my way to my father.'

'I see,' Simon said. 'He's at The Planet.'

'Yes, I know.

'We all heard he came round. Just all of a sudden.'

Simon's radio stuttered loudly and his hand reached to his hip and turned the volume down. 'I think it's changed him,' he said.

She thought about what Anne and the nurse had said. A small swirl of concern rose in her. She was about to ask in what way, when the police car passenger door opened. A lean dark-haired woman with a hooked nose got out. She wore the same uniform as Simon and looked just as neat and imposing.

'Radio room says we got a job,' she said to Simon. Drift thought she was about to hurry him up in booking her for speeding, but instead she said, 'I've told them to send another car. Give us a little more time here.' She winked at Simon then walked over to them, Drift taking in how tall she was. Half a head taller than Simon.

'Thanks, honey,' Simon said to her.

Honey? Was that her name, Drift wondered. Sergeant Honey? Simon read her face.

'Melody, I'd like you to meet my fiancée, Kerri.'

Kerri held her left hand out to her, and smiled.

On the woman's finger, Drift saw the gleam of the same diamond ring she'd once worn. She looked to them both. 'Fiancée?'

'Yes,' beamed Kerri.

'Congratulations,' Drift said.

'Thanks. Simon told me you passed him up,' Kerri said.

Drift grimaced. 'Yes. Sorry. Yes.'

Kerri laughed, sounding deep and guttural. 'No, *no*! Don't apologise! Lucky me! Women as tall as me don't have a large selection of men. I was about to get myself a third kitten for my thirty-fifth birthday. But there he was, all sad and miserable about you. I'm glad you turned him down. I got him on the rebound. Snapped him up.' She laughed again and looked at him with love. 'It's not often you find men who keep their noses as clean as Simon.'

'That you don't,' Drift said politely.

'In my line of work, I'm pretty picky about fellas nowadays.'

An image came to Drift's mind of Kerri picking Simon's nose. Drift told her brain to quit it.

'Now it's my turn to retrain him,' Kerri continued. 'Get some of that religious nonsense out of his head. Right, baby?'

'Yes, it is. Sure,' Simon said, smiling, looking at her as if she were Miss Universe.

She leaned in close to Drift, rolling her eyes. 'He expected me to give up policing so I could cook and clean for him! And make babies! Hello? Thank God we work in the same job. He has no excuses. It's Even-Stevens at home with us. Or it will be when we're married.'

'Ha,' Simon said. 'You just did it again.' He pointed at her.

'Did what again?' she said, turning to him as couple conversation came over them and covered them like a bell jar. It was as if Drift wasn't there at all.

'You just thanked God again.'

'I did not.'

'You did.'

'Did not.'

'You *did*. Didn't she?' He turned suddenly to Drift.

'Um ...'

'Well if I did, I didn't mean *God* God. I just meant thank goodness.'

'Goodness is God.'

'Oh, for fuck's sake, Simon!' Kerri looked at Drift with a gleam in her eye and snorted a laugh. 'He's fucking impossible.'

Drift hoped she didn't look as taken aback as she felt. Here was a woman renouncing Simon's God and then swearing as if she was a teenager outside a shopping centre.

'I can see why you couldn't put up with him, on some levels. But we click.' She got him in a headlock and planted a kiss on his cheek. 'He just needs an older woman.'

'Regulations, Kerri, regulations,' Simon said, trying to extract himself.

Kerri released him and straightened his cap for him. 'You're right, darling. Back on the job.'

She turned her rather fierce eyes to Drift. 'Now, I'm glad we found you. That dirtbag Kelvin Waller: I think I've got enough evidence to ping him. He couldn't help himself, even with us keeping an eye on him. He's tried it again — this time with a minor. We're an inch away from arrest. The sentence will be a long one. Thought you'd like to hear that.'

Drift was stunned for a moment at the mention of Kelvin's name, and with the way Kerri dished out the information as if she were in some kind of cop show. 'That's ... good news. Sad for his wife, though. Very sad,' Drift said.

'Yeah, maybe. Or it could be a chance for a new start for her, perhaps. One can hope. We may need to call on you as a witness, so we need a contact number for you.'

'I don't have a phone.'

'Why?' Kerri's eyes were intense, her question direct.

Drift hesitated a moment too long and emotion swelled.

'Who did that to you?' Kerri indicated the fingerprint bruises on Drift's neck and arms.

Drift had thought no one would notice them, but now she'd cut her hair, she knew they were visible, especially to a cop.

'I had an accident.'

'How?'

Drift swallowed painfully. Emotion clouded her expression.

'I think you'd better come with me,' Kerri said.

Flashing in Drift's mind came the intense discomfort she'd had in the police interview room after Kelvin had attacked her.

Kerri saw her fear. 'I don't mean down to the station. I mean over to this bench and tell me all about it. I can spot a victim of sexual violence a mile off. It's not just Kelvin, is it? There've been others?'

Drift looked between Simon and Kerri. She felt her face give away her emotional pain.

'Kerri is specially trained in this area,' Simon urged. 'You can trust her. We met on your case. She helped me understand the impacts.'

Drift read his expression as an apology. She smiled at him, letting him know she'd received it and she forgave him.

'I'll wait in the car.' He cleared his throat, revealing a little of his guilt, and the nerves caused by the simultaneous presence of his ex and his fiancée, then he moved away.

As Kerri sat, Drift looked down at the graffitied wooden bench. Apparently, according to the Texta marks, Diane was a slut and Giles woz 'ere. She looked up just as her dogs came to lie beneath it in the shade.

'I know what you need. I'm here,' said Kerri softly.

'I don't want to make a fuss,' Drift said. 'I've asked myself for a long time if maybe I'm overreacting. I mean, it's happened to loads of other women, and they seem to get over it. Don't they? I feel guilty about it all.'

Kerri took both her hands, and Drift felt the pulse of authentic compassion in her touch.

'Guilty? No!' Kerri said emphatically. '*None* of this is your fault. You have a right to make a fuss. It's never OK for a man to dominate you in such a way. *Never.*'

Drift felt the heavy weight of remorse lift inside her. Kerri was giving her permission to shed any guilt she held. She had such a sureness in how she moved and spoke that Drift felt her courage bubbling up. She knew it was time to speak up. To speak out. She'd been silent for too long. 'But why help me?'

'Let's just say putting men away who abuse women is my speciality,' Kerri said, revealing a glimpse of her own past pain in her eyes. 'It's why I became a cop in the first place. I can see you need help. I believe I can help women avoid further risks with predatory men. I've met a lot of women who grow up being taught subconsciously that they are less than a man. Then they go on to make unconscious choices to confirm that negative belief, buried deep inside them. Like partnering with, say, an alcoholic because it feels familiar if your dad was one, or pairing with a violent man, if that's what you're conditioned to as a child. But together, as empowered, fulfilled, fun-loving women, we can shift those deep old paradigms. Together we stand and united we *fly!*'

Drift felt even more relief to hear Kerri's words.

'I'll give you my card and you can come along to one of my courses —'

'But why would you want to help me? I'm Simon's ex. Aren't you jealous?' Drift asked.

Kerri laughed. 'These days, I'm too much of an egotist to get jealous. I know Simon's got the best woman for him. Even though I can see you are lovely, inside and out, I can also see you two would have been wrong together, if you don't mind me saying. That mother of his would've eaten you alive.'

Both women gave each other a knowing smile.

'Plus,' said Kerri, 'I never forget. After what happened to me, I know that women need women. We need to see ourselves as part of one big sisterhood, not being petty and jealous and separate from each other, like modern culture promotes. We need to band together. Not be divided. We need to balance the world up a bit with our solidarity and cheer each other on. So it's better for everyone.'

Drift felt gratitude and a sense of trust swamp her. Over the next hour, she told Kerri everything there was to tell about Jack Hawkins and his drugs, and Wal coming out of the shadows, his back-up rapist. She told her where the dress could be found by the turkey's nest, and the location of the phone lying at its murky bottom. She told her about the room at the cattle station where the rape occurred and Adele's name. She told Kerri of the drink spiking and date rapes Adele had alluded to and how she knew he'd done it to other girls too.

When she was done, Kerri folded her notebook and inserted the pen back into the side of it. Then she pulled out a card. 'Here. Call me when you get yourself another phone. I'll do a system search on all of those people. You can bet this coffee-machine creep has past allegations or convictions. I'll get a forensics team on to it. Drug squad too. We'll get going on it. Leave it with me, sister.'

'Thank you.'

Kerri shook her head. 'No thanks needed. Thank *you*. It's time for all of us women to say enough is enough when it comes to the likes of Jack Hawkins.'

Chapter 47

As Drift drove towards Widgenup on a dark pencil-line highway, the sky was a sulky grey. The occasional car zoomed around her slow-moving truck, distracting her momentarily from Kerri's parting sentence: 'Leave it with me, sister.' It soothed her. She was relieved she could pass the crimes of the men against her into the hands of Kerri, who was clearly a forthright woman on a mission. Drift told herself it was time to leave her memories of those men in the past where they belonged, so they couldn't keep attacking her in the now. She knew it was dangerous to let her mind wander, so she began to notice little details of beauty as she drove. A bird on the wing. The tone of the sky, as if it were watercolour washed. A graceful-looking old gum.

The truck chewed up the kilometres so before she knew it she was refuelling at the Widgenup bowser and rolling on towards the store. The doors slid open. There was the same girl. What was her name, Drift wondered. Some kind of perfume? Chanel? No. Champagne? Chenille? Cartier? That's it. *Cartier.*

'Hi, Cartier,' she said lightly as she came in.

Cartier looked up from where she was rearranging the magazines. 'Fuck, your *hair*,' she said, beginning to circle her. 'It used to be so nice. Why'd you do that? You look like you've been in prison.'

'Thanks. Well, I'm not in prison now, am I? Where's Head Bob?' Drift asked, looking to the chip stand and the cash register where he mostly perched.

'Back with Shaynene.'

'Shaynene? Where's she?'

'She came back. She's thataway,' Cartier said, nodding her head over the road.

'Whichaway?'

'Rental out the back of the servo. You go down the side, past the old tyres. Shit-hole.'

Drift thought of Kerri's words on sisterhood and her own journey — the times when other women, like Adele, hadn't stood by her. She realised Shaynene had been navigating the same rocky road in her own way in a patriarchal society. It was a word she'd rediscovered in her dictionary the day Kelvin had first groped her, as she tried to make sense of why the world felt so unbalanced. She recalled Charlie's advice on forgiving people. Charlie'd said non-forgiveness was like carrying a bag of stones about with you for the rest of your life. For her own sake, and Shaynene's, Drift wanted to make amends with her.

'Reckon she'd be home for a cuppa?'

'Reckon she would. You never see her out no more. Not since that creep ditched her.'

Grabbing up a packet of Tim Tams, Drift paid, thanked Cartier and went outside. She left the truck where it was, calling her dogs out of the cab.

*

Drift trod over the oil-stained soil down the side of the ramshackle servo, past palings sliding off the fence and allowing long grasses to seep through. There were the tyres Cartier mentioned, giving off a petrochemical stench as they heated up in the afternoon sun. Gearbox was poised to pee on one when Drift caught the glistening tail of a snake disappearing under the fence. She called him away. The place made her shudder.

The house sat in a yard full of old car bodies. A squat gumtree offered a little shade in a weedy turning circle and seemed as if it were laden with bizarre fruit — a collection of toys had been hurled into its branches. There hung a broken sun-brittle plastic tricycle at the tree's top, along with a hula-hoop, a faded Care Bear and an assortment of children's clothing. It was like a Christmas tree of broken dreams.

The house itself looked unloved, plonked there on its stumps after a mining company had finished using it as men's quarters. Drift and the dogs trod up the wobbling verandah steps, past bags of rubbish that buzzed with flies. An assortment of cheap shoes scattered the doormat. Drift opened the cobwebbed screen door and knocked. She could hear a television on. Through the side window a kids' program flashed, looming large on one wall. A giant purple bear was dancing around in a tutu on a studio set in slap-your-face vivid colours. The door opened. There was Shaynene with a snotty-nosed pot-gutted baby on her hip. He had glowing pink cheeks, was wearing just a nappy and had some kind of chewed food smeared through his jagged red hair. Drift's jaw dropped at the same time as Shaynene's.

'Fuck,' Shaynene said. 'It's you! Your *hair*!'

Drift felt like saying the same. Shaynene had let her hair grow out. There was no more colour. No more groovy shaved back and sides and flop tops. It was dull and lank. Pimples were erupting over her even chubbier face. Drift didn't think she'd ever seen Shaynene without makeup.

'Hey,' Drift said.

'What are you doin ere? I thought you'd pissed off for good. With that hair, you look like you're about to be gay married.'

There was a fluttering noise and Head Bob flew towards Drift, landing on her shoulder.

'Head Bob!' she said joyfully as he began nibbling her ear.

'Typical,' Shaynene said. 'He always gets the warmest welcome.'

Drift smiling, looked at Shaynene and her baby. 'It's good to see you too. And who's this?' she asked, indicating the boy.

Shaynene adjusted the chunky baby to the other hip. 'This is Zakk.' She paused then added, 'With a double K. He's as heavy as all fuck. Weird, considering Gup was such a skinny dick. Guess he took after me. Poor bastard.' She looked down to her own rounded form. 'What the fuck are you doing here, anyway?' she asked again. 'I thought after what I'd done you'd hate me guts.'

Drift waved her words away, as if shooing a fly. 'Oh, that old story. That's not what I'm here for. Got time for a cuppa? Can I come in?'

A flush of shame crossed Shaynene's face. She hesitated. 'Sure — you're gunna have to not mind the mess, but.'

Drift, normally not fussed by untidy spaces after living in the tiny caravan with her dad, was shocked at the chaos that lay within the small, stuffy home. She could tell Shaynene was practically dying inside with embarrassment. Drift wanted to put her at ease but she didn't know quite what to say. As Shaynene set the baby down in a playpen he promptly started screaming. Shay flamed red with frustration and went to put the kettle on.

'You want me to hold him for you, or we'll swap? I'll put the billy on?'

'Sure. Thanks. He needs a change. I'll take him. You sort the tea,' Shaynene said, setting the kettle down again and swinging around for the screaming child.

'Hard times, eh, Head Bob?' Drift said to the bird on her shoulder as she went to the sink.

'Blow me! Blow me!' the bird chirped.

'You're supposed to finish that sentence, you silly bird. It's meant to be "blow me down with a feather". Try it.'

As if offended by her coaching, Head Bob fluttered off to the curtain rail, where dried bird poo was slowly amassing into what looked like dollops of black and white puff paint. Drift turned back to the sink. Inside the cups, discs of mould grew on the surface of half-drunk coffees. She tipped them out, then cleared away bowls of crusting two-minute noodles re-dehydrating themselves in the bowls. Ants marched in rows over the feast of spilled food. Drift ran the water hot and filled the sink with frothing suds while the kettle chuggled. She tackled the glasses and baby sip-cups first, saddened to see one had flat Coke inside it; the rest, cordial.

'You don't have to do that,' Shaynene said, coming back in with a cleaner-looking child.

'I know,' Drift said. 'I want to.'

Shaynene set Zakk down in front of the television, this time handing him a rattle. She parked herself on a stool at the kitchen bench. 'Whaddya know?' she asked.

'Not much,' Drift said.

'You wouldn't tell me if you did. I might sell your story to the media,' Shaynene joked. She tried to sound light, but her voice quavered. Tears began to roll over her cheeks. 'I'm sorry! I'm such a bitch. I am so *stupid*! That bloody arsehole took the lot. What we didn't spend of it. He talked me into doing what we did to you. Then he got me hooked on fucken ice for a year. Almost got me in prison, which by the way looks like where you've been.' Shaynene nodded at Drift's hair.

'Anyway, then he got me knocked up, and right before Zakk was born he pulled some other chick and fucked off with her and with all our money. Never to be seen again. He says Zakk was my fault, as if he and his dick had nothin to do with it! And now he's denying he's his … I mean really! Look at him!'

Both Drift and Shaynene stared for a moment at the child, who, while on the chubby side was, sadly, a dead ringer for his dad. There was no mistaking it.

'I tell ya, I ought to have cut Gup's balls off. Blokes like that ought not to be breeding.'

They continued looking at the baby.

'My little Zakky is pretty cool though.'

The light of a mother's love shone through for a moment in Shaynene. Drift felt relieved to see it. But then Shaynene shut it down.

'Even though he can be a little shit.'

'He's not a little shit,' Drift said. 'How can you say that? I reckon he's just full of too much sugar. Too much TV. And too many negative words,' she said, handing a shocked Shaynene a cup of tea. Drift could see Shaynene needed help, but so did her kid.

'So you are still mad with me! You're having a go at me!'

'No, I'm not mad with you, or having a go at you. The past is the past. I've let all that go. Why would I bring you Tim Tams if I was still mad with you? But I will be mad with you if you say one more horrible thing about that poor kid.'

'You try being a single fucken mum,' said Shaynene defensively.

Drift felt another wave of anger rise. 'Don't give me that. That's an excuse. Saying you're a single mum is just a shitty way of looking at it. Zakk and you are a great team. You have each other so that means you have love. And blessings. And a chance to smile and enjoy each other. And to grow and learn together.'

'Yeah right! Even living in this shit-hole? Even after that shithead put me through all that he did?'

Drift felt as if she were channelling Charlie as she spoke. 'Even after that. We all have to learn our lessons in life. We are one hundred per cent responsible for how we view what happens to us. Everyone has shit in their lives. It's up to us to choose whether we wade through it to the other side, or if we lie down in it. Trust me. I know. At one point I almost chose to drown myself in shit, metaphorically.' An image flickered in her mind of her body smeared in mud and cow shit at the turkey's nest.

Shaynene looked at Drift's sincere face, then burst into tears again. 'I've missed you and your big fucken words!' she sobbed. 'Meta-fucken-what?'

Both girls edged closer, then held each other.

'We gotta stick together,' Drift said. 'Support each other.'

'I know,' Shaynene sniffled. 'I was such a bitch.'

'Yeah, you were caught up in the moment. But now you're forgiven. You're the only one who's bashing yourself up about it now. Let it go. After all my travels, I realised you're the only friend my age I've ever had. I need you.'

'I need you too,' Shaynene sniffled again. 'I missed you.'

They sat side by side at the kitchen bench, until Drift punched Shay lightly on the arm.

'So,' Drift said. 'Tell me how it all happened.'

Shaynene began recounting her journey after she and Gup left Pinrush Point. Then Drift sketched in her recent past, omitting the bits about Eli. She was grateful Shaynene resisted pressing her for the full story. She glanced at the time. The roos would be out thickly at dusk and she thought of her father down at The Planet.

'I can't stay. I have to get to Dad. But here,' she slid Kerri's card over to Shaynene, 'if you want Gup to be made accountable for what he's done, she'll point you in the right direction. Scary lady, but her heart's in the right place. Leave it with her.' Drift stood up to leave. 'Maybe we could do her course together.'

'Before you go,' Shaynene said, 'let me do something with your hair.'

'My hair? Really? Why?'

'*Why?*' Shaynene rolled her index finger in circles near her temple. 'Mental patient on the loose!' She pulled a mock horror face before gathering up some scissors and draping a towel that smelled disturbingly of wee over Drift's shoulders.

'Did I ever tell you I was almost a hairdresser? Almost. Once.'

'Really?'

Shaynene began to massage Drift's scalp in expert fashion before taking up the scissors.

'Are you sure you want to do this?' Drift asked.

'Leave it with me, sister,' Shaynene said.

Chapter 48

Driving deeper into Pinrush Point, Drift's heart beat faster as the truck rolled past the familiar roadside, each bend, each twisted coastal tree evoking a memory of her herd and of her horses. The days droving with Eli came alive too. Of all the places she'd travelled, she realised she loved this remote place the best, and it was here with her father and Eli near The Planet that she'd felt happiest. She came over the rise and her breath was stolen away when she saw the spread of the ocean. Home! A jewelled sea lay sparkling before her in a burst of late-afternoon sunlight, so bright she had to drag her servo sunglasses down from where they rested on the top of her head. Around the next bend she passed the place where the cattle camp had been, the grasses grown back in a flourish of sun-fed shoots, soaking up the richness of the dung and urine that had merged into the soil over time.

She passed a site where they'd set up another camp, the small grey stone ring of a long-ago extinguished campfire inviting her back. Over the next rise came the vast stretch of The Planet, off in the distance the tiny gleam of the solar panel at the gates. A short while later Drift sucked in a nervous but excited breath as she changed down gears and swung the wheel to turn in, ready to buzz the intercom, ready to go see her father.

She was surprised to see the gates wide open, as if the people within knew she was coming. Tyres thunked over the metal cattle grid. Thoughts of Eli, vivid and renewed, burst into her mind as she drove into the picturesque property. What if he was here too? Just the thought made her pulse race. Dunno too was up on the seat, his tiny triangular ears cast forward, whining a little, looking anxiously for Eli too.

'I know, mate,' she soothed. She breathed deeply to relax her body, allowing the landscape to envelop her, to calm her. The beauty of The Planet's meadows and copses spreading for thousands of acres gave her a shot of excitement. The mixed cropping paddocks had stands of emerging grain crops underlaid with the darker green tinge of broad leaf crops nestling below. The beans were waiting their turn in the sun after grain harvest, their roots feeding the microbes in the unseen Universe of the soil. In pastures, Drift spied the familiar toffee-coloured cattle grazing happily, sun glancing off shiny hides. It was hard to believe this was the same kind of country she'd passed leading to the Point, where the farms were bare-soiled landscapes with *For Sale* signs leaning sideways on equally sagging fences.

Parking the truck in the shade of a massive old peppercorn tree, Drift looked to the cattleyards where she and Serge had drafted the boxed herds. As she opened the door, Dunno practically burst from the truck and started trotting happily along the path towards the workspace and homestead, tail swinging in a low wag. A more reserved Gearbox got out and instantly began sniffing about for the scents of the station's dogs.

'Manners on, please,' she cautioned him.

He snuffed and wagged his tail as if to say, 'Got it.'

Ahead of Drift, the sun was sinking, warming the winter landscape to a green and golden glow. An orchestra of birds sounded from the canopies above. On the lawn by the pond to the left, a large group of The Planet people were doing yoga, most still in their hi-vis work gear, but all barefoot on colourful mats. The kids and dogs were included, giving the gathering an informal feel, like a crowd on the hill at the cricket. Drift scanned the group of about twenty-five adults, instantly recognising the familiar drape of Sophia's ponytail, skidding over her shoulder as she bent in a warrior pose. Drift waited patiently in the shade a little way off, making her dogs sit with her. Dunno was practically beside himself and kept glancing up pleadingly.

'No,' whispered Drift. 'Not yet. We'll wait till they're done.'

Drift saw that Serge was matching Sophia's moves to the right of her, looking fit and tanned in his work shorts and a bluey singlet on his red mat. Beside Sophia, on a green mat, a tall lean brown-haired man flexed upwards as all of them moved into a prayer pose. He wobbled slightly and Drift watched Sophia turn her head, offering him a hand, beaming a smile at him, laughing. They entwined fingertips for a moment, Sophia steadying him. Drift noticed Sophia was in no hurry to let go of the man's fingers, nor his gaze.

Patiently Drift waited, concentrating on her own breath, wishing they would finish soon so she could go find her father, who must be in one of the serene bedrooms recuperating. She wondered if she ought to go seek out someone in the kitchen and ask rather than wait. She told herself to settle and remained on the grass, rummaging her fingers in Dunno's fur to calm herself. The Earth turned for a moment, silent save for the sound of birds and a breeze in the trees. Drift looked at the dreamy scene. Humans, silent and still in a real-life Garden of Eden. A Utopia created out of someone's belief systems and their love flowing out to others. She felt any past hurt melt away about the mess with Eli and the police, as she saw clearly that Sophia wanted to help everyone she came in contact with. Her goal was to serve others. To make the planet and people's lives richer. She also saw Sophia endured her own fears as a woman and worked to overcome them daily. As she watched her move in the last vinyasa, Drift saw she was as humble as she was noble.

Standing there, under the shade of the trees, Drift had a moment of realisation. She might not have Sophia's billions, but from this moment forwards, she too would serve others and help change the world around her, starting simply with the gift of a smile, or a kind word of encouragement. For too long she'd sat on her stump of past hurts, and not seen the light she passed on with her saddlery stitching, her artful jewellery or her time at the library, where the oldies had gravitated to her warmth and her open ears. She was, already, all she needed to be. She had all she needed to have. She was whole already. And that knowledge made her feel good. Smiling, she looked up at the canopy of leaves that breathed above her and felt peace deep within herself.

A few minutes later each person came out from their brief meditation and pressed their palms together and bowed their heads with a whisper of 'Namaste' to the leader of the group. Yoga session over, people began rolling up their mats, dragging on their workboots. Then the chatter began to escalate. The kids upped their energy and started to tear about again. The dogs in the shade woke from their slumber and ambled over to say hello to Dunno and Gearbox, the flirty collie Munro among them. Drift noticed how Gearbox, normally such a prickly dog, greeted The Planet pack with wagging tail and enquiring nose, particularly liking the feathery-tailed retriever, Joel. Drift walked past the happy dogs over to Sophia and Serge, who were chatting in a group of smiling people.

'Sophia, Serge — hi,' Drift said a little awkwardly, not sure how she'd be received after all this time and the business with Eli. Serge's and Sophia's faces beamed when it dawned on them who had arrived.

'Oh my goodness! Drift, darling!' Sophia said, taking in Drift's short hair, cut in a cute little pixie style, thanks to Shaynene. 'I didn't recognise you with your hair! You look fabulous, like a blonde version of Audrey Hepburn! Beautiful!'

Serge swooped in for a hug. 'Hello, my darling,' he said.

'I guess you came to say hello to this fellow too?' Sophia said, stepping back and tugging on the white T-shirt of the tall man who'd been doing yoga next to her. When he turned to face her, Drift's mouth fell open in disbelief.

'*Dad?*' she said breathlessly.

There he stood before her, altogether changed. Altogether transformed! His eyes open with light and joy radiating from them.

'Drifty girl!' he said, his voice cracking, gathering her up. Tears came to them both as they hugged, Drift feeling his broad shoulders, and taking in the unfamiliar reduced size of him. She felt his big hands over her short hair and heard his sob. They pressed their foreheads together, laughing with relief.

'Thank God,' they said in unison.

They held each other at arm's length, letting tears fall, emotion-soaked laughter shuddering up in them.

'Everyone said you'd changed! You sure have! Where's the rest of you?' Drift asked. 'I thought you'd be in bed! Shouldn't you be in bed?'

'Bed?' He laughed. 'As if I'd want to be there! Spent too long there!'

Drift felt joy bubble in her. 'It's so good to see you, Dad!' she said. 'And awake! I didn't even recognise you! You've changed *so* much!'

Drift had seen the slimmed-down version of her father when he'd been in hospital, but he'd lost even more weight in the months she'd been gone. She'd forgotten that underneath the bulk he was an utterly handsome man. His brown hair peppered with grey was in a buzzcut and even though he'd lost his stockman's muscle tone, he was clearly on his way to gaining it back again. What was different too was the light in his eyes. He had an altogether different energy.

She saw his love for her radiating out. There was no sense of burden in him now. No sense of being trapped and troubled by the past. He just looked … joyful. Present.

'I like your do!' he said.

Instead of allowing herself to be dragged back to the reason she'd hacked off her hair, she beamed a smile, reflecting her father's joy. 'Thanks. It was just for a change. But I'm going to grow it back again. You get a sunburned neck this way.' She touched her fingertips to her scalp, knowing new memories would come as it grew. Better memories. Kinder memories, made by a mind that looked to the future, not the past.

'I was sure you'd turn up,' her dad said. 'It was the only place the hospital would let me come. I'm under doctor's orders.' He glanced over to Landy, who gave a friendly wave of welcome to Drift. 'We couldn't reach you. But I wasn't worried. I knew you'd come! I *knew*.'

'I ought to have come here months back,' Drift said, 'but I guess I needed to learn a few lessons on the road by myself.'

'I understand,' her father said, squeezing her hand. 'So did Simon set you straight and tell you I was here?'

'No. Not Simon. It was the women at the library who put me on the right path, but then Simon found me anyway. Y'know. Small towns.'

'Speaking of … did you meet Kerri?' her father asked, a glint in his eye.

'I did!'

'She's a rum'un. Good for him. Better for you.'

She took in his meaning. She'd narrowly escaped a disaster.

'Things never work out how you think they ought to. But if you trust it's all part of a bigger plan, it all turns out anyway,' he said.

He glanced over to Sophia and Serge, who were politely standing a way off, giving them some privacy. Drift noted the unmistakeable twinkle in Sophia's eye when she looked at her dad. Split returned her a gentle, fond smile.

Split noticed Drift's expression, like she was solving a puzzle. 'What?' he said.

Drift grinned and nodded a little at Sophia. 'I think there's a good moon on the rise,' she said, hoping he'd catch her meaning.

He did. He let a small smile reveal the excitement of possibility, but then frowned at her, the look he gave when she was pushing cheeky over the line. 'Steady on. In time. All in good time.'

'You and Sophia are so on the same page as far as regenerative ag goes,' Drift said. 'It makes such sense.'

He looked at her for a moment. 'A woman like her would never have been interested in the old version of me. I'm just lucky I've seen.'

Drift squeezed his hand. 'What do you mean, seen?'

Tears welled in his eyes. 'In the hospital. I saw how powerful I could be if I chose to come back. I was half in this world, and half in the one beyond, where it's ... where it's pure love. Bliss. *Home*. If I chose to come back, I knew I needed to live without guilt, without grief and to choose where I shone my focus. Sophia would have scared me before. But now ... it's like ... I know I can be on the same frequency as her. Like I've tuned my radio station to hers.'

An involuntary tear slid down Drift's face. She'd never heard her father speak this way and it filled her with hope and with love. 'I'm glad you did choose to come back and not go — well, *home*, as you call it.'

'I'm only here because of you.'

'Me?'

Her dad's deep brown eyes looked at her. 'I wanted to stay in that bliss-filled place and let go of that big lumping, aching body I had to walk in on the Earth, then I'd hear you guys, you and Wilma, carrying on. You kept me here. That same love I was feeling beyond the veil where I was without my body was actually right here in this world with me too. I saw how your love filled up the room, and I realised I'd never truly let it in before. Not properly. It was like a thread of light coming from you and Wilma. A way to find what I felt *there*, in this world. Am I sounding crazy?'

Drift shook her head. 'Not at all. You make perfect sense.' She hugged him close. 'I love you, Dad.'

'I love you too. C'mon,' he said, stooping to pat Gearbox and gather Dunno up in his arms, 'it's dinner time. Let's get you settled in. I think you and I both know, this from now on is *home.*'

They walked over to Serge and Sophia and together they all headed towards the kitchen, where an abundance of good food and good company awaited them on The Planet.

Chapter 49

'We've got a surprise for you,' Sophia said as they finished their meals on the long banquet table. The doors were open to a lovely warm winter's evening and the children were spilling outside for a last-minute play on the lawn before bed. 'We've just enough daylight.'

Drift's heart fluttered. *Was it Eli?* She hadn't been brave enough to ask. They'd been surrounded by so many people who were greeting her so warmly that she'd not found the right moment. Plus she wanted to savour sitting next to her father as he ate. Alive. Well. And now radiating an inner peace with every action. From savouring his food — 'So much better than a tube,' he'd joked — to the kindly way he passed the platters about, making eye contact with each and every person as if the interaction was a holy instant. At one point Drift had elbowed him.

'I feel like I'm sitting next to Jesus at the Last Supper,' she joked.

Her father had elbowed her back. 'Shut up, smartarse.' He'd chewed for a while on a corn cob, reminding Drift of the old days where the only yellow food he put in his mouth was crumbed, then he spoke.

'Jesus, you reckon? I had my last supper back at the abattoir and it tasted like crap. Now you're back here with me, this is the *first* supper, with many to come. Not just with you, but with

400

many other people. I'm learning.' His eyes fell on Sophia, who was out on the lawn chasing the kids with the dogs leaping at her bare feet.

'No more suffering. No more self-destructive actions. So yes, I guess I am Jesus in a way. Born again. Resurrected. And with a super-tuned sense of humour like him. You can call me Jeez-Arse, Jeez for short, and Mr Arse when you have the shits with me.'

Drift chuckled. 'Thanks, Mr Arse,' she said, looking at his handsome profile.

'No worries, love,' he said, winking at her, and then biting down on the freshest apple.

*

As her father climbed in next to her on the passenger seat of one of The Planet's utes, Drift began her teasing banter.

'There's no need for you to shove over any more is there, Jeez? No more fatty father.'

Sophia glanced over from where she sat waiting behind the wheel of the ute.

'He looks as spunky as young James Dean and as ruggedly handsome as Hugh Jackman, don't you think?' Drift stirred.

Sophia smiled gently and looked away out the window, a dreamy look on her face. 'He sure does. Ready?' Sophia asked as Split slammed the door.

Drift in the middle nodded, tense about what 'surprise' lay ahead. As they travelled along a track she wondered if they were taking her to a cattle camp somewhere. A camp where Eli was? After about ten minutes, she summoned up the courage to ask.

'Are you taking me to where I think you're taking me?' She had a bit of play in her tone. She looked to the attractive Cleopatra profile of Sophia, who looked noble and glamorous even with her hair knotted in a rough plait, jolting over a bulldust track.

'Where do you think we're taking you?'

Drift fingered the fraying edges of her cut-offs. 'I don't know. To a stock camp maybe? With someone in it?'

Sophia and Split exchanged glances. She tried to read their expressions.

Was that regret on Sophia's face? Her dad was now looking out the window at some saltbush.

'If you mean Kai — Eli,' Sophia said in her rich deep voice, 'I'm sorry, darlin' girl. We've not heard from him.'

Drift felt her heart sink. 'Since when?'

'Since the night I sent him on to your camp. We really don't know what has become of him.'

Drift saw tears in Sophia's eyes. Disappointment ripped through her. She'd almost willed him there on his handsome white horse. Waiting for her. Healing. Coming to terms with his life post-scandal. Sophia and Split felt the pain behind her silence.

'He was such a mess,' Sophia said. 'The whole thing was a mess! Serge and I felt so bad deceiving you and everyone really … Especially his parents, Sukey and Lani. How could we leave a mother and father hanging with such grief? The whole time was awful. I don't know how he talked me into it. I guess he sprung it on us, turning up out of the blue in the way he did. I felt so sorry for him and wanted to give him a chance to learn and re-emerge, awakened.' Sophia sighed. 'Serge and I decided to tell his parents he was alive. Kai was so angry. So we had a fight. That's when I sent him to you. Didn't he tell you?'

Drift shook her head.

'Then, Split told me what happened. So we could have lost him to the sea anyway.' Drift saw regret in Sophia's expression. 'And the whole world of pain opened up for everyone again. His parents too. To live not knowing.'

'We do know,' Drift said.

Sophia slowed the vehicle and glanced at her. So too Split.

'He's alive.'

Sophia hit the brakes and turned to Drift. '*Alive!* How do you know? Are you sure?'

Drift nodded. 'He must've hitched with Charlie after he left us. I found his things hidden in her truck.'

Sophia cast her face heavenwards and let out a moan of relief.

Split shook his head. 'I'll be. With Charlie? Really?'

'I think so,' Drift said. 'I can't believe he hasn't been in touch with you.' She felt the old anger rise. Eli had hidden so many things, inflicted so much worry on so many people. But then she realised it was an old practised feeling, and one she could now choose to shed.

Both her father and Sophia picked up on her plummeting mood. Sophia laid a hand on her knee, rolling the vehicle onwards, steering one handed over the lumping track with an easy strength.

'Darling girl. I'm so glad to know for certain he is alive, but that boy had so many demons to lay to rest. He had so much guilt, made worse by his culture and believing he was betraying his ancestors. He has a lot of processing to do. A lot of forgiving of himself. Until that time, we just have to leave him be. He'll come back to us eventually. And to his parents. They're in touch periodically with Regenerative International, but they never mention Eli.'

'Where do you think he might be?'

Sophia shook her head. 'I have no idea where in the world.'

Drift turned to her father, desperation creeping into her voice unexpectedly. 'Did you know he came to see you?'

Split looked at his daughter and took up her hand. 'Yes and no. I don't remember him specifically coming to see me. But I know somehow he was there. Not just in the hospital. But all the time. All I remember is feeling his love, his good thoughts towards me, and you. It was like a thread of vibration. Like a powerful prayer.'

Drift felt tears spring to her eyes. She flexed out her leg in the cramped ute cab so she could reach her fingertips into her pocket and fish out the heart stone. 'Do you remember this?'

Her father looked at it, puzzled. He thought for a moment, taking it in his hands. 'Yes. I don't know why or how, but yes.' He gave it back to her. Drift ran the smooth stone between her fingertips.

Sophia glanced at it as she drove.

'It's beautiful.'

'It is beautiful,' echoed Drift. 'The nurse said someone had placed it on your heart, Dad. It was a stone he gave me. But I lost it on the beach that night.' They fell silent for a while, the engine the only noise.

'That boy is a mystery.'

'Best he stay that way,' Drift said sadly. Then she brightened, deciding to simply be happy wedged between two of her favourite people on the planet. 'Now you've really got me. If it's not Eli, I have no idea what your surprise is.'

'Almost there,' Split said, elbowing her.

Soon they were slowing up at a set of double gates.

'Look,' Sophia said with a smile. Drift followed her gaze out over the stretch of long wavering grasses. There, peppering the paddock, was a motley herd of cows of varying crosses. The cattle mooed at the sight of them. Curiosity led the herd over. Front and centre came the cranky black cow, who looked far from cranky now. She looked happy, bold and inquisitive.

'*My girls*!' Drift exclaimed. 'But how? *Why?*'

Sophia smiled at her. 'I'll explain. C'mon.'

They spilled from the ute just as dusk began settling over the land. With the cattle was a handsome Santa bull who had clearly chosen the old black cow as a favourite: he hovered near her flank, silver drool trailing from his mouth.

Split opened the gate and ushered them through.

The three of them stood while the cattle sniffed and jostled about.

'I bought the lot,' Sophia said. 'We weaned the calves as late as we could and sold them off. But we kept the girls.'

'But why? They'd be the worst line of cattle this place has ever seen.'

'They add a bit of colour to the place.'

'But why, Sophia? Why do that for me? For us?'

Sophia swallowed. 'I realised I placed you in such a dilemma. When I heard about the abattoir and your father's accident, shall we call it, and his extended sleep session,' she glanced at him, 'I felt it was the least I could do. You'd lost your entire life. I hadn't been straight with you at all. I wanted your road cattle to end their days kindly, after all they'd been through. After all you'd been through.'

Drift felt the next question circling like a bird. She didn't want to ask. But she had to. 'And the horses?'

Split looked away again. Sophia turned to face her and took her by the hands. 'I'm sorry. I couldn't save them.'

'You mean they slaughtered them?'

Sophia's eyes welled when she witnessed Drift's pain. 'I think so.' Then she shook her head vehemently. 'No. I'm not going to say that. *I don't know* for sure. The man on the phone barely spoke any English. He said they'd done-in a pen of horses. But he couldn't be sure *which* horses. I'm sorry. He said I was a day late. It was all I could do to get the cattle.'

Misery swelled in Drift as she thought of the kind eyes of her hardworking, beautiful horses. Each one so different, so special to her.

She felt her father's arm around her shoulders. 'Another thing to grieve and then let go, my girl,' he said. 'They'll always be with us.'

She looked around her, at the cattle happy in this beautiful place. Drift saw the big brindle girl with the daggy udder. The toffee-coloured girl with the pointy ears. The brown and white lady with the white whorl on her nose that was so low it looked like she'd licked an ice-cream and missed her mouth. She looked back to the ute, where Dunno was clipped, and the memories of her stock dogs, Molly and Hamlet, rose up. She felt the weight of sadness then breathed it away, like letting a black balloon go, up to the darkening sky. No matter which way she looked, despite the loss, life was still good. Still beautiful.

'Thanks,' Drift said, 'for saving my girls. Thanks.' She hugged them both and realised they were right.

'I'm going to take a leaf out of Jeez Arse's book here.' She lightly punched her dad on the arm. 'Let the past stay in the past. Be grateful for what's in the now. And right now I'm here with you. How lucky we are!'

Chapter 50

'That's all of it,' Joey said, dumping more horse gear outside the saddlery truck under a dreamy peppercorn tree near Alphie's day yard.

'Thanks,' Drift called back. She had been concentrating intently on wrapping the gift she'd made for Sophia. Turning, she took in the sight of the wiry Joey, who spent his time on The Planet educating both horses and humans in a shared language. His lively old blue eyes looked to her with slight apology.

'I know the last lot took you a few weeks. This is older, more busted up, but I'm sure it can be resurrected. Waste not want not.' He rubbed his bony hands together, excited that some of the gear, laid aside for several years, could once again be put to use.

'Oh we're good at resurrections around here!' Drift joked. 'Aren't we, Jeez Arse?' she ribbed her father, who was leaning on the workbench beside her.

'We're good at smartarse too,' Split returned.

Joey shook his head, a warm smile on his face. 'Good good,' he said, turning away, greeting Sophia as she walked over to the truck.

'You wanted me?' Sophia's words carried a double meaning, the way she looked at Split standing inside Drift's workspace.

'We sure do,' Drift said, getting up. She cleared her throat. 'I wanted to give you this.' She held out a brown paper package that was decorated with a ribbon of leather thonging and a sprig of early wattle.

Sophia received it in her elegant hands. 'Oh, thank you!' She glanced up at Split, her expression curious and excited, like a child.

She peeled back soft green tissue paper, revealing a beautiful silver and turquoise necklace entwined with intricately plaited chestnut horse hair.

'Oh I love it,' she said, eyes moistening. 'It's gorgeous! Where did you get it?'

'I made it,' Drift said. 'Well, me *and* Charlie did.'

'You made it? You clever, talented woman!'

Drift felt a blush tingle on her cheeks. 'Alphie didn't mind sacrificing some of his tail for it either.'

Sophia peered more closely at the necklace. 'That's part of Alphie's tail?'

Drift nodded.

'Oh I love it even more!'

'I'm just trialling stuff at the moment. But I wanted to thank you in some small way for having us here these past few weeks, for giving us a home.'

Sophia smiled at her and then looked again to the necklace. 'I'm sure you know the gratitude is mutual,' Sophia said, looking at Split. 'It's helped me beyond measure. Look at me! I'm a changed woman. Fancy me being brave enough to leave the gates of The Planet open!' She unclipped the chunky cowgirl-style silver clasp and reached behind her neck to put it on.

Split dived forwards to help her, gently brushing Sophia's ponytail aside. Drift saw how Sophia shut her eyes from the pleasure of his nearness.

For the past couple of weeks, Split had been helping Sophia see how it was really important to start reaching out locally. He knew he had a client base of conservative, sometimes cranky and often stubborn farmers who would never believe her message unless they could see it. It had been Split who'd done a ring-around of his former clients and arranged the first of many field days and a government-funded bus to bring the cockies out.

On the drive in, the farmers had passed the other stations that lay in the northern section of Pinrush Point: eroded, denuded and desertifying. As the farmers ambled off the bus, cynical and seemingly reluctant to be convinced, Drift had noticed that instead of Split dumbing his words and demeanour down to fit the mould of the farmer world he had walked in, he now spoke from the depths of his vast intelligence. He now had nothing to prove ... only a path to lead others forward if they chose. Drift had listened spellbound to him, and she saw the farmers start to incline their heads, seemingly enthralled by the new version of the man they had once known, and the contrast between the land over the boundary fence and the beautiful property they now stood on.

'Barren, lifeless farms are the new normal in the Australian people's minds,' Split had said, standing in the shade of a vast old gumtree as the insects and birds on The Planet backgrounded them with a soundtrack of vibrancy. 'Most of us believe the myth that Australia is made up of poor soil and is governed by drought. But a growing number of us now know that this is untrue. The white history of our country is untrue. And the forecast for our future is untrue. We know regenerative farming practice is the best way forwards if we are to survive as a species. Technology is not the answer. It may be part of the answer, but it's not *the* answer.'

The farmers had taken in the unquestionable fact that this farm looked like an oasis in a desert. They'd seen nothing like it.

Split had swept his arm out to encompass the paddock they stood in. 'With insight into Mother Nature and with wisdom in your management, every farm could achieve what Sophia, Serge and The Planet team have created here. But unless you change the climate of your mind, your soils will keep blowing to the sea, taking with it your dollar bills and your family happiness, and community health.'

Drift had seen how some of the men were nodding. Many looked tired. Defeated. Others angry. Defensive. But she knew that the way her dad was communicating, he'd reached the tiny flame within them that held the truth of what the land and they themselves truly could become.

Split had then toured the busload of men to another section of The Planet, gently questioning their traditional beliefs, inviting them to think differently as they witnessed the ecology before them, speaking their farming lingo, speaking in economics, yet not undermining for one minute his wisdom and deep learning. Beside him had stood Sophia, radiating a calm confidence. Together, Drift mused, their energy was powerful beyond measure.

Drift found herself thinking how glad she had been that night of her twenty-first birthday to wish for change and the bumpy old road that had led them here. After the bus left that first day Sophia had said, 'Leave the gates open for good! Let the world come! Let the world see,' and Split, Serge and Drift had cheered. And the dogs had barked.

Now, as Sophia stood with her tall stockman behind her in the saddler truck, necklace in place, Split left his hand resting on her shoulder. She spun around, took his hands in hers and looked up at him. 'How did you do it? How do you do it?'

'Do what?'

'Give me the courage to open the gates? Serge has been on at me for years!'

Split returned her smile. 'Same as livestock management. Gentle pressure on, pressure off. Gentle pressure on, pressure off. Plus, I think you realised you were being a little selective ... or at least playing it safe with your own kind.'

Sophia laughed. 'So true. So now are you trying to turn me into a docile, compliant cow?' she asked jokingly.

'No. Just a very happy and self-assured supported woman,' he replied. 'One who is brave.'

They looked at each other with such adoration that Drift turned back towards her workbench, a little embarrassed to be in the proximity of such an intimate display, but glad of the love story blooming between them.

The old version of her father would never have turned Sophia's head, and he in turn would never have considered himself 'good enough' for a woman like her. It was clear now to Drift that Sophia had put on a display of courage, but underneath, the fearful little girl lingered within her. Despite her money and self-assurance Drift could now see that the gates had remained shut and locked because Sophia, like many women, found it confronting to be a woman in this patriarchal world. There were reasons to stay guarded. But that was the old way, Drift concluded. Both she and Sophia were ready to influence the wider world and stand firm and open their hearts.

A knock on the side of the truck interrupted her thoughts. They looked up.

'Split Wood,' Dr Landy called, 'it's check-up time.'

Split looked at the slight woman inclining her head in the direction of her bungalow. It was there Landy carried out trials and gathered data on the nutrition levels of the food The Planet grew. Her mini lab was also the place for The Planet team to go when they needed a stitch-up from a cut, or to have something checked. Mostly Landy spent her time treating adventurous children for potentially broken bones after getting too carefree in a tree or on a pony.

'Just one more blood pressure and cognitive function test, then you've got the all-clear.'

'On my way,' he said, before taking up Sophia's hand. 'It looks beautiful on you,' he said of the necklace lying perfectly on her warm olive skin. 'Good job,' he said to Drift. Then he turned and went with Landy.

*

Drift watched Sophia walk from the truck in her elegant unhurried way, and as she did Drift sent up a silent thank you to the

Heavens for things turning out in life. There was just one niggling sensation, though. Her thoughts kept returning again and again to Eli, despite how she tried to meditate them into silence.

On The Planet, there were plenty of cute guys who arrived at the dining table with enthusiasm, sweetness or charm. They were from many corners of the globe. But not one turned her head or made her think twice about romance.

Alone now in the truck Drift switched on the sewing machine. She set it to work, jabbing thick stitches through even thicker leather with a large silver needle. Immersed in her work so she wouldn't think of him, she settled in. A good hour later she was jolted back to the here and now when Dunno let out an uncustomary bark. Drift sat up and listened. She couldn't hear anything.

'What is it?' Dunno was spinning in circles, whining. Gearbox had picked up on his excitement and was now barking. He too could clearly hear something as he paused between his barks, straining to listen. Drift got up, stretched, looking out the door of the truck. Then she heard an unmistakeable sound. A smile lit her face. She felt like spinning in circles like Dunno when she realised who was coming. The sound got louder and louder and soon Wilma's big silver bullet bus came rolling between the arched branches of The Planet's drive.

Drift leaped from the truck and stood in the yard, and a few of The Planet people stopped their work to watch, smiling too to see the bookmobile arrive.

'Arrrrhggghhh!' Drift said, reefing open the door before Wilma even had a chance to put the park brake on. 'I'm so, so glad to see you!'

Wilma, vibrant in an orange geranium-print dress, uncrumpled herself from the driver's seat and got out. Sitting in the passenger seat was another surprise.

'Double arrrrhgggghh!' Drift said again when she saw Shaynene, with little Zakk strapped in beside her in a car seat. Head Bob was there too, in a little travel cage, quizzically taking everything in.

'Meet my new apprentices,' Wilma said, her cheeks rosy red and cheerful as she hugged Drift.

Shaynene got out and came to Drift. Her hair had been re-coloured a gentle blonde with vibrant green streaks and she wore a black denim ragged-hem mini and a cool Wonder Woman T-shirt that curved magnificently around her bosom.

Shaynene and Drift hugged.

'Thank you,' Shaynene whispered in her ear before letting her go.

'What for?' Drift asked, puzzled.

'If you hadn't called in a few weeks back, I'd still be creating my own kinda Hell.'

'What do you mean?'

'You forgave me. You showed me you cared. I realised it was up to me to become a better person, for myself and now for Zakky. And I rang that Kerri cop woman. What an awesome chick. She's dealt with those scumbags Kelvin and Jack for you, good and proper. She also made it clear it wasn't my fault. She said Gup sounded like a classic sociopath. She put me on to the child support peeps, who tracked him down. He's now supporting us with some money. It's taken a ton of pressure off. And things are better because of that. That, and giving up sugar ... for the most part. Both me and Zakk. And I've booked you and me into her course next month ... if you're up for it.'

Drift had never heard Shaynene talk so honestly before. She'd always masked herself with bluster and bulldust, a classic defence mechanism, Drift realised now as she took in the changed girl before her.

'Sure, I am,' Drift said.

'You're both doing good,' Wilma said proudly, pulling them both into a hug.

'Wilma offered ages ago to help me,' Shaynene said, 'but I never let her. I didn't know it was up to me to *allow* help. That it was *me* blocking it all along.'

'Shay's been a godsend for me too,' Wilma said. 'I've been so lonely since you and Dunno and Gearbox left. Now I've got another empowered goddess in training and a colourful bird with colourful language.'

'She's not wrong. At first I had the shits with all them books,' the old Shaynene returned for a moment. '*Those* books,' she corrected herself.

She giggled. 'Head Bob did too. He shat all over them at first. But now he goes in his library cage. He's been a real hit at the first schools we've been at and the other kids have been so good with Zakk. I started reading to the kids, and to him. He loves it. And now I'm reading books too. For myself. I never thought I would. Or even *could*.'

Drift smiled at the vision of it. Wilma on the road with Shaynene and her bird and her baby, gently giving the younger woman time and space to wake up herself, slowly, but correcting her with love when she slipped into self-hating thought patterns or bad choices. Teaching and guiding as she had with Drift.

'Shay, darling,' Wilma said, clearing her throat, 'would you give Drift and me some time? I've got a few things to tell her.'

The Shaynene of old would've protested, or hovered, or flat-out refused and stayed and bullied in, but instead she smiled.

'Of course. Zakky and I want to check this place out properly. This time without a mob of journalist dickheads.'

'Go see Dad,' suggested Drift. 'He's over there in that cottage.' She nodded to the twin-windowed dwelling shaded by a verandah draped with grapevine. 'And help yourself to the snow peas, the fruit, whatever. It's there to be shared.'

Wilma and Drift watched her go.

'She's coming along,' Wilma said, watching her picking peas for her boy. 'It's early days. She had the roughest of childhoods, but she's not using that as an excuse any more. She's learning that the past can't touch her future. That she is enough — more than enough.'

'I'm so glad. It's what you've tried to teach me. I think I'm getting it now.'

'I can tell.' Wilma reached for Drift's hand. 'Come,' she said, leading her to the bus door.

When Drift stepped inside, the colour and books wrapped her up in familiarity and love. She gladly flopped down in a beanbag, her dogs coming to lie beside her. Wilma went to her desk and opened a drawer.

'A couple of things,' she said. 'Sort of good news. Sort of bad. Sort of exciting. Sort of upsetting. But it's all how you choose to perceive it.'

She passed a newspaper to Drift. Headlines shouted at her: *MISSING SURFER SCUM!* There was a large photo of Kai, a savage flash capturing him shading his face with his jacket. Drift recognised his familiar beautiful hands. His beard was longer. His hair shaggier. He looked rough. Like a homeless man. Nothing like the Eli she'd seen astride a horse here on Pinrush Point.

The article described a shamed Kai Kaahea, who it was revealed had staged his own disappearance, tearing apart his family's lives and his surf team's prospects.

'When was this?' Drift asked, searching for a date on the page.

'It was a couple of days ago. He'll be going through the eye of the storm,' Wilma said. 'I'd like to say poor boy, but there's nothing poor about him. He just has to learn the lessons he needs to learn. Same as you and me. Same as Shaynene. Same as anyone. The only problem is his is a *very* public lesson.'

Drift searched her own self for how she felt about seeing him exposed and hounded like that. She knew he'd brought it on himself in some way, but she also knew he was so much like her. Like Kai, she too found the modern world too confronting, too confusing, too jagged and harsh. Where Kai had used drugs, drinking and sex to mask it, Drift had isolated herself and hidden in her own dream space, not fully participating in life, judging others, doubting her own self-worth.

'He's in a world of trouble from a legal perspective,' Wilma said. 'His manager is suing him. His teammates too. The sponsors are at him along with the tournament organisers he let down. He'll probably lose all his money. His reputation is definitely gone. The media frenzy and the public outcry is fierce. But I suspect it will die down eventually. Folks will find some other poor public soul to target. I just hope Kai sees we don't have to carry our guilt for things in the past. We can forgive ourselves.'

Drift looked again at the paper, a swirl of mixed emotions in her. Seeing his image again, she felt the familiar tug of something deeper than attraction. She felt sorry for him, but knew his life and hers were so far apart now in every way that she could close the chapter on him. 'Where is he now?'

Wilma shrugged. 'If you can believe the papers, he'll be on his way back home to his family in Hawaii. He'll have to hide out there and lick his wounds and hope they forgive him too. There are more articles. Would you like to see them?'

Drift shook her head. 'I've seen enough. Thank you.'

'There's one last thing,' Wilma said. She picked up another newspaper. Drift recognised it as the local Cooperville paper. Wilma began tapping her index finger on a small advertisement in the classifieds. 'Look!'

'What? Asian hottie massage?'

'No! Not that one! This one!'

Drift read the brief ad Wilma was pointing at out loud, '*FORCED SALE DUE TO FORECLOSURE. Lightway Station. Approx 5,000 hectares.*' She looked up at Wilma, wondering what she was angling at. 'That's the property next door to here? Right?' Her mind flashed to barren sand hills and slumping fences and a front gate leaning off its bottom hinge.

'Yes. It's been on the market for over a year. Not one taker. I rang and asked. They've dropped their price to a third of what it's worth. The banks don't care. They just want it off their hands. It's so degraded and salt affected that no one knows how to restore it.' Wilma paused and inclined her head. 'Except perhaps someone like you? Along with a little help from your neighbours? Imagine you and Sophia owning almost this entire point! Think of the showcase you could develop for large-scale land and water catchment management? So why not start with the idea of Lightway Station?'

Drift recalled the seeds of her dreams Wilma and she had planted so long ago, and realised they were starting to sprout. 'Me? Own Lightway Station?' She turned the idea around in her head, examining it. The concept ran over her skin in goosebumps.

'The banker told me the homestead has no roof in places and is partly ruins. The sheds are practically sideways. He said it's a real fixer-upper, and I think that's an understatement. But if there's anyone who can handle it, it's you.'

As Wilma talked, Drift felt her thoughts falling like rain on the germinating ideas in her mind. She pictured herself on a horse. Grasses wavering.

'The property has ten kilometres of beachfront, but there's a covenant on it so it can't ever be subdivided. That means there's no takers. The developers won't touch it, thank God. But if it's locked up, it will be overrun by woody-stemmed weeds and feral animals, as you know. If it isn't loved to life soon, it will cost more to restore later on, so ...' Wilma left the end of her sentence dangling like a fishing hook, her eyes twinkling.

'Loved to life, eh?' Drift said, the faint green shoots from the seeds of the idea emerging clearly now. 'Are you really suggesting I buy it? But I couldn't afford it, could I?'

Wilma took her by both hands. 'Drifty. Have you checked your finances lately? Do you realise just how much Charlie left you? The solicitor called me, looking for you. They've found more deeds. Charlie had property in Perth. In the swanky parts of town. Now you're headed towards twenty-four, and you have the support of Sophia next door, of course you could afford it.'

Drift felt a tingle run through her. Five thousand hectares of devastated land, just waiting to be restored. Her own place. A place to love back to life.

Chapter 51

The abandoned homestead on Lightway Station was built from the deep red stone of the low hills that surrounded it. Despite its dilapidated state it still held beauty that could only be gained by age. The house sat square and honest at the heart of the slumping out buildings of the farm. What was left of its red rust-stained corrugated-iron roof sloped over a deep, shady verandah. A few loose sheets of tin ticking in the breeze greeted Drift, Split, Serge and Sophia when they first arrived, but after figuring out what hardware and tools they needed, a team from The Planet returned and tacked them back on, stopping the rain entering the breezy cool stone-walled rooms within. New flyscreen gauze, re-plastered walls and a thick layer of paint soon had the place looking livable. Beside the homestead, a once-still windmill turned above the round stone base of a well, clunking the pump rod as it moved. Large corrugated tanks were now back to watertight. An hour after they'd finished re-guttering the place, a shower of rain arrived like a good omen. They had stood out in it cheering, listening to rain gushing through the downpipes into the tanks.

The garden fence was all but gone, but since a new one had been built a lawn had begun to emerge. The garden space itself had lovely 'bones' of big established gum and deciduous trees, beneath which blended vegetable and flower garden beds soon flourishing, thanks to soils and seedlings imported from The Planet.

At night, large gums with glowing white trunks twisted upwards to an expansive sky in the moonlight, giving the place a magical feel. Drift had chosen the largest, most majestic tree to park Charlie's truck under.

She slowly worked both inside and out on the Lightway homestead, and night and day, wanting to finish it in time for Christmas.

With new electric fencing and a poly pipe watering system, Drift was using her road cattle, gifted to her by Sophia, to start to return soil function using grazing. It would take time, but already, where the cattle had been, the ground was starting to respond. Some patches of pasture were even gaining growth from gentle dewy mornings during stretches of time when no rain fell. Drift knew it wouldn't be long before diverse plants covered all the soil. In her mind, with a direct seeder ordered from a specialist machinery dealer in Perth, she could now picture a functioning landscape of poa, spear and kangaroo grasses even in the dry times, along with meadows of plant diversity just like The Planet. Old Dunno and Gearbox trailed her throughout the months like faithful apprentices and loyal companions, and she felt utterly fulfilled. For Christmas, she knew a kelpie pup was on its way from her father and he'd booked them both into a Natural Sequence Farming course.

Life had settled and was growing for Drift in new ways. Each afternoon the gift of a sea breeze and the sound of waves carried across the front paddock from the beach. Drift drew in deep salty breaths from her verandah. She was no longer searching the whitecaps for her mother or Eli, but instead feeling a bigger love within. The connectedness she now felt meant she never felt lonely. She could have as vibrant a social life as she wanted next door in the hub of The Planet, just a forty-minute drive from her gateway.

Tonight though, she was facing her last night in the saddlery truck. The serene bedroom inside the homestead was now complete; the kitchen too was finished, and there was even an art space that was already creatively cluttered with her paints and pencils and her watercolours and sketches. The bathroom had been done for a while — all thanks to the help of The Planet crew. Drift knew she'd been dawdling on making the move from her truck to the house. Living in a house seemed so foreign to her, even though she knew this homestead would now suit her. The stars, moonlight and night-time breezes had been invited in with the renovations she'd added. Newly built wide wooden concertina doors and large sliding insect-proof gauze opened the house up to the landscape beyond the bedroom and the living areas to the sound of the sea.

But, even though the house was beautiful in its simple rustic way, the truck held the people she loved close to her. She would miss it.

In the truck now, as she sat up in her bed, Drift's fingers found the familiar groove behind the Namatjira print. She pulled the panel from the wall. Inside lay the items belonging to Eli. Drift contemplated yet again going to Hawaii to find him. Then, just as she had many times before, she filed the idea in the too-hard basket and settled herself down. It was all long ago. It was meant to be, then meant not to be. It was just one blip on her long journey. She resolved this would be the last time she would hold his clothing to her. His scent had long ago faded from the fabric, but still she pressed his shirts to her cheek and inhaled.

As the moonlight spilled through the truck's high windows, Drift looked to the ceiling, imagining the scenes that would have unfolded for Kai arriving home to his family, shame filled and penniless. A sudden idea caused her to sit up and switch on the light. She got up, picking up one of the boxes she used to post saddlery gear, and carefully folded Kai's clothes, placing them in the box. Taking up the heart stone that lay under her pillow, she pressed it to her own heart, then kissed it, tucking it into one of the little leather drawstring bags she'd made to sell her jewellery in. Then, rummaging in the space in the wall, she pulled out the cigar box of money, putting that in the box too. She hovered for a moment, wondering if she ought to send a note. Something light-hearted, like, *In case the lawyers have taken the shirt from your back*. Or *Thought you could use a little help and have a little heart*. She grimaced. She just couldn't find the words. Foregoing the note, she sealed the box with tape, writing on it in Texta, *Kai Kaahea* and in brackets, *(Eli) c/o Horseheart Ranch, Moloka'i, Hawaii*. Drift set the box at the doorway of the truck, ready to send the next time she was in Widgenup. She then closed up the wall for the very last time.

Chapter 52

Eight months on, Drift woke just as the sun kissed the horizon of Lightway Station's treeline. A gentle breeze lifted the curtains of her bedroom window and as her mind cleared to waking Drift remembered that a busload of farmers was due to arrive mid-morning. She and The Planet were now running tours every month with visitors staying the night at Shaynene's new motel in Widgenup.

Named 'The Regeneration Retreat', the new facility, funded by Sophia, had the best fresh food on offer provided by The Planet, plus the funniest receptionist in the form of Head Bob, who sat on the brochure stand screeching 'Faaaark orf! Faaaark orf!' each time a guest came through the doors. The obnoxious bird never failed to stir a smile or raise an eyebrow.

The bookings for regenerative farm tours were rapidly growing and Shaynene, with Wilma's guidance, was proving to be a perfect manager and host as little Zakk trailed around with her. In the afternoons, he enjoyed paddling with his mother in the new swimming pool, gardening with her or entertaining the guests and doing his best Head Bob dance with the bird. Occasionally Shaynene played the role of 'almost hairdresser', offering guests a trim if they wanted one. Ragged farmers often left the establishment feeling like Elvises born again, thanks to Shaynene's flattery, flirtatiousness and scissor snips.

Today, at Lightway, Drift was to give the visiting farmers and agriculturalists a tour of how she was correcting the areas of salinity and soil compaction. She would also show them her slides of the land's progress and the data Sophia's soil scientists and botanists were compiling about the property. She hoped the farmers could see that by using managed grazing, in a very short time she had returned life to the soil and captured and stabilised carbon there too. Following Drift's talk, the next half of the tour at The Planet would show the visitors all the goings-on there, from tree regeneration, to steam-weeding technology, to Dr Landy's stunning results on nutrient-dense food when compared to industrially grown fruit and vegetables. And then from Dr Daisy, they'd be shown the vet's stunning data on weight gain and animal health, along with the team's renewable energy systems.

Lightway Station was a perfect start, because it showed the visitors just how degraded land could be and how it could be fixed on a tight budget. Then, after being at The Planet, the visitors could see what such land could become over time. Those who were more resistant were often coaxed around when Sophia showed them just how low the farm input costs were. Sophia then gave them contacts in banks and corporations of forward-thinking people who were looking to lend to farmers who were building ecological capital on their properties. She told them soil health and pure food sources was 'the next big thing' in business. Drift smiled at the thought of all those mindsets potentially changed. More and more, people were coming to see regenerative agriculture for themselves. Whether it was debt, sickness or divorce, or a quiet niggling inside for change, people were drawn to The Planet, and month after month they just kept coming.

After a shower in the newly created bathroom she still pinched herself over how her life now looked. Drift glanced at her watch as she put it on. There was enough time to electric-fence the next grazing section of the paddock. She wanted to show the farmers at what point she took her cattle off the grass and moved them onto fresh pasture to graze. Crunching on an apple, she bounded down the steps with Gearbox and Dunno, then loaded up the fencing gear into the old ute she'd bought from Serge and set off with her dogs.

In the home paddock, Lolly, the long-socked bay with the broad blaze on loan from The Planet, whickered. She looked at the pretty mare, thinking she'd have to find another horse, not just as company for Lolly but also because she missed having her own. She'd hoped too, once the infrastructure was in place on the property, she'd have time to seek out a troubled or unwanted horse to re-educate and give a new, happy home to. But for now, she just hadn't had the time a horse like that required.

Out in the paddock on the rise above the homestead, with the sweep of the sea sparkling in the distance, she hooked the temporary electric fence onto the permanent one. The sun was pushing up higher in the sky. She looked over landscape that had been a wasteland of bare dirt, weeds and tufted woody-stemmed plants. Now there was a gentle tinge of green to it all. There was a long way to go, but by having the image in her head of what the view from the hill would look like, Drift took comfort in knowing she was on the right path. Gearbox let out a bark and Dunno joined in, despite the cloudy-eyed dog not having much vision these days. Their ears pointed to the red-dust ribbon drive that wove for a good five kilometres to the Pinrush Point road.

Drift could see a plume of dust. Surely the bus couldn't be that early? Though it might well be someone from The Planet dropping in some fresh produce, or offering her help with the visitors. She called her dogs onboard then frowned when she saw an unfamiliar white ute towing a large horse float. From the top of the hill, she waved, but the driver didn't see her. She was too far away. As she got into her vehicle, the cattle lowed at her and walked the fence, disappointed they weren't moving to fresh ground.

'Sorry, guys,' she called to them from the window, 'I need you as my demonstration models for the morning. I'll be back soon.'

She blew them a kiss before winding her way over the stony track down and around towards the homestead. As she arrived in the work yard, she saw Sophia leaning against a brand-new vehicle covered in a light film of road dust. Drift got out of the ute and beamed at her friend.

'Is this what I think it is?' Drift said, pointing to the four-wheel-drive ute with gleaming silver trim.

Sophia kinked out her hip proudly. 'It sure is! Meet our new Regen Workhorse ute ... a prototype, all set for release into the market in the next three years.'

'No way!' said Drift excitedly. 'It's here!'

'I know, right? It's a dream come alive. They've agreed to use *our* science, The Planet's work. You're looking at the first of the world's farm vehicles powered by human methane and farm organic waste. Forget the ute! Drive a Poot!'

Drift jumped up and down with excitement then hugged Sophia. 'That is beyond awesome and good timing. We can show our busload!' They stood surveying what had taken years of work, particularly for Gizmo, and hundreds of thousands of dollars to achieve.

'My daddy and my pappy would be rolling in their graves. To think we've potentially undone the oil industry's monopoly on transport ... finally!'

Drift shook her head. 'I reckon your granddad and father would be proud. You did it!'

She hugged Sophia again, knowing how hard she and The Planet people had worked to sell their concept of methane-powered vehicles to global corporates and governments. As Sophia had said, the marketing companies would find fart cars hard to sell.

'Now we've convinced one company, it's just a matter of time and the other companies will follow suit, so the infrastructure will be forced to change.'

'Welcome to the world, the Poot! Congratulations!'

'The baby steps are starting to turn into giant leaps for humankind and now we're doing the farmer tours, I feel like we're flying!' Sophia said, looking skywards as if she were up there in the blue too. Drift saw the vibrancy in Sophia's eyes. Today her hair was tamed back and she was in her most conservative clothing, in readiness for the visiting busload of conventional farmers, but there was no dimming her shine of beauty, both inner and outer.

'Where's Dad?' Drift asked.

'Setting up back at The Planet. It's pretty busy there, but I couldn't wait to show you and the visitors this, so here I am.'

From deep within the float a deep shuddering whinny sounded. Lolly called from over the fenceline in answer. Sophia grinned at Drift.

'And who's in there?' Drift asked.

'Wait right here,' Sophia said excitedly, disappearing to the back of the float to lower the ramp.

Drift cocked her head. 'What are you up to?'

She heard the angle load gate swing open, the sound of clumping hooves. Next Sophia was leading a handsome grey gelding from the float.

'Ta da! Meet Oddfellow.'

'Funny name,' Drift said, frowning, not sure what Sophia was up to.

'Funny horse,' Sophia said, stroking his neck. 'He's got a real sense of humour, haven't you, boy?'

The horse nodded as if in agreement. Drift laughed.

'What's he doing here?'

'Late house-warming and early Christmas present combined. And the float's for you too.'

'A horse! *And* a float! For me? I thought a kelpie pup from Dad was enough!' Drift looked from Sophia to the white-haired horse in disbelief, taking in his brush-stroked dark legs and mane and tail. He was so much like Minty she felt emotion swell.

Sophia waved Drift's comment away. 'Can't have a horse without transport. Oddfellow is all yours.'

'Is it Oddfellow, as in the mints?'

'As in the mints,' Sophia confirmed. She held the lead rope out towards her.

As Drift took it, tears moistened her eyes. Even the horse's energy reminded her so much of her Minty. She stroked the smoky nose of the handsome curve-necked gelding. He had a light dappling on his rump like rain clouds, and dark knees that looked as if he'd kneeled in wet black soil. Above all he had a kind calm eye. Just like her Minty.

'Why?'

'Because,' Sophia said, 'since you came into my life, I've truly known there's a bright future to be had. You, with all your curiosity about the world, like I'd hope my own daughter would've had. And of course, with you, came your dad.' Sophia blushed a little. The romance now had morphed into a firm partnership between two people who were utterly *right* for each other.

'As a woman, I felt whole before I met your dad but that wholeness came from practice and determination. But now, with Dennis by my side, I feel … like my journey is *shared*. Witnessed. That it's all worth it and it flows … rather than being forced.'

Drift smiled — Sophia was the only person in the world who called Split Dennis. At first it had sounded funny to her, but now it just sounded like love between a couple who had found each other after doing the hard work on themselves.

'Once I found Dennis, I realised I had to stop pushing with my willpower and surrender to life. I could start believing that the right thing was going to happen, no matter what it was. He helped me let go, open up, not let my fears and guilt take over, and once I did,' she swung to look at the ute, 'things started to really fly!'

Drift slid her palms over the horse's sides, feeling his warmth and steadiness as she listened.

'Den and I have been looking for ages for a horse for you. We didn't want to rush. Oddfellow is station bred, and has eight years' stock work under his girth, and when he came with that name and was a grey ... well ... we *knew.*'

Drift ran her hand under his forelock, the horse dropping his head into the pressure of her palm.

'He's gorgeous. Thank you.'

Sophia stilled herself watching them together, knowing the moment was to be savoured. Eventually she said, 'Come on, let's get him in the paddock. The bus will be here soon. I came to give you a hand with the scones.'

Together, they led Oddfellow towards Lolly's paddock, gratitude surging in Drift again.

'You know the feeling's mutual,' she said quietly. 'My whole life opened up the day I met you too. All the solutions to the farming and environmental problems Dad had been ranting about came to me the day I wandered in to The Planet. And I found out who I wanted to be like as a grown woman. What my purpose was. I even have a garden now ... something I've dreamed of since I was little.'

She scratched behind Oddfellow's ears. 'Now with this new fella, I feel like you do. My journey will be shared.'

Sophia swung about, her expression suddenly serious. 'No, my dear. You may feel *whole* in your life now. I mean, look what you're creating,' she waved her hand to encompass the blooming garden of the homestead and greening paddocks of the station, 'but it's our relationship with other humans that gives us our deepest lessons. Especially the special relationship we have with a lover. You can't hide with your animals forever. Don't make the mistake I did. I guarded my heart for years and flew solo. I shut myself down as a woman.'

Sophia opened the gate for Drift to lead Oddfellow through. As Drift pulled the rope halter from him, she listened intently to Sophia.

'I was in touch with my inner Athena ...' Sophia explained, 'the *doing, warrior* side of me ... but I was not in touch with my inner Aphrodite ... the *being*, the *loving*, *still* side of myself. Thanks now to Den in my life, I have balance.'

Silver and turquoise glistened on her fingers and wrists as she lay her hand on Drift's arm.

'Open your heart again, Drift, to love. Trust.'

Drift looked at Sophia's earnest face, unsettled by her sudden deep conversation, but knowing that there was a wisdom and a truth to what she said. Still the resistance flared. She'd be happy with a horse and a dog. What did she want in a man? A partner?

'Drift? Are you getting me?' Sophia urged.

'Yes, Sophia. Trust. I get it,' she said, not really getting it at all. Then an image of a dark-skinned, dark-haired young man rushed to her mind. A beautiful man lying under sarongs, on sea grass matts and white sand, with her next to him, her palm pressing lightly on the smooth contours of his chest at the place where his heart knocked gently. She felt annoyance rumble inside. She thought she'd exorcised *him* from her mind in that way. Apparently not.

Drift breathed in frustration as she leaned on the top rail of the fence beside Sophia, watching Oddfellow, neck outstretched, touching noses with the docile Lolly. The moment reminded Drift of the first time she'd leaned on a rail with Sophia at The Planet. It felt she had come full circle and arrived back at a different place, better than the one where she'd started. She felt Sophia elbow her.

'Come on. We've got scones to make and a busload of visiting farmers to inspire. Let's go get ready to light them up!'

Chapter 53

Gearbox barked loudly from the verandah, signalling the bus was rolling into the homestead yard. Drift glanced through the windows of the light-filled kitchen, the smell of fresh-baked scones wrapped in a tea towel wafting from the long timber table.

'It's showtime!' said Sophia, wiping her hands on a blue-checked tea towel and coming to stand beside her. She turned to Drift, saying, 'Here, let me fix you up a bit,' and dabbed the corner of the towel on Drift's nose, swiping away a smudge of flour. 'We have to have you looking your best. You're about to win some hearts.'

Drift smiled and looked down at herself. 'Ya think?' She had put on her best sky-blue workshirt and her 'good' jeans especially for the farmers' visit.

'You look beautiful,' Sophia said, eyes moist with emotion. 'I really hope this goes well.'

'Why wouldn't it?' Drift asked, wondering again why Sophia was being so emotional today. She looked at her and realised she had found what she'd been longing for all these years. A mother. *Her mother*. It wasn't *the* mother, the one who left so long ago, but she knew she had Sophia's heart and Sophia had hers. She thought of the other mothers she'd had in her life. Wilma the Wondrous and the legendary Charlie Weatherbourne, who she could still feel mothering her from another realm. Gratitude swamped her again.

'Thank you,' Drift said.

Sophia stood square on to her and held her hands. 'Always remember, my darling girl, you are always exactly in the right place at exactly the right time. That's what it is to surrender to life's journey.' She punctuated the sentence with a kiss to Drift's forehead.

'OK?' Drift said. What was up with Sophia today?

'You'd better go tie Gearbox up. He's likely to take a chunk out of someone's leg,' Sophia advised.

'Sure.'

Drift whistled the dogs, who were both sniffing about under the kitchen table on the hunt for crumbs. 'C'mon, you two,' she said, making her way to the verandah and the dogs' baskets. 'Dunno, you gotta keep your cranky friend company.' She stooped to rub behind the old dog's ears and clipped him on to his lead near Gearbox, who was prone to bark when he was tied up alone. Dogs settled, Sophia and Drift put on their stockman hats, stepped across the wide old wonky boards and out into the sun.

In the work yard, the bus lowered itself on its fancy hydraulics and the doors shushed open. Out stepped the visitors. Most were men but a scattering of women stood with them, looking about, tugging on caps and broad-brimmed hats, talking quietly among themselves.

At her shoulder, Sophia gave her a nudge and whispered, 'Go on.'

Drift stepped forwards and beamed a smile at the assembling group, knowing her energy, not her words was the most important thing to be aware of when talking to them.

'Welcome, everyone,' she said, feeling love swell her heart. 'I'm Melody Wood. Thanks so much for coming to Lightway Station. I hope you had a good trip. No doubt Shaynene and Zakk filled you up with a big breakfast with our farm-fresh produce.'

All of them smiled and a few of the farmers patted their bellies, everyone murmuring agreement.

'Good. This morning I'm going to show you what I've done to this place in the short time I've had it. It was a lock-up and walk-off property claimed by the bank. No one wanted to touch it. We're hoping it will give you an idea of how quickly degraded land can heal using regenerative ag methods. And, in my case, on limited funds.'

Her eyes scanned the typical farmer mob, until her gaze landed on the face of one man. A face she knew so well. A face from so long ago. Breath was stolen from her. Her cheeks began to burn. She looked across incredulously to Sophia, who winked at her and smiled reassuringly.

It was *him*. Eli. Kai. His eyebrows were the same perfect dark arches. His skin, smooth and tanned. His cleanshaven square jaw revealed a slightly dimpled chin, making him look younger and even more gorgeous than she remembered him. His hair was now cut shorter, but had its classic shagginess of a free spirit. She flushed with sudden shyness at having him standing there at the back of the group, his eyes roaming to her then looking away again. Drift cleared her throat and tried to remember the thread of what she'd been saying, her body buzzing at having Eli here.

Drift saw the way Sophia's eyes gleamed — Oh! Sophia *knew* ... She had known Eli would be on that bus! Drift faltered in what she was saying. She felt a prick of resentment over their plotting. But then it dawned on her ... Sophia and her dad wouldn't be part of this if they didn't know it was meant to happen. That Eli was ready. That she was ready. This time, as she caught Eli's eye, a gentle, shy smile and unmistakeable glimmer arrived on his face as his gaze locked with hers. Her words evaporated. Sophia stepped in to cover for her, introducing herself and finishing the welcome.

'We'll head to the shed for a ten-minute stretch and a lavatory stop, then we're going to get y'all back on the bus to move some cattle on Lightway. Melody's going to show you how she is bringing the land back to health using time-controlled mob grazing and the help of clever Mother Nature and her abundance of plants. After that we'll have some slides and scientific information about the process of building soil, then the promised scones, before we whisk you off to The Planet for a tour then lunch.'

As the group of about forty farmers made their way to the shed, Sophia fell in beside Eli, bringing Drift with her.

'Hello,' he said simply.

'Hello, Kai,' Drift replied, willing herself to leave it at that and not fill the space with nervous words and a string of questions.

'It's Eli these days,' he said, leaning forwards to give her a soft friendly kiss on the cheek, squeezing her shoulder lightly in greeting. 'Kai is long gone,' he added.

'Eli,' Drift corrected herself, feeling her body buzz.

Sophia filled the gap in the conversation. 'It's been too long since he's been home, hasn't it?'

Drift glanced at her. Sophia had clearly caught up with Eli before the bus trip. Drift wanted to hear Eli's story properly, and be fully present as to how it was that he was here beside her, but now was not the time. A farmer was already on his way over to ask them some questions.

Eli read the situation. 'It's lovely to be back,' he said, nodding at her. 'All of this is so exciting. I'll leave you two to focus.' He gave Sophia a squeeze across her shoulders, gave them both a grin and made his way back to the heart of the group.

Drift felt frustration rise in her. So many unanswered questions, years of not knowing what had happened to him, and here was Sophia and possibly her father knowing something she didn't. She sucked in a determined breath.

'Sophia? What's going on?' she asked quickly before the farmer arrived.

Sophia shrugged innocently. 'Wilma showed me the news reports that he'd been found and he was headed home, so I sent him a flyer a little while ago. We didn't know if he'd come or not.'

Drift remembered the way she'd packaged up the heart stone with his clothes and the money, sending it on impulse. She too had been part of this. Maybe it had been her parcel and the flyer combined that had brought him. Sophia wasn't entirely to blame.

'He's through the storm and out the other side, well and truly. Last night at dinner Eli —'

'Last night at dinner!' Drift cut across her words. 'So Dad knew too?'

Sophia nodded and bit her lip. 'Yup.'

'You two,' Drift said, exasperated. Then she saw Sophia's kind expression, one dark curved eyebrow cocked cheekily, and felt a smile bloom on her face.

'It's all good,' Sophia reassured. 'Remember. Exactly the right place at exactly the right time. You are responsible for what you see in life. Choose to see the good things. He's a good man.' She winked at her, then moved off to talk to the waiting farmer.

Drift didn't know how she managed the next hour and a half, as she gave her talk about management to the farmers on the bus and opened the electric tape gate to call up the eager full-bloom cattle. She tried to block out the fact Eli was here, looking so delicious, but questions crowded her mind. Surely a man as good looking and worldly as him wouldn't still be single? Would he?

When it was time to usher everyone back on the bus, the crowd was buzzing from what they'd seen, heard and learned.

Conversation was at fever pitch. Sophia seemed very happy with it all too and was shining even more. Drift stood waiting for the last man to get on the bus. It was Eli.

'That was fantastic, thank you,' he said. 'You were — you are — incredible! I think you've reached a good few.'

Drift felt herself melting standing near him, looking so tall and lean in his jeans and plain black T-shirt with his sexy leather wristband. He was looking at her with admiration on his face, taking in her changes too. She was fuller in the body now, and her hair, grown out, rested on her strong shoulders.

'Thanks,' she said, wanting to explode with a thousand questions. 'Well, I'll see you. Catch up some time.'

'That some time is now,' Sophia said, walking over. 'I'll hitch back with you to The Planet, Bill,' she called to the bus driver, steering Eli away from the step.

She delivered that wink again, then stepped up into the bus. 'Take it away, Bill,' she said to the driver.

'But —' Drift and Eli said in unison, but she was already moving to take her seat behind Bill.

'I'll be right as rain at home with this mob,' she called over the purr of the electric-engine bus. 'Den has got it all covered, so I don't need you, Drift. Eli, you've seen The Planet plenty. You can bring the prototype Poot back later.'

Drift looked to Eli, who was looking at Sophia, his mouth open.

'Drift, you've got a new horse to ride,' Sophia said, nodding over at Oddfellow, 'and you don't want to ride a strange horse on your own. With a name like Oddfellow he could have some habits we haven't seen in him yet. I'd like Eli to stay. Check the horse over for me.'

There was no question in her voice. In Sophia fashion it was an order, dished up with directness and good intentions.

She glanced at her watch. 'Better stick to the schedule,' and with that, the bus doors folded shut and off Sophia drove with her load of farmers who were now lively with new ideas and good cheer.

Eli and Drift stood looking at each other and laughed nervously.

'I think we've just been set up,' Eli said.

'Do you think?' Drift said with a grin.

Chapter 54

The odd thing about Oddfellow was there was only one thing odd about him — his name. In the round yard as they worked him, Drift and Eli discovered he had nice manners on the ground and under saddle he responded immediately to the gentlest of cues. He was athletic in his turns and stops, yet he was steady in his mind.

Drift was grateful for the easy way Eli and she fell in step with each other. It was just like the droving days of old. Yes, the questions burned, but his calm, gentle energy and their old friendship were back. Like they had never gone away.

'He's a champion,' Eli said as he watched Drift wind the horse up into a canter then slide him to a faultless stop.

'Shall we try him bareback?'

He looked at her, eyes bright. Drift swung off the horse and felt the buzz when Eli's shoulder touched hers as he began to unsaddle Oddfellow. They caught each other's eye. In an instant Drift felt the wave of love crash within her very being. It was still there.

'What are you doing here?' she asked, her eyes filling with unexpected tears.

Eli looked at her helplessly. 'Where do I start?' He sighed.

'It's clearly a big story to tell, but I have to know. What happened?'

Eli shrugged. 'Nothing more really, just a story from the past that's over now. Over for good.'

'What do you mean, over?'

'I mean I've changed. Grown. The story I lived isn't going to get re-run in the future. Ever.'

Drift thought of all the advice she'd had from her mothers, her wise women, about living in the moment and the power of forgiveness and having compassion. She made a decision to have compassion for Eli. She had seen in her own life's journey that compassionate love for herself and for others was the only choice that allowed life to get really good for her.

'Bunk me up,' she said suddenly to him, bending her leg. She felt his warm palm on her shin as she lobbed onto Oddfellow's broad back. Up on the horse Drift felt as if she had arrived home to her power. She smiled down at Eli. 'Like old times, eh?'

A gentle cloud of remembering crossed Eli's face, his time on the road with her softening his expression. The flutter of sarongs came to them both in memory. 'Except better,' he said.

'You getting on too? See if he'll dink? See if he's got any buck in him?' Drift had confidence in her voice. Challenge, even.

He cleared his throat. 'Sure.'

She legged the horse to the rail. As he settled behind her, Drift felt Eli's chest pressed at her back, his breath on her neck. She cued Oddfellow gently one way, then the next. He was rock solid. She turned him to the gate and leaned to unlatch it.

'Where are we going?' Eli asked, challenging her right back.

'To the water. I want to show him the beach.'

*

Tiny white grains scudded into the breeze as Oddfellow's big disced hooves walked them purposefully forwards. With a glassy sea on the horizon, a cooling light wind was easing the heat of the afternoon sun. The horse was lively under her, but he was keeping his head, clearly used to beaches. It's easier, Drift thought, to ask Eli the hard questions when I can't see his face.

'Why did you leave me that morning?' Drift asked, and felt his body tense.

Close to her ear the words came in his rich Hawaiian accent. 'I was too ashamed of who I was to stay. Guilty about what I'd done. I didn't want to burden you with that. And you were right … it was so, *so* wrong to burden the people I loved. So egotistical and young and stupid.'

Drift was glad he was admitting to the impact he'd had on her and others, but she also wanted to impart some of Charlie's wisdom. She wanted to counter his words, to say it was all just lessons, and he needed to forgive himself, but she let him continue.

'I did go surfing in that storm with a death-wish. I did lose control. I did almost drown. But then I realised I had every reason to live, to make up for what I'd done. That's when I met Charlie on the road. *Your Charlie.* She came just at the right time. It was a miracle. She spotted me on the beach from the rise. She seemed to know I was in trouble. In more ways than one. When I told her the story and that the media were after me, she turned the truck around and we drove away from your camp, the Point, The Planet. After that, I started travelling with her in the truck.'

Drift smiled, walking the horse along on a loose rein, remembering Charlie so clearly, picturing her. 'She would've got you straight,' she said dryly.

She felt the warm timbre of Eli's laugh against her body.

'She sure did. Thanks to her I started to find myself. I was ready to go home, but then I came close to getting sprung again. Someone recognised me and called the police. I panicked. I had to do a runner, in a hurry. I had no time to say a proper goodbye to her. Or say thank you. And she ran out of time to tell you I was still here.'

Drift reined Oddfellow to a halt and they both sat for a moment in silence, remembering the wise old woman who had saved them both.

'And then?' Drift asked.

'After I'd left Charlie, I settled on a station near Alice Springs ... A new name for myself, a new identity and a new life. They were good people on the place. They helped get me home to Hawaii — I didn't think the media would still be trailing me.'

'And your family? How were they?'

Eli splayed his beautiful hands on his thighs and Drift looked down to them, feeling his sadness from the memory, but also the relief.

'Oh they were stoked. Puna hugged me so much I thought she'd crush my ribs. Mum cried for a whole day.'

He turned his face to the sea and said sadly, 'Y'know, they never told me off. They never judged me. Not once. They just got on with it ... with the horses, the ranch. They helped me sort all the legal stuff out. I'd broken so many contracts. Blew all my money on legals.' He shrugged. 'I began helping Mum and Dad with the regen work, low key of course, but I was working again, at something with purpose. I began hanging out with Grandpa again, and the horses. And every time I rode from the homestead down to the sea and I saw the naupaka flowers, I thought of you. Since I got home, I've not stopped working on being a better man. Thanks to you. Thanks to Charlie. But I was too afraid to get in touch. And then your parcel came.'

He reached his hand up to Drift's face to turn her head to him. She swivelled around and saw the deep expression of sincerity in his eyes. He pulled something from his pocket and placed it in her hand. She didn't need to look down to know what it was. As she closed her palm around the heart stone she felt her own heart opening, like a flower. She sucked in a breath and leaned her head back on his shoulder, smiled, closing her eyes in both surrender and relief as his arms folded around her.

'I really missed you,' he said. 'I missed your dad, this life. Here.'

'I missed you, too,' Drift said. 'I thought about coming to see you in Hawaii. But same. Same as you. I was too afraid. Too ashamed.'

Eli spoke with such intensity, her heart leaped. 'Can you forgive me?'

'Yes,' Drift said easily, swivelling on the horse to look him in the eye. 'Can you?'

Eli laughed. 'Of course I do.'

Then as natural as the tide turning, Eli lifted Drift's chin with his finger and they kissed tenderly. It was as if time had not stretched and kept them apart at all. To Drift, the kiss felt like Heaven. Heaven on Earth. Again they leaned into each other's bodies and shut their eyes in gratitude, feeling each other's breath.

Suddenly Oddfellow started pawing the ground. Before Drift could snatch up the reins, his black knees were buckling in the sand. Eli and Drift spilled sideways from the horse, who was getting set for a big joyful roll on the beach. Laughing, they leaped clear, watching Oddfellow list sideways, then roll onto his back, writhing happily in the sand.

'Now we know he likes to roll,' Drift said.

'Now we know!'

Drift felt Eli's hand slide around her waist, then he pulled her close. She looked up to him and smiled. They stood and kissed as the waves broke on the shore.

'How long are you staying?' Drift murmured.

'Ah, that's a really interesting question,' he said, pulling back to look at her.

'Really? Why?'

'I'm not going far. You see, I'm your new neighbour.'

'What? You're moving to The Planet?'

'No. Your other boundary.

'Bright Star Station?'

'Yes.'

'What?'

'It's mine now.'

'You bought Bright Star Station?'

'No,' Eli said, 'In a roundabout way, Charlie did.'

'*Charlie?*'

'When she died she left me some money. It took a while for the solicitor to find me. It wasn't until he saw me on the news that he tracked me down. I've been saving up my wages from the ranch so I could make a new start, so I couldn't believe it when I found out. Then Sophia sent me a clipping from the paper advertising it for sale. "One giant hint", she wrote in her note,' Eli said, smiling at the memory. 'Then, when you sent all that money from the truck, it was enough to make my mind up. So I bought my flight out here so I could get started on my dreams.'

Drift took a moment to take in the news. 'I didn't even know it was on the market. It had been walked off years ago.'

'You do know the house was on another title that had already sold, up on the other side of Widgenup? My block doesn't have a homestead, so I need somewhere to live.'

Drift looked at him, her mind in a rush. Surely he wasn't suggesting he stay with her?

He read her expression and laughed quietly. 'Can I borrow the truck? Charlie's truck.'

Drift chuckled at herself. That fierce independence was still there in her. Her love of her own solitude still warning another type of life away. 'Of course you can borrow the truck. For the moment, I'm happy to have a house with no wheels!'

Oddfellow was standing now, shaking the sand from his beach-white back and snorting. Drift reached to catch his dangling reins.

'So my neighbour is Eli Kaahea,' Drift said, letting the news settle in her. 'Who'd have thought it?'

Eli shook his head. 'No, your neighbour is Eli Wood.'

Drift looked puzzled. 'Wood?'

'Yes, when I tried to disappear from the world, I chose that name. Even if you didn't want to ever see me again, I wanted to share it with you. With your dad. You were like family for a time there. You and Charlie.'

Drift looked out to sea at the distant blue sky and laughed, thinking of the way things had turned out, the stone warm and certain in her hand. 'Ah Charlie,' Drift sighed. 'Even from the other side she's still pulling Universal strings.'

'She sure is. Just think, all of Pinrush Point, from Widgenup south, will be managed by us. Sophia, Serge, you, me, your dad. The team. Think of the paradise we can create.'

'I can already see it,' Drift said, leaning into him, breathing in his scent, which was familiar yet freshly new and foreign. She pulled back from him and frowned. 'When you were staying with Charlie did she give you her lecture on special romantic relationships?'

Eli shut his eyes at the memory and nodded. 'Yes, over and over until I got it.'

'Good,' Drift said. 'So you're not pinning all your happiness and fulfilment on just me, like some kind of fairy tale?'

Eli threw his head back and laughed. 'Not in this lifetime! Not ever. Charlie bashed it into me … you gotta love with a capital L,' he said, drawing her near. 'You forget I have my grandparents too, teaching me Hawaiian *aloha kakou* … It's a different kind of love from Disney. It's an inseparable love. A love founded not on two separate Is — *owau* — but a united respectful We — *kakou*. I now know how to live as an honourable man. To honour you. My *tutu* taught me to *pule*, *mele*, *oli* and *hula*.'

Drift looked puzzled.

'To pray, sing, chant and dance to learn mana'o — wisdom,' he translated. 'I now know I have the *ahonui*, the patience, to live a life of *kakou*, of "we" thinking with the woman I love.'

Drift looked at his handsome face. In their time droving he'd rarely shared his native language with her, like he was still trying to be somebody different. But here he was, like her father, utterly transformed from the inside out. Drift frowned. She felt that old niggle of doubt rise in her again, despite his energy, despite his words. Could she trust him? Was this all too fast? Too sudden? Even though she realised she'd been wishing for this moment for an age. Just as the fear came surging in like a rip, Drift heard excited yelping from behind the dunes. Scuttling over the rise came Dunno, his lead chewed through, flapping on his old-man barrel body. The dog threw himself at Eli, wagging his entire frame. A giant dog grin was pinned from small ear to small ear. Eli dropped to his knees in the sand and drew him into his arms.

'Dunno!' Eli laughed, his delight in seeing the dog equalled.

Drift watched them both, laughing too. With clarity she realised, Dunno *knew*. That dog *really knew* … this fella before her was more than all right. He was a keeper.

Epilogue

Seven years later

Over a calm silver sea, the thirteenth moon was on the rise. It was a giant disc of crystal white in a rich sky of fading blue. A wave surged and Drift felt old Oddfellow's hooves lifted from the sandy bed beneath. The horse struck out in giant paddling movements. Beside her, Eli astride Arrowstone swam too, and with their fingers entwined in manes they both laughed at the thrill and power of swimming their two horses, horses who were alive with excitement at the sensation of the water. Not a breath of wind stirred the ocean.

After a time, Eli nodded to the shore. 'Shall we take them in?' Drift followed him, salty water dripping over her skin. The sky darkened until the two white horses, washed clean by the sea, almost glowed on the beach as they rode towards Lightway's homestead. At the track through the dunes, Eli shook his head and said, 'Not that way. This way.'

'This way?'

She saw him leg Arrowstone around so the gelding travelled in the direction of their favourite section of the beach beyond a tumble of stones on the sand. They were soon walking the horses into a tiny secluded fingernail curve of white, wedged between rocks. Drift gasped when she saw Eli's creation at the heart

444

centre of the beach, ringed with stones and brightened further with bunches of native flowers placed in silver buckets.

'Happy belated birthday, beautiful,' he said. 'I've been waiting for the January full blue moon to do this.'

He slid from the horse and put his palm on Drift's bare thigh as she took in the upright branches shaped into a tepee frame. Two mats were spread side by side within a secluded structure shrouded with Hawaiian print sarongs. Drift gasped and smiled at him as she slid from Oddfellow, her bare feet hitting the still-warm sand.

'It's beautiful.' Her fingertips brushed the pretty, vibrant fabric. 'These are lovely.'

'Mum sent them for you. Happy birthday from them.' He kissed her on her crown as arm in arm they watched the horses roll happily then stand to shake the sand from their wet, glistening coats. Drift and Eli anchored the horses' lead ropes to nothing but sand, such was the horses' willingness to be near them. Eli lit the torches so they burned gently in the still night air.

He came to stand beside Drift. Fingers caressed her shoulders, his lips gently brushing her skin. She spun around, running her palm over the back of his neck, fingers rummaging through his dark curling hair. Her head fell back in desire as he trailed kisses up her neck, along her jawbone.

'You taste like the sea,' she said.

'You smell like the Earth,' he said.

He led her to the mats. They lay down. His shorts and her bikini slipped from their bodies. Naked, pressed together, they looked deeply into each other's eyes; his the colour of dark soil, hers the colour of a summer ocean. Then the lovers joined. The moon rose. And everything balanced in the world for a moment of timeless, utter perfection.

Afterwards, Drift lay again beneath the shelter with her man, he trailing fingertips over her curves, she running her hands over the firmness of his muscled shoulders and smooth tanned skin of his broad back. In the light of the burning torches they were lost in each other's eyes until a small voice came to them.

'Mama? Papa?'

Drift heard the voice. 'Rose Wood!' she said, exasperated, pulling a sarong up and over her body and passing another hastily to Eli. 'What are you doing out of bed? Where are Puna Split and Tutu Sophia? Where is Auntie Wilma?'

'Puna is asleep. Tutu Sophia is too and Auntie Wilma is reading a book with her eyes closed.'

Drift looked to Eli, trying to smother her laughter and settle a stern expression on her face, but failing.

Eli looked grave, though his eyes also danced with mirth. 'What have we told you about wandering to the beach, Rose? Especially at night by yourself.'

The little girl smiled. 'The moon told me to come. And I'm not by myself. The lady with the long plait is with me.'

'Is she now, Rose?' Drift smiled. It wasn't the first time their daughter had mentioned her invisible old woman friend with long grey hair. Wrapped in their sarongs the couple sat up and looked towards the dunes to their daughter. Drift was about to call Rose over to them, but at that moment a gust of wind came surging through the beach grasses and the rolls of the dunes. The clear moon blazed extra brightly for a moment. As Eli and Drift looked at their daughter, she stood in her white dress, barefoot in the sand, long dark hair lifting in the wind. Her soulful gaze was fixed on both of them. The horses stopped dozing and pricked their ears at her, standing alert. Rose looked otherworldly. For an instant. Then a wave crashed and the moment was gone.

'Did you see that?' Drift said incredulously, grabbing Eli's hand as the little girl began making her way over to their lovers' tepee.

'I did,' Eli said. 'I saw.'

'Did you recognise her?' Drift asked, tears welling in her eyes. 'Did you see?'

'Yes,' Eli said.

'It was our little girl all along,' Drift whispered. 'The girl I told you about. From *that* night.'

The couple looked at each other, the pieces of life's strange puzzle falling into place. They rested their foreheads together and laughed quietly as Rose padded to them and fell into their open arms.

'She's come back for another Earth walk,' Eli whispered, echoing his dearly departed puna and tutu's expression.

Drift and Eli gathered their child to them and together they sat gazing at the moon. They listened to the sound of the sea. Every rolling wave was an out breath of joy. Every wave's inhale was the breath of love. There was remembering and forgetting with every shift of every grain of sand and every life that came and went from the Earth. But always, for all of eternity, there was Love, and that was *their Truth*.

Research resources

This novel was woven from threads of insight gleaned from many books and hours of study; however, the main texts underpinning this tale are:

Partners in Pleasure, by Hawaiian heart surgeon and author Paul Pearsall PhD, who introduces the concept of Aloha Kakou via Eli's character.

The 13 Original Clan Mothers, by Native American author Jamie Sams, inspiring each phase of Drift's learnings being based on the teachings from each monthly moon.

Women Who Run with the Wolves, by author and poet Clarissa Pinkola Estés, who helps Drift know not to believe modern-day fairy tales and to trust her inner-wildness.

A Course in Miracles, 'scribed' by professor of medical psychology Helen Schucman, is the foundation of some of the teachings of my characters Wilma, Charlie and Sophia.

The regenerative agricultural principles included in this novel are gleaned from over a decade of enquiry, study and experimentation in this rapidly growing way forward in agriculture. Some of my main mentors are: Colin Seis, Dr Fred Provenza, Dr Christine Jones, Gabe Brown, Tim Wright, David Marsh and Joel Salatin to name just a few. All of them are worth a Google for those of you wishing to create a version of The Planet on your own patch of land.

It's an opportunity to feed your soul and your soil!

Thanks for sharing the journey of *White Horses* with me. I know for some of you it will be a stepping stone into a better, kinder world.

Rachael xx

Acknowledgements

Big thanks to the core people around me who lift me up and celebrate who I am and love me. You know who you are ... the diamonds of my life. You kept my heart overflowing, mirroring to me all your good grace, humour, gratitude and love. From pony players to poodle smoochers, you know that you are my dearest friends. You who have stepped in to become family for me. Thank you. I love you with all my heart.

To my animal friends: from the Kelpies at my feet, the chooks at the breakfast window, the poodle by my side, the divine Dexter cattle and Aloeburn Poll Merino sheep, and the fuzzy coated ponies, you give me inspiration and companionship every day and ground me in unconditional love and hilarity.

For my literary agent and dear friend, Margaret Connolly — you are the most integrious, insightful and supportive agent an artist like me could wish for. Thank you for encouraging me to be brave and stand as a powerful woman. And above all, for helping me to laugh at the most challenging situations.

Thanks to my publishers, HarperCollins. I am so blessed to be teamed creatively with you — I thank you for supporting not just my novels, but also encouraging me to share my vision for a regenerated agricultural landscape and to express my writing-self in other creative endeavors. James Kellow and Catherine Milne, and the entire team — I'm so, so grateful.

To Derek and Mary and your tribe, you have given me a safe harbour and a beautiful garden where I can grow and bloom as much as the flowers! I am so blessed to be part of your family.

For Jackie Merchant, my midnight help friend and now a fellow author — I'm so lucky you now can walk with me on this creative journey and help me limp to the finish line of a novel. I thrive because you are here.

And to my incredible Daniel and my vibrant children, Rosie and Charlie. We have shared the deepest journey together and the adventures of life continue for us. You are my world. You are my everything. I love you with a capital L … Love. Unconditionally. That is my *Truth*.

Thanks to my recently departed mum, Jenny. Mum, I'm living a free-as-a-butterfly life for both of us now and I shall teach your grandchildren well about empowerment and the power and value of feminine nurture.

And lastly, thank you to Mother Earth. You speak to me — so I can whisper your stories into others' ears, and so hopefully all your children will come to hear you.